Kyona Jiles

Copyright © 2024 by Kyona Jiles

2nd Edition

All rights reserved.

ISBN (eBook): 979-8-9898052-4-2
ISBN (Paperback): 979-8-9898052-5-9
Library of Congress Control Number: 2024901670

No part of this book may be reproduced in any form or by any electronic or mechanical means, including information storage and retrieval systems, without written permission from the author, except for the use of brief quotations in a book review.

Title Production by The Bookwhisperer

Cover Design by Sandy Robson

*For Eunice
because I think you would have liked it the most...
We love and miss you.*

Chapter One

THE UNIVERSITY OF WASHINGTON campus is beautiful in the daylight and downright creepy at almost midnight.

Shelly Wright walked briskly from the library to her dorm room, mentally cursing herself for ending up alone and walking. She also cursed herself for being scared. She was on a safe campus; it wasn't like someone was going to attack her.

There was no sound as the man moved from the shadows and stalked Shelly. If he didn't want her to see him, she wouldn't. This time, he wanted her to see him, to feel and fear him.

It increased his fun to hear their hearts beat faster, feel their blood pump rapidly, and taste their fear. That was what he really wanted: the taste of her fear.

He moved quickly. Anyone watching Shelly would have thought she just disappeared. He pulled her into the shadows, fisting his hand into her dark brown hair, ripping her head back. Resting the knife at the carotid artery on the side of her neck, he put his nose into her hair and breathed in her essence.

"Don't make a sound." His menacing voice echoed in her skull.

He dragged the knife lightly across Shelly's throat and the thin line of blood looked black in the shadows. The cut was deep enough to escalate her fear and cause her to whimper.

Closing his eyes, he relied on thousands of years of evolution to take over. His tongue snaked out to lick away the blood and the small slice instantly healed, leaving behind only a welt-like mark.

He decided to show her exactly what he was capable of. Exactly what he was.

***

IT TOOK over an hour for Shelly to die. She never did make any noises above the terrified pleading sounds he loved to hear. Her bloodless corpse would be found propped against one of the many trees that dotted the UW campus, her naked body entirely covered in welt-like burn marks.

The first mark on her throat would never be seen because most of her neck was now missing. It would also be blamed for her death by bleed-out.

Seattle didn't know Death had come to the Emerald City. But soon His wrath would be known to all.

Seconds from the end, Shelly's pale lips had tried in vain to mouth the impossible word.

"Vampire."

Chapter Two

IT WAS MY 21ST BIRTHDAY. Hot damn! I was celebrating at Seattle's newest nightclub, Screamers. Aptly named, the place was kind of Goth meets Grunge meets Seattle Preppies. I know, sounds strange. However, it seemed to be popular. Screamers had only been open for a month, and on a Wednesday night in May, the place was packed.

I was with my best friend, Rachel, my parents, and my aunt. My parents and aunt had driven in from our hometown of Paradise. Yes, I said Paradise. Forty-two miles north of Spokane. Population 2,471.

My parents own a small farmhouse that has been passed down in my dad's family. My mom is a seventh grade teacher and my dad runs a consulting company from home. I don't actually know what he does. How there is even a thriving consulting business in Paradise is beyond me. Dad says he gets a lot of out of town business from cities in the Pacific Northwest. People have certain problems and he helps solve them. He wants me to work with him this summer and learn the business. I don't have any desire to move back to Paradise. That place is not exactly my idea of a paradise.

Rachel grew up there, too. She's going to be a lawyer and I'm going to be a teacher.

I watched my mom sip her soda and my dad order a shot to do with me. I don't know why they stay in Paradise. They don't fit in with anyone in that town.

Their only real friend is my Aunt Marie. She's not really my aunt, though. She's my mom's best friend who has always lived with us. She's somewhere around my parents' age of forty, doesn't look a day over eighteen, and is completely, totally, insane. No, really. I've seen the court documents declaring her legally incapacitated.

She was at the bar with my parents because they can't leave her alone. You never know what kind of trouble Marie will get into. She was currently doing a little bump and grind on the dance floor with a couple of college guys I secretly think would have kidnapped her if my dad hadn't been watching so closely. They had Aunt Marie sandwiched between them and I was afraid I was going to have nightmares for a month.

"Come on, Kinsley, let's have our traditional birthday shot!" I could barely hear my dad over the noise.

I stepped to the bar and eyed the shots. There were eight. "I can't drink all of these, Dad. Where did they come from?"

Dad saluted me with his drink. "All the gentlemen at the bar bought them when I mentioned you were single."

My mom winked at me.

"I figure you can do four and Marie can do four." Dad laughed. "Pick your poison."

Marie has super hearing. She floated up to the bar. "Did I hear something about shots?" She knocked back each one with barely a breath in between.

The bar was so caught up in chanting and cheering for Marie, they didn't see Rachel take two of my shots for me.

I did pretty well for the rest of the night. I kept a soda in my hand and sipped it. Even though I like to drink, I really don't like to get drunk. When I drink too much I have these bizarre dreams about people dying.

I knew we'd be going back to our room soon and Mom, Dad, and Marie would be going back to their hotel. Mom wanted me to stay with them, but I couldn't.

Rachel and I still live in the dorms because we're resident advisors. We monitor floors, mentor students, and keep order in our section. It's a new thing the university is trying.

Mom and Dad are so overprotective. Mom says it's because I don't know how dangerous the rest of the world can be. She didn't even want me to go to college. She wanted me to stay with her and get a job as a para-educator at the school. Dad finally convinced her I needed to go out on my own and that I would be safe.

In the beginning, Mom wanted to see me every weekend possible. Since I'd made it two whole years without being attacked in the 'big city', we were down to once a month visits. Because of Rachel's and my job in the dorm, they had to drive to Seattle to see us. I don't know where my parents came up with the money for gas and hotels. Apparently Dad's consulting business was going better than I ever gave him credit for. I knew Mom's teaching salary wasn't supporting their 'smother our daughter' campaign.

We left Screamers at almost two in the morning. Mom, Dad, and Marie had to get back home the next day. They would be back in two and a half weeks to help Rachel and me move our belongings home for the summer.

Not only did Mom and Dad need to get some sleep before their drive back, Rachel and I had classes in a few hours. It was going to be a long rest of the week; all two days of it. We also had finals coming up.

Rachel and I said our goodbyes and took a rideshare back to campus.

Pulling up to our dorm, we noticed several police cars and crowds of people.

As we got closer, we overheard comments like:

"Did you see her body?"

"It's crazy! Her throat is missing but there's no blood."

"My roommate saw it; she said it was awful!"

"This is so awesome! Wait till I call my parents. They're gonna freak!"

The police were asking people to return to their rooms so Rachel and I joined in and ushered a group of pajama-clad girls back to the dorms.

At four in the morning, the ASB and University Presidents issued the protocol for the remainder of the school year. No one was to go anywhere alone, there was a strict curfew to be in rooms by midnight, and everyone with a cell phone and defense spray needed to have it on their person at all times.

Someone had been murdered on the UW campus.

Chapter Three

ALMOST A WEEK AFTER THE MURDER, I was walking to my room from the campus library. We had made it to Hell Week. The week before the end of school when everyone was cramming for finals. I knew I wasn't supposed to be alone, but there hadn't been any other incidents, as the police were referring to it. The problem was that Rachel had been called to her old job at the bar across from where the Mariner's play. She'd left the library at nine-thirty and I'd promised I'd leave by ten.

I'd lost track of time studying and it was just after midnight. Usually the library closes at eleven, but during hell week, it stays open late. My dorm wasn't that far away and I'd left with a group of other late studiers so the campus police wouldn't think I was alone. Their group had veered off toward the parking lot and I had just a few minutes until I was at my dorm. I could see the lights shining above the door.

It took me a minute to realize that it was absolutely silent around me. I couldn't hear any of the sounds of spring that are usually present. No crickets, no traffic, no people sounds. It was like I was in a bubble of silence.

A breeze blew across the back of my neck, like a breath, and

I turned. Behind me, about ten feet away, was a man dressed all in black, his face hidden in the shadow of a nearby tree. A scream began to bubble up from my throat as he held his hands up in a non-threatening gesture.

"I did not mean to startle you," he said in a soft voice. "I was worried about you walking out here all alone."

"I'm not alone," I said. "I'm meeting my roommate at the entrance to the dorm." My hand shook as I pointed behind me to the poorly lit dorm in question. How come what had looked so bright moments ago seemed so dark now?

"That is wonderful," he said, his voice coming from right next to me. "Perhaps I shall accompany you?" He must have walked up when I turned away. I was nervous and scared but determined to keep him from seeing my discomfort.

"That's okay," I said just a little too loud. "It's only a bit further. Thanks, though." I spun around and began to walk quickly. I couldn't hear any footsteps and when I glanced behind me, he was gone. I breathed a sigh of relief and turned forward. I ran headlong into the same mysterious man. This time the scream made it out of my mouth and I almost fell down.

"Again, I am sorry," he said as his hands on my shoulders steadied me.

He had olive skin and straight black hair that brushed his shoulders. His eyes were so black, I couldn't see the pupils. If I hadn't been scared, I might have thought he was handsome. He looked to be in his mid-thirties and I could think of no good reason why he would be on a college campus at midnight. Except to rape and murder me. At least, that was the only reason that came to mind.

"Please, just let me go to my dorm." My voice shook.

His hands on my shoulders sent a kind of electrical jolt through my body. Like when you go to unplug something and accidentally touch the prongs while you're pulling the plug out of the socket. He watched me carefully and then dropped his hands and stepped back.

"I do not mean to frighten you." He had some kind of an accent and his speech seemed too formal. "It is not safe for you to be out here alone. Please, let me walk you the rest of the way." He stepped to the side and waved his hand in front of him. I figured he couldn't kidnap me a few hundred yards from the front of my dorm, right?

When I didn't talk, he tried to strike up a conversation. "Are you from the area?"

"Um, no," I answered.

He nodded. "Myself, either. I moved from London a few years back and accepted a position teaching history with the university."

I relaxed instantly. If he worked for the university, he couldn't be a psycho-serial-killer-rapist. They did background checks on professors. It also explained his rich, English accent.

"I am Dr. Beckford Alexander. Dr. Alexander to my students, Beck to my friends."

"My name's Kinsley Preston," I said. I could be polite now that my heart wasn't trying to beat out of my chest.

"Kinsley. A little old fashioned."

"My mother's last name." I looked at him out of the corner of my eye. "Besides, Beckford? That's more old fashioned than Kinsley."

He tipped an imaginary hat. "Touché."

"Wait, you're the one who owns Screamers, aren't you?" I stopped to get a better look at him.

He nodded and looked over his shoulder, then back to me. "You had your 21st birthday party there."

When I raised a brow at him, he said, "I make it a point to

know what happens in my club." He raised his right hand as though he was going to touch me and I stepped back.

"Your eyes are a very unique color. An almost silver," Dr. Alexander said as he dropped his hand, peering intently at my face.

"Uh, yeah," I mumbled. Great comeback. He was handsome, a professor with the university, owned a night club, and was walking me to my dorm room. I think there are porn movies that start just like this. I hid a blush by looking at my feet and started walking again.

We arrived at the door to my dorm and I pulled out my keycard. "Thank you for walking me, Dr. Alexander."

"Please, call me Beck." He reached into his jacket pocket and handed me his card. "What is your major?"

"I'm going to be a teacher." I took the card and our fingers brushed. That strange electricity thing happened again. I quickly pulled my hand back and looked at the professor to see if he felt it too.

"If you need an advanced history class or you would like a job as an assistant, please do me the pleasure of contacting me." Before I could ask why he was offering someone he didn't know a job, Beck looked over his shoulder again.

I gasped as another man seemed to appear out of nowhere and step into the soft white rays of a sidewalk light. He had dark hair with white at his temples and a pointy little salt and pepper goatee. He was also dressed in black.

Beck turned so his back was to me and he partially blocked my view of the newcomer. "Kinsley," he said, "I would like to introduce the Head of the History Department, Dr. Gabriel Finch."

"Seems like the History Department is out roaming the campus at midnight." I know I didn't sound as relaxed as I wanted to. Dr. Finch made my hair stand on end, literally. I looked down at my arm and all the little hairs I could see were standing straight up.

It was like the electricity I had experienced with Beck was multiplied by one hundred. In fact, lightning flashed in the sky and I didn't see a cloud in sight. This was getting too weird. My porn movie scenario switched to a slasher movie.

"It does appear that way, doesn't it?" Dr. Finch bowed at the waist but his dark eyes never left mine. I shivered and another flash of lightning broke the sky. Dr. Finch and Beck both looked up.

"Kinsley, I believe it is time you went inside," Beck said without turning to me.

"No, Kinsley. I think you should stay and chat," Dr. Finch said. He also had an English accent. It didn't sound nearly as sexy as Beck's.

"She is not a threat, Gabriel. Leave her be." Beck's words made no sense. Of course I wasn't a threat.

"Alexander, this does not concern you," Dr. Finch said while taking a few steps closer to us. Lightning flashed across the sky one more time and when I looked up, I saw clouds moving in like they were living beings. I could feel a change in the temperature of the air.

Beck stepped backward, closer to me, and his hands gripped mine. I felt the electricity, but felt something else as well. Heat. The clouds opened and rain began to fall. Dr. Finch hissed, actually hissed.

Beck pushed me toward the door. "Kinsley, go inside and stay there. I will not let anything happen to you."

I turned, sprinted toward the door, and slammed my keycard on the sensor box. I heard what sounded like growling behind me but I didn't turn around. I tripped in my haste to get inside and started falling toward the stairs.

Oh, this was so gonna hurt.

Chapter Four

POUNDING ASSAULTED my aching head as I raised a hand to my face. I wasn't laying in a broken heap at the entrance to the dorm. I was on a bed. I slowly opened my eyes and realized that I was in my room.

Knocking...that's what I heard. The pounding in my head started when I tried to sit up. I slowly laid my head back on my pillow and the person at the door knocked again. Morning light filtered through the curtains of our room. Rachel mumbled something from her bed.

"Go *away!*" she finally yelled at the door. She sat up, threw her pillow at it, and flopped back.

"Open the door, Ms. Preston. We need to speak with you. This is the King County Sheriff's Department." The knocking continued.

I sat straight up, ignoring my aching head this time. "King County Sheriff's Department? Rachel, what did you do?"

Rachel uttered from under her comforter, "Nothing, I swear. You're the one who was on your bed fully clothed when I got home. Maybe you did something."

I looked down. I wore my jeans and UW sweatshirt I had

put on before walking to the library to study. My shoes were on the floor next to my backpack.

I pushed the hair out of my eyes and looked at the clock. It was six in the morning. What in the hell were the police doing here? Why couldn't I remember how I got in bed? Beck and Dr. Finch. Had something happened to them? I stood and slowly walked to the door. This couldn't be good.

When I opened the door, two men in uniform stood side by side with the dorm advisor from upstairs. She looked at me and burst into tears. "I'm so sorry, Kinsley, so sorry."

I took one look at the officers and instantly knew something had happened to my parents. They had that look, the one that held pity. I covered my ears with my hands, started screaming 'no' over and over again, and dropped to the floor so hard my teeth clicked. This couldn't be happening. Maybe they were wrong. Maybe I was wrong.

I refused to listen to the words they said. If I didn't actually hear them, maybe it wouldn't be real.

I felt Rachel next to me. Her familiar perfume was a small comfort. She wrapped her arms around my shoulders and cried with me as I rocked on the floor. She kept whispering in my ear that I was going to be okay, that she loved me, and that we'd get through this. All I could do was cry harder.

Rachel practically carried me downstairs to the police cruiser. We sat at the police station for hours and waited for the Pend Oreille County Sheriff's Deputy to come explain what had happened. I couldn't form complete thoughts, let alone coherent sentences. Rachel did all the talking.

I don't even know what time it was when the Deputy finally showed up. He handed me belongings to identify. Two blackened rings and a charred locket.

I threw up.

I heard the words, but it was like they were coming from down a long, tinny tunnel.

Car accident.

Fire.

Explosion.

The words echoed in my head over and over as the Sheriff's Deputy pointed to all the lines I had to sign for the official paperwork.

TWO DAYS PASSED. I didn't eat. I didn't shower. Rachel drove us to Paradise so we could finish all the paperwork with the police department and the lawyer. I also had to find Aunt Marie and make sure she was okay. The accident scene had only two bodies and my parents were never without Marie. Where was she?

We got to the farmhouse and I sat in the car waiting for my mom to run out on the porch to greet us. She didn't. The gravity of her death hit me like a physical blow. It was as though someone had reached into my chest and ripped out my heart. The pain was so intense, it was hard to breathe. Rachel opened my door and rubbed the side of my face.

"Kins, honey," Rachel said softly. "We have to go in the house and find Marie." She rubbed my arm. "You know she's hiding in there. And I know this hurts. I hate to see you like this. Come on."

I nodded and let Rachel pull me from the car. The police told me they'd searched the house and yelled for Marie, but she wasn't there. Rachel was right, though. Marie was hiding.

When I was little and asked questions about why Aunt Marie was so different, mom had explained to me that someone very mean had hurt Marie a long time ago. Now she didn't trust anyone but our family. There was a special hiding place in the house for Marie and me to go if anyone ever came to the house that we didn't know.

Rachel and I went upstairs and moved the panel from the hidden door. I braced myself for what I'd find and slowly pushed the door open. Marie was curled on the cot, wrapped in a blanket. I went to her and the pain in my chest intensified. She had scratches on her face and she'd been crying.

She rocked back and forth, arms wrapped around her body. "Oh, Kinsley, I tried. I tried to save them. I'm so sorry that I failed you all."

I pulled her to me and rested my cheek on the top of her head. "Aunt Marie, it's okay. Shh." Having something to do and someone to take care of helped me to not feel as much of the pain.

"I tried," Marie kept saying.

We sat for over an hour in that little room while Marie alternately paced, cried, and mumbled.

Rachel called the deputies to come to the house and talk to Marie. It looked to us like she'd been attacked.

When the deputy got there, he questioned Marie. "Ms. DeVoe, were you in the vehicle with Mr. Preston and Ms. Kinsley?"

"Yes. No." She looked at me questioningly. "I don't know."

"Ms. DeVoe?" the deputy said.

"I tried to save them," she sobbed, her hands fisting the hem of her shirt.

"Listen, Deputy Knox," I said, "she isn't in any condition to answer your questions; she never will be. Even on a good day she can't usually tell you what she had for breakfast."

"Miss Preston," the deputy said, "our investigation shows no sign of foul play. We're ruling this an accident. You can come by later today or tomorrow to have the bodies released for the funeral."

His words sent Aunt Marie into another crying jag. I think I was finally cried out, if it were possible.

THE FUNERAL SERVICES WERE SIMPLE. I chose to have my parents' remains cremated and placed together in one urn. It made me feel like I still had a piece of them with me.

As I picked up the urn, one of the gentlemen I hadn't recognized approached me. "Your dad said he would be teaching you the business this summer. I don't suppose he had time to do that?"

"Excuse me?" I said. "My parents are dead. I don't care about your consulting needs." I considered the merits of hitting him in the face when Rachel stepped between us. Good thing, too. I probably would have dropped the urn and then I really would have been mad.

"I'm sorry, sir," Rachel said, "you're going to need to find another consulting business. Kinsley's going to be a teacher."

The man's forehead scrunched in confusion. "Do you know anything about the business?"

"No, and I don't plan to." I turned to walk away.

"Miss Preston, I don't mean any disrespect. Please, accept my apologies. Your dad and I were very good friends. Here, take my card. If you ever need anything, call me. I mean anything." The man handed me his card and walked to a black Lincoln Town Car with tinted windows.

It was a classy business card and had the title "Masters Security" and the name Scott Masters, Owner. There were phone numbers, fax numbers, and cell numbers to reach him. He was based in Bellevue.

Rachel wolf-whistled. "If we weren't at your parents' funeral, I'd be impressed by the width of his shoulders, the dimple in his cheek, and the cut of his suit." She fanned her face with her hand.

I smiled at Rachel, grateful for the distraction.

When everyone was gone, we drove back to the farmhouse and sat in the driveway staring out over the property. Thoughts rolled in my head like lottery balls. I perversely got the giggles.

"What?" Rachel asked.

"It's not funny," I said through my laughter.

"What's not funny?"

"Any of it. Yet all I can sit here and think is I've inherited a one hundred fifty year old farm house, fifteen acres, a few beat up cars, and a Crazy Aunt Marie." I laughed harder and then the tears started.

"Crazy?" Aunt Marie said from the backseat. "Do not call me crazy!"

Rachel started to laugh now. The situation was not funny. But listening to Crazy Aunt Marie try to defend her sanity was, well, funny.

"I prefer the term *nucking futs*," she told us haughtily.

This caused Rachel and me to laugh harder. Finally, Aunt Marie started to laugh, too. We sat in the driveway of my parents' home, the urn clutched in my arms, and mourned them the only way we knew how. By living.

Chapter Five

BY THE TIME we got back to Seattle, it was the week after finals. Against our better judgment, we had brought Marie because we didn't know what else to do. She couldn't be left alone and there was no one in Paradise we could leave her with.

Rachel went to see if she could make up her finals. I sat with Aunt Marie in our dorm. She looked around and smiled.

"I loved university. It was such a great time."

"Aunt Marie, you went to college? Where? When?"

She sighed. "Hoover was President. It was such a rough time."

"Hoover? Herbert Hoover? Marie! That was like 1930!" I stared at her.

"1931. The Great Depression was in full swing. I don't know why they called it Great, there was nothing *great* about it. I almost felt bad that my family could afford to send me to Yale."

"Wait, Yale? 1931? How old are you? Better yet, how old do you think you are? I didn't think you were that much older than Mom and Dad." Before Marie could answer, my cell rang.

"Hello?" I was doing the math in my head. There was no

way she was actually talking about her life. She had to be talking about a book she read or a movie she'd seen.

"This is Judy from the Ed Department. We want to schedule your finals." Her chipper voice was a little annoying.

"Excuse me?"

Judy said, "Dr. Alexander contacted us regarding your circumstances and requested an extension for you."

I pulled the phone away, stared at it, then put it back to my ear. "He what?" Why would he do that? I didn't even know the man.

"Miss Preston, didn't you recently lose your parents?" Her voice took on that tone I knew I was going to have to get used to. The 'your parents died, you poor thing' tone. "Dr. Alexander told us about your loss and gave you glowing recommendations."

I took advantage of the gift that had been handed to me. I scheduled my finals, hung up, and called Rachel.

"You're not going to believe this," she said as soon as she answered. "Dr. Alexander from the History Department got me an extension on my finals! Isn't that awesome?"

Rachel was so happy, I couldn't burst her bubble. Why didn't she think it was unusual? "That's great, Rach. Can you get back here to be with Marie so I can go get my finals set up?" I hoped I sounded normal and calm.

Not that I knew what normal and calm were anymore.

"You bet, chica. I'll be there A.S.A.P." She hung up.

When Rachel got back, I left Marie in her capable hands so I could track down Dr. Beckford Alexander and his *glowing recommendations*.

I found his office and stood outside the door. What was I going to say? 'Thank you' seemed like a good idea with 'why?' close behind.

I pushed open the door. His secretary looked up as I entered. The name tag on her desk said Meredith Jones.

"Is Dr. Alexander here?" I asked.

"Are you Kinsley Preston?"

I took a step back. "How do you know my name?"

"Dr. Alexander thought you might stop by to see him when you returned."

"He did?" How did Dr. Alexander and his secretary know so much about me? "Where is he?"

"He's teaching class in the basement."

I left the office and found the stairs.

I pushed through the double doors of Dr. Alexander's classroom and found myself the object of at least fifty sets of eyes.

Dr. Alexander stopped speaking and stared at me for a moment. Then he addressed his class. "Ladies and gentlemen, this is my assistant, Kinsley. As you can see, she needs to speak with me. So, she has saved you from my droning for the next fifteen minutes. Class dismissed. I shall see you tomorrow."

The students chuckled, gathered their items, and shuffled from the room.

He moved toward me. "Kinsley, my dear, what can I do for you?"

I held up my hands. "Dr. Alexander, I don't understand what's going on."

"Dr. Alexander? Only a few weeks ago you thought of me as Beck."

"A lot has happened in a few weeks."

He clasped my hand between his two larger ones. "I know, Kinsley, and I am so very, very sorry for your loss."

That's all it took. I dissolved into a puddle of tears at Beck's feet. He came down next to me on the floor. After a few moments he produced a handkerchief from somewhere and handed it to me. I wiped at my eyes and nose.

He touched my cheek. "It is not healthy to hold in all your grief."

I clutched his handkerchief like a lifeline. I looked into his black eyes and asked the question that had brought me to him. "Why did you vouch for Rachel and me to our professors? You don't even know us."

"That is not true. I met you a few weeks ago."

I shook my head. "You know what I mean."

"I did some research on you when I found out about your parents' deaths. I know you are here on academic scholarships and you will lose them if your GPA drops below a 3.0. I spoke to your professors and they agreed to let you take your finals upon your return. I vouched for you because you needed it and for Rachel because she is your best friend. I would have done it for any of my students." He brushed some hair back from my face and I suddenly felt awkward.

I scooted away from him and rested my back against the leg of one of the desks. "But I'm not one of your students."

"I know that. I would like to offer you a job as my assistant, Kinsley. I think your education is important to you and it was important to your parents. You cannot drop out of school and move back to where you grew up."

It was like he was reading my mind. I had already thought about quitting, selling the house, and moving to Spokane with Marie. What I was going to do after that, I didn't know. My talents included waitressing, making a kick-ass mocha, and professional student. Whoop-de-frickin-doo! None of that was going to land me a decent paying job.

I swallowed and wiped the corners of my eyes again. "I have to be moved out of the dorms by this weekend. I'm going home to figure out what to do. I have an aunt to care for." Possibly elderly, but that was another issue all together.

"An aunt?" His eyes widened and he leaned back.

"Well, she was my mom's best friend."

"I see," Beck nodded.

I chewed on my lower lip. "I have another question. What in the hell happened outside my dorm room the night we met?"

"What do you mean?" He was looking at me strangely.

"The unusual lightning and rain? You and Dr. Finch fighting?" Duh.

He chuckled. "Fighting? That is absurd. Dr. Finch and I were not fighting. I think the stress of the next day must have affected your memory of that night."

"I heard you guys—" I stopped. What was I going to say? That I'd heard them growling and hissing at each other? Maybe I didn't remember exactly what had happened that night because of everything that came after it.

"You heard us what?"

I ran my hands over my face. "Never mind. You're right; I don't remember that night clearly. In fact, the last three weeks are a blur. I'm kind of numb."

"Which is completely understandable. You have been through a lot. Let me get you the names of some lawyers and real estate people I trust on that side of the mountain."

"Real estate? I didn't tell you I want to sell the house." I hadn't said it out loud, had I?

"I figured you would want to sell. When my parents died, I sold everything."

"How did your parents die?" I asked quietly.

"In an accident. Not like your parents, but still an accident that caused their deaths. That is why I am doing so much for you and trying to be your friend. Please, Kinsley, let me help you. I fear there is no one else in your life to do so."

I waved my arm in the air. "Rachel's been helping me. And I have Aunt Marie." So I was twenty-one, and my parents were dead. I could take care of myself.

He shook his head. "Another twenty-one-year-old and an aunt that your parents took care of are not help. They are more work."

"That's not true. Without Rachel, I wouldn't have been able to do anything these last weeks. She's like the sister I never had and she's my best friend." I stood and started walking to the doors.

"Kinsley, wait, I apologize." Beck was behind me. "I do not intend to demean the relationships you have. I would just like to be one of your friends." He put his hand on my shoulder and guided me toward a desk in the back of the classroom.

"My condominium is only a few miles from campus. It is a high security building, has a view of the mountains and the bay, and many services. There just happens to be an open unit. Sell the house and property, buy the condo, bring your aunt over, and complete your education here. Then you will have time to figure out what to do after that."

It all sounded so easy. The plan he laid out, the idea of staying in Seattle, having a home for Aunt Marie and me. I was so desperate for a chance at something easy that it made me wary.

"I need to talk to Rachel and Aunt Marie," I said as I stood.

Beck nodded his head. "Of course you do. You are a family now."

I practically ran from the classroom to get back to Rachel and tell her what Beck offered. I needed to talk it through with her so I didn't jump into the deep end. The way things were going, I'd probably drown.

Chapter Six

"AM I CRAZY?" I asked Rachel for the hundredth time. We sat at the kitchen table of my parents' house. We'd already been through two pots of coffee. Marie darted through the rooms like a hummingbird.

"I think you're taking a calculated risk?" Rachel said.

I rolled my eyes. "Not helpful. Are you asking me or telling me?"

When I'd left Beck's classroom I'd immediately interrupted Rachel and Marie's movie to tell Rachel about Beck's idea. She hadn't looked as worried as I'd felt. She'd said, "What a great plan!" hugged me and asked when Marie and I were moving.

I'd been shocked at her easy acceptance of such a huge decision. The conversation that had ensued was quite similar to the one we were having now.

"Can I really just sell everything and move to Seattle?" I set my coffee cup on the table.

"That's what you were going to do anyway. Sell everything, I mean. You were just going to move to Spokane. Then what? Enroll at Eastern? Whitworth? Get a fast food job?" Rachel shuddered. "Let's look at our pro and con list again." Rachel liked to make lists.

Her list had started in the dorm room and she'd been working on it for a week between taking finals and moving our stuff back to Paradise. Not much new had been added in the last three days. Rachel had moved into the farm house with Marie and me instead of going to her parents' house.

"Cons," Rachel said in her lawyer voice, "One: Kinsley thinks it sounds like a crazy idea." She rolled her eyes and I glared at her. "Two: emotionally difficult to sell family home."

"We're selling the house?" Marie's voice came loudly from two rooms over where she was watching *True Blood* on Rachel's computer.

I dropped my head to the table and smacked it down a couple times. "She's like having a five-year-old," I said. I picked my head up slowly and met Rachel's mischievous grin. "Just shut up," I said.

"Marie," I stated calmly, my voice loud so she could hear me. "We've been talking about this. I'm not sure we can keep living here. The property and house are too much for me to take care of." My voice cracked a bit, but I ignored it and forged on. "You never said if you preferred to live in Spokane or Seattle."

Marie didn't answer.

"Pros," Rachel continued. "One: perfect opportunity to continue education at university where scholarship is. Two: perfect opportunity to get away from Paradise. Three: job opportunity with smokin' hot university professor. Four: you and I will live in the same city so we can still see each other all the time. Five—"

"Okay. I get it. There are way more pros than cons." I put my head back on the table. "This is just so hard."

When I needed advice or something important, I'd been able to call my mom and dad. They were always there for me no matter what I needed and now they were gone. I choked on a sob.

Marie came into the room and stood behind my chair. "We should sell the house. We can't live here without Tom and Claire. I can mow the lawn but I don't know how to change the big sprinklers."

Mentioning we had an automated sprinkler system seemed pointless.

"How about Nevada? The weather is hot and the sun is out a lot," she said.

"Nevada?" I choked out into my hands. "You want to move to Nevada? You freak out when we change the coffee brand and you want to move to another state?" I picked my head up from the table and met Rachel's gaze again. She was doing her best not to laugh but it was a losing battle.

"Can you go to college in Nevada?" Marie asked. "I would think they have schools there. If not, you could go to Mexico and finish school. Maybe I should find the map." She ran from the room, her long, dark ponytail bouncing.

Rachel smothered a laugh with her hand.

"Yeah, laugh it up, girl," I told her. "You get to help me raise her." This made Rachel laugh more.

Marie came back with a bag of cookies instead of a map. "Have you tried these? They're amazing!" Marie ate more than a college football team and never gained an ounce. It probably helped that she rarely sat down.

"I'll take one," Rachel said, snagging an Oreo from the bag.

"What are you guys doing?" Marie asked as she looked at our list on the table. "What is this list for?"

"Her topic changes give me whiplash," Rachel whispered.

I realized right then it wouldn't matter what I chose to do. Marie lived in her head and would have to deal with whatever I decided.

My terrified gaze met Rachel's. "I'm going to need your help, Rach. I can't do all this alone."

"I'd never let you do anything alone, chica, you know that. All kidding aside, I want you to look at this from an outside point of view. You can't live here by yourself. The place is paid off and even in this horrible housing market, you're going to walk away with more money than you've ever had.

"Why in the world would you quit school or change universities? You've been offered a job that will allow you to finish your degree. I know it seems like it's all too easy, but what you've been through has been rough. You need to do what will make your life easier." Finally Rachel took a breath and gripped my hands.

She was right. I knew she was right. Marie put her hands over ours and yelled, "All for one and one for all!" Then she lifted her arms in the air like we were doing a sports team huddle. "So, what's the list for?" Marie asked again around another cookie.

I groaned and Rachel laughed.

I picked up my cell phone and the business card for Dr. Beckford Alexander. I dialed his cell and waited for it to go to voicemail since it was almost ten at night.

"Hello," his melodic voice answered with no hint of tiredness.

"Dr. Alexander?" I said.

"Kinsley, dear, we are beyond formalities. Must I remind you again to refer to me as Beck?"

"Beck," I said with a little more steel in my voice. "I'd like to take you up on your offer."

"Which one?" he asked.

I made eye contact with Rachel and she nodded her head. I watched Marie turn ballerina circles in the kitchen.

"All of them," I said.

Chapter Seven

I USED my own real estate agent to sell the farm as a slight show of defiance on my part to Beck. My way of saying, "See, I can take care of some things myself."

However, I had to concede to his expertise when it came time to buy the condo. The real estate agent and escrow company Beck set me up with were efficient. They took care of everything.

I lived in the farmhouse with Marie and Rachel for the month of July while we cleaned and packed. It was wonderful and horrible at the same time to go through all my parents' belongings and all the items they'd kept from my childhood. One picture would make me laugh out loud and another would make me break down into uncontrollable sobs.

Rachel was amazing. She helped me box up everything to be donated and carefully pack all the items I felt like I had to keep. My father's knife collection and my mother's ruby ring were the things I wanted with me and not in storage.

There were eight knives, daggers, really. They were all silver blades ranging in length from two to nine inches. Each dagger was different. The handles were hand carved from bone and had designs engraved in them. They had been well used at one time. Some of the engravings were almost worn away. Dad told me they had been passed down in his family for hundreds of years.

The case that held them resembled a small suitcase on the outside. The inside, however, was lined in silver and covered with crushed velvet. It had to weigh over fifty pounds with all the daggers in it. I'd once asked Dad about all the silver and he reminded me that not too long ago, many countries were superstitious of creatures that go bump in the night. Things like vampires and werewolves.

Even though my mom never wore the ruby ring, I knew it was special. She kept it in her jewelry box and said it had belonged to every first born daughter in her family since the early 1500s. She had been telling me since I was little that I'd get the ring when the time was right. I figured losing my parents, while not right, was a time to try and celebrate life. I slid it on my left hand ring finger. It looked like an exotic engagement ring and felt warm and heavy on my hand.

I wore my mom and dad's rings on a chain around my neck. While they'd never gotten married, they had both worn wedding rings. My mom's locket was tucked safely in my jewelry box.

It was harder than I expected to stand in the driveway of the farmhouse for one last time. While the sorrow of their deaths had lessened to a throbbing ache, anger was now bubbling to the surface. I wanted the world to feel my pain, to hurt as much as I hurt.

As I stood and stared at my childhood home, I wondered how many years it would take for the damage inside me to heal. Or if it ever would. I felt like I was in a twelve step program, like AA, where step one is admitting you're powerless over alcohol. Except my step one was just admitting I was powerless.

"Time to go," Rachel said as she led me to the passenger side of her dad's truck. We were using it to haul a horse trailer full of our possessions.

"Where are we going?" Marie asked as she climbed in the backseat. I rolled my eyes as Rachel told her again that we were moving to Seattle.

I spent as much of the drive as I could looking out the window trying to think about nothing. I kept thinking about my parents. I envisioned the holidays and special occasions to come. How was I going to survive without them? How could any of it be special without my parents?

As the city came into view, I realized things had gone much smoother than I ever could have imagined, considering the circumstances. From a business standpoint, I had money in the bank, a new, amazing home, and a semblance of stability.

The keys to the condo had been mailed to us last week. At times, I was excited to begin this new chapter of my life. Then I immediately got upset with myself for being happy. I shouldn't be happy. My parents were dead.

To anyone who didn't know me, outward appearances would show a well adjusted, calm, young woman ready to take on the world. Appearances can sometimes be deceiving.

"Everything will be okay, chica. Wipe that look off your face." Rachel could only look at me for a brief moment before she had to put her attention back on the road.

"What look?" I asked, but Rachel knew me too well.

"The look you get when you spend six hours thinking about all the changes going on in your life."

Marie noticed how still I had become. She undid her seat belt and sat forward to wrap her arms around me. "Your parents loved you very much and just wanted you to be happy. It's okay to be happy." She kissed my cheek and sat back.

Tears gathered in my eyes and Rachel took my hand in a silent show of support.

We pulled up to the front entrance of the condo. It resembled an upper class hotel.

"Whoa," Rachel said.

"The pictures didn't do this place justice." I stared out the windshield in awe.

The building was old in style but current in beauty. It was a five story brick building with picture windows along the bottom floor. The vegetation surrounding the building was green and contrasted beautifully with the brick. Flowers, trees, and shrubs were everywhere.

Rachel put the truck in park. "I'm a little jealous. I still have to find an apartment."

I put my hand to my mouth. "Oh, Rach. You spent so much time helping me, I forgot we were going to get a place together for our senior year." I felt horrible. "You should live with us. We have that extra bedroom."

She reached over and squeezed my shoulder. "Quit trying to do what you think is the right thing. You don't need me living with you. You and Marie need your space while you deal with everything." She smiled sadly. "I will miss being your roomie, though."

The doorman came out to greet us. He opened my door before I could try and convince Rachel I really needed her to live with us because I didn't know how I was going to handle Marie alone. Actually I wasn't sure how I was going to handle *anything*.

"Miss Preston, I presume?" The doorman wore a dark red pea coat and white gloves. It was like we were in a movie. He took my hand, helped me out of the truck, and shut the door. "Dr. Alexander has a moving crew ready for your belongings and asked me to give you this. My name is Gerald. Please let me know if anything is not to your liking." Gerald handed me a thick parchment envelope.

I looked through the open window at Rachel and she winked at me. "He's gorgeous," she said. "He helped you get this place. He's a professor. He's gorgeous. He hired a moving crew. He's drop-dead-gorgeous. He's your neighbor. I don't think I need to say more. Did I mention he's gorgeous? You are soooo lucky, Kins."

I shook my head. "You're a hopeless romantic."

She threw her head back and laughed. "And you're just hopeless."

Rachel got out of the truck and helped Marie out of the back. I opened the envelope. The letter was written in elegant writing I didn't expect from a man.

My Dearest Kinsley,

Please accept my apology that I cannot be here to greet you personally. As you know, I have classes to teach. Allow Gerald to assist you ladies with whatever you need. The moving crew have already been paid and tipped, so do not worry about that. I would like to invite the three of you to dinner at my residence tomorrow night. I know you will still be settling in, however, I would like to see how you are doing. I would very much like to meet Rachel and your Aunt Marie.

Fondest Regards,

Beck

The formality of his writing seemed to be laced with something more personal. A shiver rippled up my spine.

"Hey, Kins. Wake up."

I turned to see Rachel, Aunt Marie, Gerald, and four large men staring at me.

Rachel reached for the letter. "What in the hell did he write? You're, like, in another world."

"We're invited to dinner tomorrow night," I said before I thought better of it. Rachel would make such a big deal out of this.

"He invited you to dinner? Where?" She started to squeal and jump up and down. Gerald and the moving crew lost interest in us and opened the back of the horse trailer to get to our boxes.

"Not just me, all of us. He wants us to come to dinner at his place tomorrow night." My voice sounded strange to my own ears.

Rachel clapped her hands. "This is great. What are you going to wear? I can pretend to have a headache halfway through dinner and Marie and I can leave. You'll be alone and —" If she kept jumping up and down, she was going to take flight.

"And what, Rachel? He's not interested in me like that. He's just being nice. Besides, it's not like I'm emotionally stable enough to have a relationship right now."

"Who said anything about a relationship? I was just thinking you could have sex."

Gerald cleared his throat loudly and one of the men almost dropped a box.

"Rachel," I said. "Stop it. I'm not interested."

"Sure. You'd have to be dead not to be interested." Her face went slack when she realized what she'd said.

"It's okay, Rach, I know what you're trying to say. Yes, he's hot and yes, he's been very helpful. But that's where it stops. I don't want to just have sex, not that he would, and I am not going to start a relationship with anyone. I have you and Marie to help me."

Before I burst into tears, I turned. "Show me my new home please, Gerald."

Chapter Eight

IT TOOK the movers two hours to get our belongings upstairs and set up. They didn't unpack the boxes, but they put our beds together and placed the furniture.

By the time we had the beds made and the kitchen mostly unpacked, it was almost midnight. Rachel was still going strong. I watched her bounce around the kitchen to the music on the radio. I say 'bounce' because that's how Rachel moves. She's about 5'4", curvy and cute. Her long, blonde hair was swept up in a ponytail on top of her head.

We'd ordered pizza when we first arrived and I grabbed the last piece when Dave Matthews started singing. Rachel squealed and tried to grab me to dance around the kitchen. I barely avoided her and took a big bite.

"I can't dance and eat at the same time," I told her with my mouth full.

Rachel laughed and went to pull Marie from the couch.

There was a knock on the door and Rachel and I froze and stared at each other. Who in the world would be knocking on our new door at midnight? Aunt Marie jumped up and opened the door before I could stop her. We never locked our doors and windows in Paradise. I realized it was going to take a while to train Marie.

Beck stood in the doorway with a bottle of wine and a bouquet of flowers. Aunt Marie instantly dropped into some kind of defensive crouch and started babbling words I couldn't make out. Beck stepped back and raised his hands. The bottle of wine dropped to the floor and shattered on the tiles. Rachel and I ran to the door.

"You must be Marie. I mean no harm to the girls. I come as a Protector not a Slayer," Beck said, arms still up.

"What in the hell are you talking about?" I practically screeched. This was ridiculous. For some unknown reason, my mild-mannered, crazy Aunt looked like she was going to attack a man almost three times her size. Why was he using words like slayer?

I put my hand on Marie's shoulder, trying to calm her, but she spun on me. Her hand shot out and hit me in the chest and her leg swept mine out from under me. I landed on the floor. I gasped, struggling to get enough air into my lungs for my next breath.

Beck was by me in an instant and Rachel was trying to wrestle Marie to the ground. Rachel ended up on the floor not too far from me.

Beck growled something at Marie and she stood straight and took in the sight of us on the floor like she didn't know how we had gotten there.

Her eyes widened and she started to cry. "Oh, Kinsley, Tom and Claire knew this was going to happen. We were supposed to teach you. We were supposed to show you everything this summer." She knelt beside me, opposite Beck, and stroked my arm. "What have I done? Are you okay?"

I still struggled to breathe and Beck placed calming hands

to my face. "Look at me. You are fine. You can breathe. Nothing is broken."

My lungs filled with air as I concentrated on the sound of his voice. My chest didn't ache anymore and my head cleared.

Seriously, what had just happened?

"Kinsley? Rachel?" Marie looked back and forth between us. Then, as if a switch had been flipped, her face turned to stone and she yelled at Beck, "You need to leave!"

"Leave? Marie, you just tried to attack him in our doorway. What is wrong with you?" I sat up and Beck supported me.

Beck closed his eyes and took a deep breath. When he opened them, they were blacker than I'd ever seen anyone's eyes. He turned his body slightly and spoke to Marie in a low voice. I didn't understand a word he said. Obviously, neither did Rachel.

"Are you speaking in a different language, Dr. Alexander? Marie doesn't understand anything but English, does she?" Rachel was looking wildly at the three of us.

I was just about to say no when Marie said "Nein." Apparently she was answering whatever Beck had said.

I whipped my head to her. "Did you just say *no* in German, Marie?"

She looked at me. "Ja." Then she walked to her room and shut the door.

"No! I cannot handle any more surprises. Beck, I am so sorry." I tried to stand up.

He helped me to my feet and smiled. "Why are you apologizing? You are the one who was attacked by your aunt."

"Kins?" Rachel asked as she went on shaky legs to the table.

"I don't know, Rach. Dad was supposed to teach me about his consulting business this summer. That's all I know." I pulled myself from Beck's hands and walked to the sink. I got a washrag and started trying to clean up the broken wine bottle.

"Be careful, I do not want you to cut yourself." Beck took the rag from my hands and led me to the chair next to Rachel. He made sure I was going to stay there and then went to clean the mess.

"Where did Marie learn to fight like that?" Rachel said. "Holy crap, that was cool! Think she'd teach us?"

Leave it to Rachel to think that nucking futs Marie leveling us in my entryway would be cool.

"You should have her teach you everything she can," Beck said. He'd picked up the last of the glass and was dumping it in our garbage can. "I think we have had enough excitement for the evening, ladies." He reached down and picked up the bouquet of flowers that had fallen to the floor. It was a dozen red roses.

"I would still like you to come to dinner tomorrow night, if your aunt is not too offended by my presence." He turned to leave.

"Wait, where are you going?" I jumped to my feet and walked toward him even though he'd already turned away and was reaching for the doorknob. "Were you speaking German to Marie? What just happened? I need an explanation and I feel like you know something you're not telling me." The shock of being attacked by Marie was subsiding. Why did everything strange in my life keep coming back to this man?

He shoved the flowers into my hands. "Marie will need to explain that to you. It is not my place." He walked out the door. I shut it behind him, locked the bolt, and turned. When I lifted my eyes to look at Rachel, she was frowning.

We stared at each other in shocked silence for a moment. "Kins, your life just keeps getting weirder and weirder."

"Yeah, I noticed. Listen, Rach, I need you to think about something. I'm not saying this because of what just happened, either. I meant it earlier when I said I want you to live with us. I don't want to be alone." I put the roses on the table and took her hands. "Please. Marie can be a handful. More than I knew, obviously. And I don't want to be without you. We've been roommates since we started college and best friends since we were five. Would you think about maybe moving in with us? Please? You won't be a babysitter or anything like that. You're my rock and I just don't know what I'd do without you." I started to tear up.

"Are you sure? I really thought you might want some space." Rachel's eyes were wide.

I squeezed her hands. "I'm sure. I'm going to have to reevaluate this living situation with Marie now that I know she's potentially dangerous. I may have to hire someone to be here when I'm gone. Having you here will help everything feel normal." A brittle sound emerged from my throat. I think I was trying to laugh.

"Oh, Kins! Of course I'll move in. This place is huge. How can I pass up my own bedroom and bathroom?" She smiled and hugged me. "Go talk to Marie and figure out what flew up her ass. I'll go over and try to mend things with Beck. He seemed a little upset when he left."

"Thanks, Rach. I'll try to talk to Marie." I rubbed my temples. "I'm a little pissed at her right now, though. She could have knocked me out. It was bad enough she knocked the breath out of me. She also could have hurt you. Or Beck. He's done so much for us and I repay him by siccing my crazy aunt on him."

"You didn't sic her on him, Kinsley! Damn, that was bizarre." She slipped on a pair of sandals and opened the front door. "Good luck with Marie. You have to tell me everything she says."

"Yeah. Good luck to you, too. Beck will probably want to fire me before I've worked a day as his assistant."

Chapter Nine

AS I APPROACHED the closed door to Marie's room, I could hear her sobs. My anger faded as I tried to put myself in her place. Everything she knew had been changed and she wasn't right in the head. I couldn't be mad at her for acting strange. She was strange. I'd lost my parents and she'd lost her family and best friends. I was twenty-one and she was, well, who knew how old. But I was in a better frame of mind to deal with the loss than she was. For once, I was the strong one. Man, it sucks to be an adult sometimes.

I knocked lightly on the door and pushed it open. "Marie, I'm coming in."

She was curled up on her bed. "There is so much you have to learn, so much you need to know. I'm not supposed to be the one teaching you."

I rubbed my forehead. I was tired, stressed out, and confused. "Teach me what? About the consulting business?" She hadn't even helped my dad.

"The consulting business is a front, Kinsley. It's all a lie. The only thing we consult on is—" she stopped and burst into tears again. This was getting old.

"What? What is going on?"

"I have to start at the beginning. This will make more sense if I start at the beginning."

"Oh, yes, please! Let's make sense."

"Your mom and dad were going to tell you everything this summer. I was going to train you how to be a Shadower. It's our destiny."

"Geez, Marie, I thought you said you were going to start making sense." I turned and she jumped off the bed and grabbed my arm.

"Please, just listen to what I have to say. You don't have to believe a word of it. Just let me tell you." The Marie I remembered from my childhood stood before me. The woman who had kissed my owies and woven tales to put me to sleep. I backed up and slid down the wall to sit on the floor.

Marie went back to her bed, pulled off the comforter, and grabbed the pillows that were underneath. She threw them all to the floor and pulled me to the softness. It reminded me of when I'd had 'sleepovers' in Marie's bedroom when I was younger. She had told me tales then too. Tales of princes and princesses, dragons and witches, vampires and werewolves. What was she going to tell me now when it was supposed to be real?

She looked at the ceiling, as though searching in her mind for words. "My family left Germany in the late 1800s. I don't always remember the exact date. We spoke German in our home, that's why I know German now."

I stared at her. I'd never heard this, never heard her talk about a family before mine. I wasn't counting her ramblings about President Hoover. She'd never spoken German with my family. How did she remember it? Wait. 1800s?

"We were being hunted and had to flee. We figured America would be the safest place."

Why did she keep saying 'we'? She was talking about over a

hundred years ago. Before I could make my mouth form the words, she continued.

"We moved to the east coast of the new America. That's how I ended up at Yale. We were in Connecticut when they found us." She trembled and looked away.

"You're not making any sense, Marie. You keep saying things like *we* and *us*. You weren't there. That was over a hundred years ago. You. Weren't. There." One of the things I'd learned about Marie's illness was you had to be gentle but firm. When she was confused, you had to make her see reason.

"Oh, Kinsley, it was horrible." She turned her head back to me and there were tears rolling down her cheeks. "There were only four of them. He held me while the other three murdered each of my family members. My mother, my father, my little brother and sister, and our maid. They ripped their throats out and feasted on their blood while making me watch. Isaac kept telling me how it was all my fault. I'd trusted him and it killed my whole family." Her sobs ripped through the room and she collapsed, burying her head in the pillows.

I racked my brain for a book or movie that was even close to what she was saying so I could convince her she was remembering something, but not her life. I tried to bring her back to the present so she could focus on something real. "When did you come to live with my family? You were there when I was born. I have pictures."

She smacked her forehead. "Pictures! Oh, I'm so silly. Why didn't I think of the pictures?" The tears stopped immediately. Sometimes Marie's mood changes were scary. She crawled on her hands and knees to her bed and rooted around underneath until she found a wooden box. After pulling off the lid, she cradled an old book to her chest. It was bound in leather and was the size of a giant dictionary.

She knee-walked back to me and set the book reverently

between us on the comforter. She opened to the first page, an old, worn, brown photo of a family. I looked at each face and drew in a surprised breath when I saw a young woman who looked shockingly like Marie.

I looked up and Marie stared expectantly back.

"Is this your great, great, great grandmother? You look just like her. Were they murdered and you've heard the story?" I said.

"This is so much harder than I thought." Marie let out a breath and turned the page. There were photos and descriptions from Germany. A laughing family and the life of a young Marie. She was betrothed to marry a man named Isaac. He was a striking, aristocratic man. You could almost see the love between them.

Then there were no more pictures of Isaac and Marie. There were letters, though. Letters about love and spending eternity together. I felt like a voyeur as I read each one.

Marie put her face next to mine, eyes wide. "Do you see? Do you see who the monsters were that murdered my family?"

"What are you talking about? What monsters?" I'd been so caught up in reading the love letters I hadn't realized Marie held another book. This one was older than the first.

She poked a finger to my chest. "We're Shadowers. Our family is responsible for protecting the Monarchs. Claire, you, and me. Amazingly, Claire found Tom, who was also a Shadower. We protect the Monarchs. Our blood is sacred. Now you and I are all who are left." Her eyes slid back to the new book. She opened it and flipped to the first page.

There was a graphic pencil drawing of a creature that looked like what you'd expect the Devil to look like. He hovered off the ground on dragon-like wings, his naked body covered with sinewy muscle and ropy veins. There was a pile of bodies below him. Men, women, and children.

The artist had smeared reddish brown color over the pile of bodies. The Devil-creature had fangs and the same reddish brown color running down his chin. Marie handed me the book and a shiver rippled through me. I realized the pages were parchment and the pencil was actually charcoal. I think the color was real blood. I shuddered again.

Marie turned the page.

The writing was in another language. I was able to pick out a few words that looked slightly familiar. I think the language was Latin-based. Whoo-hoo to high school Spanish class. I glanced at Marie with question on my face.

"Romanian."

"Can you speak this too?" I asked with a hint of disbelief in my voice.

She ducked her head and nodded. "Part of the early training is languages. You didn't get that."

"Romanian and German. Any others?"

She lifted her head to meet my eyes. "Greek, Portuguese, Spanish, French, and Italian."

"That's enough." I stood, leaving both books on the floor. "This is going beyond the point of insanity, even for you. I can't deal with this. I won't."

Marie followed me to the bedroom door and blocked my exit with the strength she'd shown in the foyer. "The picture! What does he look like?" She was angry now, something Marie seldom was.

"The Devil," I blurted.

She stared at me for a moment then went back to the ancient book. She flipped back a page and shoved the picture of the hovering, winged figure into my face. "Look at him! What is he?"

I didn't answer, but she wasn't really expecting me to.

"*Vampir*, Kinsley," she said in a thick accent. "He's a Vampire. We're Shadowers. Do you understand now?"

"Understand? What could I possibly understand? That you're delusional? Insane? There's no such thing as vampires! I don't care what pictures you have in your stupid little book."

"You won't even listen to me!" Marie yelled. "This is why Tom and Claire should be here. They were supposed to explain everything then I was going to train you."

"Are you trying to tell me my parents are a part of your delusion? Now you've gone too far. I am *not* going to stand here and let you talk about them like this." I started to cry and tried to push Marie out of the way of the door. She held her ground with her new freakish strength.

"You are not going to leave until you've seen this whole book and believe me! Legends, myths, folklore, it all comes from somewhere! Vampires are real. They've been here since the dawn of time. Some are evil, some are good. Just like humans. Shadowers protect the Monarchs of the Royal family. We have been trained since the beginning to protect the Monarchs!"

Marie pushed me backward until I stumbled over the pillows on the floor and fell on my butt. "Damn it, Marie! I've had enough of all this nonsense."

"You will listen to what I have to say! I love you and I'm not going to let them kill you like they did your parents. I will teach you what you need to know and you will be able to protect yourself!"

This new Marie standing in front of me was bossy, talking in complete sentences, and had said the one thing that would make me listen to her. She'd told me someone had killed my parents.

Chapter Ten

AS I STARED at Marie in shock, I heard the front door open and Rachel call to us. Marie looked at me then opened the bedroom door. I got up from the floor.

Marie yelled to the other room, "I want you to be in here, Rachel. You'll believe me and I need you to help me convince Kinsley."

Rachel bounced into Marie's room. "You will not believe how awesome Beck's condo is. There are plants, artwork, and a view of the city to die for. Not that your view isn't great, Kins, but his is of Elliott Bay." Rachel looked at my pale face and the mess of Marie's floor. "What's wrong? What's going on?"

"Marie was just getting ready to tell me that my parents were murdered." I turned to Marie and resisted the urge to shake her. First all this nonsense about vampires and now lies about my parents.

"Marie! What are you doing?" Rachel put her arm around my shoulders. "Don't do this to Kinsley."

"Do what? I didn't kill Tom and Claire. I tried to save them."

"I've had enough. Quit making up these stories." I was starting to shake.

Marie shook her head. "They're not stories. The vampires are real. They killed your mom and dad."

"Vampires? What the hell?" Rachel stared at Marie.

Marie gripped Rachel's shoulders. "Rachel, you have to help me convince Kinsley about what's going on. Look at my books. Read them. You'll understand."

That was all it took. I ended up in Marie's bedroom on the floor with her and Rachel until well after the sun came up. Rachel is impulsive and trusting. She completely believes in the idea of life on other planets, ghosts, unicorns, mermaids, witches, and anything supernatural. She took one look at the picture of the *Vampir* and didn't even think to question it. She now believed in vampires.

Marie translated some of the main parts of her 'Vampire Bible' to us while Rachel diligently wrote it all down in a notebook. By ten o'clock I'd had all I could take. I stood to go to bed. Rachel still sat on the floor with Marie, flipping through the pages of the photo album and the book of vampire secrets.

"Where are you going?" Rachel asked, almost absently.

"Gee, how about bed? We drove here yesterday, unloaded everything, and then were attacked by my crazy aunt. Now, I'm supposed to believe in ghastly fairy tales. My head hurts. I'm tired. I'm going to sleep."

"But we're not done going through stuff." Rachel looked up at me, wide awake and alert.

"I can only take so much."

"Oh, honey. I didn't even think about how hard all this would be," Rachel said. She stood and stretched her arms toward the ceiling. "You still don't believe any of this, do you?"

I rubbed my hand over my face. "I'm trying."

"No you're not. You're stressed out and dealing with the loss of your mom and dad." Rachel stared at me. "But you've never been willing to think outside the box. Why can't you just for one minute accept there's something in this world besides us? Why can't you even consider there might be vampires?"

"Why can't you grow up?" I yelled.

Rachel took a step back as though I'd slapped her. "Grow up? Because I'm willing to open my mind to other possibilities, you think I need to grow up?"

"Girls," Marie stepped between us. "I didn't want you to fight with each other. I just wanted you to understand."

I held up a hand. "Listen, Marie, I need some time. You told me vampires are real and then you tried to tell me my parents were murdered. If vampires killed them, why were they killed in a car accident? Why not just rip their throats out and drain them of all their blood?" I was being sarcastic but I couldn't help it. I'd been up for almost thirty hours straight.

Marie scoffed. "They're smarter than that. What would people think if they found dead bodies with fang marks in the necks? Duh."

"Who knows? I don't care right now. I'm going to bed, hopefully until tomorrow morning." I turned to go to my own room.

"Um, Kins," Rachel stopped me with the sound of her voice, almost apologetic. "You have dinner with Beck tonight at seven. His place. He wants to talk about you working for him. I recommended Marie and I take a rain check this time."

"Okay, then I'll sleep until at least six. Good night." I walked to my room and shut the door. I put my back to the wall and slid down to the floor, resting my forehead on my knees.

Was Rachel right? Was I so closed-minded that I couldn't even entertain the idea of vampires? Holy crap, what was wrong with me? Was I actually considering that there was some truth to what Marie said?

"I have to get some sleep."

I stumbled over boxes and landed face first on my bed. But

sleep wouldn't come. I kept playing the pictures of Marie's photo album in my head like a movie reel.

I finally slept. It was fitful and I had dreams that mixed with reality. I dreamed of Rachel and Marie. I dreamed of my parents. I also dreamed of Beck.

As Beck and I walked in my dream, a man came out of the shadows. He was dirty and wearing a black trench coat. I could tell he was going to approach us for a handout. Beck pulled me behind him and spoke in German to the bum. Then the bum jumped in the air and flew toward us. I screamed as Beck was thrown from me and the bum grabbed my neck and lifted me from the ground. His eyes glowed red and when he opened his mouth, he had fangs.

I sat straight up in bed and tried to orient myself. My hands went to my neck. I knew it had just been a dream but my heart was still beating a mile a minute. Damn it. Now vampires were going to be part of my dreams and not just Marie's crazy world.

I dug in my sweatpants pocket for my cell phone. It was five o'clock. I waited for my heart to slow and then walked to the kitchen for some water. I stood next to the fridge for a few moments and held the cool bottle against my forehead. Glancing to Marie's room, I saw the door was partially open.

Marie and Rachel were sacked out on the floor covered with the sheets and blanket from the bed. The books were next to them. They looked like two children sleeping peacefully. Why weren't they having nightmares?

I went back to my room, swallowed two Tylenol, and took a shower. I finally felt awake as I dried my hair.

I needed this job and I didn't want Marie's strange behavior to ruin it. Of course, Beck's behavior toward Marie had also been odd. I wondered if I'd get any real answers from Beck or if I should let it go to see if he would bring anything up first.

At six-thirty, I went back into Marie's room and tried to

rouse Rachel. She didn't move when I said her name. I squatted next to her and put my hand on her shoulder. "Rach, wake up."

She mumbled something and pulled the sheet over her head.

"Can I go to Beck's early?"

"Tired. Go away." She rolled from her side to her stomach and buried her head in her pillow. I had always been jealous of Rachel's ability to sleep through anything.

"Rachel." Nothing. Not even movement or grumbling this time.

Marie slept, oblivious. I went back to my bedroom and took the blanket off my bed. I put it over the two of them and the books, adding to the mess. Couldn't have Psycho and Sleeping Beauty getting chilled.

I was half an hour early but wanted to get this meeting started. I pocketed my key, along with my cell phone, and opened the door. There was a young man in the hallway, just opening Beck's door. He jumped and almost dropped the bag he was holding.

"Miss Kinsley, you scared me." He didn't look a day over sixteen.

"How do you know my name?" I was curious what this kid was doing going into Beck's condo.

"I'm Nathaniel. I run errands for Dr. Alexander. I thought you weren't going to be here until seven." He juggled the bag he was holding and I reached out to help him.

He moved so quickly I was caught off guard.

"I've got it," he yelped.

"I was only trying to help."

"Wait here. I'll see if Dr. Alexander is ready to see you." Nathaniel rushed through the door and closed it.

Thirty seconds passed and the door swung open.

"I'm sorry for my behavior, Miss Kinsley. Please come in."

He stood to the side so I could enter. Beck was nowhere to be seen. But, holy shit, Rachel had been right about his place.

Although it had the exact same layout, only reversed, as my condo, there was nothing similar about the feel. He had artwork, throw rugs, thriving plants, and candles. His walls had been painted with accent colors; dark reds and shades of brown were opposite beige walls.

The man had incredibly elegant taste and obviously had money. Nothing was flashy, but it did shout wealth.

Nathaniel cleared his throat behind me and I turned to look at him. He was maybe two inches taller than me which put him at about 5'9". He still looked really young, but maybe eighteen instead of sixteen.

"Would you like a glass of wine while you wait for Dr. Alexander to join you?" When I nodded he asked, "Red or white?"

"I prefer white, thank you."

Nathaniel turned, walking to the kitchen, and I followed. There was a small wine fridge on the marble counter top. While he selected a bottle and then began to open it, I had a thought. "If you work for Beck, what does he need me for?"

Breath stirred the hair by my left ear and Beck's musical voice filled my senses. "You shall be taking care of other needs, Kinsley."

I swallowed. Oh my.

Chapter Eleven

I QUICKLY TURNED. I hadn't heard Beck come into the room. He was wearing pressed black slacks and a maroon silk shirt that was buttoned to just below his throat. I suddenly felt very underdressed in my jeans and sweatshirt.

Beck noticed me looking down at my clothes and smiled as he took one of my hands. "Do not worry. You look beautiful."

I snorted when I laughed then ripped my hand from his to cover my mouth. Would I always be at my worst with this man?

"Kinsley, this is not a formal interview. I already told you that you were hired."

"What do you mean by *other* needs?" I swallowed again.

Beck laughed. "If only you could see the look on your face. Nathaniel has been my, for lack of a better explanation, personal assistant for quite a few years."

I glanced at Nathaniel. "Is child labor legal in England?"

"I assure you, he is older than he looks. I have become busy since arriving in the States and Nathaniel cannot efficiently take care of both my workload and my personal needs. I would like to have him continue to take care of my business affairs. You will take care of my school schedule and needs since you'll be on campus anyway. I would also have you run some errands, such as shopping, on your way from campus to here." Beck reached around me to pick up the glass of wine I'd been waiting for.

He handed it to me and I was careful to make sure our hands didn't touch. As I took a sip, Beck named my weekly salary. I almost spit wine on his polished Italian shoes.

It didn't take me long to calculate a monthly amount and then yearly. "That's ridiculous! That's more than I'm going to make as a first year teacher." I wiped my lips with the back of my hand.

"If that is true, then maybe you should quit school and be my assistant. Teachers are not paid nearly enough."

I poked my finger into his chest. It was like poking granite. "Listen, mister, I am going to graduate. Besides, I wouldn't quit school when I haven't worked for you yet."

Beck tucked my hand into his. The electric feeling from the night we met coursed up my arm. "I think you're electrically charged. You shock me every time we touch," I said.

Nathaniel cleared his throat behind us and stepped around me with the bottle of wine. His movements caused Beck to drop my hand and step back.

"What do you think of the wine, Miss Kinsley?" Nathaniel poured more into my glass even though I'd only taken a small sip.

"It's very good, Nathaniel. Thank you."

"I prepare the meals. I was hoping if I gave you daily shopping lists, you could pick up the items we need from the natural foods market. I would also include you in dinner so you won't have to cook for yourself." Nathaniel smiled.

This was all so bizarre. "I have to feed Aunt Marie and Rachel, so thank you for the offer, but no."

"He can make dinner for all of us each night," Beck said. "I plan to keep you busy and worrying about food is not something you will have time to do. Will Rachel be living with you as well?"

Beck's ability to problem solve was amazing, yet I wasn't willing to be railroaded. "I don't need Nate to make us all dinner. Yes, Rachel is going to live with us. And I don't think Crazy Aunt Marie is very good company at the moment. Wouldn't you agree?"

"Did she explain to you why she acted the way she did?" Beck asked.

I gulped down some wine and held the glass out toward Nate so he could fill it back up. "Thanks, Nate."

He scrunched his face in confusion. "Why do you call me Nate when my name is Nathaniel?"

"It's a nickname. Hasn't anyone ever called you by a nickname?"

"We're very formal where we come from," Nate said.

"England?" I asked.

Nate looked to Beck and back to me. "Yes, England."

"Kinsley? Did Marie explain her odd behavior?" Beck seemed oblivious to the side conversation Nate and I were trying to hold.

"Yes." Now what did I say? That she believed in vampires and was supposed to teach me karate, jiu-jitsu, or some other crazy fighting style to defend myself? Like that would go over well.

I went with as much of the truth as I could bring myself to say. "She thinks my parents were murdered. She believes Rachel and I could be in danger and need to defend ourselves."

Beck nodded as though this were perfectly normal. "You do not need to tell me of her ideas about the death of your parents. Do you think she is right about you needing to know how to defend yourself?"

I saluted him with my wine glass. "I think any woman

living in a city needs to know how to defend herself."

He pursed his lips. "True. Did she say why she considered me, personally, a threat?"

Oh, wow. I hadn't even thought of that. Did Marie think Beck was a vampire? No way. He didn't come close to resembling the picture of the nasty *Vampir* the drawing had depicted.

"I don't think it was you, personally, as much as a strange man in our kitchen. That's what I get for letting her answer the door." I tried to laugh.

He seemed satisfied for the moment. "Let us go over my proposal for your daily schedule while Nathaniel makes dinner. You are a little early."

"Sorry about that. Rachel was sleeping and I couldn't get her to tell me if I was allowed to come early."

He raised his hand, as though to touch my cheek, but pulled back before making contact. "If this arrangement works to your liking, you can come and go as you please at any time, night or day."

Oh my.

For the next hour, Beck went over his daily schedule. All his classes were evening classes no matter what quarter he taught.

I tried to protest when he started sharing all the technological items he was going to be giving me. He talked over my objections and rationally explained why I needed an iPhone, iPad, and laptop. He also told me I was going to earn every cent of the overpriced salary he was planning to pay me.

Beck walked me through how to work the phone since I'd been using a different brand. He showed me how to sync my phone to his computer and phone, that way I could update his schedule and he could update mine. The phone was already programmed with numbers: his, his secretary at the University, Nate's, and a number of local businesses. Part of Beck's job with the History Department was as a liaison with local museums and art galleries.

Just when my head was starting to spin, Nate came into the office and said dinner was ready. I hadn't noticed the wonderful smells in the air until that moment.

"What are we having? It smells delicious."

Nate beamed at me. "Beef flank steak, baked potatoes, and tossed green salad."

"If it tastes as good as it smells, I might take you up on the offer of being our cook."

Nate nodded. "Nothing would please me more, Miss Kinsley."

"Why do you both speak so formally?" I asked.

"As Nathaniel mentioned, where we were in England was a formal setting. I taught at Oxford."

"I bet that's a little more stuffy than U-dub." I smiled. The University of Washington and Oxford University were probably polar opposites. I mean, UW is a good school but Oxford is a distinguished university. "Why in the world would you give up working there to come to Seattle?"

Beck touched a finger to his lips. "We tend to covet what we cannot have. Seattle offers, new blood, if you will. England had become boring."

I swear Nathaniel made a noise from behind me but when I turned to look at him, it was as though he wasn't even listening to the conversation.

Beck held out a dining room chair for me. I had finished three glasses of wine in the hour we went over my new responsibilities. That was a lot for me so I put my hand over my glass when Nate tried to pour me more.

"Come, Kinsley, you can have more wine. You have only to walk across the hall," Beck said.

"Maybe after dinner. I've had enough for now. This is

supposed to be business. I'll take a glass of water though." I stood and Nate stopped me.

"Part of my job entails meals. Please sit."

"If I'm really going to be coming and going as I please," I looked at Beck for confirmation and he nodded his head, "then you're going to have to quit treating me like a guest."

Nate held out a hand. "Let me treat you like a guest for the evening. It has been so long since we've had dinner company." At my nod, he got me a glass of water then went back to the kitchen for dinner.

I thanked Nate when he put a plate of food in front of me. At first bite, I groaned my approval as Beck and Nate looked on expectantly. "Pour me more wine, Nate. It would be a shame to ruin this steak with plain water."

"Wait until you taste dessert," Nate said with a smile.

"If you can put up with Marie's bipolar mood swings, Nate, I will let you cook for us every night."

"Bring Marie and Rachel tomorrow. Everything will be fine." Beck smiled and drank his own wine. His goblet was dark and the wine stained his lips a dark red. I stared fascinated as he wiped his mouth with a linen napkin.

"Why aren't you eating?" I almost hadn't noticed Beck was only drinking wine instead of eating the delicious food.

"I ate on campus. One of the downfalls of teaching late classes."

I tilted my head. "I can't believe you would pass up Nate's cooking."

Nate sat down next to me and poured his own wine. "Thank you, Kinsley."

Beck nodded. "I will eat with the three of you tomorrow night."

Tomorrow night. Another night with Beck.

Hopefully Marie would behave herself.

Chapter Twelve

AFTER DINNER I tried to help clean up, but Nate wouldn't let me. He insisted I eat dessert, drink more wine, and relax with Beck.

I told Beck about growing up in Paradise and how Marie had always been part of my life. He let me talk about my parents and it was easier than I thought. Maybe because he hadn't known them.

I finished my last swallow of wine and stood. "I really should be going. It's been a long day. Well, two days."

Beck stood. "I understand. I hope I did not overwhelm you."

"No. I'm actually a little excited to start. It will be nice to focus on someone else's problems instead of my own."

"I am pleased to offer the distraction." He put his hand on the small of my back and guided me toward the kitchen.

Nate appeared from down the hall. The kitchen was spotless and a dim light was on above the stove. I set my glass on the counter. Next to the empty bottle of wine.

"I drank a bottle of wine?" I was appalled.

Nate looked at the clock. "In about five hours. Is that a problem?"

"Yes," I said at the same time Beck said "No."

"Yes, it is," I said. "I can't usually drink that much. I get tipsy and I get a headache." Oddly, I didn't feel the least bit drunk.

"It was spread out over a long period of time. Do not worry about it. No one here will judge you." Beck shook his head, as though I were being foolish. "Besides, as I mentioned before, you only have to walk across the hall."

"Is it really midnight?" I asked.

"Close enough," Nate said.

"Isn't midnight the witching hour or something?"

Nate laughed. "Witches aren't the scariest things out roaming at midnight."

I laughed. "You're a little different, Nate. Fortunately you're also very sweet and an expert cook, so it makes up for it." I leaned in to give him a hug.

Startled, Nate moved away from my embrace. Then he said something under his breath and pulled me into a bear hug that lifted my feet off the floor.

"Put her down, Nathaniel, you will crush her," Beck said from behind me.

Nate put me on my feet. "Sorry. I'm just not used to all the friendliness and compliments. Please pardon my rudeness, Miss Kinsley."

"You're not being rude and stop calling me Miss, okay?" He nodded and I realized I hadn't been this comfortable around virtual strangers in my life. Being the outsiders my family had been in Paradise, we weren't exactly invited to lots of social functions. I was usually much more guarded with my emotions.

"Plan to arrive here between six and six-thirty in the evening," Beck said. "I insist Rachel and Marie be here. Everything will be fine."

"Can I bring anything? More wine?"

"I have all the wine you could ever drink. Please, go get some more rest." Beck opened the door for me. "Good night."

I turned in the small hallway and looked at my door. I dreaded going inside because I was pretty sure I knew what would greet me.

I opened the door, it wasn't locked, and saw just what I had expected. Marie and Rachel were awake and sitting at the kitchen table. They had Marie's books out and were busy at work again. I sighed my disapproval and Rachel looked up.

"Oh, knock it off, Kins. I've decided I know how to get you to look at this stuff with us. You're going to treat it like a school assignment. If you want it to be fantasy, that's fine. We won't spend any more time trying to convince you it's real. But you are going to study it with us."

I shut the door and leaned against it. Rachel was like a dog with a bone when she decided on something. I knew I wasn't going to change her mind. She would keep throwing all this in my face if I tried to ignore it. She'd let me go at my own pace if I agreed. Sometimes it was hell to have such a good best friend.

"But first," Rachel said, "tell us all about dinner with Beck. Does he cook? What did you eat? Isn't his condo great?"

Since we'd been friends for over fifteen years, I was used to the way Rachel talked and the way her thoughts moved like whitewater rapids. She could leap from one subject to another and back without missing a beat. She was going to make a great lawyer.

"You didn't meet Nathaniel?" I asked.

"Who's Nathaniel? Where would I have met him?" Rachel was back to looking at the books in front of her.

"Nathaniel works for Beck. He cooked dinner."

This got Rachel's attention. "Works for Beck? Like a maid or something?"

Nathaniel was kind of like a maid but with more responsibilities. "I don't think so. He does the cooking and he cleans up afterward, but he's also Beck's assistant."

"I thought you were going to be his assistant." Rachel stood to get a beer from the fridge.

"I'm going to be his school assistant since I'll be on campus everyday. He needs help keeping his schedule for university functions organized. He's really involved with the local museums and art places. Oh, get this, he used to teach at Oxford."

Marie looked up from one of the books and said, "Oxford is lovely this time of year. We should go." Then she went back to the book.

I almost asked how she knew anything about Oxford but quickly changed my mind.

"Okay, Kins, sit down. Do you want a beer?" Rachel reached back toward the fridge.

"No thanks. I had quite a bit of wine during and after dinner. I'll take a bottle of water, though."

Rachel handed me the bottle and sat in the chair with her knees pulled to her chest. "This stuff is so cool, even if only from a historical standpoint. You wouldn't believe the information Marie knows."

I decided to play along, just to appease the two most important people in my life. I sat at the table. "Okay, tell me about the vampires. While you're at it, tell me about the werewolves, witches, goblins, and devils." I took a big swallow of water. Maybe I did need a beer. Maybe I needed something stronger.

"Don't be bitchy," Marie said.

I choked on my water.

"I have the Book of Protection," Marie said. "It has been passed down in the family with the silver daggers. The ones you have now, Kinsley. Silver has always been the one weakness of almost every mythological creature."

"Exactly. Mythological," I said.

"Then why did your dad have a case full of silver daggers?" Rachel asked me.

"Why does your dad have a box full of family bibles? Because it's important to the history of your family. It's the same with the daggers," I said.

"Just read the damn book and then tell me what you think," Rachel said. "Well, you can't read the book because it's not in English, but at least read what Marie has translated for us. I wrote it all down in a notebook. We've only made it a quarter of the way though, but everything at the beginning explains the history of Shadowers and Vampires.

"There's a tiny bit about your family's role in it, but we haven't gotten to that part yet. Each family adds to the book, so your family's history is toward the end." Rachel handed me the notebook. She'd written about ten pages of information. It was mostly listed with bullets. It wouldn't take me long to get through it.

"Fine. I'll read it." I didn't want to admit it to them yet, but I was getting curious.

The silver daggers had always been my weak spot. From the moment I'd laid my eyes on them, I'd been creating stories in my head about their uses. In elementary and junior high, I'd even written stories about battling creatures with the silver daggers. I couldn't believe I'd forgotten that. I must have had an imagination at one point in my life.

I took the notebook from Rachel and headed to my room.

"Where are you going?" They both asked me.

"I'm going to read this in the confines of my room where you two can't bug me. Maybe you can make yourselves useful and unpack some boxes. I'll see you when the sun is up."

I went in my room and looked at my own boxes. I should unpack them. I kicked off my shoes and started ripping tape off boxes until I found the one with my bedside lamp. I put the lamp on my headboard and plugged it in. I switched on the lamp and shut off the bedroom light. I changed into my pajamas.

Pulling the sheet over me, I rolled to my side and started reading Rachel's notes from the Book of Protection. I owed it to my best friend and aunt to at least listen to what they had to say. They'd do it for me without question.

Chapter Thirteen

Translated from The Book of Protection by Marie DeVoe and Rachel Fredericks.

Written by Rachel for my best friend, Kinsley Preston, who is currently a non-believer...prepare to be amazed, chica.

Dictated by Crazy Aunt Marie (as read from The Book). Side commentary by Rachel (because even though I believe, some of this is just really weird)

- Since the beginning of life itself, there have been good and evil forces at battle.
- The Creature of Shadow created beings of darkness to prowl from sundown to sunup.
- The Creature of Light created beings to protect the earth from the shadow beings...blah,

blah, blah...some of this is really boring and kind of 'end of the worldish'....

• When humans became part of the world, their blood was the food for the beings of darkness and light (eww...gross)

• The beings of darkness learned they could feed off emotion from the blood and would become stronger and more powerful if they took the life of the human.

• The beings of light discovered that there were humans with different blood...more crap about blood being a lifeforce (wow, I forgot how Marie rambles about nothing sometimes)

Here are the main points and the good stuff that I think I've gotten from the beginning of this 'Vampire Bible':

1. Vampires DO exist!

2. There are good and bad vampires. All of them must feed off blood but do not have to kill the source: humans (I wonder if they'd drink animal blood? wow - can't believe I just asked that)

3. Blood has different 'flavors' depending on the emotion being felt by the human. Vampires are similar to incubus or succubus (demons) in the sense that they feed off the blood and emotion.

(well, that explains why they probably wouldn't drink from animals)

4. Shadowers (what you guys are) have 'special' blood. This blood allows the Monarchs to become stronger and be in the sunlight without adverse side effects.

5. This is soooo cool!!!

<u>Shadowers and The "Good" Vampires</u>

• Shadowers have a rare blood disorder that allows them to be special food (do you have a rare blood disorder, Kinsley?)

• Shadowers come into their 'powers' between the ages of 18 and 22 (that's you!) Powers may include, but are not limited to: prolonged lifespan, mind control, control of the weather, and some other stuff (Marie was mumbling again)

• There were ten original family bloodlines that claimed to be Shadowers. Monarchs (royal Vampire family) offered protection to Shadowers in exchange for their blood. The Shadowers agreed as long as a life would never be taken during a bloodpact.

• The Shadowers realized they couldn't be helpless against any vampires so they learned to fight using martial arts and weapons made of silver. They also learned to fight because a Monarch is vulnerable just after a bloodpact exchange as their body metabolizes the Shadower's blood (it's kind of a symbiotic relationship).

• Shadowers can only give blood to a Monarch every few days (no exact count). Their body produces more blood than a regular human but not enough to allow for a daily bloodpact.

• Monarchs also need the blood of regular humans because it's still their diet.

• All Vampires can eat 'normal' food in order to keep up the appearance of being human, but it is believed the food has no taste and offers no nutrients.

The "Bad" Vampires

• Goal - world domination. They call themselves the Sovereignty. They feel they are superior to humans and only need them for food.

• About 2,000 years ago, the Sovereignty split from the Monarchs because of being punished for killing humans. They have been at 'war' ever since.

• Vlad the Impaler was a real vampire. He wanted to be the leader of the Sovereignty. Vlad was destroyed by the Monarchs and Shadowers.

All Vampires

• Can heal themselves almost immediately from a wound, unless that wound is caused by a silver weapon. Anything inflicted by silver takes days to heal.

- Stake through the heart is a myth. The only thing that can kill a vampire is cutting off their head and burning the body.

- NOTE: Silver weapons (cuts made with silver blades or bullets made out of silver) will slow the vamp down long enough for you to get away or try to cut off their head.

- It's true that sunlight will kill a vampire but it doesn't happen instantly. Prolonged exposure to sun will cause them to dehydrate and turn to dust. The older a vampire is, the longer they can withstand the sun. As mentioned before, the blood of a Shadower allows a vampire to be immune to sunlight.

- The Sovereignty Vampires DO NOT know who the Shadowers are. Only Monarchs hold this knowledge. They can smell you or something. (aren't those called pheromones? Kinsley, this means that your blood is weird and you secrete smells... I don't think you smell funny...)

**So I asked Marie - what about the vampires that aren't Monarchs or Sovereignty? She just stared at me. I explained that it sounds like the Monarchs and Sovereignty are the ones who are in charge and aren't there just plain old vampires wandering around the world. She said we'd get to that later.

<u>Shadower Families</u>

• According to the book, Shadower Families become part of the world of the Monarchs. Not only do they supply blood, they protect the Monarchs from danger.

• Your family had not bonded with a Monarch Family. Translation - your parents weren't food for anyone. Marie's family thought they were bonding with a Monarch Family, but it was actually a Sovereignty posing as Monarchs. Isaac tricked Marie into believing he was a good vampire when he was actually a bad one.(Marie talks about this in the first person. I know she's crazy and all, but can she really be like 150 years old? Even I don't know if I believe that.)

• Your dad was using his consulting business as a front to go out and hunt vampires. (hunt vampires? seriously? this is so awesome!)

Here's my personal opinion and what I want you to think about. I'm your best friend and I love you like family (probably more than my real family!) I want you to be safe from any dangers in the world. Even if there aren't vampires, there are icky and dangerous people out there.

I think we should keep translating this book and take some self-defense classes. We need to be safe from the world, whether there are vampires in it or not. Who knows, maybe now that we know what to look for, we can find the proof to convince you they're real. The point is that you, Marie, and I will be safe from anything or anyone. Okay, chica?

Love, Rachel

I CLOSED the spiral notebook and looked at my phone. It was two in the morning and I'd read the damn notes three times. I actually found all the information interesting.

The book and movie-loving, creative person inside me had come to life. Everything Rachel wrote was fascinating from a fictional, mythical standpoint. Thinking that vampires could be real? It was amazing.

The logical person in me still couldn't be convinced. I needed to see things with my own eyes. I decided to do what Rachel had suggested. I'd enroll the three of us in some self-defense classes and maybe some kickboxing lessons. It appeared Marie could take care of herself, but I wanted her with me.

Maybe I'd even do some research on vampires and other creatures of lore. As Marie said, myths and legends come from somewhere. It would make Marie and Rachel happy if I was taking them seriously. To a point.

I put the notebook on my headboard and turned off the lamp. I could hear Rachel and Marie moving around in the rest of the condo. I stayed in bed because I wasn't ready to talk about what I'd read.

If my family were Shadowers, that meant my mom and dad

were fighters, killers, and vampire food. I tried to think of any peculiar happenings at my house. All that came to mind was anything dealing with Marie. My dad traveled every other weekend for his business and my mom was always home. Where had Dad traveled to? Rachel said his consulting business was a front for hunting vampires. Had my dad really been out slaying vampires?

I sat up in bed, "My dad was Buffy!" I flopped back down. "This is insane."

I kept going over in my head anything that would point to some kind of secret life my parents had been living. That's what I fell asleep to.

I knew I was dreaming because my mom and dad were in the living room of my new condo. They were laughing and helping Rachel and Marie hang pictures on the walls. I watched from the bedroom door, feeling like an outcast.

All four had bite marks on their necks. Blood ran down into the collars of their shirts.

Chapter Fourteen

I WOKE to sun shining through the window of my bedroom. I groaned as I rolled over and buried my head in my pillow. It felt like I hadn't gotten much sleep. My eyes were gritty and my body was sore.

My dreams played back in my head. I'd had the dream about Beck and the bum again. Maybe the bottle of wine was to blame. I put my hand to my throat, feeling foolish, then shook my head.

I got out of bed. It was time to go for a run. I needed the exercise but I needed to clear my head more. After putting on mesh shorts and a tank top, I laced up my Nikes and grabbed sunglasses.

I checked on Rachel and Marie, asleep on Marie's floor. I needed to convince the girl to move in and get her stuff here. I took the single key for the door and slid it in the inside pocket of my running shorts. Last, I grabbed my ancient iPod and put it in my exercise armband. I'd have to get my music transferred to my new phone today or download some music apps. It would be too bulky to carry both and I needed my music right now more than I needed a phone.

I slipped out the door. As the elevator took me to the main floor and lobby area, I did some stretches.

Gerald was working at the front desk. "Miss Kinsley, what are you doing out so early?"

I pulled my sunglasses low on my nose so I could look over the tops of them. "I like to run early in the morning before the humidity gets too bad."

"Is anyone going with you?"

I looked behind me. "Obviously not."

He blinked rapidly and I realized I sounded rude. Too bad. I hadn't gotten much sleep over the last few days and I didn't like dreaming about vampires or my dead parents.

"I always ran in the mornings around campus. Here won't be any different. See ya." I pushed my glasses into place, turned on my running mix, and headed out the doors.

Nickelback blasted in my ears as I ran and thought about all the things I was going to need now that I wasn't living on campus. I either had to get a car or figure out the bus schedules. Was I going to need a more professional wardrobe working for Beck? What kinds of people would I be meeting with?

The more I thought about everything, the harder I ran. I was supposed to empty my brain, not clog it up with more issues. The next thing I knew, I was in a neighborhood I didn't recognize with sweat pouring off me, and I was breathing hard. I shut off my music.

I turned and began to walk back the way I'd just come. It was dumb to leave the house without my cell phone. I started to jog. Even though so much had gone on since Rachel and I had left campus, I knew there had been at least three other murders in Seattle during the summer. They'd all happened between midnight and four, but that didn't mean I should be careless. I should have downloaded a music app on my new phone before I left the condo instead of sticking in my comfort zone of using the iPod. My excuse was it had been my mom's. I'd always given her a hard time for not embracing new technology. None of that mattered now; I'd been stupid.

The sound of a car caught my attention. A black Mercedes with tinted windows was headed right for me. The car slowed as it came closer and my heart began to beat faster than it already was.

When the car stopped and the door opened, I took off running. I didn't look back.

"Kinsley! Wait, it's me!"

I slowed and turned. "Nate? What the hell?" When he reached me I punched him in the shoulder. "Jesus, you scared the crap out of me!" I hit him again.

"I'm sorry. I didn't mean to frighten you. It's not safe for you to be out alone." Nate tried to take my arm.

I ripped away and got ready to blast him about how I'd been taking care of myself in the city for years when squealing tires drew our attention. Behind Nate, coming right at us, was a huge, black military-style Hummer. It didn't look like it was slowing down.

Nate wrapped an arm around me, jumped in the air, and we hit the ground like a bag of bricks. It didn't hurt as much as I expected but I still had the wind knocked out of me.

"Are you okay?" Nate looked up at me. He had his arms wrapped around me and I was sprawled on top of him. He had taken the brunt of the fall.

A voice I didn't recognize yelled at us over the sound of the engine. "Stop moving! Let go of Kinsley and keep your hands where I can see them!"

Nate growled and didn't release his steel arms from around me. Finally my breath came back. "They know my name. Let me see who it is." I tried to roll off him, but he wouldn't let me.

Instead, Nate rolled his body and I was now under him. He

sat up slowly into a crouch and turned so that he blocked my body with his. "Who are you and what do you want?" The meek, young Nate from the night before was not next to me. This man was powerful and vibrating with energy.

"Get your hands off Kinsley and then we'll talk!"

I looked over Nate's shoulder and saw a big man standing behind the passenger door of the Hummer. He aimed a giant gun at us. I stared. He looked familiar, but I couldn't figure out from where.

"I think I know you. What's your name?" I yelled.

He didn't take his eyes from Nate and his gun never wavered. "Scott Masters. We met at your parents' funeral. Kinsley, I'm here to help you. Move away from the kid slowly. I'll shoot him if he tries to hurt you again."

"You will not! Get that gun off Nate and quit acting like I can't take care of myself!" I screeched at him.

First Nate scared the crap out of me and now this Scott Masters guy was trying to protect me when I didn't need it. I stood and pushed Nate away when he tried to stop me.

"You don't know who that is. Stay by me." Nate kept trying to block my body with his.

"If you get shot because you're both being morons, I am so going to be pissed!" I moved closer to the Hummer. "Mr. Masters, quit pointing that gun at us or I'm calling the police!"

Masters finally made eye contact with me. He said something to the driver of the Hummer then lowered his gun. "I want you to get away from that guy and come over here. I'll take you home." His deep voice shook slightly. Was he that worried about me? Why?

"Mr. Masters, Nate is my friend. He lives next door to me and we work for the same person. While I appreciate your concern, you went a little overboard. No, you went a lot overboard."

"Your friend?" Masters said something to the person driving the Hummer again. The engine shut off and the driver's door opened. A gigantic man got out and started toward us. I could actually see his muscles ripple when he walked.

"Stop where you are. I don't want to hurt you." Nate sounded like he meant it, but he was about a third of the size of the giant coming toward us.

"Stop it! All of you just stop it!" I screamed. The three men stopped moving and looked at me. "I am not a damsel in distress. I didn't ask for any personal bodyguards. Go away!"

I brushed the dirt off my hands and knees, noticed my right knee was bleeding. I saw mom's iPod, even though it had been in the armband, was cracked. That brough tears to my eyes. My sunglasses were gone, too. "I'm going home."

I turned and started to jog. My knee hurt, and stupidly, the tears started running down my cheeks. Not because I was in pain but because my life had become something I didn't recognize anymore. I could hear two male voices calling my name; Nate and Mr. Masters. I ignored them.

Nate in the black Mercedes and Masters and his driver in the Hummer were following slowly behind me. I'm sure we made quite the parade.

It took over an hour for me to get home. I ignored every plea the men made. By the time I got to the entrance of the condo, the blood had run down my leg and my sock was stained. It wasn't gushing, but I'm sure jogging for an hour hadn't helped.

Gerald took one look at my disheveled appearance and his mouth made an 'O'. I walked to the elevator and stabbed the up button. Gerald grabbed the phone and I heard him say "Dr. Alexander," just before the elevator doors closed.

When the doors opened on my floor Beck was standing there. "What happened and where is Nathaniel?"

"Nathaniel is what happened to me. Nathaniel and Scott Masters."

"What?" Beck yelled. Then he saw my leg. His nostrils flared and his face hardened. "Who did this to you?"

Before I could answer, Beck swung me up into his arms and carried me down the hallway.

"What in the hell do you think you're doing?" I said.

"Nathaniel was supposed to watch over you, not injure you. He will be punished." The coldness in Beck's voice scared me.

"Beck, stop, please, and put me down." He stopped walking and looked at me. For a moment, we just stared at each other.

"Kinsley," he said.

The door to the stairwell flung open and Nate sprang through. Masters and the other man were right behind. Nate ran to us, spun, and dropped into a crouch like he was protecting Beck and me.

With his back to us, he addressed Beck. "Sir, I did not mean for Miss Kinsley to be injured. These two set off my protective instincts."

I sighed in frustration. "I wasn't injured, I don't need protection, and put me down."

Beck slowly set me on my feet, our bodies close.

"I don't know who you are, but Kinsley needs to come with us. Now," Mr. Masters said.

I spun away from Beck and glared at everyone in the hall. "Hello? I'm. Right. Here! You all need to stop treating me like a pet or a child." I rubbed my face. "Beck, don't be too mad at Nate. I think he was trying to protect me from the lunatic driving the Hummer." I glared at him then I transferred my stare to Scott Masters. "Mr. Masters, you had no right to scare me like that or point a gun at my friend."

He sighed and shook his head. "I promised your parents if anything happened to them, I'd look after you."

I waved my arms in the air. "Did you think of calling and checking on me like a normal person?"

He looked at his shoes. "Um, well, no."

I put my hands on my hips. "I live here and Dr. Alexander and Nate are my friends. This condo has great security. And most importantly, I don't need looking after. I'm an adult."

"Did you say Dr. Alexander?" Masters put his hand in his jacket like he was reaching for his gun again. "Dr. Beckford Alexander?"

Beck stared at both men for a moment. "You worked with Kinsley's father."

"How did you know that?" I asked Beck.

Beck met my gaze then looked back at the men at the end of the hall. "I make it a point to know about the different security firms in the area. I shall explain the whole story later, Kinsley. The condensed version is if you are going to work for me you will need security. I know some distasteful characters who do not like the way I do business."

Mr. Masters snorted. "She doesn't know."

"Know what?" I asked, looking back and forth between the men.

"You have two days to let Kinsley know what goes on in your business, Dr. Alexander, and then I get to talk to her."

"A week," Beck countered.

"Three days," Masters said.

"What in the hell is going on?" I asked.

"Three days, Dr. Alexander, and then I tell her the truth. By the way, I'm glad I know where you live now."

With that parting shot, Mr. Masters and his buddy went back down the stairwell.

Nate started to say something. I stopped him with my hand

out. "I don't want to talk to you right now." I looked at Beck. "I know I'm going to regret this, but I expect an explanation at dinner. I'm going to take a shower."

"I am relieved you still wish to talk to me," Beck said.

I huffed and opened the door to my condo. Then I slammed it behind me.

Chapter Fifteen

THE SHOWER MADE me feel worse because it gave me more time to think. First all the cryptic stuff with Marie and now more mysterious crap with Beck and this Scott Masters guy. I felt like I was living in a movie.

When I got out of the shower, Rachel was laying on my bed with her feet dangling off the end.

"The cute maid, Nathaniel, is waiting to talk to you in the living room," she said. "He woke me up pounding on the door and yelling for you. Can you believe something woke me up? It sounded like he was going to break the door down."

I had a towel wrapped around me. "Tell him to go away. I don't want to talk to him."

"I tried telling him you were in the shower and that I'd have you call him or come over when you were done but he said he'd wait." Rachel rolled over so she was on her stomach and looking at me. "Then I sat on the couch and tried to talk to him. I got some grunts but that was about it."

"I went for a run this morning and between Nate and Scott Masters, I didn't have a very good time." I pointed at my raw knee.

"Did you say Scott Masters?" Rachel sat up. "Isn't that the

hunk who was at your parents' funeral? The one who said he worked with your dad? What was he doing here?"

"I don't know. I was jogging and a car scared me. It was Nate. Then another car almost ran us over."

"What?" Rachel shrieked.

"Yeah. Welcome to my new world." I sat down next to her. "When did my life become a sci-fi soap opera?" I rested my head on her shoulder.

"Um, somewhere between the death of your parents and Marie showing us that crazy book?" Rachel said. "Let's go out and talk to Nathaniel together. Put on some clothes, though." She patted my uninjured knee.

"Thanks for being here. I don't know what I'd do without you."

She rested her head against mine. "You'd be strong just like you always are."

"I'm not strong," I said.

"That's not true. When I needed you, you were there for me. You were strong when I went through all that shit in high school. I'm just returning the favor now."

We shared that memory together in those few seconds. Rachel coming to me with the knowledge she was pregnant and her dad was going to have a fit. The heart wrenching discussions about whether or not to have an abortion, give the baby up for adoption, or try to keep it. She had only been sixteen.

I watched Rachel's face as she remembered her dad beating her within an inch of her life and my parents and me taking her to the hospital in Spokane. It was the only time I'd seen my dad lose his temper. He'd looked mad enough to kill Reverend Fredericks.

Four broken ribs and abdominal trauma had caused Rachel to lose the baby. Deep down, we knew it was for the best, but it didn't make her any less devastated. My parents had tried to get her to press charges. When she wouldn't do that, we'd tried to get her to move in with us. She wouldn't do that either. That was when I'd realized Rachel and her mom were being abused.

Since I couldn't protect Rachel any other way, I made sure that I was always there for her. She'd spent almost every weekend at my house our junior and senior years of high school and then we'd gone to college across the state.

She gave me a one-armed hug. "Nobody's life is perfect, Kinsley. Maybe I believe in all this crazy stuff because I need something to believe in."

She slipped out of my room so I could get dressed.

When I stepped out of the bedroom, she was in the kitchen making coffee and Nate was standing at one of the big windows. I walked over and saw that Scott Masters's Hummer was in the parking lot.

"Annoying man," Nate mumbled.

"You're both annoying," I said sweetly.

Without turning around, Nate said, "I never meant for you to get hurt. I was trying to protect you. Gerald called and said you'd gone for a run. I followed you from a distance just to make sure you were okay. Then I noticed that the Hummer was following you, too."

"First of all," I said, "why does it matter if I run alone? Why did Gerald call you? Secondly, it bothers me that you were following me. That's stalking."

Nate spun and glared at me. "You don't know how dangerous it is out there. You need to make sure one of us is with you at all times."

"Everyone keeps telling me how dangerous it is *out there.*" I made air quotes. "Maybe someone should be more specific. And what's with the attitude? You threw me down on the ground. You followed me like a stalker. You—"

Before I could finish my sentence Nate grabbed me by the shoulders and shook me. My teeth clattered together. I don't know why I thought he was a boy before. Nate was solid muscle.

"Nathaniel!" Beck's voice boomed from behind me. I didn't know how he'd gotten in, and at the moment, I didn't care. The hair on my arms stood up and the electricity feeling flowed over my skin. Nate backed away from me and looked like he was cowering against the windows.

"You will never manhandle Kinsley!" Beck walked toward us. His accent was much more pronounced when he was angry. "Are you okay?" he asked me, glaring at Nate.

I stepped back. "No. I'm not okay. I was almost run over by a car and you men seem to think I'm helpless. Someone better explain why I'm not supposed to be alone or else I'm done with all of this. I'll move." I crossed my arms. "You also need to explain what the deal is with Scott Masters. What did he mean by saying I didn't know about something and you needing to tell me in a few days. I'm tired of all the secrets and strangeness in my life!"

Marie chose that moment to come into the room. She had the stupid Book of Protection clutched in her arms.

I covered my eyes. "Not now, Marie, I can only handle one frickin' thing at a time. You and that book aren't it."

"Actually," Beck said, "now would be a wonderful time for Marie to bring the book in. Nathaniel, take Rachel to breakfast somewhere while Marie, Kinsley, and I talk about The Book of Protection."

I dropped my hands and stared at Beck with my mouth hanging open. How in the hell did he know about the book and why was he trying to get rid of Rachel?

"Rachel stays," I said. "I don't care if Nate does."

"Nathaniel's behavior is because of me. Please do not be

mad at him. We only want what is best for you." Beck turned toward Marie. "How much have you told her?"

"I told her everything, but she doesn't believe me." Marie was whining. "I showed her the book, the pictures, I even told her about her family legacy. She won't listen." She slammed the book onto the table.

Beck turned curious eyes to me. "The daughter of Tom Preston and Claire Kinsley does not believe?"

"Tell me what you know about that book and my parents. Now."

"I'm a history teacher, Kinsley. I study everything there is to know about history, legend, myth, and lore. The Book of Protection has been a hot topic for thousands of years. People have died to reveal or hide its existence. I wish I would have known your family had it. I might have been able to protect them."

I stumbled forward and dropped on shaky legs to the couch. "So, you believe in..." I couldn't bring myself to say the word out loud.

"Vampires?" Beck asked me. "I do believe in them. I have seen them, hunted them, killed them. When you are ready to believe, I will show them to you."

I sucked in a breath and put my hand to my throat.

"Until then, you have to understand your blood is precious. You should not go anywhere without Nathaniel or me at your side." Beck glared at Nathaniel. "However, if he does not start doing a better job, I will find a replacement."

"Hey," Nate protested, "It's really hard to protect someone who doesn't know they need it."

I wondered if I was dreaming again. Maybe that was it. I was dreaming, not losing my mind. I made eye contact with Rachel and I think she sensed my approaching breakdown.

"Okay, everyone. You really need to do a better job of

explaining mystical things to Kinsley. Marie, you know she's a realist. You didn't even try to introduce this topic to her in a good way. Beck, if you know anything about Kinsley's family at all, you'd know that they were rational and logical. You don't just throw non-rational things at my girl.

"Finally, Kinsley." Rachel sat down next to me. "Chica, you need to listen to what everyone has to say. You owe it to yourself and your parents to hear this out. Just listen, that's all we ask."

I held Rachel's hands in mine. We'd been through so much together and she was, and always would be, my best friend. She was right. I owed it to myself and my parents to hear what Marie and Beck had to say.

Then I could decide if *I* was crazy, or if they were.

Chapter Sixteen

BECK FINISHED READING Rachel's notes and I swear his lips twitched in a smile. "Very creative, Rachel. You would make me believe. It also shows Marie does not know as much about The Book as I thought she would."

"Marie has a mental condition," I said. "She doesn't know much about a lot of things. That's why I couldn't believe her to begin with."

"Let me add to what Rachel and Marie translated for you." Beck took a drink of water. He'd convinced us all to go over to his place so Nate could cook breakfast.

I'd changed to sweats and put my hair in a ponytail. Marie and Rachel were still in their pajamas. Nate was wearing what I'd consider workout clothes. There was a gash in his Adidas pants and his brown hair was mussed. I took some small comfort in the fact that he hadn't walked away from our tumble unscathed.

Beck, as usual, was dressed casually but impeccably. His dark hair brushed his shoulders because he hadn't pulled it back.

Beck turned and met my eyes. He smiled. Now he was downright gorgeous. I shook my head and got my mind firmly back on track. I needed to be processing the disturbing story, not checking out my new boss who was possibly a lunatic.

Beck raised an eyebrow. "Anything you would like to share? You seem deep in thought."

It wasn't like he could read my mind, or anything, but I blushed anyway. I looked away. "Just trying to take it all in," I lied.

"For the last two thousand years," Beck said, "the Monarchs, Shadowers, civilian fighters, and a few other groups have been trying to destroy rogue vampires and members of the Sovereignty. The rogue vampires are those who have been turned and not taken in by a group."

"How do you turn someone into a vampire, Beck? Is it like on movies and TV?" Rachel, while eating her eggs, was asking these questions like they were normal.

"I suppose," Beck answered. "A vampire must be at least one hundred years old before their blood is strong enough to bring The Change. Monarchs have strict rules about who is allowed to create others. If a vampire is not a member of the Monarchs, or does not have permission, the penalty for turning a human is death. In order to turn someone, the human's blood has to be almost drained and then they have to ingest the blood of a vampire. It causes a genetic change in the human. A vampire's blood produces cells almost a million times faster."

"How do you know all this?" I asked.

"I lost my family to vampires. Since I have money, I have invested a lot of time into the genetic research of blood. The Monarchs heard of my research and approached me to help their cause." He shrugged. "If we can create synthetic blood, we can give the vampires an alternative food source and maybe find a way to wipe out the Sovereignty."

"What does this have to do with Scott Masters and my

parents?" My head was spinning, but I needed to know if I could believe any of this.

"Scott Masters also wants to destroy the vampires. He started his security firm as a front to get into sensitive locations and learn valuable information," Beck said. "Your father helped him do that with his consulting business. Mr. Masters works for important individuals who have unexplained breeches in their security. Vampires have many different talents depending on how old they are and what they have learned throughout the years.

"Mind control, some degrees of invisibility, and teleporting, are just a few. Your father and Mr. Masters would find out which person in the company, or whatever location, was the vampire and they would, well..." Beck stopped, finally at a loss for words.

"Dispose of them. Tom and Scott would dispose of them." Marie's voice was strong but quiet in the uneasy silence. "Your mother was the better hunter and Shadower, but she refused to leave you and me alone. She could sense when a supernatural being was close. Just like you can."

"No I can't, Marie." This was getting weirder, yet in a way, it almost made sense. My dad had been gone a lot for work. My mother never went with him. Was this why they'd driven to Seattle almost every weekend when I'd gone away to college?

"You just don't know how to read your powers yet," Marie said. "That's what I meant when I tried to explain about you being trained this summer. Your mom said you were going to be stronger than any Shadower had been in hundreds of years."

"How could she possibly know that?" I demanded.

Beck cut in before Marie could answer. "Shadowers are usually trained from the moment they can walk. They had to be ready to protect themselves at all times because the Sovereignty gains almost unlimited power if they drain the blood of a

Shadower. The young Shadowers had to know when danger was near and be able to defend themselves."

"We moved to Paradise because there had never been a vampire sighting there," Marie said. "It's so small that missing people would be noticed. We could have a normal life. The people around us wouldn't be in danger. That's what Tom and Claire wanted for us. They thought they could let Kinsley live a normal life until she turned twenty-one. Then we'd introduce her to the world of vampires and Shadowers." Marie scooted from the table.

"I told them it was wrong. That it was your destiny and you had to learn about it early. Some Shadowers train from the time they're three until they come into their full powers and they're still not good enough. They still get tricked by the Sovereignty and get their entire family killed." Marie started crying. "They have to watch everyone they love die right in front of them."

"I'm taking Marie to our place," Rachel said. "Beck, I really want to hear the rest of this. Can you wait and not give too many details until I get back?"

Beck looked at me.

"You'll want Rachel to know everything so she can convince me," I said.

"Should we just wait until dinner?" Nate asked.

"No," Rachel and I said at the same time. When Beck raised an eyebrow in question, I shrugged my shoulder. "I'm listening now and want to know. Take advantage of that."

Rachel left with Marie.

"Are you a vampire?" I asked Beck.

He looked at me but didn't answer for several tense seconds. "Kinsley, I help kill vampires for a living. Do you really think I could be one?"

I turned to Nate. "What about you?"

"I am not a vampire," Nate vowed.

"When are you going to show me a real vampire?" I asked.

"Only when you are ready," Beck said.

"What kind of an answer is that? When am I going to be ready?" This was getting cryptic again.

"I shall have you and Nathaniel meet with Scott Masters so he may tell you about his and your father's working relationship. While I believe he really does have your best interests at heart, I prefer you not meet him alone."

"Are you going to tell me why I'm in danger?" I finally asked the question I'd been wanting to.

"Your parents were well known in the vampire communities. They were somehow able to keep you a secret for many years. I do not think anyone knew about Marie. I believe the Sovereignty killed your parents and they want to kill you and Marie."

I stifled a sob.

"When I saw all of you at my club on your birthday, I could not believe it. I put security on you but not on them. I figured they could protect themselves. I was more worried about your safety."

I wiped away a tear. "Are you a Shadower?"

"No. I am a Protector."

"You said that the night Marie attacked you. What does it mean?" I sat at the kitchen table, food forgotten, honestly thinking all this could be real.

"Exactly what it sounds like. I protect. So does Nathaniel."

"Who do you protect?"

"Anyone who needs it," Nate said. "Humans, vampires, others."

Before I could ask what 'others' meant, Beck started talking again. "The murders that have been happening in Seattle are because of the Sovereignty. I want to keep you safe."

"Oh my, that night, on campus. Was there a…" I still couldn't say it.

"Vampire? Yes. I frightened him away," Beck said.

"Then Dr. Finch was there and you two…" I stopped as realization dawned. "You *were* fighting that night! Is he? Is he a —?" Still couldn't bring myself to say the 'V' word. How pathetic.

"Oh, yeah. Finch is a vampire," Nate said. "I don't trust him one bit, but Beck thinks he's useful and trustworthy."

"Dr. Finch has never given us a reason to distrust him," Beck said.

"Don't you think trying to kill Kinsley is enough of a reason?" Nate said.

"Kill? Dr. Finch tried to kill me?" My hand crept to my throat.

"No. He explained that he was there to protect you that night." Beck glared at Nate. "Besides, the point is you were safe. We made sure of that."

Beck took my hands. "Kinsley, please spend the next few days thinking about everything. Get Marie to translate more of the book. Then you need to meet with Mr. Masters."

"I trust Masters more than I trust Finch," Nate said.

"I know your feelings about Dr. Finch, Nathaniel. That is enough on the subject," Beck said.

Nate went down the hall and slammed a door.

"Does he live here with you?" I don't know why the question was important now, but I asked anyway.

"Yes. He also has an apartment downtown, but he rarely stays there."

"Beck," I started hesitantly.

"I need you to learn that you can ask me anything at any time. I have seen good people get hurt because of their reluctance to ask what they require."

"Did you just hire me to protect us? Is this a pity job?"

"I hired you to keep you close and protect you. I also hired you because Nathaniel is a horrible organizer and double books my schedule all the time."

That was the first time I smiled all morning.

Chapter Seventeen

WITH BECK'S words running through my mind, I went home. Rachel met me in the hallway.

"Oh, come on, I was hoping to get more information." She stomped her foot.

"I've had all I can take for the morning. You go shower and we'll plan our day. I think I could use some retail therapy to clear my head."

Rachel and I always went shopping when we were stressed. We joked that it had to be cheaper than going to a therapist.

"You're not going to let me ask or talk about vampires all day, are you?" Rachel asked.

I shook my head. "Nope. There will be no talk of vampires or anything else strange or depressing."

"Well then what are we going to talk about? You know we have to take Marie with us so *something* freaky will come up in the conversation."

I laughed at her and went to my room.

Two hours later Rachel and Marie were finally ready to go. I texted Beck to say the three of us were going to the mall. He called me moments after I'd sent the message.

"What, Beck?" I answered the phone, annoyed.

"Nathaniel should go with you."

"I don't need a babysitter. It's a public place and it's the middle of the day. I don't think the vampires will want to risk death by sun," I said.

"You learned that some vampires are immune to the sunlight for short amounts of time. Your safety is a priority."

I walked to the window and looked down at Scott Masters's Hummer. "I'm sure Scott would go with us," I teased. I didn't know where my audacity was coming from. Maybe it was my way of dealing with the situation.

"I would prefer you did not do that," Beck answered through what sounded like clenched teeth.

"I'm sorry I'm being a pain," I said. "I'm having trouble with all this."

"I know. How about a compromise? Nathaniel can be your chauffeur and bag boy for the day. You can use my company credit card to buy some work clothes and an evening gown."

I almost drooled at the thought of getting to shop for important clothes. "I don't think that's a compromise. You're just bribing me."

"Yes, I am," Beck chuckled. "You will need a black dress for the Seattle Art Museum gala at the end of this month. You shall accompany me so I will not have to deal with finding a date."

"Glad to be of service. You're lucky you already offered to buy me clothes or my feelings might have been hurt about not being your date." It was so easy to banter with Beck. It was like we'd been friends for years.

"I thought it would offend you if I insinuated you would be my date." Beck's voice caused shivers. What did it mean that he could affect me like this over the phone?

Rachel was watching me closely so I tried to act like his voice didn't make me tremble. "If you let me buy an outfit for

Rachel and something small for Marie, you have a deal." Hardball. I could do hardball.

Rachel raised her eyebrows.

"You play hardball, Kinsley," he said.

I pulled the phone away and looked at it then put it back to my ear quickly so I wouldn't miss what he was saying.

"You may have Nathaniel, my car, and the company credit card with a limit of $10,000 to buy whatever you choose."

I almost choked. "Are you always this easy?"

"It appears, with you, I am much easier than I ever believed." He hung up before I could think of anything to say to that.

"So?" Rachel said.

"So, we have Nathaniel as our driver for the day, Beck's car, and the company credit card. I need to buy work clothes, an evening gown for the SAM gala, and I get to buy you and Marie something as long as I don't spend over ten grand."

"What the F? Why don't I ever find cool jobs like this?"

"So far, this job has come with some very interesting side issues. Anyway, you're reaping the benefits." I waved my hand around our living room.

"That's true," she conceded. "I suppose I'll just have to live vicariously through you for once until I can find my own sugar daddy."

"He's not a sugar daddy," I said.

"He could be," Rachel answered with a wiggle of her eyebrows.

I rolled my eyes and pulled the card for Scott Masters out of my purse. I called his cell.

"Masters," he answered on the first ring.

"Mr. Masters, this is Kinsley."

Nothing.

"Mr. Masters?"

"Kinsley, sorry. I'm a little surprised. I wasn't sure you'd be talking to me."

"There are a lot of things I'm unsure about right now, but talking to you is going to take precedence, Mr. Masters." I sighed.

"Do you think you could call me Scott? I know we just officially met, but you calling me Mister is going to get old."

"You worked with my dad." No point beating around the bush.

"Yes," he answered carefully.

"Are you a Shadower?"

Scott let out a huge breath. "They told you?"

"Well, Marie's been trying for a few days, but I thought she was just on one of her crazy rambles. She showed me the book. Then Beck convinced me. I need more information from you, though."

"Beck convinced you," he mumbled under his breath. Then, "What do you need?"

"I just want to know about my mom and dad and what they did. You also didn't answer me. Are you a Shadower?"

"No, I'm not. But your dad and I had been working together for the past seven years. Even if I don't have his crazy strength, I'm still a force to be reckoned with."

"I believe that. Especially after seeing you and your bodyguard in action this morning."

"Bodyguard?" Scott laughed. "Are you talking about Oliver?"

"Is that the name of the Michael Clarke Duncan look-alike who almost ran over me?"

I heard Scott say, "She thinks you look like the big black dude from *The Green Mile*." Then he laughed. "Yes, that's Oliver." Scott said to me. "He's been part of our team for three years. He's quite handy to have around."

"Handy? Is that what you call three hundred pound, six and a half foot tall monsters? Seriously? Handy?"

"Kinsley," Scott became serious. "I considered your dad my best friend. He always made me promise to look out for you if anything ever happened to him or your mom. I've been trying to protect you and keep my distance. Considering everything, I can't keep my distance anymore. Please let me explain what I know."

I hesitated. This fantasy world became increasingly real the more I learned about it. Was I ready to find out details about my dad's secret life? How did I know that Scott Masters really worked with him?

"How come I'd never seen you before the funeral?" I said.

"I can understand why you don't trust me yet. Your dad wanted to keep anything dealing with vampires away from you. I never went to your home in Paradise because we wanted to keep you safe. Your dad would come to Seattle. From there we traveled where we needed to go. Your family's safety was always our first concern."

"When can you meet with me and tell me what I need to know?" I asked.

"As soon as possible. However, I have to be out of town for the rest of this week. I'll be back Sunday night. Can I call you as soon as I know when I'm flying in? We can meet for drinks or a late dinner and talk."

"Beck's going to want me to bring Nate."

Scott growled. "You get to make the decisions about who you go places with, not Beckford Alexander. If you want Nate to be there, fine. Oliver will be with us, too. I've made some enemies over the past few years, just as Alexander has. We both have our bodyguards and we'll share them with you."

"I don't think Nate's really a bodyguard," I said. I thought of Nate's wiry frame. Yeah, he had more muscle than I'd given him credit for, but he was no Oliver.

"What do you think he was this morning?" Scott asked.

"Well, uh, I don't know," I said. "I have to go. Marie, Rachel, and I are going shopping. Nate will be with us, I don't need you and Ollie following."

"I have to get ready for my trip anyway. Please keep Alexander or Nate with you at all times. If Oliver and I can't be here to protect you, they're going to have to do."

"I don't need protecting!" I said.

"Yes, Kinsley, you do. Alexander should have explained that to you. I'll explain it again on Sunday."

"He explained it," I snapped, "but that doesn't mean I believe it or agree with either of you." I took a few deep breaths to calm myself down. I knew everyone was trying to help. "Scott, have a safe trip. I look forward to seeing you on Sunday night."

"I almost believe you," Scott said. "Be safe. Call or text me if you need anything. I'll be in southern California but my jet can make it back quickly." He hung up.

I was not only living in a world with vampires, I was living in a world with rich, overprotective men. It wasn't as glamorous as the books and movies made it out to be. It was a pain in the ass because they thought they could order me around.

There was a knock at the door and Marie answered without looking out the peephole. I still hadn't told her to ask who was there first. Nate walked in. His hair was damp and he wore dark slacks, shirt, and shoes.

Every time I saw him, he seemed a little older and a little bigger.

Rachel popped out of her new room in a skirt, baby doll shirt, and sandals. "I'm so glad you're going with us,

Nathaniel." She strutted over to him and I recognized her intent.

Rachel liked men. I could psychoanalyze the hell out of it and say she was looking for acceptance from a male because her dad didn't offer jack-diddly-shit. She'd just say she likes sex.

"I wish nothing more than to spend the day with three lovely ladies." Nate bowed and kissed Rachel's hand. He obviously knew the score and didn't need me to rescue him.

"You're not a vampire. What are you?" Marie asked.

"Marie!" I said. "Beck and Nate have shown us nothing but kindness and respect. Don't be rude." I was appalled with Marie. Probably because I'd asked almost the same thing a few hours earlier.

"You're right, Miss Marie, I'm not a vampire." Nate wrapped his arm around Marie's slim shoulders and led her toward the door. "I promise I won't hurt you."

"It's not me I'm worried about, it's Kinsley," Marie said.

Stupidly, tears gathered in the corners of my eyes. She may be certifiably insane, but she was still my Marie.

"I would kill myself before I'd hurt Kinsley," Nate answered.

The statement reminded me how different my life had become. "Okay, no more talk of death, nothing about vampires, and shopping is our goal."

We walked to the elevator. Instead of choosing the lobby, Nate chose the 'P' button.

"Where does that go?" I asked.

"Parking garage."

The four-door black Mercedes was one of three vehicles in the garage. The other two were also black Mercedes. One an SUV, the other a two-door coupe.

"Are these all Beck's?" I said.

Nate smiled sheepishly and I knew the answer. What had I

gotten myself into? I didn't know a single teacher, college or otherwise, who could afford three Mercedes, two personal assistants, and a penthouse condo. Especially at the salary he offered me.

"Does anyone else park down here?" How many other people lived in our building?

Nate surveyed the ten parking spots. "Beck has exclusive parking rights," he said without meeting my eyes.

I let it go. These were questions for Beck, not Nate. Soon Beck would be telling me about his other business if I was going to keep working for him.

Chapter Eighteen

BELLEVUE SQUARE MALL and its excellent combination of exclusive and chain stores was exactly the therapy I needed. I had a black evening dress and some casual business suit skirt outfits. As Rachel, Marie, and I had tried on clothes for fun, I hadn't known what to get for work.

I'd explained to the woman helping us that I needed casual, yet classy, outfits for any occasion. When I'd produced the credit card with 'Alexander Antiquities' on it, she'd practically salivated at the thought of her commission sales.

Nate, Marie, and I had picked out a sweet little black and white dress for Rachel. It was a total clubbing outfit and it accentuated her curves. Not that I knew a lot about men, but I could have sworn that Nate was taken with Rachel.

For Marie, I'd picked out a simple gold necklace. I felt she deserved something for everything she'd been through. I paid for that myself.

Nate pulled the car around to the front of the condo and got out to open our doors. He placed a chaste kiss on Marie's cheek and a lingering kiss on Rachel's. When he opened the front door for me, he kissed my hand.

"I can't believe you actually like to shop, Nate," I said.

"It wasn't the shopping I liked. It was the company."

"Whatever. Beck made you come with us."

"There are a number of Beck's employees who would give their right arm to be your bodyguard for the day." He smiled.

I scowled. "So, you are my bodyguard. Scott was right."

"I consider myself your friend and protector."

Before I could answer, Rachel slid next to Nate. "You can be my protector," she said in his ear, but loud enough that I heard her.

"Miss Rachel, my first priority is Kinsley, but you will always be just as important." He kissed her cheek again.

"Get a room," I mumbled and headed to the trunk to get my bags.

"Miss Kinsley," Gerald took everything from my hands, "do you want these delivered to your place?"

"Where else would they go?" I said.

Gerald lowered his eyes.

"You think my clothes would go to Beck's?" I asked.

"He doesn't mean any disrespect," Nate said.

"Because other women's clothes go to Beck's?" I covered my mouth as soon as the words were out. Beck could have as many women as he wanted, I didn't care. Did I?

Gerald looked back and forth between Nate and me.

"Never mind. I don't care. It doesn't matter." I yanked the bags away from Gerald and marched toward the doors.

Marie skipped up beside me, fingering her new gold necklace. She acted so childlike and innocent sometimes. "Thank you, Kinsley. It's beautiful." Marie stopped walking. "Don't worry. I won't let Beck hurt you."

Whoa. I stopped. "Beck won't hurt me."

Marie watched me closely and then reached out her hand to smooth down my hair. "I don't think he'll hurt you physically. Sometimes more than our bodies can be hurt, honey."

As Marie walked away I let out a big breath. She needed a user's manual. Had she always been like this? Maybe since I'd never had to be an adult around Marie I hadn't noticed how gone her mind really was.

"Kinsley," Rachel called to me. "I'm going to help Nathaniel make dinner. I'll come get you and Marie when it's ready, okay?" She smiled and looped her arm through Nate's.

"No problemo, Rach, have fun."

Gerald opened the big glass doors for me.

Marie was already in the condo when I got there. She was at the table with The Book of Protection open. I went straight to my room and avoided eye contact.

My evening gown had to be dry-cleaned, but the rest of my purchases could be machine washed. I took off the tags and made a pile of laundry.

I loaded the washing machine and adjusted the settings. The condo had come with a new front load washer and dryer. I wasn't really sure how it worked since we'd had the same washer and dryer at home for twenty years. Being a Vampire Shadower must not be a lucrative business. I laughed at myself. I was actually considering my parents were, like, superheroes or something.

"Kinsley," Marie called from the dining room. "Would you come here and look at these maps?"

Great. Maps. Wonder where this conversation was going to lead.

I went to the dining room and Marie was crouched in a kitchen chair, her finger moving over the pages of the book in front of her. As I came closer, I could see she was tracing a path over a very old, hand drawn map of Europe and Asia.

"What does it look like?" she asked.

"A map."

She narrowed her eyes. "You're doing it again. You just need to believe."

I was tired of arguing with her. Also, if she thought I did believe a little bit of it, she'd bombard me with more than I was ready to deal with.

I stared at the map and the path Marie's finger was traveling.

"I don't know what you want me to see," I said.

"This is the path we took when we fled. Sometimes we stayed at inns along the way, sometimes we slept in the carriages."

I listened to Marie retell the story from the first night. But this time I listened and pictured her as the Marie from the story; not a great, great, great grandmother.

"It was July 1881 when we ran. Isaac had convinced me he was a Monarch and I was sharing blood with him. I didn't realize he was a member of the Sovereignty. I saw him kill a group of humans one night. I'd gone to his home to surprise him because I was ready to be his wife. He had a group of men, women, and children. He just, just, slaughtered them.

"I ran home and told Mother and Father what I'd seen. We left immediately. Isaac should have been able to track me because we shared a bloodpact, but he never came. We made it to Liverpool and sailed to America." Marie wiped a few tears from her cheeks.

"You don't have to tell me all this."

"Yes, I do. It will help you understand." She took my hand. "We lived in America for sixty years before Isaac came. He left us alone for *sixty* years. Kinsley, we aren't like the vampires in the sense of having immortality, but we live longer and we're harder to kill. Our blood helps us heal quickly and live longer." She paused and looked out over the kitchen, not really seeing anything.

This was the most I'd ever heard Marie talk about one subject without getting off track.

She focused back on me. "The children, Harold and Anne, came into their powers early, so they were stuck as adolescents. Father thought it had something to do with our fleeing from a threat. The children's bodies sensed they needed to be protected.

"We moved every few years so people wouldn't be able to tell we weren't aging. We got a new maid in each city so no one knew our secrets. It was 1941 when the Sovereignty found us. We were living in Connecticut. I told you that." Marie wrapped her arms around her knees while she crouched in the chair. "We'd lived for so many years without the threat of vampires, I think we'd gotten lazy. You know they were all killed. I told you that, too."

I nodded and reached out my hand for Marie's. She placed her trembling hand in mine; it was ice cold.

"Marie, why—"

"Why didn't they kill me?" She asked for me.

When I nodded, she began to cry harder. Tears on her exotic face seemed so out of place.

"I asked Isaac for twenty years, almost every day, why I was alive. He told me it was because he loved me. *Loved* me. He kept me as a blood slave for twenty years and every day he told me he loved me." Marie stood and went to the kitchen sink. Her small body shook with the force of her tears.

"Your parents saved me. They were part of a small group who had banded together to try and destroy the Sovereignty. By the time they found me I was insane. Isaac had taken blood from me every day, sometimes twice a day. He kept me on the verge of life and death for all those years and my mind couldn't take it. My mind also couldn't take the fact that I had loved him once and he had betrayed me. Killed my family." Marie finally turned from the sink to look at me.

"Your parents took me in when the rest of the group wanted to kill me. God, I wanted them to kill me. Anything to end my torment. It took a few years for me to start acting even remotely close to normal." She laughed. It held no humor.

"Your mother, bless her soul, kept a weekly journal to let me know about my progress as I came back from the brink of insanity. Tom and Claire are the only reason I'm alive today. When your mom got pregnant, we all knew it was time to hide. We couldn't bear the thought of what had happened to me, happening to you."

Suddenly Marie undid the button of her shorts and pulled them down to her ankles. I was too shocked at first to realize what she was doing. Her thin, muscular legs were marred with scars on the insides of her thighs. It looked like shark bites or the mauling from a bear. I inhaled quickly at the shock of seeing her scars.

"He drank from every part of my body and then healed the wounds. But not here. Here, he ripped my flesh open and watched me bleed and then wouldn't let it heal for days. Isaac told me no man would ever touch me but him." Marie pulled up her shorts, ran to me, and dropped to her knees.

"You can't fall in love with a vampire, Kinsley, you can't!" She was almost yelling. "It doesn't matter if you think they're good or a Monarch. They're evil and they can't be trusted. You can't fall in love with a vampire!" Then she put her head on my knees and began to cry harder.

I ran my hands over her hair and down her back trying to soothe her. Those scars were horrifying. Marie had been held captive and tortured for twenty years after seeing her family slaughtered. That would explain her state of mind.

I urged her up and led her to her room. She didn't protest as I pulled back the blankets and lowered her into bed.

As I was leaving her room, she sat up. "Promise me."

I turned and looked at the only family I had left sitting like a small child on her bed.

"I promise I won't fall in love with a vampire," I said.

Her face relaxed and she flopped down.

I went back to the kitchen and pulled Marie's photo album out from under The Book of Protection. As I flipped through the pages, I looked closely at the woman in the photos. It was my Marie. Her eyes were the same, her hair was the same, her dimples when she smiled were the same. This was all real.

Holy shit, it was real.

Marie was almost two hundred years old, my family was part of some secret society that killed vampires, and I was one of them.

Anger surged through me. How could my parents keep something like this from me?

I went and got my own photo album and flipped through the pages. I relived my life from birth to my twenty-first birthday. It was like looking at photos from someone else's life. The girl in the pictures was young and innocent, not vampire food or a vampire killer. She was normal, not a Shadower.

Grief overtook my anger.

I'd had an amazing, normal childhood. Would that have been the case if I had been trained to be a Shadower? Quite simply? No. Mom and Dad had done what they thought was right and I couldn't change that now.

I rested my forehead on the photo album and tried to fight the tears and panic threatening to overtake me.

It startled me when the front door flew open and Rachel came in laughing and holding Nate's hand. She saw the photos and stopped laughing. "Are you okay, chica?" She came to me.

"Yes. No. I don't know." I rubbed my face.

"You're starting to believe it all, aren't you?"

Damn Rachel and her best friend superpowers of observation.

"Maybe. I don't want to talk about it right now," I said.

"Okay. I'll wake Marie up and then we'll go have dinner." Rachel kissed my forehead and went to Marie's room.

"It gets easier, Kinsley," Nate said quietly.

"I don't want it to get easier. I want my life back."

Chapter Nineteen

MARIE WAS ACTING like a normal person.

It probably shouldn't have shocked me as much as it did. I watched her float around Beck's kitchen and living room, sipping wine and visiting. She flirted shamelessly with Nate and told stories to Rachel.

I wasn't feeling very sociable. My whole world was crumbling around me and the people in my life acted like everything was fine.

Beck glided up to me. "You are not well tonight. Would you like to go home?" He reached his hand up like he was going to touch my face but then stopped.

"Kinsley will do no such thing. She doesn't have enough fun in her life," Marie said. She moved in between Beck and me and I had to step back to give her room. "Have more wine, darling, it's fabulous," she said.

Marie took the bottle from the ice bucket and poured more wine into my glass. She filled it to the top and I had to take a sip to make sure I wouldn't spill it.

I set my glass on the counter. "Excuse me, I need to use the restroom." I walked to the bathroom and locked myself inside.

I leaned against the door and stood in the dark. A candle

caused shadows to flicker across the ceiling and walls. I was taking at least three minutes of solitude to try and pull myself together. I took some deep breaths and closed my eyes. I was doing that a lot lately.

I enjoyed all three minutes of silence and darkness. Until there was a light knock on the door.

"What?" I snapped.

"Kinsley?" It was Beck.

"Just give me another minute, I'll be right out."

"Tell me what is wrong."

I unlocked the door and flung it open. Beck stood there calm and handsome, as always. His hair was back in a leather tie tonight. It made him look like he was from a different time period.

I tossed my hands in the air. "What's wrong? Almost two months ago, my parents died. This week, my crazy aunt wants me to believe they were murdered by vampires. You, Nate, and this job are all too good to be true." I took a breath. "Then I meet Scott Masters. You both insist I'm in danger and now you want me to believe in vampires. Don't I have a good reason to seem upset? This is insane!"

Maybe I wasn't handling things as well as I thought.

I walked down the hallway toward the bedrooms. I could hide in his office.

"Go to the master suite and sit down," Beck said.

He ushered me into his room. The king-sized bed had a canopy with dark, billowy curtains around it.

There was a settee in the corner and Beck sat me down on it. He pulled a ladder-backed chair from the desk against the wall, lowered himself into it, and took my hands in his.

"This is a very hard world to live in, Kinsley. If you want me to, I shall keep you out of it." He stared at me with those intense, black eyes.

"How? Now that I know about it, I can't just ignore everything."

"Yes, you can. You can still work for me, although Nathaniel will have to be your bodyguard. I can make sure you are safe and that you do not have to be a Shadower. The thought of you out fighting the vampires or entering into a bloodpact with one of them makes me crazy."

This was the first time I'd seen Beck's iron control slip.

"Beck? Are you worried about me?" He hardly knew me. Why was he being so protective?

This time when he raised his hand he did touch my face. His fingers traced my cheek and then lowered to my lips. The electric current that was always present, zapped to life.

"You do feel that, don't you?" I whispered. I didn't know what was happening but I didn't want to ruin it.

Beck's eyes dilated and he leaned toward me. "From the moment I saw you at my club, I knew you were special. I protected you that night on campus. I will always protect you." He tucked a strand of hair behind my ear. "The electricity between us is a sort of bond. When you are ready, I will tell you about it. For now, we will have to see where this—"

"Kinsley!" Marie shouted down the hallway. She marched into Beck's room, pushed him aside and pulled me off the settee. "Dinner's ready." She dragged me away with her.

I turned to see if Beck had the same shell-shocked look on his face I had to have on mine. He stood leaning in his doorway with his feet crossed at the ankles. He winked. I stumbled behind Marie. What was happening to me?

The table had been set by Rachel and Nate, who were practically joined at the hip.

I watched with morbid fascination. How did Rachel do it? How did she act so comfortable around men? I'd never had a real boyfriend in high school. I'd gone to two proms and three homecoming dances with Rachel and whoever she was dating at the time. Third wheel, that was me.

I sat at Beck's table feeling out of place again. Rachel and Nate had connected, Marie was always in her own world. And Beck? Well Beck was a force all his own.

As though I had summoned him, he appeared from the hallway. He retrieved my wine glass from the counter where I'd left it earlier. When he set it in front of me, he kissed my cheek.

Marie glared at him. He walked to her, kissed her cheek, then whispered something in her ear. I couldn't hear what he said but Marie sized him up for a moment then nodded sharply.

Nate was on his second serving before any of the rest of us had finished our first. Everyone at the table talked about our shopping trip.

"Did you find what you needed, Kinsley? I assume you had no problem using the company credit card?" Beck asked.

"Every store we went to was happy to help Kins use that card," Rachel said while I sat there like an idiot.

"Tell us about your business, Beck," Marie said around her wine glass.

"Alexander Antiquities is an upper class antique store," Beck said. "With all my connections around the world, I acquire items to sell. I have several collectors who shop there quite often. Whenever I come across something very rare, I donate it to a museum or art gallery, the University of Washington, or Oxford."

"I'm sure the public loves that," Marie said. It sounded snotty to me.

Beck saluted Marie with his wine glass. "I always donate anonymously, Marie. I cannot have certain people knowing how to find me, now can I?"

"No, can't have that," Marie said.

"You should see Kinsley's dagger collection," Rachel cut in, noticing the undertones between Beck and Marie. "Go get them when you're done with dinner, Kins."

"Yeah, okay," I said.

Beck and Marie were still glaring at each other.

I finished my salmon, not really tasting it. When I stood from the table, Beck and Nate also stood. "It's okay. I'm done. I'm just going to get the daggers."

"Shall I accompany you?" Beck asked.

"No," Marie said before I could answer.

I shook my head and went across the hall. The daggers were under my bed. I slid the case out and hefted it back to Beck's. I could hear arguing through the door. Maybe Beck had had enough of Marie's attitude.

As soon as I turned the knob, the voices stopped. All four of them were still sitting at the table. Marie had a fake smile plastered on her face.

"Don't stop arguing just because of me," I said.

"We were not arguing, merely discussing the recent events," Beck soothed.

"Sure," I said. "Nate, can we have dessert now?"

While Rachel and I cleared the table, Nate cut pie and dished it out.

"May I look at the daggers, Kinsley?" Beck asked as I was getting ready to take a bite of pie.

"Have at it," I said. "The case is silver, so it weighs a ton."

Beck's hands were almost on the latches but he stopped and jerked back. "I am going to wear gloves so I do not get fingerprints or oil from my skin on anything."

"Don't worry about it," I said. "We've all been touching them. My dad used them for throwing in the backyard. I'm not worried about them being dirty."

"Nevertheless, the curator in me wants to wear gloves."

Beck pulled black gloves from the pocket of a jacket that was hanging in the closet by the front door. He slipped the gloves on and flipped open the case.

I watched his face as he looked reverently at the eight daggers. He ran his fingers over each handle until he came to the largest one; the nine inch blade. He pulled it from the case and Marie hummed in pleasure.

"That blade was used to kill the first leader of the Sovereignty, Kinsley. It's rumored it was also used to kill Vlad the Impaler," Marie said.

I almost dropped my bite of pie.

"Silver is one of the only substances that can render a vampire helpless," Beck said as he studied the blade. "If a vampire is wounded by silver, they take much longer to heal. They can also be shackled with silver and unable to break it. If you can stab a vampire in the heart with silver, it will render them immobile long enough for you to cut off their head and burn the body."

"Cool," Rachel breathed.

Nate looked at her then shook his head and laughed.

Beck put the dagger back and closed the case. "You have a ruby ring, do you not?"

I stared at my hand and my mother's ring. "Yes."

"I told you I would keep you out of the supernatural world if I could, but this changes things. You are not just a Shadower. You are descended from the first family of Shadowers."

Marie laughed in triumph and crossed her arms over her chest. "I told you, Dr. Alexander, she could not change what is to be. And neither can you."

Oh great, crazy Marie was back. I didn't know if I liked overprotective, party hostess Marie, but at least she was predictable. Crazy Marie just confused the shit out of me and was a little scary.

"I would like to request that we take a break from all things vampire for a while." I stood and grabbed my case of daggers. "Marie, Rachel, stay as long as you want. Nate, thank you again for feeding us. It was excellent as usual." I turned to Beck. "I'll be here tomorrow morning at eight so we can start going over your fall schedule."

I walked across the hall and went straight to my room. I opened the case and pulled out the dagger Marie said had killed the vampires. I stared at it. Could a person turn their back on their birthright? Could they ignore the past and try to forge their own course? I didn't know if I'd be able to, but I was going to try.

I didn't believe in vampires and I wasn't going to be a Shadower.

Chapter Twenty

WE SPENT the week avoiding anything that had to do with vampires. Rachel drove to Paradise to get her stuff. Then we spent time making the rest of the condo resemble a real home. We hung up pictures and curtains, filled a bookcase with our assortment of books, and set up our bedrooms. Rachel and I would share the bills and take turns keeping an eye on Marie.

Rachel was going to start waitressing at Screamers. Since the night of dinner with the five of us, Rachel and Nate had spent every spare moment and night with each other.

I had my phone calendar open to the month of August and was double checking the time for the Seattle Art Museum benefit gala when the date jumped out at me.

I stared at the digital calendar. Somehow I'd made it through over two months without my parents. I thought about how much my life had changed.

Even if I continued to ignore The Book of Protection, things were screwed up. I could throw myself into working for Beck and planning my senior year. I had Rachel and Aunt Marie. But I was alone.

I was sitting on my bed listening to music and still staring at the calendar when Rachel bounded into my room. Her blonde hair was a halo of ringlets that fell to the middle of her back and she had on her party-girl makeup. I acted like I was fifty and she acted our age.

"Come on, chica, we're hitting the town. There's no way I'm going to let my best bud sit around and mope."

"I'm not moping."

"Yes you are. You're staring at that calendar thing listening to Sarah McLachlan. That's moping."

Rachel came over and dropped to her knees in front of me. She clasped my hands and looked in my eyes. "I really do love you. We're worried about you." She squeezed my fingers. "You've hardly talked this last week. You've had to process a lot and we know you miss your parents, but we've given you a few months. It's time to move on."

Move on? Of course she could say she wanted me to move on. She didn't go to sleep at night with visions of exploding cars and screams. She didn't wake up in the morning and feel the weight of a necklace with two wedding bands on it.

"I can see you're thinking too hard. You want to yell at me? You want to scream? That would be great, because then at least you'd be showing some emotion."

I stared at Rachel. She was right, but I didn't want to admit that. It was easier to be angry at her than face the truth that I was becoming a shell of myself.

"Just leave," I said. "If you're going to try and tell me how broken I am, then I don't need you."

Rachel tried to smile. "Does it make you feel better to be mad?"

"No," I said as I dropped my head.

She tugged on my hand. "C'mon. You need to go out and live."

"Don't you see? I don't know how to live? Do I pretend that none of this has happened?"

"No," Rachel said, "you dust yourself off and move forward."

"I don't know how," I said again.

"Yes you do. But you're not even trying."

"Just leave me alone," I said as I pulled away from her.

Hurt flashed in Rachel's eyes as she stood. "Sorry I wanted you to act like a person. I'm going to Screamers," she said as she left.

I stared at the closed door. What had I done?

I got ready for bed like a zombie. I'd been so tired but the minute my head hit the pillow I was wide awake. I thought about all that had been going on since that horrible morning in June.

I tried to let my body relax. Rachel and I had had little fights all our lives. We were going to be fine. I drifted off to sleep thinking of how I would apologize in the morning.

I STOOD on top of a building across from Screamers. I could see Rachel in an alley with two guys and another girl. They smoked cigarettes and laughed. One of the men pulled the other girl toward him and they started necking. I watched the girl's legs buckle.

I could hear Rachel screaming. The other guy was trying to pull her to him. The first guy lifted his head from the girl's neck and he had blood on his face.

Then I was screaming.

"KINSLEY. WAKE UP." The accented voice drew me from my nightmare. I didn't care how Beck had gotten into my room, I only cared he was here. He gripped my shoulders and shook me gently. His hands were fire on my cold skin.

"It was horrible! It was like the nightmares I used to have when I was little. But this one had Rachel in it. We argued and I have to apologize." I sobbed as I sat up. Beck pulled me to him.

"If Rachel were here, she would have heard you screaming." Beck ran his hands over my hair and wiped the tears from my cheeks with his thumbs. The electricity, that was always present when he touched me, sparked to life.

He drew a deep breath but didn't move. Ever since the night in his room I hadn't thought about much else than his intoxicating scent. I'd been trying to do as much work as possible through email, texts, faxes, and handwritten notes. He kept coming up with more things for me to do at his house, though.

"What time is it?" I brushed his hands from my face so I could turn to find my phone. "It's four in the morning? Why isn't she home?"

"You said you argued. Is there someone else she might stay with besides Nathaniel?" Beck asked.

I shook my head. "She was hurt. I have to check hospitals."

"It was just a dream. And even if it was not, there are many hospitals in King County."

"Beck, please, she was going to Screamers. Call and see if anyone was hurt. Please." Rachel was hurt, I knew it.

Beck pulled his cell from his pocket and frowned at the screen. He looked at me. "You said she was going to Screamers?"

When I nodded, he stood. "Give me a moment."

He left but I followed him to the living room. I could hear him talking to someone explaining he'd been busy all night and his phone had been set on silent. After a few more tense moments, he ended the call and met my gaze.

"Two women were attacked outside the club. One woman is dead and one was taken to Sun Memorial Hospital. The police wouldn't give my manager any names until the families were notified."

The world tilted. It was like getting the news about my parents. Spots peppered my vision and I thought I was going to pass out. Beck grabbed me before I fell to the floor. Tears flooded my eyes.

"Kinsley, we do not know if it is Rachel."

"Either way, she's hurt or dead! I can't stand this!" I pounded on his chest. "Why do the people I love get hurt?"

"Let us go to the hospital. I am sure she is fine."

His confidence helped me feel calm. It was odd how his simple presence could affect me. As I stood in the circle of his arms, the electric charge flashed to life again. I watched his eyes dilate and that blackness drew me in.

"The feeling of electricity when we touch, is that part of the bond you say we have? I felt it the first night we met when you touched me. And then last week at dinner."

"I do not think we should talk about this now. We need to get to the hospital."

"Rachel." How could I forget about Rachel for even thirty seconds?

"We will leave Marie here," Beck said. "Write her a note and I will call Gerald to have one of the staff sit in the hall to make sure she does not leave."

Marie would be in the way at the hospital. I agreed and scribbled out a hasty note without giving any information about Rachel while Beck made the phone call.

We rushed to the hospital in Beck's SUV. The dark tinted

windows made the hour before dawn seem even darker. We parked and I ran inside with Beck behind me.

There were police talking to a doctor and I went straight to them. "Rachel Fredericks, is she alive?" I begged.

"Let me handle this." Beck pushed me gently into one of the ER waiting room chairs.

The air of authority that Beck commanded got results. The Chief of Staff soon joined the police and other employees. After a few exchanges, Beck came to me.

"She is alive and in surgery."

I burst into tears and threw my arms around Beck.

Nate came running down the hallway covered in blood. "Sir, where is she?"

The police drew their guns on Nate and told him to put his hands on his head.

"Nate, what happened?" I said.

People in the waiting room screamed at the police and their guns.

"Calm down!" Beck bellowed. "Mr. Chase was the one who called 911. He is covered in Miss Fredericks's blood. He is also my employee. Put your guns away."

The police hesitated then holstered their pistols.

Beck looked at Nate and then back to the Chief of Staff. "Take us to Miss Fredericks's room now, please. We would like to be there when she is released from surgery."

No one questioned Beck's orders. That's what they were, too. He told the police how to handle the investigation then he told the hospital staff what to do until the specialist from England could arrive.

When the mayor showed up to find out what was going on, Beck pulled him to the side and they were laughing and talking like old buddies.

While I waited for Rachel to come out of recovery, Nate changed his clothes from a spare set that were in his car.

I bumped his shoulder. "Nate, why don't you go home and take a shower?"

"I've done all I need to do."

"What do you mean?" I asked.

"I killed the two vampires that did this."

"Vampires?" I whispered.

Beck was suddenly behind me. "That is why I am bringing in my specialist. We need to find out how badly she was hurt. We also need to find out if this attack was random or aimed at you or me."

"Is Rachel a Vampi—," for the second time that morning, my world tilted. I watched Beck's face fade from my vision.

Chapter Twenty-One

I OPENED MY EYES. I didn't know where I was. Beck's smell surrounded me. The black curtain canopy of his bed circled me like a tent. I could hear Beck's voice.

I got to my knees and moved to the end of the bed. I pushed back the heavy curtain and saw Beck pacing the room talking on his cell. As soon as he saw me he stopped moving and locked his eyes with mine.

"I will call you back this evening." He disconnected the call. "How are you feeling?"

"I'm not sure," I said. "Is Rachel okay?"

"How much do you remember?" Beck asked.

"Rachel in surgery, Nate covered in blood saying he'd killed two vampires, you telling me about a special doctor from England. Then I'm pretty sure I passed out."

Beck's lips lifted in a small smile. "That is everything. Impressive."

"There's nothing impressive about passing out." I moved so I was sitting on the edge of the bed. The curtains kept falling toward me.

Beck tied back one side and then the other.

"Is Rachel okay?" I repeated.

"She will be."

I looked to the closed curtains. "What time is it?"

"Almost noon."

I slowly climbed off the bed.

"Nathaniel is at the hospital with Rachel. After you have rested and explained everything to Marie, we will go back." He blocked my exit from the room.

I put my hands on his chest. "I have responsibilities. You can't keep me locked in here."

His eyes narrowed. "Watch me."

That caught me off guard. "What's going on?"

He curled his hands over mine. "I think Rachel was attacked on purpose to get to one of us. It was a vampire."

"I don't believe you."

"I had the video footage uploaded to my computer. You are not going to like watching it."

I swallowed. Was this my moment of truth? "Show me. It can't be any worse than my dream."

Beck regarded me intently. "It is."

We moved to the desk. He did some clicking on the laptop. The video footage was slightly grainy but high quality and in color. It was on a still frame of four people in the parking lot outside Screamers.

Beck pointed at the screen. "Rachel waited for Nathaniel to get some items from my office. He told her to wait inside, but she went outside with these three." He started the video.

I watched as the other woman lit a cigarette and Rachel laughed at something she said. There was no sound on the video. Then one of the men moved toward cigarette woman and nuzzled her neck.

"No." I watched as Rachel's mouth opened in a scream and the man pulled away from the neck of the woman. He had blood on his face. In my dream, that was where I woke up. In this horrifying video I watched the second man rip Rachel's head back and attack her neck.

Beck went to stop the video and I put my hand out. "I have to see the rest."

"I want you to see the infrared video."

He clicked on some other icons and brought up a greenish-gray video picture with two red-filled bodies on the screen. It was the same scene, but the men were missing.

I watched as the woman's knees buckled and then I watched the red-filled body of the man appear in the picture. It took my brain a moment to process. The men weren't missing. They didn't have a heat signature until they had the blood of the women. When Rachel's attacker slowly appeared, I knew I'd just watched vampires consume blood.

"This is not how I wanted you to see vampires for the first time." Beck turned off the computer.

"You have to show that to the police," I mumbled, suddenly feeling very cold.

He laughed. "The police? What are the human police going to do? Shadowers, Protectors, and Monarchs are the supernatural world's police."

I stumbled back to the end of Beck's bed. I started to shiver. Beck was by me in an instant, pulling a blanket around me. He acted like he was going to say something when his phone rang.

He looked at the screen. "It is Nathaniel. He may have news for us."

Beck answered the phone while I stared at the blank computer screen. I'd just seen vampires on video and still my brain couldn't process everything. Rachel had been attacked, almost killed, by a vampire. What was I going to do?

"Kinsley," Beck said quietly. "Nathaniel said the doctors have some questions about previous injuries Rachel may have sustained. Was she in a car accident?"

It took me a moment to decide how to answer.

"No, she was in a Reverend Fredericks accident," I said. "When she was fourteen, she had a broken arm. When she was sixteen, four broken ribs and a miscarriage. When she was seventeen, a fractured jaw. I'm sure the devil has been exorcised from her body, though."

I was already angry and thinking about all Rachel had suffered at the hands of her father made me want to hit something.

Beck quietly relayed the information to Nate as I stared at the wall. He ended the call as I pulled the blanket tighter around my shoulders and my teeth started to chatter. "Do you have super duper air conditioning or what?"

"You are in shock. That is why you feel cold. The adrenaline that has been coursing through your body is crashing. You need food and you need sleep."

"I need to go home," I said through clenched teeth. I released the blanket and stood.

"Until we know how much of a threat this attack poses, I need to keep you with me. Marie is in the kitchen baking cookies. I told her Rachel was at the hospital and you would explain everything when you woke up."

"Is Marie okay?"

"Besides blaming me for hurting Rachel, she is fine. Marie is easy to distract."

"Why does she not care for you?"

Beck laughed. "She hates me, Kinsley, but thank you for trying to make it seem less harsh. Shadowers and Protectors have rarely gotten along. We are too much the same and yet too different."

I hit his arm. "Thanks, that cleared everything up."

"You will not understand completely until you start your training."

"Training. What do I need to do to protect myself and my family?"

"We are going to start with reading the signs of your body. You need food and rest." As though he'd willed it, someone knocked on the bedroom door.

Marie and a tiny woman with short black hair came in carrying a tray with food and a bottle of water.

"Kinsley, this is Raven," Beck said. "Marie picked her as a personal bodyguard from my bouncers at the club. I figured it was best to let Marie make the decision."

"Nice to meet you, Raven. I've never met a bouncer before." I stared at the Smurf in front of me. A bouncer?

She was shorter than Marie, which put her at five foot nothing. Fun-size. She wore exotic black makeup that couldn't hide a pixie face and was dressed in dark leather clothes. Her short black hair was an array of wild wavy spikes. She had beautiful dark green eyes.

Raven raised her head to sniff the air. Considering everything I'd been through in the past week, I didn't find this odd. What it said about my sanity, I'm not sure.

"She's not a vampire, Kinsley," Marie said.

"She doesn't know how to tell?" Raven said in a voice as tiny as her body.

"No one's had time to teach her," Marie said.

"A Shadower has to know how to tell the difference and how to protect themselves," Raven said with a frown.

"The difference between what?" I asked.

Marie and Raven continued to stare at each other as though I hadn't spoken.

"We have to start training her right away if she's going to protect—"

"Raven," Beck cut in, "I think Kinsley has had enough to

deal with the last few days. As soon as we know Rachel is on the mend, we will start introductory training."

I looked back and forth between the three. "The difference between what? Who do I have to protect? And is Rachel okay?" I figured I'd only get one answer. I was right.

"Rachel will be fine. She came out of surgery a few hours ago. My personal physician has arrived and he is with Nathaniel at the hospital," Beck said.

"How did your doctor get here so fast from England?" I asked. "An airplane would take a lot longer than that."

"Not everyone has to fly commercially," Beck said.

I wanted to ask how people could get across the Atlantic and entire United States so quickly, but figured he wouldn't answer me anyway. I was learning how to play the Beckford Alexander word game.

"I want to go see her," I said.

"I told you she'd want to go," Marie said.

"No one's going anywhere," Raven said. "You are my current responsibility, Marie. When Beck says it's safe for us to go to the hospital, then we'll go."

Marie stomped her foot. "Oh, phooey. Do you all do what he says?"

"Yes," Raven said. "He's our boss. He's always done what's best for us." She turned to me. "Kinsley, I look forward to getting to know you better and being one of your training partners. I will take care of Marie's safety as though she were my own mother or aunt."

They left the tray of food and Beck handed me the bottle of water.

"Drink. I know you are dehydrated," Beck said. "You should eat the food they brought and try to take another nap before we go back to the hospital."

"Tell me what the police have to say about the attack." I

grabbed the tray and climbed back onto Beck's bed like it was my own. If he was going to keep me locked in his room then I was going to act like it was mine. I picked up a croissant sandwich.

"The police confirmed the woman in the alley with Rachel is the seventh victim of the *Seattle Ripper*. That is what they are calling him. Rachel would have been victim eight. Of course they do not know they are dealing with a cadre of rogue vampires."

I felt sick to my stomach and dropped the sandwich back on the tray. "There have been that many murders since the attack on campus?"

"Yes."

"And it's being done by a vampire?"

"I think it is a small group. They know it is forbidden to kill so blatantly. Either they are newly turned and do not know the rules or they do not care. However, that does not mean Rachel was targeted on purpose. Word spread when I opened my club that it would be considered a safe haven. No fighting, no bloodshed, no attacks on humans."

"You run a vampire club?" I was having trouble breathing.

"No. I run a club which vampires can visit."

I scrubbed my hands down my face. "I have to accept this as my new life, don't I?"

He nodded. "Yes, you do."

"Then you and Nate are going to have to quit treating me like glass and start treating me like a Shadower." I had some force back in my voice. Point for me.

"Marie said you would say that. I do not like it."

"Deal with it. I won't be a victim. If I'm going to protect Rachel and Marie from whatever is out there, I need to know what I'm up against."

"You need to protect yourself first." Beck moved toward the

bed. "You are a Shadower and I will not allow anything to happen to you."

I wasn't sure why Beck was so worried about my safety. "Why would vampires want me dead?"

"They do not want you dead, Kinsley. They want you very much alive, preferably chained up somewhere so they can have your blood. They will try to kill everyone around you so you will not have any reason to fight back. They will make you a blood slave.

"Then you will spend hundreds of years as a food source until your body cannot handle the blood reproduction anymore. You will slowly bleed to death. All the while you will be giving the Sovereignty the powers of the Monarchs. They will win the war."

"You're trying to scare me."

"Yes, Kinsley! I am trying to scare the living hell out of you so you understand why you cannot be unprotected. You are too important to fall into their hands."

"Well, then, you better teach me what I'm up against and how to defend myself."

He growled and stormed from the room.

"Can't I make you happy?" I yelled after him. "I thought you wanted me to believe!"

He didn't answer.

Chapter Twenty-Two

FOR TWO INCREDIBLY LONG days I avoided Beck and sat vigil by Rachel's bedside. Nate didn't leave the room either. I figured he was there because Beck wanted him to watch me. I also knew Nate was there to be with Rachel. He held her hand and read magazine articles to her still body.

Raven came in a few times with Marie to check on us. Beck visited once to try and get me to leave but I ignored him. I knew I was being childish. He'd tried to scare me on purpose and had succeeded. Until I knew Rachel was going to be okay and I'd had time to process all he'd told me, he was going to have to deal with it.

Rachel looked worse than she was, the doctors assured me. Her throat was bandaged so thickly you couldn't tell she had a neck. Her arms had been secured to the bed so she wouldn't wake and pull any of the tubes from her neck, throat, or nose. The drainage tubes were the worst. She was a mass of tubes that were draining what Beck's fancy British doctor called poison.

Dr. Benjamin Karlof was a tiny man. He was shorter than me, had a white hair comb over and frail body. His teeth were yellowed. He didn't have the bedside manner of a stellar physician. I expected someone who worked for Beck to be more refined. Dr. Karlof gave me the creeps. I couldn't put my finger on what it was though. He watched me out of the corner of his eye and made the hair on the back of my neck stand up when he came in the room.

Nate wasn't very talkative when I tried to ask him about the man. All I was able to get out of him was Karlof had been the Alexander family's personal physician since Beck had been born. I found that odd. Did the obscenely rich just buy doctors to be part of the family until the doctor died? If so, Karlof had to be nearing the end of his job.

I sat in the darkness of Rachel's room and listened to the beeping of the machines. She was being pumped full of antibiotics for infection and morphine for pain. She'd also received a transfusion since being admitted because she'd lost so much blood.

For the murders, and Rachel's attack, none of the blood had been found at the scene. The police were calling the *Seattle Ripper* a member of a cult who used blood for weird Satan-worshiping reasons. Apparently, that was more believable than saying it was vampires.

I watched Rachel's heart rate spike and her eyes begin to twitch. Nate was by her side before I was out of the chair.

"Rachel, honey, wake up. You're okay, just wake up." He held one of Rachel's hands and stroked her hair with the other.

"Kins," Rachel's voice sounded like it was being scraped over sandpaper as she tried to talk around the tube in her throat.

I went to her side. "Don't talk, Rach. Nate and I are here and we're not going anywhere."

Tears leaked from Rachel's closed eyes. "Hurts."

"I know, baby, and I'm so sorry." Nate's voice held an edge of pain.

"They made me call your parents, Rachel. They're coming." I had to tell her now so it wouldn't be such a shock.

I couldn't wait to see Nate and Beck take on Reverend Fredericks. The man was finally going to be put in his place by someone more imposing than my family.

Rachel groaned and that made her start coughing which caused her to start gagging. I went to the hall to find a nurse or doctor and Nate pressed the call button.

Moments later, Dr. Karlof came in with two nurses. He looked at Nate and me, fully intending to tell us to leave. I could see it on his face.

Beck appeared in the doorway. "They will not go, Benjamin, you may as well save your breath."

I stood by Rachel's bed while Karlof did all his doctor stuff and removed the restraints from her wrists.

"I recommend you do not do any talking. You are not to eat or drink for a few days. We need to keep you hooked up to IVs for nourishment and hydration." Karlof's voice was nasally. His accent didn't sound nearly as elegant as Beck or Dr. Finch's.

Karlof turned to Beck. "I assume you want her moved to the condo as soon as she can be transported?"

"Of course," Beck said. "We cannot protect her adequately in the hospital."

"If you would listen to me, you would not have to deal with any of this."

"Duly noted, Karlof. Now, do your job so we can take Rachel home," Beck said.

Karlof and Beck had a staring contest then Karlof left the room.

I wanted to apologize to Beck for ignoring him. I started to speak when the door to Rachel's room slammed open with enough force to rattle the tacky landscape pictures on the wall.

Reverend Harper Fredericks and his wife, Molly, stood in

the doorway. Well, the Reverend stood in the door. Molly cowered behind him a few steps. There might have been a time when Molly was a good person and a good mother, but Harper had beaten it all from her. How Rachel was even normal was a miracle. Of course, what did I know about normal?

Harper used to scare me half to death. Not anymore. I was learning about true evil and this man was a flea.

"I knew you'd be the death of my daughter, you harlot!" Fredericks said.

Rachel tried to protest from the bed but Nate held her down and silenced her.

"Leave," Beck demanded. "I will not have you upsetting Rachel and Kinsley. They have been through enough."

"How dare you order me around! Do you know who I am? I'm Rachel's father. Only God and I decide what is best for Rachel. Not her so-called whore friend or anyone associated with the Prestons."

Beck strode to Reverend Fredericks. I'll give ole Harper credit, he didn't flinch, but he did take a step back.

"You will never refer to Kinsley, or her family, with anything less than civility and respect. Do I make myself clear?"

Harper paled and took another step back, bumping into Molly. "I see the devil on your soul."

"You are going to see more of the devil if you ever speak about Kinsley that way again." Beck's voice scared me a little. He towered over the Reverend.

I couldn't see Beck's face, but I could see Harper and Molly's faces. I'd never seen anyone look so terrified.

"This isn't over," Fredericks blustered. "She's my daughter and I'll be getting her out of your evil clutches immediately." He stormed away, leaving Molly.

"Come see her, Molly. Talk to her." I'd given up trying to save Molly from Harper, but I wasn't mean to her.

Molly stumbled to the bedside and began to cry. "Oh, Rachel, are you okay?"

"Isn't much worse...than four broken ribs...or a fractured jaw," Rachel rasped.

Molly's eyes got huge. "He only does what he thinks is right. You needed to be put in your place."

"Go home, momma. I don't want...either of you here. Kinsley, Marie, Beck, and Nathaniel...take care of me better...than you ever have." Rachel turned her head and closed her eyes. I could still see the tears running down her cheeks. I knew she was in horrible pain and not just physical.

"You heard her," Nate snarled. "Any mother who would let a man treat her daughter the way you've let him treat Rachel doesn't deserve to be here. Leave."

Molly burst into sobs and ran from the room.

"Thank you," I said to both Nate and Beck. "Harper never acknowledges my presence, so anything I say to him goes unheard. He was scared of my dad, but not as scared as he seems to be of you."

"That man thinks he saw the devil in Beck, he hasn't seen me." Nate was breathing heavily and clenching his fists. Then he looked at Beck. "We've got to get her out of here, sir. Please. Rachel is an adult and doesn't have to be released to her parents. Besides, you donated all the money to have the blood bank and rare blood disorders wing built. Doesn't that mean you can do whatever you want at this hospital?"

"Not whatever I want, but very close." Beck pulled out his phone and made two calls. One was to Raven and the other was to the hospital Chief of Staff.

Raven arrived within ten minutes accompanied by a man. He was short, stocky, Asian, and his head was shaved. Dark sunglasses and a gold hoop earring completed his 'I'm a badass' look.

"Where's Marie? Who's this?" I asked Raven.

"Marie is safe at the condo with Mya. This is Ian."

Ian nodded, but didn't remove his sunglasses.

I looked at Beck. "Who's Mya?"

"You left Marie with Mya? That was just dumb," Nate's comment didn't inspire confidence.

"Marie chose Mya. It'll be fine," Raven said.

I turned to Nate. "Why is Mya not a good choice?"

"She is a vampire," Beck finally answered. "I think Marie chose her because Mya is currently angry with me. I am sure Marie could sense that."

"Why is Mya angry with you?"

"This is not the time nor place for that discussion, Kinsley." Beck sounded annoyed.

"I already told you that Marie and Rachel are my number one concerns." I turned to Raven. "From now on, I really want to meet anyone who will be left alone with Marie."

Raven looked to Beck. I'm pretty sure he discreetly indicated his approval since Raven looked back to me and said, "You're absolutely right, Kinsley. I'm sorry I didn't check with you. It's just that I'm better for this assignment than Mya would have been."

"What assignment?"

Raven waved an arm around the room. "Getting all of you out of the hospital without any bloodshed. Mya likes bloodshed."

"I also think Rachel should not be around vampires for a while," Beck added.

I agreed. "When can we get out of here?" I asked.

"Right now the Chief of Staff is explaining to Rachel's parents that they cannot take her against her will. I am going to have Karlof set up ambulance transport. Raven is going to take you home. Nathaniel and Ian are going to stay here with me to get Rachel back to the condo."

"I'm staying with Rachel," I argued.

"Kins...go. Be with Marie...I'm in good hands." Rachel reached for Nate.

"Okay. I'll make sure you don't have to talk to your parents." I left the room with Raven behind me.

The Chief of Staff was walking away from Rachel's parents. Harper was clenching his fists. Molly was dabbing at her eyes with a tissue.

"Molly, Rachel is going to be moved back to our condo. She'll have a great doctor on hand twenty-four hours a day and I'll take care of all the expenses." I was proud of myself for sounding so grown up and in control.

Her father had to have at least one good bone in his body to realize Rachel would be better taken care of here than in Paradise. I'm not sure why I thought he'd be understanding for once.

"I don't want your vile money and I don't want you near my daughter!" Harper screeched at me. "You should have died with your parents, you evil bastard-child. They paid for their sins, and you will pay for yours."

My vision narrowed and the world moved in slow motion. Reverend Fredericks raised his hand and slapped me. I heard Molly gasp and I heard Raven say a few choice swear words.

Fredericks raised his hand to slap me again and my body moved of its own accord. I grabbed his right hand with mine, twisting and squeezing. I felt and heard bones snap under my grip.

Suddenly Beck had his arms wrapped around me and was pulling me from the Reverend, who was now lying on the floor of the hospital reception area curled in the fetal position sobbing.

Holy shit. What happened? I stared down at my hands. Had I just broken Harper's hand?

"You broke most of the bones in his hand and his wrist."

"How did you know what I was thinking?" I stared at Beck. Then I realized he still held me off the ground tight in the embrace of his arms. "Put me down, please."

"I know what you are thinking because it is written all over your face. You are coming into your powers, Kinsley. This is why we must start your training. You need to learn how to control your new strength."

"You mean, I have like, superpowers?" I looked from Beck to the sobbing jerk on the floor.

"I do not think the Shadowers would call their gift super-powers, but you are not quite human anymore." Beck regarded me intently.

Not quite human.

I wasn't sure what to think about that.

Chapter Twenty-Three

RAVEN DROVE while I stared out the window reliving the horrifying moment when I'd broken Harper's hand and wrist. I could still feel the bones snapping like a handful of dried spaghetti noodles in my grip. I don't think I felt bad that I'd hurt him. I felt uncomfortable because it had been so easy.

"Don't let it bother you too much," Raven said. "First of all, he deserved it. Second, it was a good way for you to see how strong you're becoming."

I murmured something that sounded like I agreed.

When Raven stopped in front of the double glass doors, Gerald came out and opened my car door. "Miss Kinsley, I hope you are well. I'm sorry about Miss Rachel."

"Thank you, Gerald," I managed. I went to the elevator and stood at it. Then I remembered I had to press a button to get it to open.

Raven helped me into the elevator. She pressed the button for our floor and I rode up in silence with my eyes closed. When the car slid to a stop and dinged, I was leaning heavily on Raven. My little friend was stronger than she looked.

"You're going to be okay. It's a lot to deal with. When we

start training, I'll tell you about my past and what I've been through."

We started down the hallway when an inhuman scream pierced the air.

Raven took off running to my door and kicked it open with one stomp of her foot. She'd drawn a nasty looking gun from under her shirt. I ran after her even though I didn't have a weapon. I almost laughed when I thought about my hands. They could be weapons, I suppose.

The sight that greeted me was not even within my realm of comprehension. Marie stood in the middle of the dining room holding one of my dad's silver daggers. A woman with fire-red hair was chained, almost naked, to the top of our kitchen table. Chained. It wasn't until I looked closer that I realized she wasn't human, not really.

She was screeching and speaking in a language I didn't recognize. Her face was contorted, somehow too big for her head, and it was like the bones of her face were moving under the skin. I could see two sets of fangs, top and bottom, like a dog, every time she opened her mouth to scream.

Her body was covered in ropy veins that I could see the blood pumping through, like the picture Marie had shown me. I noticed Marie's neck was bleeding.

"Mya! Did you attack Marie?" Raven seemed stunned.

The voice coming from the body of the vampire chained to my table sounded like a possessed person. "I just wanted the blood of a Shadower. I was going to make sure she didn't remember." Mya squirmed and howled in agony. The chains were silver and causing burns.

"Marie?" I asked in a whisper.

"I thought Beck was the evil one until I met this." Marie lunged toward Mya with the silver dagger.

Raven tackled Marie as she stabbed the blade down. It

drove into Mya's shoulder. If I thought she'd been screaming in pain before, it was nothing compared to the sounds she made now.

While Raven held Marie down I went to Mya. "How do I get the chains off?"

"No!" Raven and Marie yelled at the same time.

"Do you trust me to take care of this?" Raven asked.

"Make her shut up!" Marie yelled while covering her ears with her hands. "If you had let me cut off her head she wouldn't be making that horrible noise."

I looked to where the knife was buried in Mya's shoulder. Marie had been trying to cut off her head?

"I'll make her shut up if you'll stay put," Raven said.

Marie narrowed her eyes then nodded.

I moved to the floor next to Marie when Raven stood.

"You stupid bitch," Raven accused Mya. "We trusted you. I trusted you."

"I just wanted to try the blood," Mya squealed again. "I wasn't going to hurt her."

Raven elbowed Mya in the face. She quit howling and didn't twitch.

"Thank you," Marie said. "Although I had it all under control before you got here. A few more minutes and she would have been headless."

"Marie, are you okay?" I grasped her head and turned it so I could look at the wound on her neck. It wasn't ripped open like Rachel's. There were two small puncture marks.

"Of course I'm okay," Marie scolded me. "I let the vampire bite me on purpose."

"You what?" Raven and I demanded.

Marie looked at Raven. "You know that a vampire is vulnerable while it digests the blood of a Shadower. I made her think I was cooperating so I could chain her."

"That was very risky," Raven said.

"She can't be trusted. I knew it the moment you brought her in here with your furry friend."

"Furry friend?" I asked.

"Ian," Raven said.

"But he's bald," I replied. This was such a dumb conversation to be having right now. "Never mind. Where did you get silver chains?"

"My room," Marie said.

It made we worry about what else she might have hidden. Was I going to have to start doing a bed check every night?

Marie grinned like a fool. "I haven't had this much fun since the spring of '82." She switched from reminiscent to commanding. "Call Beck. He needs to know there are untrustworthy blood suckers in his ranks."

"What's going on?" I demanded of Marie while Raven made the call.

"What do you mean?" Marie asked.

I pointed at the knocked out vampire on my kitchen table. The chains had burned her skin everywhere they touched because Mya was only wearing a bra and underwear. Whoa. Her body and face were back to looking like an ordinary woman.

"A normal vampire is no match for a Shadower," Marie said.

Raven ended the call. "Beck's furious."

"Marie was defending herself. He can't blame her—"

"He's not mad a Marie. He's mad at himself. And Mya."

"Mad at himself?" I asked. "Why?"

"Beck considers it his job to make sure innocents are safe. He put Marie and you in danger. He doesn't forgive himself easily for such mistakes." Raven gazed at Mya. "This is a death sentence."

"That's what I was trying to do," Marie said.

"It's not your sentence to carry out, Marie. It's the Protector's."

"It's the Shadower's," Marie argued.

Raven shook her head. "You're not an active Shadower because of your mind. You don't get to determine the death sentence of any beings."

There was a knock on the door. The three of us looked at each other stupidly. Even though the deadbolt had ripped through the door when Raven had kicked it open, it was still attached to the wall. Marie went for the door before I could stop her.

Raven jumped in the air and landed in front of Marie just before she reached the door. I knew it was impossible for a human to move like that.

"What are you?" I asked.

"Does it matter right now if my job is to protect you and Marie?" Raven stared at me for a moment.

"No."

"Thank you for your acceptance," Raven nodded then sniffed the air. "It's Dr. Finch."

"Gabriel Finch? The vampire?" I said.

"Beck must have sent him for cleanup. That was fast." Raven opened the door.

He looked just like I remembered from the night Beck had apparently saved my life from a vampire. Nate's distrust of Finch was in the forefront of my mind as he came through the door. But Beck trusted him. Who did I believe?

"Kinsley, how lovely to see you again." Finch bowed. "I was sorry to hear about the death of your parents. They were important people."

"Um, thanks. I really miss them." Something flashed in

Finch's eyes and I wished I hadn't revealed that small weakness.

Marie stood stone still and stared at Finch.

"And who is this beautiful, young lady?" Finch asked as he floated toward Marie. He took her hand, turned it over, and kissed the inside of her wrist. Marie stood there like a mannequin and let him nibble on her skin.

"Stop," I said so loudly it was on the verge of shouting. I swear I saw fangs and there was no way I was going to let Marie be bitten by another creature tonight.

Finch noticed Marie's neck. "Mya took from you?"

Marie dropped her eyes and whispered, "I invited it so I could chain her."

Finch narrowed his eyes. "Remove the chains so I can dispose of her."

Marie didn't move.

"Where's the key?" I finally asked.

"I can't touch the chains. Neither can Finch," said Raven.

Marie held out the small key to a padlock. I walked to the body on my table. First, I pulled out the dagger embedded in her shoulder. She didn't move.

I knelt down and found the lock up under the edge. It clicked open and I removed it. I started to slide the chains off when someone came busting through the door.

I turned to see Beck and the next thing I knew I was flying through the air. I slammed against the refrigerator and slid to the kitchen floor. Mya was on me. She wrapped a clawed hand around my throat.

"I bet you taste better than Marie. She's been used; you're pure."

I watched Mya's fanged face move toward my throat. That's when I remembered I wasn't helpless. I'd broken a man's hand tonight without even trying. I grabbed the hand that was wrapped around my throat and squeezed. While nothing broke under my grip, Mya's eyes widened in surprise. That moment was all Raven and Finch needed.

Raven wrapped the silver chain around Mya's throat while Finch held her still. I smelled burning flesh and heard Mya scream again. Beck came to me and put his cold hands on my throbbing neck.

"You are bleeding," Beck said.

Marie cowered in the corner as Finch carried away a hog-tied and unconscious Mya. Beck kept talking about my throat bleeding but that didn't make any sense. She hadn't bitten me.

Raven fell to the floor and I crawled to her. She held her hands out and they were covered in angry blisters. It was like she'd shoved her hands into a fire.

I winced. "The silver?"

Raven nodded. She wasn't crying in pain like Mya.

"Are you going to be okay?"

Raven met my eyes. They looked different. The irises were jade green and her pupils were small black ovals instead of perfect circles.

"I will be." Her voice was deep and growly.

This woman wasn't human. I kind of wanted to run screaming into my bedroom. The part of me that had always been accepting of people's differences stayed where I was.

I cradled her injured hands in mine. "Raven, what can I do to help? You saved my life."

Beck came and pulled me slowly to my feet. I released Raven's hands so I wouldn't hurt her.

"Gabriel will take care of Mya. I am so sorry that one of my employees put you and Marie in danger," Beck said, wrapping me in his arms.

I rested my head on his chest for a moment. "I'll take care of Marie and myself. You take care of Raven."

"I don't deserve to be taken care of," Raven said.

I pulled myself from Beck's arms and squatted back down by Raven. "What? I just told you, you saved my life."

She shook her head. "I shouldn't have left Marie with Mya and I shouldn't have had you remove the chains."

"You didn't know she was going to attack me. She was knocked unconscious and had a knife in her shoulder." I looked on the floor at my father's dagger. At least the vampire bitch hadn't gotten away with that.

I scooped up the dagger and went to Marie. "Come on, let's get you cleaned up."

"How long has Dr. Finch been with you, Beck?" Marie asked.

"Is there something you want to tell me, Marie?" Beck asked.

"Not right now. Maybe later." Marie went to walk to the bathroom. "Raven, I can sense your shame. There is no need. Kinsley will not judge you."

"Is she telling me the truth, Kinsley? Can I trust you with my secret?" Raven asked.

I shrugged. "Right now I only seem to have prejudice against vampires. Marie already told me you weren't one of those. I'm willing to listen. That's more than I could have promised two weeks ago."

Raven regarded me intently then looked to Beck.

"You have to change in order to heal. The secret is yours to share, not mine." Beck said.

"Change into what? Are you a werewolf?" I couldn't believe these words were coming out of my mouth.

Raven laughed. "Thank you, Kinsley, I needed that. Why does everyone think shapeshifters are wolves?"

"Hollywood?" I mumbled, wondering what else I was getting myself into.

"What did you see in my eyes, Kinsley."

"They were different. They looked like cat eyes."

Raven let out a breath.

"You're a cat?" I asked. "What kind of cat? Like a house cat?"

This time Beck laughed. "Raven is no one's kitty cat."

Raven closed her eyes. I watched in astonishment, mixed with some horror, as she began to change. Her body became hunched and I heard and saw the bones and ligaments move under her clothes. She fell to her hands and knees and her clothes kind of blew off her body as golden fur grew from her skin.

In a matter of seconds, there stood a mountain lion in place of Raven.

Chapter Twenty-Four

I STARED in shocked silence at the giant cat in front of me and the shredded clothes on the floor. There was a tuft of black hair on its head and that made me laugh. The cougar turned its head as though asking a question.

I asked Beck, "Can she understand me?"

Raven's cougar body walked to me and rubbed against my legs. Her fur was silky smooth. I gently touched the tuft of black hair. "You didn't tell me you dye your hair."

The cougar butted its head against my legs. I almost fell down. "Raven? Is it really you?"

She rubbed against my leg again. I dropped down on the floor and ran my hands over her body. I froze when she stuck her flat face up against my neck. I could feel hot breath on my skin. "Beck?" I asked trying not to show fear.

"She is asking permission to clean and heal your wound."

"Wound? What wound?" I tried to touch my neck but Raven wouldn't move her big fat cat head.

"Mya pierced your skin with her claws." Beck was talking through clinched teeth again. I could see the anger on his face.

"Um, okay." I directed my attention to Raven. "You can

clean my wounds." At the first pass of her tongue over my throat, I squeaked in surprise.

Beck knelt down next to us on the floor. "Did she hurt you?" He had his hand wrapped in the fur at Raven's neck.

"No, it uh, kind of tickled." I put my hand out for Raven to sniff. She licked my fingers. It felt like, well, like a giant cat's tongue. It was warm, wet, and like soft sandpaper. I laughed. "I can't believe this."

Raven licked my neck again and it kind of tingled. "What's happening?" I asked Beck.

"Vampires and most shapeshifters have an enzyme in their saliva that heals wounds. Raven is healing the puncture."

Raven stepped away from me and sat back on her haunches. Seeing this giant cat was amazing. She had the flat, round face with the small ears just like the cougar I'd seen at Woodland Park Zoo.

"How much does she weigh?"

Raven stepped to me and sprawled herself in my lap.

"Okay, I'm sorry for asking. That's like asking a woman how much she weighs. Get off me, cat!" I laughed as I pushed at her huge, muscular body.

"She weighs a little bit more than her human form because of the muscle in her cougar body," Beck said while he dragged Raven off me.

"This is amazing," I said as Raven put her head on my shoulder.

"I told you she wouldn't judge," Marie said.

Raven started to walk toward Marie when her body became tense, her tail poofed out, and a line of fur stood up along her spine.

"Someone's in the hallway," Marie translated.

Suddenly Raven's body relaxed as the front door swung open. It was Nate.

"Whoa." Nate stopped walking.

"It's okay, Nate. It's just Raven," I said.

Nate smiled at me.

"You already knew that, didn't you?"

"Yeah. I was just wondering what brought about her change." Nate noticed the table, the blood, and the silver chains on the floor. "Did Marie throw a party?"

"Mya," Beck explained with the single word.

"You're kidding me? Where's Finch?"

"He is taking care of her."

Nate shook his head. "You don't really believe he'll kill her, do you? He's always had a soft spot for Mya."

"He will do what he is told," Beck said.

While the exchange was engrossing, I had more important things to worry about. "Where's Rachel?"

"Ian and Dr. Karlof are bringing her up in the elevator. We left her in a bed instead of trying to put her in a wheelchair. Kinsley, I need to ask you something," Nate said.

I waited patiently. Sort of.

"I know Rachel is very important to you. She's become important to me in a short amount of time," he paused, waiting for me to interrupt. When I didn't, he went on. "I'd feel better if we were all in one place. I'd like to have Rachel over with Beck and me. Raven and Ian will stay here with you and Marie. Or you could all come to Beck's."

I thought for a moment. "I need some normalcy for Marie and me, Nate. I'll feel better knowing Rachel will be with you. I can't protect her."

Nate let out the breath he'd been holding. "Thank you for understanding, Kinsley. Although, I think Fredericks would argue you could protect just about anyone."

I laughed without humor. "Yeah, maybe from a measly, chicken-shit human, but not from anything supernatural."

"You'll be able to," Nate said.

"Go to bed, ladies. I think we have had enough excitement for one day," Beck said.

I shook my head. "I'm not going to bed until I've seen Rachel and get to talk to her."

"She was sedated. I don't think she'll be doing much talking," Nate said.

"That's fine. I still want to see her."

Nate turned his head to the door. "They're here."

"How do you do that?" I asked.

"Do you really want to know right now?"

"Are you a werewolf?" I blurted.

Nate turned around and mumbled something about movies giving the paranormal world a bad name. Beck smiled.

"Marie, will you make up a bed for Raven?" Beck asked.

"We're all sleeping in my room," I said. "Marie's sleeping with me tonight." I looked down at Raven. "You're on the floor or at the foot of the bed if you'll fit." I rubbed the top of her head, enjoying the softness of her fur when a thought occurred to me. "When can you change back?"

She couldn't answer me, of course, so I looked to Beck. "She will need to stay in her animal form for a few hours in order to heal completely," he said.

Marie was walking in circles around the dining room table.

"Marie. Marie!"

She finally realized I was talking to her. "Yes, dear?" Her voice had taken on that flighty tone she got when she wasn't really paying attention to what was going on.

"Sleepover in my room."

"Will Rachel be coming?" Marie clapped her hands together and bounced up and down like the internal eight-year-old she was.

"No, Rachel's going to sleep over with Nate. Raven will stay with us, though."

"Oh, goodie. I'll go get ready for bed." Marie ran to my room and shut herself in the bathroom.

I looked down at Raven. "Watch her and make sure she doesn't decide to curl her hair and catch the bathroom on fire." I was only partially kidding. She'd done that once.

As Raven padded into my room I turned to Beck. "Any other surprises I should know about?"

"Always. We are going to leave it at this for now."

"As long as I don't have to deal with any vampires, I think I'll be fine."

Beck stared at me for a moment and opened his mouth to speak.

"Kinsley, Kinsley!" Marie came running from my bedroom with the cougar right behind her.

"On any other day, that might seem weird," I said.

"Did you know there was a vampire here tonight? Actually, there were two. Finch reminds me of someone, but I can't remember who."

"I was here, Marie, I saw the two vampires. One threw me against...the fridge..." I turned and looked at the refrigerator. Our magnets and fast food menus were scattered around the floor. I looked at Beck. "Shouldn't I have broken bones or internal bleeding or something? Not that I'm complaining, mind you, just curious."

Beck hesitated before saying, "Along with your strength, you have some protection from small injuries. You are still going to bleed, but it will take more than a thump to hurt you."

I rubbed my temples. "I need to go to bed."

"That is what I have been trying to get you to do," Beck said.

I scowled at him. Turning to my bedroom I said, "Marie,

stay here with Raven. Do not answer the door. I'll be back right after I check on Rachel."

Marie looked at the cougar sitting at her feet. "Rachel? What happened to Rachel."

I closed my eyes and counted to ten. "Remember, Marie, she's been at the hospital? She was attacked almost three days ago." Had it really only been three days? The exhaustion I felt made it seem like more.

"Oh, that's right. Sorry." Marie ran back to my bedroom.

Beck followed me across the hall. Rachel appeared to be asleep as Dr. Karlof plugged in the various machines that were attached to her. He pulled out a syringe and injected it into the IV at her hand.

"More sedative. She's been having nightmares. I'll be at the hotel if you need me," Karlof said. He walked out without saying a word to me.

"Odd man," I said.

Beck nodded. "Yes, however he has been useful for many years."

"Nate said he was there when you were born. Is he human or vampire?"

Beck regarded me for a moment. "Vampire. A very old, very strong vampire who has been helping me try to develop synthetic blood. I know you do not care much for vampires right now, Kinsley, but he is one of the good ones."

"It's going to take a little more than your word to convince me of that. Vampires killed my parents, tried to kill Rachel, and Mya didn't impress me much."

Beck looked down then back to me. "There are good vampires, Kinsley."

"Uh huh. Sure there are. Let's not talk about this right now."

Ian stood a few feet away from Rachel's hospital bed which

was situated in Beck's living room. "Are you sure you don't want her at my place? This is an inconvenience for you."

Beck shook his head. "Nonsense. Besides, Nathaniel is smitten with Rachel and does not want her out of his sight. She will heal quickly, I shall make sure of it."

"How? Her throat was practically ripped out." I stopped. "Raven."

"Well, probably not Raven specifically, but yes. As soon as Rachel's neck quits bleeding when we change the bandages, I will have one of the cougars heal the wounds. She will still need time to mend her hurting body and mind, but that is what her best friend is for." Beck took my hand in his.

"You're freezing," I said. Without thinking about it, I wrapped his hand in both of mine. The electricity sparked. "Tell me what it is."

Beck didn't try to pretend he didn't know what I was talking about. I was thankful for that. "Part of your Shadower powers are to help you tell when a supernatural creature is near you."

"That's what Raven meant by me being able to tell the difference."

"Yes. The more emotionally attached you are to a being, the better you will be able to sense their presence."

I tilted my head. "Are you a cougar, too?"

Beck said nothing.

"Am I going to have to guess?"

"I would prefer not to tell all secrets yet."

"I won't think any less of you. You've done nothing but wonderful things for me since I met you. I accepted Raven, I'll accept you."

He shook his head. "We will see how you feel when the time comes."

"Beck, please."

He put his finger over my lips. "This is not up for discussion. Not now. We need to get Rachel well and I must make sure Gabriel took care of Mya. We also have the Seattle Art Museum gala to prepare for. The regular world goes on."

Beck left me alone with Rachel for about ten minutes. I sat and held her hand. Nate appeared fresh from the shower and made up a bed on the couch. Ian never moved from his corner in the living room.

I dragged myself across the hall and found Marie asleep in my bed. Raven lay curled on the floor next to my bedroom door. She yawned, showing impressive fangs, as I walked by.

I got ready for bed then stood in the dark for a moment. Raven walked over to me and bumped my thigh with her head.

"I'm just confused, Raven. Why won't Beck tell me what he is?" I said.

She rubbed against me and herded me toward my bed. Marie emitted a ladylike snore and I smiled. I climbed into bed and pulled the sheet over me. Marie didn't move.

I rolled to my stomach and let my arm hang off the side of the bed to where Raven was stretched out. I buried my hand in her thick, soft fur. She purred like a house cat. A very loud house cat.

I fell asleep wondering what kind of creature Beck was that he didn't think I'd understand. Did he not trust me? What could be so awful?

Chapter Twenty-Five

I WOKE with countless thoughts already spiraling through my head. I'd agreed to meet with Scott Masters as soon as he returned from his business trip, but I couldn't remember when that was. I knew that I had to start training mentally and physically to be a Shadower and I didn't know what that meant.

I supposed I should start with having Marie translate more of The Book of Protection. I was still laying on my stomach when I remembered Raven. I looked to the floor and she was asleep, back in human form, and naked.

Awkward.

I didn't want Beck or Nate to show up and find her naked on my floor so I slid the comforter off the foot of my bed onto her. The minute it touched her skin, Raven jumped to a crouch and evaluated the threat situation. At least that's what it looked like to me.

I held up my hands. "Raven, it's okay, I just didn't want one of the boys to come in and find you naked."

She looked down at herself and then at me. "Sorry. We sleep deeply when we need to heal. I'm relatively young, so I don't bounce back as fast as some of the others."

"It's okay. You don't need to apologize. You were amazing

last night. I imagine being a shapeshifter is hell on your wardrobe, though."

Raven pulled the comforter over herself. "I usually take off my clothes when I'm planning to shift. I didn't think I should strip in your kitchen. You'd been through enough."

I laughed. "Thank you for that. Can I see your hands?"

Raven tucked the blanket around her and held out her hands. There wasn't a trace of blistering or scarring from the silver chains.

"Incredible," I said.

"Sometimes it still shocks me, too."

I sat up and crossed my legs. "Tell me about your life."

"I've always been an outdoor girl," Raven sat back. "I was hiking outside of Bellingham, near Mt. Baker, almost three years ago. I don't remember everything that happened, but I woke up in the hospital. I'd been attacked by a mountain lion. My injuries healed much faster than the doctors expected, but no one said anything about it.

"I went about my life even though I felt different. I couldn't put my finger on what it was. I convinced myself it was because I'd suffered a near death experience and I was living my life more rebelliously or something like that.

"I was at a club when this guy started hitting on me. I didn't like the vibe I was getting from him so I brushed him off. He followed me out to the parking lot when I left and tried to drag me into his car. I had my eyes closed and swung my hands at him. I hurt him bad, Kinsley."

I shuddered at the look of horror on Raven's face.

"Luckily, Nathaniel found me in the parking lot. The guy was bleeding from four slices across his abdomen. Nathaniel knew what I was. It took a lot of work, but Beck and Nathaniel took me in and helped me control my *inner cat* as I like to call her."

"So you can change when you want to?"

She nodded. "Now I can control it. In the beginning I changed when I got scared or angry."

"Beck told me that vampires have a process to go through before they can change a human. But the animals, for lack of a better word, infect a human by biting them?"

She nodded again. "There's a little more to it than that, but basically, yes. Dr. Karlof is studying all the shapeshifters who work for Beck. He tests our blood at least once a month to see if there are any changes or anomalies."

"How many shapeshifters work for Beck?"

"I trust you, Kinsley, I already do. But shifters have made a pact we don't share information about each other. If someone wants to share their secret, they do."

"So you won't tell me what Nate and Beck are?"

"It's not my secret to tell. While every one of us was human, our animal instincts demand self-preservation."

I whispered, "Are there any werewolves?"

Raven laughed. "Yes, there are wolves."

My doorbell rang before I could ask any more questions. "I think you should find some clothes, Raven."

"All my stuff is down at Screamers."

"My clothes are all going to be too big for you but I should have something you can wear." I opened a dresser drawer and threw a pair of shorts and a shirt at Raven. Then I went to the front door.

"Thanks," she called after me. "Ask who's there before you answer."

"You already know who it is, don't you?"

"It's Nathaniel. But you need to be in the habit of asking who's there."

"It's not like it matters. Someone broke my door last night and it's barely hanging on the hinges."

Raven laughed at me.

I opened the door to Nathaniel, just as Raven said I would. "Good morning," I said.

"Good morning. Rachel slept through the night and I had her wounds healed this morning. She handled it well, considering. I know she's still a little sore, but her throat doesn't look like a vampire ripped it open."

I threw my arms around Nate and hugged him for all I was worth. He kind of made a noise like he was clearing his throat then picked me up and walked me into my condo. He kicked the door shut behind him.

"Kinsley, you're stronger, remember? Don't squeeze so hard."

"Oops, sorry!" I loosened my hold and planted a kiss on Nate's cheek. "Thank you for taking such good care of Rachel."

I let go of Nate as Raven came out of my bedroom. The shirt hung almost to her knees. She looked like a kid playing dress up.

"Nice look, Raven, you should go clubbing like that. The guys will be dropping at your feet."

"Ha ha, you're almost funny, Nathaniel." Raven went to my fridge to get a bottle of water.

"What happened to my kitchen?" I asked.

"What do you mean?" Nate said. "It's clean and you can't tell there was a vampire chained to your table last night."

"That's what I'm getting at." He was right. My kitchen looked like nothing had happened. "I'm missing a chair."

"Yeah," Nate said. "Only one got broken. That's pretty good. Ian put it in the dumpster. It wasn't worth saving."

"Ian cleaned my kitchen? Where was I?"

"You and Marie were sleeping. Ian is quiet and trustworthy." This time Raven answered. She closed my fridge and all our magnets were back. They were in a blob in one corner, but they were there.

"Why are you all taking such good care of me? Of us?"

"Because you're a Shadower, Kinsley. You're our Shadower." Nate took my hand. "When you meet your Monarch, you'll understand better. The Monarch and the Shadower join together and protect the innocent. You do that with help from your shape shifting followers. Think of it as being our queen." Nate smiled.

I shook my head. "I don't want to be a queen. Queens have responsibilities. Can't I be a princess? And what if I don't want to join with a Monarch? I'm not sure I like vampires."

Nate looked worried. "You need to wait and see. Don't make any hasty decisions."

"I'm not making *any* decisions. I don't think I've made a single decision about my life since June." I left them in the kitchen and went to my bedroom. I closed the door behind me so Marie would hopefully keep sleeping.

I took a shower and dressed quietly.

Raven was sitting on the couch reading a book. "Nathaniel said you could go over and see Rachel."

I went across the hall and walked into Beck's condo. I'd decided we were beyond the formalities of knocking on doors.

Rachel was sitting up on Beck's couch. Ian stood in the corner like a statue. When Rachel saw me she smiled.

I walked over and sat down next to her. The tubes and bandages were gone from her throat. There were small, raised scars on her neck. It looked like a month of healing instead of a day.

"Have you seen any of the cougars?" Rachel asked. Her voice was low and raspy but didn't sound as bad as yesterday.

I nodded.

"They're amazing, aren't they?" Rachel ran her hands lightly over her neck.

"Are you okay?" I had to ask. It seemed like such a lame question considering she'd been attacked by a vampire.

She smiled and reached out to take my hand. "You know what, Kins? I am. Nathaniel's been worried about me all night, but I'm fine. I had some dreams about it. In my dreams you and Nathaniel save me."

"But I didn't save you," I said.

"Kinsley, we save each other. You know that. You didn't have to be there ripping the vampire off me. Your friendship saves me. Once I realized I would live, I knew you'd take care of me. That's what we do for each other."

This is what family did for each other, accept and love unconditionally. Rachel was my family.

I ended up with my head on Rachel's lap while she rubbed my neck and shoulders. "Isn't this backward?" I finally asked. "Shouldn't I be comforting you?"

"No. I'm fine. Nathaniel did this for me all night. He told me about the vampire that Marie chained to your table. I'm sorry I missed that." Rachel continued to rub my shoulders.

"Things just keep getting weirder if that's possible. I'm not sure I'm going to be shocked by much of anything soon."

Ian suddenly burst from the corner and was at Beck's front door in a split second. Then I heard a man's voice yelling in the hallway.

Scott Masters.

I walked to Beck's door and pushed Ian aside. Scott was yelling at Raven in my doorway.

"Scott, I'm right here. Scott!" He finally heard me and turned around.

"Jesus Christ. I try to call you for two days and you never answer your cell phone or return my messages. I get back and find out from Oliver that Rachel's been attacked by a vampire and no one's seen you. Your door looks like a battering ram went through it and the garden gnome, here, wouldn't tell me where you were."

Raven growled at Scott's comment. I guess I shouldn't tell her I thought she looked like a Smurf.

I waved an arm at the door. "Scott, I'm fine. I've been at the hospital and here."

"Here as in Beckford Alexander's home?" Scott's voice was accusing.

"Listen, buddy!" I poked him in the shoulder and he flinched.

"You're stronger," Scott said.

"Yeah, so don't piss me off. I've had a bad few days."

"You've been crying. What's wrong?" He tried to touch my face but I backed away from him.

"Yes, I've been crying. My best friend almost died. That upsets some people."

He looked over my shoulder. "I want you away from these monsters."

I poked him again. "They're not monsters. They've protected us."

"That is more than I can say for you, Masters." Beck's voice drifted across the room. I turned.

He was standing at the end of the hallway wearing a pair of silk pajama pants and that was it. His hair was damp and brushed his shoulders. His skin was dark and covered a very impressive set of eight-pack abs. I'd never seen a body so toned that wasn't grossly muscled.

"You're both fresh from a shower, I see," Scott was vibrating with anger.

"Yes, we are," Beck said.

"Stop it, both of you." I glared at Beck and tore my gaze

from his body. I looked at Scott. "Not that I need to explain myself to you, but I took a shower at my place and then came over here. I didn't even know Beck was home."

Scott stared back and forth between Beck and me. "You can do whatever you want on your own time, Kinsley. I'm not your keeper."

"If you keep accusing me of things I haven't done, I'm going to ignore you for the rest of your life. Quit being a chauvinistic jackass."

Scott quit meeting my eyes. "You're right, I'm sorry."

"Okay then," I said. "Now, how about if we meet for drinks like you planned before you left? Tonight? Screamers?"

Scott narrowed his eyes. "Does it have to be Screamers?"

"Yes," Beck answered.

"You bring Oliver," I said, "and I'll bring Raven."

"Who's Raven?"

"A new friend who is also a bodyguard. You just yelled at her." I lifted my chin so Scott would look behind him to where Raven still stood in my doorway.

"Great. Can't wait," he said.

"Me either," Raven added in a cheerfully sarcastic tone.

This was going to be an interesting night.

Chapter Twenty-Six

AFTER SCOTT LEFT, I closed Beck's door and turned to him. "Did you have to insinuate that we'd showered together?"

Beck shrugged. "I find it fun to watch that man squirm."

"Well, it's not fun to make me squirm. Don't do that again."

Beck nodded and my attention drew back to his body. There were small scars on his abdomen. "What happened?" I asked.

"The war against vampires does not come without consequences."

"Beck," Rachel said. "You have one fabulous body. How in the world do you and Nathaniel stay in such good shape?" Rachel looked at me. "Nathaniel looks just as good as this, Kins. You could bounce a quarter off his ass."

I blushed. Beck standing there in only his pajama pants was the closest I'd ever been to a naked man and Rachel was talking about how tight Nate's butt was. I didn't want to have this conversation.

"Well, thank you," Nate said from behind me. Nate lowered himself next to Rachel on the couch. After looking at her neck and running his fingers over it, he framed her face in his hands and kissed her.

I don't mean a little kiss either. This kiss had tongue and slobber and little moaning noises.

Rachel pulled her head away and rested her forehead against Nate's. "We're embarrassing Kinsley."

I figured they were sleeping together, but I hadn't really paid attention to how close they'd become. I could see the look on Rachel's face. She thought she was in love with Nate. Rachel had been in and out of love so many times since we were twelve. I hoped they wouldn't hurt each other.

My stomach growled and Nate laughed. "Is this your way of guilting me into cooking you breakfast?"

"I don't know what's wrong with me. I'm starving all the time."

Beck guided me to the kitchen and poured me a glass of orange juice. "It is part of your body changing to accommodate the Shadower blood you are producing. Your metabolism has almost tripled to help your body adjust. You are going to need to change your eating habits drastically."

"Yeah," Nate added. "More protein, carbs, and sugars. You're going to be an eating machine."

"I'll gain a ton of weight!"

"No you will not," Beck said. "I just told you your metabolism tripled. You are going to need to eat three times more than usual."

"Let me get this straight. I'm stronger, can't be injured easily, and get to eat all I want without gaining a pound?" When Nate nodded, I looked at Rachel. "Sweet."

Rachel laughed with me and I went back to join her on the couch. While Nate made breakfast, Rachel and I talked about what had happened with her parents. She told me her phone had fifteen voicemails from her dad. She'd tried to listen to the first few, but he had just called us names so she'd deleted all the messages.

Raven showed up with Marie just before Nate was ready to serve breakfast. Everyone sat at the table except for Rachel, who stayed on the couch, and Ian, who was back to standing in the corner.

"Ian, come have breakfast with us," I said.

"I'll eat when everyone else is done, Miss Kinsley."

I looked to Raven. "As bodyguards, we try to make sure at least one person is always on guard," she said.

"Okay. Speaking of bodyguards, should I start some training today?"

Beck asked, "Are you sure you are ready?"

I shrugged. "I don't know if I'm ready, but I have to start sometime."

"I need to do some shopping," Marie said.

I whipped my head to her. "What could you possibly need?" I asked.

She buttered her toast. "Some new clothes and maybe some hair products. I wouldn't mind getting some makeup, either."

I rolled my eyes. Could she be more out of touch?

"I will have someone take you shopping after breakfast, Marie," Beck said.

"No more vampires," I said.

Beck nodded. I was grateful he'd put on a shirt before sitting down to breakfast. It was disturbing to find myself staring at his chest when there was a lull in conversation.

Raven finished eating. "Let's go down to the gym."

"The gym?" I asked.

"Kinsley, have you even noticed that you never see anyone else in the building?" Nate was grinning at me.

The only other person I'd seen had been Gerald. I opened my mouth and then closed it.

"Oh my!" Rachel said from the couch. Then she laughed. "Does anyone but us live here?"

"No," Beck said. "I bought this building about four years ago and had it remodeled. From the outside it looks like a five story complex. There are only three units. Yours, mine, and Gerald's. You have seen the parking garage. There are some offices, a shooting facility, a pool, and a gym."

"And you're just telling me this now?" I said.

"I could not tell you when I was trying to get you to move in. You would have thought it strange. The money you used to buy your condo is in a savings account gaining interest. When you are ready, you can buy your own home. Just not yet. We needed to make sure you knew about being a Shadower."

When Beck said there were always going to be surprises, he wasn't kidding.

"Come on, Kinsley, I'll show you around." Raven stood. She was still wearing the borrowed clothes. She saw me looking at her. "Don't worry, I have clothes down in the gym. Go change into something comfortable for working out."

"Kinsley," Rachel said. "When Marie's done shopping, I'd like to translate more of the book for you."

"Are you sure? You need rest."

"I'll go crazy if I don't help somehow."

"I will help you translate the book, Rachel. Marie sometimes leaves out important details." Beck looked at Marie.

She had two forks, one in each hand, and was making them 'dance' across the table. At least there wasn't food on them. I shook my head.

"Thank you, Beck."

"My pleasure, Kinsley." He gave me a lingering kiss on the cheek.

I touched my cheek where his lips had just been and backed to the door. Needing space, I went to my place and quickly changed into a tank top, running shorts, and tennis shoes. Raven met me in the hallway and we took the elevator down.

I shook my head as I stared at my reflection in the elevator doors. "I can't believe I never noticed no one else lives here."

"Don't be so hard on yourself," Raven said. "You've had a lot on your mind since you moved in."

The doors opened to the lobby. "We have to take a different elevator," Raven said.

There was a door that said 'Authorized Personnel Only' with a keypad on it behind Gerald's desk. Raven told me the five digit code and then typed it in. The door opened to a small hallway and a different elevator.

"What is this place? The FBI?"

"Wait 'til you see the armory," Raven said. I don't even think she was kidding.

The elevator took us down to a huge room with no windows. The bulk of the floor and walls were covered in mats. It resembled a giant dojo combined with state of the art exercise equipment. There were four weight machines, six elliptical trainers, six treadmills, and four stationary bikes. Against a wall of mirrors, there were free weights and benches. Boxing bags hung from the ceiling in another corner.

While I admired the setup, Raven went to the locker room and came out in an outfit similar to mine.

"We're going to start with basic self-defense," Raven said.

She led me to the center of the room and started stretching. I copied what she was doing.

"Despite your new strength, your hands aren't your best weapon. You can squeeze and you have good grip, but you need to use the strongest parts of your body." She walked to the red boxing bags. "For example, your elbow can deliver a crushing blow to someone's head, throat, sternum, ribs, and groin." Raven demonstrated by twisting at the waist and throwing her weight into one of the bags. Her elbow made contact and the bag swung a good two feet out from her.

I moved over and tried to copy her movements. I twisted too far and fell to the floor on my side. I looked up at Raven to see if she was laughing at me. She wasn't.

"You need to plant your feet before you twist so you stay balanced." She helped me up and positioned my feet. Standing behind me, she helped my body feel how to twist. When she stepped back, I did it on my own.

My elbow connected and the bag swayed slightly.

"Good," Raven praised. "Again."

I hit with four more elbow blows and each time the bag moved a little more.

"Now, let's talk about knees." Raven turned so we faced each other. "For an average woman, the legs are the strongest part of their body. Being a shifter, my strength is spread throughout. You have more strength than a regular woman, but you're still built like one."

She reached out and grabbed my head with both hands. She gently pulled my head down as she raised her knee to my nose. "The cartilage in the nose is delicate and dangerous. A hit to a shifter or human face will break their nose and maybe even drive the cartilage back into their brain. You could kill a human and slow down a shifter enough to kill them or get away."

I processed that information then asked, "How do you kill a shifter? I know you can kill a vampire by cutting off its head."

"There are a few different ways to kill vampires and shifters. Right now, I just want to concentrate on defense, not killing blows. Is that okay?"

I put my hands together and bowed. "I trust your training, oh wise one."

"Ha ha. Funny girl," Raven said dryly as she pulled my

head down to demonstrate again. Then she put my hands on her head and had me practice pulling her face toward my knee.

"Most human attackers are going to grab you from behind. Your skull is thick, hard bone. Slam the back of your head into someone's face and they'll usually be stunned enough to let go. If someone grabs you from the front, do the same thing with the top of your head or your forehead, like a head butt. Just don't use the front of your face."

We practiced this a few times, too. Then Raven had me go back and hit the boxing bag with my elbows and knees.

The next thing I knew, I was sweating and it was almost noon. We'd been down here for three hours.

"Let's do a cool down," Raven said.

We walked to a treadmill and Raven showed me how to adjust the speed and incline. It wasn't as relaxing as running outside, but it would have to do. I got the feeling my days of running outside had come to an end.

Not even breathing hard, Raven said, "For the rest of this month and the beginning of September, we'll meet six days a week and do weight training, defense practice, and the treadmill and elliptical for endurance. I think we need to go at least five hours a day."

I groaned.

She chuckled at my resistance. "The payoff will be an hour in the pool and hot tub when we're done. We'll have Marie start with us tomorrow and Rachel as soon as she's ready. We'll have to come up with a schedule when classes start at the end of September."

I stopped running and was almost thrown from the treadmill.

Raven stopped her treadmill. "What's wrong?"

I braced my feet on each side of the moving track. "Classes. My senior year. I forgot." How could I have forgotten about my education? "I can't be a teacher and a Shadower." I switched off the treadmill and looked at Raven.

"Your mom was," she said.

I waved my arms around. "In a town with no vampire activity. What if I'm with my students and vampires show up? Hell, what if at the U, vampires came to my classes? I can't put innocent people in danger like that."

Sensing my impending breakdown, Raven walked me off my treadmill. "Let's go sit in the hot tub. You don't have to make any decisions right now," she said.

I let her take me to the pool area and the changing rooms. She handed me a one-piece suit that I put on without paying attention. All that was going through my head were thoughts of my future. I'd wanted to be a teacher since I was in first grade. I'd never wanted to do anything else. I didn't know what to do now that it wasn't an option.

The hot tub felt great, just as Raven said it would. I sat in the heat and watched her swim endless laps in the pool. When I was pruny, I went to take a shower in the locker room.

Beck was in the pool when I walked out twenty minutes later. Raven was nowhere to be seen. I watched the play of muscles in his back as he swam. After ten more passes he came to the edge of the pool where I stood.

He surfaced and slicked his hair back. "Raven said you became upset about starting classes in the fall."

"Not about starting classes. About becoming a teacher and putting my students at risk. I can't be a teacher anymore can I?" I wasn't going to cry about this. I wasn't.

"You can do whatever you want. No one is going to tell you you cannot try and have a regular job."

"What's your opinion?"

Beck braced his hands on the edge of the pool and effortlessly lifted himself out. He was wearing regular swim shorts that stopped at mid-thigh. Water sluiced off his body as he reached for the towel on the bench.

"Why?" he said.

"Why what?" I asked. His nearly naked body had distracted me again.

"Why do you want my opinion?"

"Because it's important. You and Marie are the only ones who understand what it means to be a Shadower and she doesn't know where she's at or what year it is most of the time. I want to know what you think."

He sighed. "I think you are correct."

I knew he was going to agree with me but it didn't ease the ache in my chest.

He rubbed the towel over his head and draped it across his shoulders. "Do not dwell on it right now. You and Raven are meeting with Masters in a few hours. One thing at a time."

"You're right. I'll try not to worry about it right now. Hell, with the workout plan Raven's putting me on, I could become a professional body builder as my new career."

Beck laughed.

Chapter Twenty-Seven

IAN DROPPED Raven and me off at the front entrance to Screamers. We strode past the line waiting to get in. Two large men ushered us through amidst the rude comments about cutting in line. One of the men smiled at me and I realized they were two of the four guys who had moved all our stuff into the condo. I wondered if they were shapeshifters and then brushed it off. So what if they were?

I followed Raven's Lycra covered backside through the crowd. She had on a one piece tank style dress in sapphire blue that barely covered her important girl parts. Lace-up stiletto heeled boots that went to her knees completed the outfit. She had dyed her hair pink and there was no trace of the black left. I wondered what her cougar would look like with a pink tuft of hair and had to stifle a laugh.

We went to the back of the club and through a set of sheer curtains. It was a small, private room that still afforded a view of the bar but the sounds from the club were muted. Four small, two-person couches surrounded a low table. I sat on one couch and Raven sat on the one right next to me. The waitress breezed in as our butts hit the cushions. Raven ordered us Appletinis.

"I don't usually drink martinis," I told her as the waitress left.

"You'll like these," she said.

Our drinks arrived in minutes despite the crowded floor and other tables. Knowing the owner had its perks.

I sipped the drink. Raven was right, I did like it. I ate a maraschino cherry from the little sword and finished the martini in four swallows. Raven stared.

"What?" I asked.

"You said you don't normally drink martinis but you finished that one in less than three minutes."

"You were right, it was good. Can I have another?" I asked as I set the glass on the table.

"Are you trying to get drunk?" Raven raised an eyebrow at me.

I shrugged. "Maybe." My life had gone to hell in a hand basket. If I wanted to drink more than usual, I could.

Raven flagged our waitress and ordered more drinks.

I was sipping when Scott appeared with Oliver. Scott looked at my empty martini glass and the new drink in my hand. "Been here a while?" he asked.

"Nope. The service here is impeccable." Raven saluted her glass at him and drained the contents. "What would you boys like this evening?"

"Nothing," Scott said, "we're working."

"That doesn't sound like much fun," I said. Two new drinks were placed on the table. Scott sat down next to me and Oliver sat opposite Raven, peering at the entrance to the room. Body-guards never get to relax.

I stared at Scott over the rim of my martini glass. His light blonde hair was cut in a military style buzz. He wore a suit, but he wasn't overdressed. My mind couldn't help but compare Beck and

Scott. While both were muscular, Scott was wider through the shoulders but a few inches shorter. Beck was lean muscle and Scott was prominent, defined muscle. I knew what Beck's body looked like. I wondered what Scott looked like without his shirt and then promptly got embarrassed and almost dropped my drink. Where in the world were these raging hormones coming from?

I broke eye contact and cleared my throat.

"We need to talk about the future, Kinsley," Scott said, thankfully oblivious to my perverted musings. "Would you like to stay in business with me?"

"Scott, I don't even know what you and my dad did together. How could I possibly know if I want to be in business with you?" I finished my second drink and picked up the third. After two swallows, I turned to Raven. "I can't get drunk, can I?"

She cocked her head in thought. "Well, Nathaniel experimented once. He drank a fifth of whiskey like it was a bottle of water and he got a little light headed. A shifter's metabolism is too fast; the alcohol doesn't stay in our systems. I figured you'd be the same." Raven watched me set the drink back on the table.

"Well this sucks. The one time in my life I actually want to drown my sorrows and I can't. I may as well just have water." I signaled the waitress over.

"Why were you trying to get drunk?" Scott asked.

"Why do people usually get drunk? To forget their problems for a few hours. I wanted to try and forget I was a Shadower. Is that so wrong?"

"No, it's not wrong. It's not the best way to deal with your problems, either." Scott glared at Raven.

"Well thank you, Dr. Phil," I said.

Scott regarded me for a moment. "I'm sorry. I'm handling

this all wrong. I'd like for you to move out of Alexander's building and live closer to me."

Raven sat up and growled at Scott. Oliver reached under his jacket.

"Stop it!" I shouted.

Raven sat back and Scott narrowed his eyes at her. Ollie didn't move his hand.

"This is ridiculous. I'm tired of everyone bossing me around," I said. "I'm staying where I'm at for now because I'm not going to uproot Marie again and Rachel is safe with Beck and Nate." I pointed at Scott. "Quit trying to tell me what to do and start talking to me. Can you prove I'll be safer living closer to you than Beck?" I let out a huge breath and was relieved when the waitress arrived with our water. I drank half the glass and slammed it down on the table. I was surprised the glass didn't shatter considering my new strength.

Scott watched me. Oliver slowly moved his hand from under his jacket.

"This was a bad idea," I said. "I never should have agreed to meet with you. You're not my father, Scott. You may have told him you'd try to look out for me but I have to make my own decisions. I'm in this mess now because my mom and dad didn't explain what I was destined to become."

Maybe that was my problem. Maybe I was mad at my parents for not being here to help me deal with this. Great. Now who sounded like Dr. Phil?

"You're right about one thing, Kinsley. I want to look out for you and take care of you, but I damn sure don't want to be your father." Scott stood and grabbed my hand. "Come on, we're going to dance." He dragged me on the floor and pulled me close to his body.

I wasn't wearing anything nearly as revealing or tight as Raven but I was wearing club clothes. I had on a purple baby-doll tee, black miniskirt, and strappy sandals with a heel. My face was level with Scott's shoulder.

"Do you know what the *people* are that you're practically living with? shapeshifters and vamps. Your parents would be appalled," Scott whisper-yelled in my ear because of the loud music.

"I don't think you get to tell me what my parents would or would not think," I shot back. "How dare you drop into my life and try to tell me what to do. I thought my parents protected the humans and non-humans who needed it and destroyed evil vampires. I'm not living with any evil vampires."

I tried to pull away from Scott but his arms locked around my body. His hands were wrapped possessively around my hips and he wasn't letting go.

"I learned some self-defense today, Masters. I don't think you should test my new-found strength."

Surprise flared in Scott's eyes. "Good, that's what I've been waiting for. For you to tell me someone has started teaching you to protect yourself."

"I'll be working out and training for more than five hours a day." I almost groaned when I said it.

"Are they going to teach you to use weapons? Guns, knives, bows?"

"We haven't talked about that yet." It was hard to dance and hold a conversation when every inch of his muscled body was plastered against me. The heat from his hands felt like a brand through my skirt.

"Here's my thought," Scott said. "Let Alexander and his shifters teach you how to deal with your new strength. Your mom and dad kicked my ass many a time because I was no match for them. Let Oliver and I teach you to use weapons and silver." Scott's hands tightened on my hips.

I found myself once again comparing the two men. What

the hell was wrong with me? I tried to pull away again, but Scott wouldn't let go. Suddenly Raven and Ollie were on the dance floor next to us.

"Kinsley's done dancing," Raven said to Scott.

"No she's not. We're still talking."

I shook my head. "I'm done, Scott. I want to go home."

Scott reluctantly released me as Raven took my arm.

"Call me tomorrow so we can set up a schedule." He stared at me intently. Then he walked toward the exit of the club with Oliver following.

"Set up a schedule for what?" Raven asked.

"I'll talk to you about it in the car. He has a good idea. I'll want to share it with Beck, too. Can you call Nate or Ian? I do want to go home." As though I'd summoned him, the crowd seemed to part and there Beck stood, leaning against the bar, facing us.

He was dressed in black slacks with a black button up shirt and a deep red tie. He stood out from all the people in the club.

And he looked delicious.

Delicious? When did I start thinking like that?

Almost like he could read my mind, Beck smiled and crooked his finger at me. When I reached him, he twirled a lock of my hair around his forefinger. "Was Masters a complete gentleman?" he asked.

Raven snorted a laugh. "Gentleman? If I hadn't been here he would have whisked her away on his white horse and locked her in his palace. Saved her from the evil creatures and made her his queen." Raven winked at me. "I'd let him whisk me away."

"What are you talking about?" I said.

Her eyes widened. "Hello? Kinsley, that man had sex and hormones oozing from his pores. He wants you. Bad."

Beck growled. I was beginning to think he had to be a cougar or a wolf.

I looked back to Raven. "He does not. He feels a sense of responsibility to my dead parents. That's it."

"Uh huh, sure," Raven said.

"Enough. I want to know what he wanted." Beck turned to the bartender, said something I couldn't hear, then took my hand. The electricity moved between us like a live current. This time it wasn't so much of a shock as flowing energy.

He pulled me to the edge of the room and we went through a keycard access door being watched by a pair of male and female body guards. Raven was right behind us as the door closed and cut out all sound from the club. We went up a wide flight of stairs to an office overlooking the lower floor through one-way mirrors.

The office had a huge desk, a conference table with numerous chairs, two couches, and a bed in the corner. There was also a small bathroom. There weren't any windows to the outside.

"I ordered bottled water. I know you do not want any more martinis." Beck glared at Raven.

"What? She had to see for herself the alcohol wouldn't have any effect," Raven said.

Beck sat behind his desk. "I also requested a fruit and cheese tray."

I sat in one of the chairs and explained Scott's idea of adding weapons training to my daily schedule. Raven seemed pleased by the idea. Beck did not.

"It's a good idea, Beck. Who better to teach me about using weapons than the people who need them to survive? I doubt any of your people carry guns."

Beck leaned back in his chair. "Raven does because she

feels more comfortable with a weapon. Though we do not usually need to."

"Exactly. But I should. I'll have a better chance of blowing some vampire's head off with a gun than I will attempting to wrestle it to the ground. Mya already proved that for me." I started eating as soon as the food and water arrived.

Fruit and cheese wasn't going to cut it. Maybe I could get Nate to barbecue me a big, juicy steak when I got home. I pulled out my phone and called him. He laughed at my request then immediately agreed.

Beck steepled his fingers in front of his face and watched me. "I will need to remember to keep a better assortment of food here."

"If I'm going to be here often, then yes you are."

Beck finally smiled. "Once again, I find myself agreeing to things I would not normally do. Always for you, Kinsley, only for you."

I wasn't sure how to respond to that, so I didn't.

"I will allow Scott Masters and his guard, Oliver, four days a week to work with you on weapons training in our facility," Beck said. "Raven, Nathaniel, or I must always be in attendance. You are not to be alone with Masters."

Raven began to laugh, but a look from Beck silenced her.

I couldn't wait to share the 'rules' with Scott. It would be interesting to watch the dynamics of these strong-willed individuals as they tried to teach me what they wanted me to learn. Hopefully Rachel would be healed enough in a few weeks so she could be with me all the time. That would make my life easier.

"Did you and Rachel do any translating of the book?" I asked Beck.

"Yes, it is waiting for you at my house."

"How much were you able to get through?"

"We made it about halfway. Rachel got tired but would not admit it. She wanted to try and finish the book, but I refused," Beck said.

"Thank you for knowing what's best for her. Rachel can be bull-headed."

He nodded. "She cares deeply for you, Kinsley. I do not think I have ever seen a more genuine display of love from someone who did not have anything to gain from the friendship."

"We've always taken care of each other," I said, shrugging.

Beck's eyes seemed to look into my soul. "Will you ever let anyone else close to you like that?"

I stared at Beck for a moment. I decided my best tactic with him when I didn't know what the hell he was talking about was to ignore him.

"Let's go home," I said to Raven. "I can eat while I learn some more about those nasty vampires."

Chapter Twenty-Eight

More translation from The Book of Protection by Rachel Fredericks and Dr. Beckford Alexander. (I just like to write and say his name)

Marie is currently occupied playing Wii with Nathaniel and Ian. It's a good game for her. Keeps her moving.

Thank you for giving me something to do, I'm going crazy being stuck in bed or on the couch.

<u>Vampires that are not Monarchs or Sovereignty.</u>

- There are vampires that have been created by the Sovereignty for purposes of killing humans and fighting the Monarchs. These vampires are not all bad...it depends how they feel about being turned and what kind of person they were as a human.
- There was a time when members of the Sovereignty were turning as many people as they

could and leaving them on their own. Most of these new vampires died from lack of food (blood) or being exposed to sunlight because there was no one to teach them or explain what they were.

• The Monarchs took in the ones they could find and helped them become members of human society and live secretly as vampires.

• When the Sovereignty realized their plan to turn everyone into a bad vampire wasn't working, they started 'training' their newly turned vampires to be killers of humans and Monarchs.

Beck explains this stuff so much better than Marie and I just love to listen to him talk! (you know I've always had a thing for accents)

shapeshifters

• As we've seen, there are people who can take animal form. It's been documented over the last four thousand years that almost every large predator in the world is also a shapeshifter.

• Current known mammal shapeshifters in North America: Mountain Lion (of course), Wolf (can't wait to meet one of those), Grizzly Bear, Black Bear, Giant Rat (I wonder if they look like R.O.U.S.'s from "The Princess Bride"? - if so, ewww!), Fox, and Coyote.

• Current known reptile shapeshifters in North America: Alligator, Crocodile, and a (not officially documented) giant snake that's like a cross between a viper and an anaconda. So basically it's venomous and constricting and really freakin scary (my description, not Beck's). It's been reportedly seen, but there has never been a shifter come forward and say they're one of these giant snakes.

● This isn't everything about shifters. There are South American, African, and European species, too. We're stopping on page 265 so I can get you non-book info that's important.

<u>What Beck knows about the history of your family (with a few random tidbits thrown in by Marie):</u>

● As you remember (hopefully) there were ten original Shadower bloodlines. Over the last thousand years, those bloodlines have been weakened and the Monarchs have not had a pure source for blood-pacts. This has caused Monarchs to become weak. The Sovereignty DON'T know this.

● Marie still claims your parents found her and saved her from someone called Isaac in 1962. (was your mom even alive in 1962?) Beck and Marie said your parents were older than you thought because of the Shadower blood slowing their aging process.

● Beck does not recognize 'Isaac the vampire' who was leading the Sovereignty. Beck also thinks Marie has the details from when she was captive wrong. He said there's no way she could have survived having blood taken every day, let alone twice a day. (we all know Marie doesn't always keep her facts straight)

• Marie's family (all dead but her) and your family (sorry - all dead but you) are two separate Shadower blood lines; possibly the last Shadowers alive with almost pure blood. Marie commented that if you had been a boy, she was supposed to marry you. (I find that kind of disturbing and hope to erase it from my mind as soon as possible - you owe me multiple drinks when I'm off bed rest, chica).

• Your parents tried to have more kids, but couldn't.

• Beck says Dr. Karlof wants to take samples of Marie's blood and your blood so he can compare it to regular human blood. Karlof also wants to see if he can synthesize your blood.

Other Stuff

You need to look at the drawings on pages: 12, 14, 20-25, 32, 47, 96-104, 152-172, and 215-225. There are maps and diagrams that go with the two sets of notes I've taken.
We're halfway through the book!!!

Love you, chica!

Rach

THERE WAS a small piece of parchment paper tucked in the notebook.

Kinsley,

This has been a lot for you to deal with. Please know that while I can be overbearing, I have your best interests at heart. Even though I am not her favorite person, I want to do what is best for Marie. I think it is obvious Nathaniel and I also care for Rachel. Please accept my help and all I can offer you.

Yours Always,

Beck

I didn't know if Beck still felt the same considering the meeting we'd had at the bar about my training. I did believe that he had my best interests at heart. But people didn't do things for nothing. Was he just getting close to me so he and Karlof could have Marie's and my blood? There had to be an alternate agenda besides keeping me safe, didn't there? He hadn't shown me anything but kindness, but I'd only known him for about two months. How much do you really know about a person you've just met?

Everyone was in Beck's condo except for Raven and me. She had been my silent shadow since we'd gotten back from Screamers. I'd thanked Nate for the food then promptly taken it to my kitchen so I could eat and read Rachel's notes.

Raven had gotten her dinner and followed me without saying a word. I think she recognized my need to be alone even if I couldn't have it completely.

After I cleaned up my dinner dishes, I glanced at the maps Marie had already shown me. I skimmed over the drawings of dissected vampire and shapeshifter bodies. They kind of creeped me out.

I couldn't bring myself to look at the rest of the pictures because I just wasn't in the mood to know how to kill things. Maybe I'd look again when Beck, Nate, or Scott pissed me off.

I put the book on the table then decided I needed to bite the bullet and call Scott. It was after ten, but I didn't care. Someone with a security firm needed to be awake whenever anyone called, right?

"Kinsley," Scott answered after a few rings. He sounded wide awake.

"I spoke with Beck and Raven. They both agree you were right."

There was silence for a beat. "They did?" He didn't sound like he believed me. "There's a catch, right?"

"I don't know if it's actually a catch. Beck stipulated you have to do the training here. Raven told me about their indoor shooting range. I think you'll like it. We thought you could come in the morning to check it out. Then you can decide what weapons to bring in. Beck requested he see what you brought since there are shifters and sometimes vampires on the premises."

"Don't want me going crazy and killing all the monsters?" Scott asked.

"You'd want your employees to feel safe in their training facilities. Beck wants his to have the same consideration."

"You're right. I'm sorry I was rude. If this is going to work, I need to play nice." Scott didn't sound too happy about it either.

I laughed. "You know how to play nice?"

His voice dropped. "I know how to do a lot of things, Kinsley."

Three hours earlier I wouldn't have thought anything about it. But after Raven had put the unwanted image of oozing hormones into my mind, I couldn't help but wonder if he was hitting on me.

I didn't know how to respond so I did the next best thing. I said, "Be here at eight tomorrow morning. Good night. Bye. Sleep well. Bye." I hung up.

I groaned and covered my face with my hands. I heard Raven chuckle. Without looking at her I said, "Don't say a word. I'm pretending you're not here." She kept quiet, thank goodness.

My new motto: *Ignore comments from overbearing men.* It was working so far. I hoped it would continue working in my favor.

Chapter Twenty-Nine

THE NEXT MORNING I got up and dressed just before eight. Raven, Marie, and I went across the hall to gather Beck and Nate. Ian was staying with Rachel since she wasn't quite up to training or working out yet.

Scott and Oliver were waiting in plush chairs by Gerald at the front desk. Both stood when we came out of the elevator.

Scott nodded to me. He kissed Marie on the cheek and said, "Nice to see you again."

Oliver stood with his feet braced apart and his hands behind his back. The sun glinted off his dark, shaved head.

Beck turned and punched in the code for the door. We went into the small hallway. Beck led our group to the armory and shooting range.

The facility was so huge I didn't know how it fit in the building. I looked at Raven. "Where are we?"

"Underground," she said. "Isn't it amazing?"

One section had a shooting range. Six different people could stand in their own little cubicle areas and fire at targets which could be placed out to one hundred yards away. On the opposite side was an open area with an obstacle course setting.

It had walls like a maze, fake people for shooting at, and half walls for jumping over or hiding behind.

"Holy shit," Scott said.

"Can we practice here every day?" Oliver asked.

"Think of the things we could accomplish if you would agree to work together," Beck said to Scott.

"Work together?" I asked.

"Alexander seems to think if my security firm worked with him and his animals, we'd have a better chance at destroying the Sovereignty. The problem is I don't trust his cats or vamps."

Raven and Nate growled.

"I'm tired of being referee," I interrupted before someone said something mean. "Get along or I won't train with any of you."

Scott and Beck engaged in a stare down.

"I'll train her," Marie said. The tension in the room was so thick you could cut it with a knife. "I won't do as good a job as any of you or Claire or Tom, but I'll do it." Marie glared at the two men. "If Kinsley has to deal with your testosterone wars, she won't be able to concentrate. Do you want to be the reason she gets killed?"

Beck broke eye contact first. "You are correct, Marie."

Scott stuffed his hands in his pockets, rocked back on his heels, and let out a huge sigh. "I won't say my whole team will come work here. But I'd appreciate the use of your facilities and the opportunity to train Kinsley."

"That is acceptable," Beck nodded. "Your team may have access to the sparring room, the weight rooms, and the pool."

Oliver didn't speak but he looked like he was about to start drooling at any minute.

"Thank you," Marie said. Then she wandered over to one of the shooting cubicles and raised her hand up like it was a gun. She started to shoot at invisible targets using her finger and thumb.

"Is she always like this?" Scott whispered.

I rubbed at the twitch in my right eye. "Yep. It used to be funny because you never knew what she was going to do. Now that I'm responsible for her, it's just tiring." I looked at Beck. "Where do we start?"

We went to a conference room near the weight room and sat down to make a schedule. Starting today, we'd spend two hours a day doing cardio, two hours sparring, two hours on shooting and weapons training, and one hour for cool down. I wasn't sure when I was going to sleep with this schedule, all the eating I needed to do, and the actual paying job for Beck.

I demanded this Friday off so I could sleep in and get my hair done before the Seattle Art Museum gala. I also agreed to only follow this schedule Monday through Saturday until classes started back up at UW.

The thought of working out for seven hours a day, six days a week for one month made me want to pass out. Then I thought of how defenseless Rachel had been and how I had Marie to take care of. I was doing what was necessary.

Scott and Oliver spent an hour bringing weapons into the facility while Raven and I practiced the self-defense moves from yesterday. We sped things up a little this time instead of going in slow motion.

While Scott set up targets and weapons, Raven and I worked on take-down techniques for another hour. She showed me how to sweep with my legs without hurting my knees. She also showed me how to use the momentum of an attacker against them. It would allow me to throw someone bigger than me over my head.

Beck watched from the corner and occasionally made a comment about technique or the attack style of different shifters and vampires. He didn't offer to show me anything and I was glad I didn't have to touch him. With the electric tingle we shared and my hormones out of whack, space was a good thing right now.

I was sweating and had a few scrapes and bruises at the end of my and Raven's two hours. Considering I'd been bounced off a fridge and hadn't been hurt made me realize Raven was not taking it easy on me because I was new at this. I appreciated that. A vampire trying to rip my throat out wasn't going to be nice because I was a new Shadower.

Marie, Raven, and Nate went back upstairs. Beck, Ollie, Scott, and I were alone for the rest of the time.

Scott and I went over more guns and bows than a sporting goods store could carry. The different pistols and rifles were all state of the art ranging from single-shot to fully automatic. He also had some flame throwers but Beck wouldn't let him use those in the building. Bummer.

My favorite part was using the bows. Scott had crossbows and compound bows. The only bows I'd ever used had been longbows at summer camp.

I practiced with the compound bow up to fifty yards. My shoulder and arms started getting tired. Scott and Oliver demonstrated their shooting ability up to one hundred yards.

The crossbow looked like a miniature compound bow set up sideways on a rifle stock. It didn't have the range of a compound bow, but the short arrows were ideal in close fighting situations. It was also easier to aim in a hurry.

The final thing we went over for the day was ammunition: gun rounds and arrow broadheads. We'd been shooting with lead bullets and practice tip arrows. Scott showed me his ammunition for when he was on the job. Everything was made of silver.

"That must get expensive." I looked to Beck. "Can we use some of my house money to help fund ammunition?"

"It is taken care of," Beck said. "Masters and I already came to an agreement about funding. I think what he does is important. Not to mention the fact I am going to arm you, Nathaniel, Ian, and Raven with these weapons."

"Silver ammunition can kill most shifters," Scott said. He held up a silver-tipped round. "This is a semi-wadcutter."

"What in the hell does that mean?" I asked.

"Dangerous," Oliver said, crossing his arms. "They're basically controlled expansion hollow points. The round pierces the body and holds capacity until the vital organs are reached."

"A human," Scott said, "will die instantly if shot almost anywhere in the body. A shifter will die if it's hit in the head or the heart. On the other hand, a vampire probably wouldn't die."

"As long as there is blood in a vampire's body and its head is still attached, it will not die," Beck said.

"I once hit a vamp in the head with a silver round," Scott said. "I blew off part of its skull but it kept coming at us. Oliver was able to cut of its head and we burned the body."

Finally, we were done for the day. Beck told me he'd teach me how to use my dad's daggers and eventually swords if I wanted. Since removal of a vampire's head was the ultimate goal, I figured blades would be a good thing to learn.

After Scott told me he'd see me tomorrow, he and Oliver left. Beck and I went to the pool.

I swam laps with Beck but his speed was unbelievable and I couldn't keep up. I left the pool and moved to the hot tub. Beck joined me after about fifteen minutes.

"Did we push you too hard today?" Beck asked.

I shook my head. "No. Luckily I was already in shape. We're going to kill Rachel, though. She hates to work out."

Beck laughed. "We will go easy on her. She should be one hundred percent in a few weeks. She is healing quickly thanks to Dr. Karlof and Nathaniel."

I looked at my hand making patterns in the hot tub water instead of looking at Beck and his bare, wet chest. "Thank you for bringing Karlof to take care of her."

"It was my pleasure. He has wanted to move over for the last two years anyway."

"How long have you lived in the States?" I asked.

Beck braced his arms on the edge of the hot tub. "This is my third year. I took leave from Oxford for a year when the University of Washington started to recruit me. I knew I wanted to be here and waited until a teaching opportunity arose."

"Why Washington state?" I finally looked at Beck.

"There has been increased vampire activity in the area. Nathaniel and I wished to investigate. Gabriel had been here for a few years before me but had not noticed anything out of the ordinary."

"Why doesn't Nate trust Finch?" I asked cautiously. I was enjoying the sharing of information and didn't want to step on Beck's toes. I wanted to tell him what I thought about Finch and Karlof, though.

Beck thought for a moment before answering me. "As a general rule, Nathaniel does not care for vampires. There are only a few he deems worthy of his trust."

"What does he think of Karlof?"

"He tolerates him because of all he is trying to do for the vampires and shifters. Why do you not like either of them?" Beck surprised me with his perception.

I shrugged. "I'm not sure. They've been fine, especially Karlof and what he's done for Rachel. There's just something in my gut that makes me feel...uncomfortable."

Beck nodded. "We will have to address that soon. I trust your Shadower instincts."

I sat up. "You do?"

"Of course. Those instincts have kept your kind alive for thousands of years. I also trust you. If it came down to choosing between Karlof and Finch or you, I would always choose you, Kinsley."

At my usual crossroads of confusion, I didn't know what to say. So I got out of the hot tub and asked, "What do you think Nate's going to make us for dinner?"

"Do not think for a moment I have not noticed your tactic of evasion when you wish to avoid something, my dear."

Great. "I learned from you," I said.

Beck smiled. "Maybe we will need to learn how to talk about sensitive subjects with each other."

Maybe so. But not right now.

Chapter Thirty

FRIDAY MORNING I lay in bed cataloging my various aching muscles. It hadn't been a full week, but I'd made it through my first major chunk of training. The only thing motivating me out of bed was the thought of the spa day I had planned. At ten, Rachel, Marie, Raven, and I were going to Gene Juarez Salon and Spa in Bellevue.

Even though Beck, Raven, and I were the only ones attending the SAM gala, I wanted us girls to have a day of pampering. I was pretty sure I'd earned it. The thought of a massage, facial, manicure, and pedicure made my body shiver with anticipation. While Rachel was way more of a girly-girl than me, I looked forward to this as much as her.

I also planned to get my hair trimmed and highlighted. Raven insisted on me getting color. I quickly learned she changed her hair color weekly. Black when I met her, pink this week, and flame red for the gala.

Nate drove into Bellevue and dropped us off at the front walkway. We got smoothies from the little espresso and sandwich bar outside the doors and enjoyed the morning sun. It was fun for me to see Raven do girl things since she was always having to be one of the boys.

The four of us checked in, were given our robes, then went into the shower rooms. It was the most amazing bathroom I'd ever been in. The floors had radiant heat tiles. The individual shower stalls were covered with multiple shower heads for maximum body coverage. There were also heated towel racks.

"I could live in here," I said to Rachel.

"It does remind me of our dream bathroom," she agreed.

"You have a dream bathroom?" Raven asked with something close to a look of horror on her face.

"Yeah. Don't you?" I asked. "What full-blooded American woman doesn't have a dream bathroom?"

"No. That's just weird," Raven said.

We laughed.

After six hours of pampering, we strutted out the doors of Gene Juarez to where Nate was waiting with the SUV. He whistled and scooped Rachel into a bear hug.

"Mmm, mmm, mmm, you ladies look delicious. Can I take you all back to my place?" He wiggled his eyebrows.

"I suppose," I tried to sound bored, but Nate picked me up and swung me around until I started to laugh. "Put me down, you big oaf!"

On the drive back to Seattle, we giggled and told Nate about our day of indulgence while he listened intently. Yet, by the time we got to the condo he kind of had the glazed-over look guys get when they're on girl information overload.

It was four o'clock and Nate promised to make me a big early dinner before I started to get ready for the gala. Since my hair was done, all I had to do was put on makeup and get into my dress. Beck wanted to arrive at seven so he could look over the displays before the doors opened at eight.

At five-thirty, I couldn't wait any longer. I had enjoyed a day of being a girly-girl and I was ready to put on the rest of the costume. That's what it felt like, too. Rachel and Raven crowded in the bathroom with me and did my makeup. I could have had it done at the salon, but I hadn't wanted everyone to wait around especially since Rachel had begged me to do it herself. After endless brushes of this and swabs of that, they stepped back and let me see.

I almost didn't recognize the woman in the mirror. My hair was full of blonde, brown, and caramel highlights that accented my already dark blonde hair. With the new cut, it fell to just below my shoulders. The woman who'd done my hair had straightened it and put some shine protection stuff on. It was like a waterfall of softness that I'd seen Rachel walk around with for many years but had never been able to do myself. I think I was in love with the staff of Gene Juarez.

The makeup was dark and smoky around my eyes. The mascara, eyeliner, and eye shadow made me look like a 1920s flapper. The silver of my eyes stood out and made me look exotic and sexy. My lips were buxom and dark mauve thanks to Rachel's plumping lipstick.

"Oh my," I breathed.

"Do you like it?" Rachel asked hesitantly.

I squealed, "Like it? I love it! I think we should live at Gene Juarez and dress like girls every day."

Rachel and Raven whooped with laughter and Marie came in to see what was going on.

"You're gorgeous, Kinsley. You look like your mom."

I looked back in the mirror and realized I did.

"Now don't be mad at me," Marie started.

My eyes got huge and a feeling of dread settled over me. I hated when she started sentences like this.

"It's okay," Rachel said. "Raven and I know about this and we helped."

"I don't know if that makes it better or worse," I admitted.

"Better," Raven said.

They guided me to my bedroom where there was a dress bag hanging on the door of my closet. It wasn't the dress bag holding my black gown for tonight's party.

"We found it yesterday while you were training with Scott and Beck. Beck hasn't seen it, but we told him about it so he could accent his tux to match." Raven slid the bag off the dress and I almost fell over.

It was the most beautiful silver evening gown I'd ever seen. It looked like two pieces, from just under the bust to the hips was a silk netted see-through fabric. The top was halter style and embroidered in crystals. It was long and had a slit in the front that went over halfway up the dress.

"Put it on!" Marie yelled.

I turned to the girls.

"Don't cry," Rachel said. "You'll ruin your makeup."

So I laughed and went to the dress. Then I stopped. "I bought a black bra and underwear to wear under the other dress. I don't have anything to wear with this."

"Taken care of," Raven said. She produced a bag from behind her back.

I grabbed everything and ran into the bathroom. I carefully stepped into the dress. It fit like a second skin.

When I stepped out of the bathroom, the girls shrieked, oohed, and ahhed at me. Nate came in to see what all the fuss was about.

"What the—" he was wearing workout clothes and looked as though he'd just walked up from the gym. The bottle of water he was holding dropped from his hands and bounced on my floor. "Holy shit, Kinsley."

"I think I'll take that as a compliment." I said.

"Ignore Mr. Can't-give-a-real-compliment." Rachel laughed as she picked up the spilled water bottle and grabbed a towel from the bathroom to put over the puddle.

Nate shrugged. "Sorry. I'm usually better with words. You look smokin'!"

"Yes, that was a much better description," Raven said, shaking her head.

"Shoes!" Marie said. She ran to the living room and came back with a shoebox. Inside were open toed four inch heeled shoes which matched the dress perfectly.

I laughed as I pulled up the dress to slip them on. "I feel like Cinderella going to the ball. Do I have to be back by midnight?"

"I hope not," said Beck, from the door.

I looked up and couldn't miss the male appreciation in his eyes. I dropped the bunched up handfuls of fabric and watched his eyes zero in on the slit that went halfway up my left thigh. Being the focus of all this attention was a little disconcerting.

"You look beautiful, amazing, and elegant my dear Kinsley," Beck said as his eyes moved up my body and finally to my face.

"Now, that's how you give a compliment," Rachel said, punching Nate in the arm.

Beck in a tux could run circles around James Bond. I'd always had a thing for the spy movies. Something about saving the world and looking sexy while doing it. Beck's bow tie and cummerbund were silver, matching my dress.

"Thank you," I finally managed to say. "You look handsome, amazing, and elegant, Dr. Alexander."

"I think we will leave even earlier than planned so I may show you off to my colleagues. They will all be green with envy." Beck bowed and held out his arm for me. I took my time as I walked toward him. I didn't need to ruin the elegance of my look by tripping before I'd made it out of my bedroom.

The heels put me at just under six feet tall and I could

almost look evenly into Beck's eyes. There was a ring of gold around his irises I'd never noticed before.

"Wait," Marie said. "We need to cover you in one more layer of hairspray and some perfume."

Beck smiled and kissed my cheek. "I shall meet you in the lobby in five minutes." He looked once more at me, then left. Nate followed.

We moved back to the bathroom. Raven spritzed hairspray over my head while Marie sprayed perfume. I turned to leave and Rachel dusted sparkly powder across my shoulders and neck.

"There ya go," Rachel said. "Now, we won't wait up. Well, Nathaniel might because that's what he does, but you better have a fabulous time."

"It's work, guys. Do you keep forgetting that?"

"I wish I could go to work dressed like that," Rachel said.

Uncaring of her nudity, Raven put on a strapless black sheath dress.

"Beck's going to be the envy of every man in that room tonight," Rachel said.

"He does like to be center of attention," Raven said as she adjusted her cleavage. Marie and Rachel sprayed her down and brushed sparkles over her, too.

"I want to go to the next one," Rachel said. Then she yelled to the living room. "Do you hear that, Nathaniel? I want to go the next time there's some fancy shindig!"

As we left Rachel said, "Don't do anything I would!"

I laughed. "That doesn't leave me much to do."

Gerald greeted us and commented on how stunning Raven and I looked. I glanced outside and saw a black stretch limo instead of one of the Mercedes.

"We have to arrive in style," Raven said.

I didn't recognize the driver as he opened the back door.

Beck was already inside. Raven took the seat opposite so I slid in next to him.

"This is incredible. Do you always go all out for events?" I asked.

"I only go to three or four a year. This is the first time I have been to the Seattle Art Museum and I wished them to know how important their facility is."

"And how important you are," I added with a smile.

"Of course," Beck agreed.

Chapter Thirty-One

WHILE BECK CONVERSED with Raven about work, he hardly took his eyes off me. The interior of the limo felt darker. The air thicker. Beck poured us champagne. The bubbles tickled my nose, mouth, and throat. My senses were on overdrive.

I tried to look out the window, but I could feel Beck's gaze like a caress on my bare skin. I wasn't cold, but goosebumps ran up and down my arms.

When we arrived at the Seattle Art Museum, I opened the door to the limo before the driver could. I gulped in air as though I'd been drowning.

"Pheromones," Raven whispered to me when she stepped from the limo. "You two were practically swimming in lust."

"Were not!" I whispered back as Beck stepped over.

"Anything you need to share, ladies?" he asked.

"No. Let's get to work," I said, turning to the entrance and pulling my shoulders back.

He smiled a knowing smile as he led us to the building.

Beck, Raven, and I met with the curators of two different museum collections. For half an hour we went over the three items that Beck had donated to the European Art collection. There were two paintings and one small sculpture. I knew nothing about fine art, but the curator was excited about what Beck had given.

The second curator we met with was ready to kiss Beck's feet and anything else she may have been able to get her lips on. Apparently the Ancient Mediterranean and Islamic Art collection hadn't been donated to in a while. The single tapestry-like picture Beck offered was a big deal.

After listening to the woman gush over Beck's kindness and greatness for twenty minutes, I'd had enough. "Dr. Alexander, we need to go over your notes one last time before your speech."

Beck looked at his watch and frowned. "We still have forty-five minutes."

"Well, yes, however, um, I think I may have spelled something wrong. Can't have you stuttering over any words in front of the crowd." I looped my arm through his and dragged him away from Ms. Curator-flirts-a-lot. I saw her glare at me out of the corner of my eye.

Raven caught on and smirked at me. I carefully rubbed the side of my nose with my middle finger so she'd know how I felt about her silent judging.

When we took our seats and the event officially began, I found out Beck was a brilliant public speaker. He made small jokes, promoted the importance of keeping history alive and sharing it with children, and announced his plan to donate money for funding arts and music in schools. He asked others to donate to causes they believed were important to help keep funding available to floundering non-profit organizations. I was impressed and I was used to his suave ways.

Beck spoke for ten minutes longer than they had him scheduled. At the end of his speech he looked directly at me.

He said, "Thank you to the Seattle Art Museum for

keeping history alive in our city. And thank you to my personal staff. Without your dedication, mental strength, and passion, I would not be able to do my job."

He kept eye contact with me through the standing ovation from the crowd. The hair on my arms stood at attention and my knees were a little weak.

Apparently the SAM had never thrown a ball, but Beck had asked to make it an evening unlike any they'd done before. They decided to make it a ticketed event to raise more money for the foundation. Hundreds of people were in attendance. By the time everyone moved to the main room for hors d'oeuvres, champagne, and dancing, it was after nine.

The movers and shakers of Seattle and the surrounding areas were there dressed to impress and rubbing elbows with anyone of importance. And everyone wanted a piece of Dr. Beckford Alexander. Men and women alike clamored for his attention.

Raven finally offered him a break when she asked the orchestra to play. They began with a classic piece, slow and melodic. The crowd made a circle around Beck and Raven as they began to waltz.

Their ability to float around the floor was amazing. The gracefulness of both their bodies demanded attention as they moved across the dance floor in perfect synchronization. When they finished their dance, the crowd erupted into applause. Then other couples moved to the floor.

Beck kindly declined when women tried to get him to dance with them and kept walking toward me.

"You're incredible," I said.

"Thank you. I taught Raven to dance. Since we took her in, she has always been my female escort to public functions." Beck never took his eyes from mine.

"You look good together." Was that jealousy I heard in my voice? No, couldn't be.

Beck tilted his head. "I am currently single."

Why was he telling me this? I didn't care. Did I?

"Dance with me," he said, pulling me to the floor.

"I can't dance," I blurted.

"That is the wonderful thing about most slow dances. You just have to follow my lead."

Beck pulled me into his body. I tried to relax and let him lead me around the floor. I felt so feminine in his arms.

"Are you dating anyone?" He whispered in my ear.

"You know I'm not," I replied. "You, Nate, or Raven haven't left me alone for the past two months. I think you'd notice if I brought anyone home."

"Would you bring anyone home?" Beck's breath was hot on my neck. He lowered his head and lightly nuzzled my throat.

I tried to pull back but he wouldn't let me. I was going to avoid the question, then decided to tell him the truth. "I've never brought anyone home with me. I really doubt I'll start now since I live in a building with a crazy aunt and a bunch of shapeshifters."

Beck laughed quietly against my neck and said, "Good answer."

We moved to the music for endless minutes. The song changed and two different women tried to cut in but Beck wouldn't let them.

"You're being rude," I smiled at him. "All these beautiful women want to dance with the most handsome man in the room and you won't let them."

"I am already dancing with the most beautiful woman in the room."

My heart beat faster and I got butterflies in my stomach. I didn't know how to respond, what to do.

I felt Beck place an open-mouthed kiss on my neck and scrape his teeth gently across the skin there. My whole body shivered with desire. I pulled back slowly and looked into Beck's eyes. By some trick of the light, the small ring of gold that I'd noticed earlier was bigger, making his eyes appear half black and half gold.

Suddenly the hair stood up on the back of my neck and the electricity flowed between us like a one hundred-twenty volt current. "What's happening?" I asked, barely above a whisper.

Beck's eyes narrowed as he looked over my shoulder. I turned my head. Scott strode toward us across the dance floor.

"Lord save me from male egos," I said and stepped out of Beck's arms.

"Time for me to dance with Kinsley," Scott said as he took my arm. "You've monopolized enough of her time."

Beck looked into my eyes, then nodded with a sigh. As Scott pulled me into his body, I saw Ms. Curator-flirts-a-lot throw herself into Beck's arms.

"I hope you know what you're doing," Scott said into my hair.

"Dancing?" I asked innocently.

He shook his head. "You're flirting with death, sweet thing. That's what you're doing."

"What are you talking about? Beck wouldn't hurt me. He and all the other shapeshifters have been protecting me."

"shapeshifters are predictable. It's the vampires you need to be careful with."

"Are you talking about Finch and Karlof? I wouldn't be alone with them if someone paid me."

"Finch and Karlof?" Scott leaned back and looked at me in confusion. "I'm talking about Alexander."

"What? He's not a vampire, he's a shifter."

Scott stared at me for a moment and then said something

under his breath that sounded a lot like the f-word. He let go of my waist and dragged me toward the edge of the dance floor.

When we were away from the people, he gripped my shoulders. "Did that lying son of a bitch tell you he was a shifter?"

"Well, he hasn't come out and said it, I just assumed that's what he is. I know he's not completely human." I tried to think back so I could figure out when I'd decided he was a shifter. He'd told me he killed vampires.

"Not completely human? He's not human at all. That man is a bloodsucker. He's a vampire, Kinsley."

"No he's not," I said. "I'd know if he was a vampire."

Scott's grip tightened. "How? How would you know?"

"I just would." I was starting to second-guess my instincts. Beck hadn't actually said he was a shifter. He'd never answered me when I'd asked him if he was a vampire. Marie hated him and the shifters seemed to obey his every command.

Oh holy hell, what if he *was* a vampire?

Scott saw the moment it registered on my face. "I want you out of there and with me," he demanded.

I pulled free. "You don't get to tell me what to do. I've got to talk to Beck and get this all cleared up."

"Get what cleared up?"

"Scott, if someone came and told me something bad about you, I'd want to talk to you about it. I wouldn't just run screaming the other way." I took his hands in mine. "I know you want to keep me safe. But I'm an adult."

He narrowed his eyes. "I don't like it."

"I know. Tough shit." My language shocked him, I could see it on his face. But I meant it. He didn't get to boss me around.

He squeezed my hands. "Promise me that you'll come to

me if anything bad happens. If he or one of his cats tries to hurt you."

"It won't happen like that, but I promise." I kissed Scott on the cheek and tried to turn away.

"Where are you going?" He pulled me back into his arms.

I put my hands on his chest. "To find Beck and Raven. I think I'm ready to go."

Now he kissed my cheek. His breath was warm on my skin as he said, "I hope I didn't ruin your evening. You look absolutely stunning. I watched you for most of the night."

"Thank you. You look very nice yourself." My hands flexed on his chest.

Scott looked like he was going to say something else when Oliver sidled up next to him and whispered something in his ear.

"I have to go." As he leaned toward me, I offered my cheek again. Scott, instead, went straight for my lips. It wasn't an erotic kiss. He barely brushed his lips with mine. But it was still a kiss.

He and Oliver left. I stood there with my hand pressed to my lips. I felt a hand on my shoulder and I turned to tell Beck I was fine.

But it wasn't Beck.

Dr. Gabriel Finch's dark eyes were narrowed on mine. Due to my heels, he was a few inches shorter, and had to look up at me.

"Come. We need to have a chat." He pulled me toward a set of doors that led outside to a patio. There were a few other people out there talking. Finch briefly looked at each person and they walked back into the building.

"Did you make them do that?" I asked.

"Make them do what?" he said.

Something wasn't right. "I want to find Beck." I tried to pull away but Finch had both of my wrists gripped in one of his massively strong bony hands.

"Mya said Marie tasted like heaven." He leaned in to smell me.

I shuddered and tried not to show my fear. "Mya's death was what she deserved."

"Who says I killed her?" Slowly, Finch's face began to change. I wanted to scream but nothing came out. His black and gray hair lightened to brown. The bones of his face shifted until it looked rounder. The goatee was still there, but I could see who he was.

He smiled, showing me his fangs. "Of course, I told Mya I already know Marie tastes like heaven. She was, after all, my blood slave for twenty years."

Beck and Raven burst onto the patio. Finch—Isaac—whatever his name was, pulled me in front of his body and clamped the steel bands of his arms around my midsection. He held me so tight I had trouble breathing.

The evil vampire ran his nose along the side of my neck up to my cheek. "Nice of you to join us, Beckford. I was beginning to wonder how long you were going to allow her to be alone with Masters. I arranged a little *emergency* for him so he would have to leave early. I like to know where all my enemies are."

Beck took a step toward us then stopped. "What is going on Gabriel? Why are you doing this? After all these years of working together and trying to bring down the Sovereignty, why are you trying to hurt Kinsley?"

I tried to wiggle away but it was no use. "Look at him, Beck," I said. "Look at his face! He's Isaac!" I barely got the words out before Isaac squeezed me harder. I heard my dress rip.

Beck started to circle us. "Let her go. Kinsley has nothing to do with this." I noticed his eyes were glowing. Then I saw his fangs.

"Scott was right, you are—" Isaac squeezed me so hard my ribs popped. I screamed in agony and Beck stepped closer.

Isaac took a step back, pulling me with him. "Don't move or I'll squeeze her so tight her insides will explode."

Beck stopped and looked at me. "I am sorry, Kinsley."

I tried to nod or say something, but the pain in my body was making it hard for me to move, let alone think.

"This has always been about Kinsley. About her parents. They took my Marie from me." Isaac kept his eyes on Beck and Raven while we slowly moved back toward the greenery at the edge of the patio.

"You cannot have either one of them. They are mine now." Beck's voice was a growl.

Beck lunged and Isaac squeezed me again. I howled in pain. Why weren't any people coming to help us? Couldn't they hear me scream?

Beck stopped moving again.

I heard a whisper of fabric and then Mya stood next to Isaac and me.

"You had to pick her over me, didn't you Beckford? I could have given you everything and made you love me, but you had to pick the weak human." Mya grabbed a handful of my hair and ripped my neck back. She licked the side of my throat.

"Get your hands off me," I managed to say. I didn't sound very dangerous.

"I'm going to rip your throat out and feast on your blood. And Beckford's going to watch me do it." Mya's fangs extended and I wondered how long it would take for me to die.

Isaac tore me from her grip just as she went for my neck. She was so close I heard her teeth click together.

"You can't kill her until I have Marie!" Isaac snarled.

Mya hissed and grabbed for me again.

The distraction was what we needed.

Raven jumped in the air and shifted as she landed on Mya. The shreds of her dress floated in little pieces around us. Isaac stepped back and his grip on me loosened. I slammed my head back like Raven had taught me. I heard him yell as I felt his nose break.

Beck flew toward us and Isaac threw my body at him. Beck caught me and we fell to the grass on the edge of the patio bricks. I grunted in pain as the impact jarred my ribs.

I looked over as Raven roared. Mya had her mouth latched onto Raven's throat, ripping and tearing at her.

"Save Raven," I wheezed to Beck.

He looked like he was going to protest but Raven cried out again. When Beck let me go, Isaac's face was back in my line of vision and I flew through the air once more.

Chapter Thirty-Two

MY BODY SLAMMED against a tree and there was another roar. A cougar larger than Raven was attempting to pin Isaac to the ground. I lay at the base of the tree unable to move and barely able to breathe. I wanted to scream, I wanted to cry, but I couldn't get any part of my body to cooperate.

Lightning ripped over the sky and thunder crashed. Rain started to fall. I realized we were at least a hundred yards from the back patio.

As rain started to fall harder, my world moved in slow motion. Beck's body materialized from the mist. Drops of water balanced on my eyelashes then fell to my cheeks. I couldn't raise my arms to wipe them away. The lights from the building were a soft glow, reflecting off the raindrops like tiny prisms. Beck looked scary and beautiful at the same time as his body was bathed in the rainbow colors.

He flew through the air, his feet inches above the ground, landing next to the cougar still fighting to hold down Isaac. Beck's hand shot out and wrapped around Isaac's throat, lifting him from the ground like a rag doll.

The cougar bounded over to where Raven and Mya were

fighting. I heard Mya's inhuman scream as the cougar grabbed her throat and ripped her away from Raven's unmoving body.

I watched through a haze of pain and rain. Beck flung Isaac into the brick wall lining the property of the gardens. Part of the wall crumbled and Beck grabbed the evil vampire again before all the pieces of brick collapsed to the ground. He threw Isaac's limp body against another part of the wall.

"Beck," I tried to yell. It came out as a squeak. "Beck," I said again. This time I was able to say his name, but it was barely above a whisper. Beck turned his head from Isaac and looked at me. His eyes were flaming gold and his mouth was open in a snarl. I could see his fangs.

I should have been scared, but I wasn't. It was still Beck and he was protecting me. He dropped Isaac to the ground and in one leap knelt in front of me on the grass. The tree was the only thing holding my body upright.

"Don't kill," I garbled. My mouth was full of blood. "Don't kill...him," I repeated. "Need answers...for Marie."

There was another scream. Beck and I watched in astonishment as Isaac jumped from the ground and flew through the air toward Mya. He grabbed her body and disappeared into the night sky.

Beck started to go after them then looked down at me. "Nathaniel," he yelled. The other cougar came to us.

"Nate," I whispered. I tried to raise my hand to pet him. He was beautiful.

Nate rubbed against my body and I winced in pain. He pulled back and Beck cursed.

"There are not any external wounds for Nathaniel to heal. I must get you to Karlof."

I tried to nod, but couldn't. "Kay," I managed.

Beck had a look of pain in his eyes. "I did not want you to find out this way. You do not even like vampires."

It took every ounce of energy I had to move the fingers of my right hand. Beck noticed and lifted my hand gently to his face.

I traced his lips with my shaking fingers. "You're still...my Beck."

He closed his eyes and kissed my fingertips. "This is going to hurt." He lifted me in his arms before I could protest.

Hot coals rolled around inside me. I sucked back a scream because I knew Beck had to move me. I buried my head in his chest and tried to relax and breathe. It didn't work.

"Stop," I cried.

Beck quit moving. "Kinsley, I do not know how fast your body heals. I have to get you to Karlof so he can do x-rays and see what is broken. If any of your bones start to heal wrong, he will have to re-break them and set them. I do not want you to have any more pain than necessary." Beck's face was a mask of agony.

I'm sure my face mirrored his. The thought of getting my ribs broken on purpose almost made me throw up. "Can't you use...some kind of vampire...mind control...make me pass out?" I tried to laugh and ended up spitting blood on Beck.

He shook his head. "It does not work that way with Shadowers. We have no power over you."

"Just ignore me...and get to Karlof." I closed my eyes and took fast, shallow breaths because deep breaths were so out of the question.

I don't know if he ran or flew, but every time his body bumped mine, I had to bite my lip to keep from crying out. I even tried to embrace the pain in hopes of making myself pass out. Didn't happen.

We arrived at a dilapidated building in an area I didn't recognize. Beck yelled for Karlof as he burst through the doors. The pain had become so intense I couldn't feel any individual part of me. I was a giant ball of painful nerve endings.

Sounds came and went while I kept my eyes closed. I hummed a song my mom sang to me when I was little. It went with a bedtime story but I couldn't concentrate long enough to remember what it was. I couldn't even remember the words to the song, just the tune.

I think Beck said something to me, but I wasn't sure. I could tolerate the pain if I didn't focus on anything.

"Kinsley," his voice kept coming to me and I couldn't ignore him any longer.

"What?" I croaked.

"Thank the Gods. I knew you were alive, but you did not respond."

"I'm trying to keep from spitting my insides on you," I snapped.

"At least he did not break your sense of humor." There was a bit of a chuckle in Beck's voice.

I pried open one eye to see where we were. Beck's face swam in and out of my vision.

"There's two of you," I said and giggled.

"Karlof is pumping you full of enough narcotics to sedate a herd of horses. How do you feel?"

My body was kind of tingly. I tested my breathing and was almost able to take a deep breath. I could wiggle the fingers on both hands.

"How long has it been?" I expected Beck to tell me it had been days or maybe even weeks. The continuous pain from when I had been a crumpled mass at the base of the tree was gone. In its place was a dull throb with occasional sharp pains.

"Almost an hour," Beck answered.

My other eye came open and I sat up. Big mistake. The room spun. I managed to lean over the bed and throw up on the floor. Even if you're full of enough drugs to stop a herd of horses, throwing up with broken ribs is not a good feeling.

"Give her more, Karlof, she is metabolizing it too fast," Beck said.

"I've already given her more than I'd give a shifter. I'm not going to accidentally kill her because you don't want her to feel a little pain." Karlof's accent was harsher than I remembered.

"I'll be okay. I shouldn't have moved." I tried to wipe my mouth and couldn't. Beck used a corner of the sheet to do it for me.

He helped me lie back down. "Do not move," he said through clenched teeth.

"Not planning on it," I whispered.

I OPENED MY EYES AGAIN. Everything was stainless steel and white. There were four additional people, dressed in scrubs, looking at computer screens while having an intense discussion.

One of them walked toward me. "Kinsley, how does your chest and stomach area feel?" It was Dr. Karlof. I could see his beady little eyes over the mask that covered his nose and mouth.

"Like I got run over by a train. And then a bus. And then thrown from an airplane where I bounced to the ground. And got run over by a train again." The drugs made me say all this. Really.

"Your x-rays show your ribs have already healed." Dr. Karlof had a note of awe in his voice.

"What?" Beck said. "How can she possibly be healed?"

"I don't feel healed," I mumbled. "Hey, that rhymed." I giggled.

"Maybe you should cut back on the drugs, Karlof."

Hadn't he just told the doctor to give me more?

Beck looked at me and held up three fingers. "How many?"

I glared at him. "Three. My eyes work fine, it was my insides that got scrambled." I took a breath. "Have you found Finch and Mya?" I watched Karlof fiddle with my IV.

Beck shook his head. "No. You are my priority."

"Marie. Where's Marie?"

He took my hands gently in his. "She is safe. I sent Nathaniel and Raven back to the condo to be with Ian, Rachel, and Marie."

"Raven's okay?" I asked.

Beck nodded. "She will be. She could not move well enough to run so I had a car pick her and Nathaniel up."

I closed one eye in hopes the room would stop spinning. "The gala. Why didn't anyone hear us fighting?"

"Do you remember how quiet it was the first night we met?"

"Yes," I said.

"One of Gabriel's talents is the ability to control the air around him. That is the best I can explain it. He is able to block out noise and sometimes even physical features from humans. Their eyes and ears are forced to miss what is going on. Gabriel never explained to me how he does it."

"That's because he's an untrustworthy son of a bitch." I was getting feeling back in my legs and feet. The pins and needles sensation of when your limbs go from being asleep to awake worked its way up my body.

I groaned.

"Are you okay?" Beck asked. When I glared at him, he shrugged. "I know you are not okay, but you were talking and then looked as though you were in pain."

"I'm getting the feeling back throughout my body and it's a

little uncomfortable."

He squeezed my fingers gently. "Karlof stopped administering the drugs through your IV."

My mind raced as it cleared. "How did Finch—Isaac—change his face? Why didn't you know who he was? Why didn't Marie know who he was?"

"I do not have all the answers, Kinsley. The very old and powerful Monarchs have been said to do what Finch—Isaac—did tonight. He is much more powerful than I ever thought." Beck shook his head.

"How long have you known him?"

"Almost four hundred years."

"What?" I couldn't even fathom what he was saying.

"We have crossed paths, working together over the last four hundred years. He would disappear for years at a time. Then word would come through to the Monarchs that he had killed another member of the Sovereignty. Now I must wonder how long he has been a member of the Sovereignty. And who else has been lying."

"Her blood and ability to heal are absolutely amazing, Beckford. I've never seen anything like this. Not from other Shadowers nor from shifters," Karlof said. "Think of the things we could do with her blood."

I wasn't so sure I liked the sound of that.

"Nothing will be done with her blood. A Shadower's blood is sacred and it will not be taken without her consent. This is not up for discussion," Beck said.

Karlof walked away, but not before glaring at me.

"When can I go home?" As I asked, Karlof looked back at us.

Beck shook his head. "I want you to stay here for a few days. You are safe here and Karlof can make sure you heal properly."

I motioned Beck toward me. He leaned in, but not close enough. I put my hands on his neck and pulled him down so my lips rested against his ear. "Don't leave me here alone."

Beck pulled back enough to look in my eyes. While there was a look of confusion at first, he then seemed to remember my earlier comment about not liking Karlof.

Louder, for Karlof's benefit, I said, "I really need to see that Marie and Rachel are okay. And I want to see Raven. Please, Beck, I'm fine."

He nodded a fraction of an inch and pulled out his cell phone. He asked to have a car sent over.

I closed my eyes and relaxed back into the soft mattress. That's when I realized I was naked. I had a sheet over me, but I was naked. I hoped Karlof hadn't been the one to take my clothes off.

At the thought of taking clothes off, Scott popped into my mind. I didn't know why and I didn't really want to think about it at that moment.

"Beck, you have to call Scott. Isaac said something about distracting him. He needs to know that Finch is Isaac and he needs to know what happened tonight."

I shivered as Beck looked at me with those black eyes.

"He is going to try and use that to get you to move in with him so he can protect you," Beck said.

"You've protected me just fine."

He closed his eyes for a few seconds, then opened them. "No, I have not."

"Stop arguing with me and call Scott or give me your phone so I can call him."

"I will call him. It is my duty to admit that I failed you," Beck said.

"You didn't fail anyone. We're all still alive."

"This time," Beck said.

Chapter Thirty-Three

SCOTT TOOK the news of my attack just how I expected. A lot of yelling, screaming, cursing, and throwing things. He waited in my living room for me to get out of the shower. I could hear him arguing with Beck and Nate.

Marie and Rachel were in Beck's condo with Ian. Raven was asleep in cougar form on my bed. She'd been so badly hurt she couldn't change back.

I stood looking at my naked body in the bathroom mirror. I'd felt my ribs break and I'd spit up blood. Karlof was sure my lungs had been punctured. A normal person would have died.

While I was grateful to be alive, it was scary to look at myself. There wasn't a bruise, scrape, or cut on me. I wasn't truly human and that terrified the hell out of me. I needed to know more about my body and the healing process but that meant I'd have to talk to Dr. Karlof. I didn't trust him. At this point, I wasn't sure who I could trust.

Someone Beck had known for four hundred years had been evil and Beck hadn't known. Even though they'd been good to me, could I trust the other people who worked for Beck? Could I trust Beck? He'd lied to me as well.

I put on sweats and went to see how Raven was. She

opened one eye when I touched her tuft of red hair. "Thank you," I whispered.

She yawned, growled, and licked my hand.

"I wish I could help heal you like you healed me."

Raven closed her kitty eyes and took a deep breath.

I took a deep breath of my own and went to deal with Scott and Beck.

The three men in the living room went silent as soon as I opened my bedroom door. Beck and Scott surveyed me from head to toe.

"I'm fine. My ribs hardly even hurt and there's not a scratch on my body." I turned to Nate. "Raven woke up and licked my hand. I think she's going to be okay."

"She will be. I'm going next door to be with Rachel and Marie. I'll feel better with both Ian and me over there." Nate turned to Beck. "Play nice."

Beck growled at Nate then walked to me.

"Move away. You almost got her killed," Scott said.

I waved my hand. "Stop it, Scott. Beck isn't the one who attacked me."

"No, but one of his vampire brethren did. You can't trust the vampires. Your mom and dad knew that."

"I'm not my mom and dad! They had time to process everything. I haven't had that luxury. There have to be good vampires or there wouldn't be a point to Shadowers. We were created to protect good vampires."

"If every vampire were dead you could lead a normal life," Scott said.

I shrugged. "But they're not and I have a purpose."

Scott looked back and forth between Beck and me. "Do you really want to be vampire food? Do you want to be bound to Beck for the rest of your life?"

"Bound to Beck?" I looked at Beck. "Why on earth would I be bound to you?"

"Oh, that's right," Scott said. "Since you didn't even know he was a vampire until I told you, you wouldn't know his other big secret."

"That is enough, human!" Beck yelled. "My relationship with Kinsley has nothing to do with you. Leave!"

Scott didn't move, appearing satisfied. Beck's eyes glowed gold and his upper fangs extended. He looked like he'd rip open Scott's neck without thinking twice.

I stepped closer. "Beck, what's going on?"

"He's a Monarch," Scott said.

Beck jumped, landing on Scott. He grabbed him by the throat slamming him against the wall.

Scott grunted but didn't stop talking. "He's tracked you for years, Kinsley. The Monarchs want your blood. Your parents were from two separate Shadower bloodlines. That makes you as close to pure blood as any Shadower left." Scott groaned in pain as Beck pulled him back, slamming him against the wall twice more.

Scott gripped Beck's wrists. "The Monarchs want you kept with them just like Isaac kept Marie. You'd supply the ones who are left making them practically invincible."

"You have said enough!" Beck yelled.

"What are you gonna do? Kill me? That's not going to get you into Kinsley's good graces." Suddenly Scott went limp and Beck let him fall to the floor with a crash.

Raven's cougar form limped from my bedroom and came to stand by me. "I'm fine, Raven. Go next door. I need to talk to Beck."

Raven walked to the door and scratched against it. We quickly went across the hall to Beck's. Marie and Ian played

Wii while Rachel and Nate cuddled on the couch watching and laughing.

I pinned Nate with a glare. "Did you know Beck was a Monarch?"

"Uh oh," Nate said.

"I'll take that as my answer." I looked at Marie. "You knew he was a vampire but didn't tell me."

"I told you. I explained how you couldn't fall in love with a vampire like I did."

"That wasn't telling me he was a vampire!" I yelled. "You're the only one who can help me navigate this mess, Marie. I need you to act normal!"

"You can't fall in love with him!" she said.

"Oh, I don't think that's going to be a problem." I looked at Nate again. "Beck knocked Scott unconscious. Call Oliver to come get Scott."

I slammed the door and walked back to my condo. Beck stood where I left him and Scott still lay on the floor.

"Tell me," I said.

Beck turned to look out the windows instead of at me. "When you were born, the Monarchs took notice. Your mother was the last Shadower they knew of, and she refused to come to Greece to meet with them. I think she knew they would not let her leave."

"You're supposed to be the good guys, Beck."

"The Monarchs have lost focus because they believe the Sovereignty has become stronger. The Sovereignty was killing off Shadower families. That is what happened to Marie's family. No one knew Isaac was Finch or that Marie was still alive. Until Isaac figured it out, the Sovereignty did not know how important Shadower blood is.

"It was discovered your father was blood related to Marie's family. Your dad tried to bury it, but we have ways of learning everything. Four years ago, the truth was learned. You are the offspring of two Shadowers. Instead of having weaker blood, you have stronger blood. I did not really believe that until I saw you heal tonight."

I did the math. "Four years ago? That's when I was choosing a college. That's when you bought and renovated this building. You've been stalking me!"

Beck slumped his shoulders. When he looked back at me, his eyes still glowed but his fangs were gone. "I am supposed to make you my Shadower and bring you to Greece," he whispered.

Scott lurched from the floor. "Over my dead body," he yelled as he tackled Beck.

They fell to the floor in a mass of arms and legs. I knew Beck was stronger and wasn't surprised when he ended up on top. What happened next shocked me beyond belief.

"I should have killed you when I had the chance," Beck roared. His fangs elongated and he drove his mouth into Scott's throat.

"No!" I screamed as I jumped on Beck's back. I wrapped my arms around his neck and pulled. My front door crashed in and Nate, in human form, and Raven, still in cougar form, ran to us.

"Sir, stop!" Nate yelled.

I pounded on Beck's back until he released Scott.

Then he turned on me.

Beck threw me to the floor and loomed over me. His breath came fast and hard as Scott's blood dripped from Beck's mouth onto my chest.

I was terrified. Not once had I ever thought Beck would hurt me. But what did I know? He was a vampire and both Marie and Scott said vampires couldn't be trusted.

Beck lowered his head and licked my throat but when he

pulled back he looked like he was in pain. "The Monarchs want me to take your blood, Kinsley," his voice was strangled. Each word bit out as though it hurt to talk. His eyes were no longer warm gold. Twin indigo orbs stared at me. Swirls of black flame danced through the dark blue.

"Nathaniel," Beck growled. His body settled over mine and he pushed himself into the cradle of my thighs. The movement was incredibly intimate and it was so not the right time or place for my body to respond to his.

Nate moved slowly toward us. "Kinsley, the Monarchs are trying to control Beck. Don't move. Don't show any fear."

Easier said than done. "You won't hurt me," I said to Beck.

"He'll kill you," Scott said from next to us.

"Shut up," Nate said through clenched teeth. "You're not helping."

Out of the corner of my eye, I watched Scott cover his bleeding neck with a hand. "I'm not trying to help. She needs to see what a monster he is."

"You won't hurt me," I repeated. The whites of Beck's eyes began to appear. Gradually a thin ring of gold circled the blue-black flame.

I slowly lifted my hand and caressed his face. He tilted his head into my palm. My fingers gently slid over his lips.

"Kinsley, do you trust me?" Beck hissed.

"I don't know," I said.

"Nathaniel," Beck said again.

Nate knelt but was still over five feet away. "Kinsley, I know you're scared. But if you give Beck your blood of your own free will, instead of the Monarchs forcing him, he'll come back."

I slowly turned my head to look at Scott. Blood trickled between the fingers on his neck. His eyes pleaded with me to ignore Nate. When my eyes found Nate's face, it held a look I couldn't quite read. Finally, I turned back to meet Beck's piercing gaze. He fought a battle; I could see it in his expression and feel it in his tense body.

I took my right hand and pushed my middle finger against one of Beck's fangs until it broke the skin. He groaned low in his throat and sucked my finger deep into the hotness of his mouth. His eyes closed.

It was the most erotic feeling I'd ever had. And in the same instant, it was the most horrendous. What in the hell was I doing? "Beck," I whispered.

He opened his eyes. The black flame was gone. His eyes glowed brighter gold than I'd ever seen. He licked my finger one more time and slowly pulled his mouth back.

"Thank you for trusting me."

"Get off me," I managed, ignoring the look of hurt on his face. When he moved, I rolled over to Scott. "You're going to be okay," I said to him. Then I turned to Raven. "Heal him," I demanded.

Raven didn't look at Beck. She walked over and nuzzled my hand, licking my finger. She put her face into Scott's neck and bathed his wound in her healing saliva. Scott tried to roll away but I wouldn't let him.

"Either she licks your neck or Beck does. I chose the one I thought you'd prefer." Scott quit moving, letting Raven heal his wounds.

"Kinsley, let me explain," Beck said.

"I've heard enough for one day," I said. "Oliver is on his way, right Nate?"

Nate looked at Beck, then me. "Yes."

"I'm going with them." I moved to my knees. "Can you sit up?" I asked Scott.

He sat and put his hand back to his throat. "I owe you, Alexander. Blood for blood."

Beck didn't respond. He looked at me with pleading eyes. "I would never hurt you, Kinsley."

"You almost killed her," Scott said.

"No, I almost killed you. And that was only because the Monarchs wanted me to rip off your head and feast on your blood. You are lucky I am strong," said Beck.

"Kinsley, please think about this," Nate said.

"I need a break," I said. "I need to go be with humans. Be somewhere that doesn't remind me of what I've become."

"Take someone with you," Beck said.

"If you think I'm going to let one of your vamps into my home, you're crazier than I thought," Scott said.

"Take Nathaniel or Raven," Beck said. "Mya and Finch—Isaac," he quickly corrected himself, "are still out there. You need my people to help you."

"I don't need anything from you. I'll blow that son of a bitch's head off if he even comes near Kinsley." Scott stood and pulled out his cell phone.

He pressed a button and started talking. "Oliver, where are you? Good. We'll meet you out front. Yes, we. Kinsley's coming home with me," Scott said as he stared at Beck.

"I'll be back," I said to Beck. "I just need a few days. Raven needs to stay here and heal. I won't take Nate away from Rachel." I turned to Nate. "Don't let anything happen to Rachel or Marie. Someone should probably tell her she's my blood aunt." I laughed without humor. "She won't remember in the morning, but someone should tell her."

I went to my room and grabbed a duffel bag. I started throwing clothes in it. I felt Beck before I saw him.

He stood in my doorway, his face full of anguish. "I would never intentionally hurt you, Kinsley. The Monarchs all have a connection. They want your blood."

I shook my head. "I really don't think you'd ever intend to

hurt me, Beck. But Marie is right. Not all hurt is physical. Just give me a little time to think."

"Does it have to be with Masters? Would you go somewhere with Ian and Raven? A hotel?"

"I'm going with Scott."

He dropped his head. "I do not like it."

"Well you know what? This isn't about what you like." I brushed past him into the living room and ignored the spark that pinched my skin.

Scott limped slightly so I wrapped my arm around his waist, offering physical and moral support. As we left, I didn't look back. I knew Beck watched me walk away. Gerald didn't hold the door for us as we went out to Ollie and the Hummer.

It was past midnight. My life had changed even more in one short evening.

I looked up to see Beck watching from the window of my living room.

Lightning forked across the sky.

Chapter Thirty-Four

DURING THE TWENTY minute drive to the outskirts of Bellevue, Scott and I rode in complete silence. He gripped my hand the entire trip, sitting with his head back and his eyes closed. His measured breathing was the only sound. I almost asked Ollie to turn on the radio but was afraid if I tried to talk I'd turn into a crying idiot.

Oliver helped us out. As I shouldered my bag, I stared at the newer home in the gated community. Scott owned a house. I'd expected him to live in a condo, like Beck. Would I compare the two of them forever?

When Oliver saw Scott could walk on his own, he glared at me and got back in the Hummer.

"I'm not his favorite person, am I?" I asked as we walked to the front door.

"He'll come around," Scott said.

As I watched Scott fish his keys out of his suit pocket, I noticed Oliver only drove a couple hundred yards, pulling into the driveway of another house.

"Oliver lives here?" I asked. Then I answered my own question. "Of course he lives here. He's your bodyguard."

"There are six houses in this gated community. Each one sits on three acres and my employees live in them."

"Convenient," I said as he finally pulled his keys out and then dropped them on the porch.

I made sure he was steady then leaned down to pick them up. I unlocked the door and walked us across the threshold.

I looked around noting vaulted ceilings, stairs to the second floor, a living room, a dining room, and a corner of the kitchen. There were pictures of landscapes on the walls but nothing personal.

"I really want to take a shower and go to bed. Will you just stay close for a while? I need to make sure you're really here and finally safe."

"I'm not going anywhere," I told him. "Where should I put my stuff?"

"Let's go upstairs. I'll show you." Scott leaned on me as we went up the stairs to the bedrooms.

"I don't think you lost that much blood. Are you really leaning on me for support?" I tried to sound light, but I felt Scott's body tense.

He shook his head. "I can't believe that bastard bit me."

"Beck said the Monarchs made him," I said.

"How can you believe anything that monster says or does?"

"We're not going to have this conversation tonight, Scott. I'm sorry I brought it up. I was just trying to joke about how a big, strong guy was still leaning on me for support." I tried to loosen his arm from around my shoulders but he wouldn't budge.

"You're right, I probably don't need to lean on you, I just like the feel of your body next to mine."

I ignored him as we walked up the stairs. We passed two bedrooms and a bathroom before Scott took me into what was obviously his bedroom.

"We're both going to sleep in here," he said. "I'll sleep on the floor, at least for tonight. I need you in the same room as me."

I didn't argue. He needed to sleep in his bed, not on the floor. I figured I'd get him showered and in bed and he'd fall asleep before he knew what hit him. Then I'd sleep in one of the other bedrooms.

Scott turned on the light. "Don't go anywhere," he said to me. He patted his bed and handed me the TV remote. "I'll be quick."

I dropped my bag by the door and turned on the TV, finding a music station.

Scott put a handgun on the nightstand next to his bed on the way into the bathroom. He didn't shut the door and I turned my back when he started to peel out of his tuxedo. I kept my back turned until I heard him groan in pain. I looked before I thought better of it. Scott's back was to me, covered in bruises. When he turned, I saw more bruises on his chest and neck.

"Oh, Scott," I walked to him. "Can I get you ice?"

"No, sweet thing. Unless you plan on joining me in the shower, I suggest you plop yourself on that bed."

I quickly left the bathroom to Scott's amused chuckle.

I didn't mean to fall asleep. Scott woke me by putting me under the covers, ignoring my protests.

"Kinsley, we were both attacked by a vampire tonight. You may not want to, but we're going to sleep in this bed. I thought I could sleep on the floor, but my body hurts too damn much. You're going to be under the covers and I'm going to be on top of them. No big deal."

I felt the mattress dip as he climbed into the bed and moved around a little. I'd never shared a bed with anyone other than Marie or Rachel when we'd had sleepovers. This felt too intimate.

"Go back to sleep. I'm not in any condition to try and jump your bones." He shifted once more.

I rolled to my side and switched off the lamp. I lay down with my back to him and pulled the covers up to my chin. Within minutes I was too warm and sweating. I sat up.

Scott didn't move.

I snuck out of bed to find my bag. I grabbed it and quietly moved down the hall to one of the bedrooms. The first one was an office. I went to the next room and saw that it held workout equipment and no bed. Damn it.

I started back down the hallway and ran into a big, hard body. "Going somewhere?" Scott asked me.

"I wasn't leaving, if that's what you mean. I was going to sleep in one of the other bedrooms, but they don't have beds."

Scott dragged me back to his room and shut the door. "You're sleeping in here. What's the problem?"

"I was too hot and it's not proper!" I said, sounding like an 1800s maiden.

"Change into something else and get into bed. No one is going to know but me. And I'm not telling anyone I had a hot chick in my bed and didn't have sex with her."

"Do you have to be so crude?" I asked as I marched into the bathroom.

"Sweet thing, you haven't seen crude."

When I came out of the bathroom in shorts and a t-shirt, Scott was back on the bed with his eyes closed. I looked around the room and wondered if I could just pull the pillow and blanket onto the floor.

Scott opened an eye. "You've been through hell tonight. Just quit thinking and get in this bed. We're both tired."

I sighed, realizing he was right. I wanted to sleep. My body hurt and I was exhausted. I climbed in, rolled to my side so my back was to him, and closed my eyes.

Sometime during the night I woke to the realization I'd kicked off the covers and Scott was plastered to the back of my body. One of his arms was by my head and his fingers were tangled in my hair. The other arm was draped over my waist with his warm hand on my stomach under my shirt. I should have moved his arms, but I was too tired and too comfortable to care.

I woke up again to the sun shining behind the curtains and a hand lightly rubbing my hip. I stretched my body and froze when I realized I was still practically stuck to Scott. His grip tightened on my hip and moved down to bunch the hem of my shorts in his hand.

I should have slept on the floor. Downstairs in the living room.

"Scott," I whispered.

"Let me touch you, Kinsley. I've waited for so long." His breath was hot on my neck. I trembled as his fingers slid to the edge of my underwear.

"I can't," I finally said.

"Yes you can. It will feel good."

"Scott, I can't." This time I said it like I meant it.

His hand stilled. "Why?"

"Because I promised myself when I had sex it would be with someone who I loved and who loved me. I'm not going to mess around with you because my life has gone to shit and last night was so horrible." I hadn't moved away. It felt good to have his body against mine. Safe.

"What do you mean *when* you have sex? You've never had sex?" Scott's hands leaped from my body like I was on fire.

"You don't have to act like I have a disease. Being a virgin at twenty-one is perfectly normal."

"No it's not," Scott said, eyes wide in shock.

"This was such a bad idea. This is why I didn't want to sleep in the same bed with you. I didn't want you to think I was a tease."

Scott rolled to his back. I sat up on the edge of the bed and looked at him. What I assumed was a very impressive erection was tenting his shorts. He covered his face and groaned.

"Seriously? You've never had sex?" He sounded like he was in pain. Good. Served him right.

"My parents raised me to be respectful of myself and my body!" I said. "Quit treating me like I'm an alien. Sorry I couldn't be your latest conquest." I started to rise.

Scott's hand snaked out and circled my wrist. He gently pulled until I was sprawled across him with his arms wrapped around me.

"I'm sorry. I'm being a total jackass. When men wake, all the blood has rushed to areas other than our brains. I woke to a warm, soft woman in my bed and I reacted."

I didn't respond. Partly because I was a little miffed. Partly because it felt good to be cradled in his arms. Again. Was it possible to be a hussy virgin? Beck and Scott muddled my brain.

"Kinsley, please? I'm sorry, okay?" He kissed the top of my head.

"Okay," I mumbled.

"How about we have some breakfast and talk about what to do with Marie."

I pushed out of his arms, sat up, and stared at him. "What about Marie?"

"Well, I can turn my office into a spare bedroom. Do you want to share a room with Marie? Originally I thought I could convince you to share a room with me," he said.

"What are you talking about?" I demanded. "I'll be going home."

"Home where? Didn't you sell the house in Paradise?" Scott appeared confused, the stupid man.

"Home to my condo."

He sat up. "You're going back to him?"

"I'm not going back to him. I'm going back to my home," I argued.

"Did the fact he bit me and wanted to bite you not open your eyes at all?" Scott moved to the edge of the bed.

I watched his muscles flex and noticed a dusting of blonde hair across his chest.

Jeeesus. Focus. I needed to focus.

"I'll be fine," I said.

"You're being stupid!"

Stupid? Had he really just called me stupid?

"It's amazing I'm still a virgin. I can't believe I haven't thrown myself at someone as sweet and charming as you." I climbed off the bed and grabbed my bag.

"Just listen to reason," Scott began.

"Reason? Is that what you call bossing me around and calling me stupid? I don't think so." I marched into the bathroom, slamming and locking the door.

I changed into jeans and a t-shirt. When I came out of the bathroom, Scott was dressed and standing by his bedroom door.

"I can't let you leave like this," he said.

"Like what? Pissed off? Angry? Or maybe you're referring to the fact I don't want to look at your face?"

"No, going back to Alexander without acknowledging he's a monster." Scott stood blocking the door with his hands on his hips.

"Monster? A monster killed someone with Rachel standing right there. A monster tried to kill Rachel. Monsters tried to kill

Raven and me. Who saved Rachel, Raven, and me from all those monsters? Beck! All you've done is boss me around and try to get in my pants!" Now I had my hands on my hips.

Scott narrowed his eyes. "If you leave, don't ask to come back."

"Quit throwing ultimatums at me! Have you forgotten I can kick your ass?" I walked to him and stood silently seething. Finally he stepped to the side and let me pass.

I went down the stairs and to the front door. That was when I remembered I didn't have a way to get home. I smacked my head on the door and just stood there.

Scott's voice came from behind me. "If you're going to leave, at least let me call Oliver."

"Always the white knight. Raven was right."

"What?" he asked.

"Nothing, never mind. Can I just borrow the Hummer? I'll have Nate and Ian bring it back. Oliver doesn't want to drive me."

Scott pulled out his cell phone. "Oliver? Will you drive Kinsley back to *her* condo?"

"I'll wait outside," I said.

I went out the door and sat on the porch. The late summer sunshine hurt my eyes, so I bent down to get my sunglasses out of my bag. I didn't see Oliver get in the Hummer but I heard the engine start.

The next thing I knew, a loud noise and an explosion of heat barreled into me. The Hummer was a huge ball of flames. Almost every door flew open, men running toward the fire. Scott's door opened and he dragged me back inside.

"Are you okay?" he yelled.

"I'm fine. Oliver—" my cell rang. I pulled it out and looked at the screen. It was Rachel. I contemplated ignoring it, but decided I should see what she wanted.

"Kinsley, my precious, you owe me some blood."

I quickly switched the phone to speaker and stared at Scott.

"Isaac?" I said.

"Come to your condo. We have some things to discuss." The phone went dead.

Chapter Thirty-Five

"I HAVE TO GO," I said.

"No, you don't," Scott argued.

"Scott, this isn't about Beck. This is about Rachel and Marie. Isaac called me on Rachel's phone. I have no reason to live if I lose Rachel and Marie." A sob caught in my throat.

Scott's mouth was a hard line, hands clenched. He pulled me through a side door into his garage, containing both a truck and a sports car.

Scott opened a gun safe and pulled out numerous pistols and shotguns. He loaded each with silver ammo and handed me two pistols and extra rounds.

We got in the black Ford Ranger. Scott made a call on his cell as he opened the automatic garage door and backed out. We whipped through the streets on the outskirts of town, carefully avoiding traffic and stoplights.

"Oliver wasn't in the Hummer," Scott said.

I looked over and realized he was off his phone. "How?" I asked.

"Oliver usually parks the Hummer in the garage. I don't know why he didn't last night. We have remote start in all our vehicles. Oliver was standing in the living room when the

Hummer blew. He got some glass cuts from the explosion but he's fine."

"Oh, thank you, God," I said. "He may not like me, but I don't want him to get killed."

"Oliver likes you fine. He doesn't care for the company you keep."

We turned onto the street that led to the condo and Scott pulled into an alley about three blocks away. "Kinsley, whatever happens, keep yourself safe first."

I shook my head. "Rachel and Marie are the priority."

Scott stared at me then we climbed out of the Ranger. It took three agonizing minutes to walk to the condo. We stayed along the backs of the buildings that were across the street. There was no sign of anyone outside or in the lobby.

"I don't like it," Scott said.

"Something's wrong," I agreed.

A series of explosions rocked the building. I watched in horror as all the windows on the upper floors blew out. Then the glass windows and doors of the lobby exploded.

I screamed, running across the street. Something swooped down and slammed me to the pavement face first. I could feel from the size of the body that it wasn't Scott or Beck. I turned my head slightly and felt gravel dig into my face. It was Mya.

I wrestled the pistol from my waistband, slid my arm up between our bodies and fired. Mya screamed and jumped away.

"You bitch!" She snarled and came at me again.

I heard the shotgun and watched her body slam back. Scott pumped in another shell as Mya withered on the ground. Silver buckshot wasn't going to kill her but it would sure hurt like hell.

I heard more glass break and looked up to see a cougar burst through the flaming mass that used to be the front doors. Nate.

He landed on Mya, biting at her throat.

I went to stand and was grabbed from behind.

"Hello, my dear," Isaac whispered in my ear. Then he drove his fangs into the side of my neck.

I screamed in pain as Isaac's fangs pierced my skin and he began to suck. Electricity flowed through my body, but it was different from when Beck touched me. This hurt. I tried to raise the gun in my hand, but Isaac was too fast. He squeezed my wrist until the bones cracked, forcing me to drop the pistol.

Nate roared and Scott yelled. I closed my eyes and tried to keep my knees from buckling. Hadn't Rachel's notes said vampires fed off emotion? I couldn't show fear. I tried to think of the love I had for Rachel, Marie, and my parents. I felt Isaac's mouth slow on my throat and he growled.

He raised one clawed hand and waved it toward Scott. Scott convulsed in pain and dropped the shotgun. Scott wrapped his own hands around his throat like he was pulling at invisible restraints.

"Stop," I said. "I'll do whatever you want, just stop."

Isaac dropped his hand and Scott fell to the pavement unmoving. Isaac pulled his mouth from my throat. "You taste better than Marie," he said. "I'll enjoy having you both."

Mya rolled from the ground. Before I could warn Nate, she was on him.

"We're going for a little trip." Isaac waved and a silver car with black tinted windows pulled up to us. A man got out of the driver's side and Mya threw Nate's limp cougar body in the trunk. The driver pulled out a syringe and injected Nate with something then slammed the trunk closed.

Isaac patted me down and threw my other pistol and clips in the bushes. He found my phone and dropped it, crushing it under his heel. He pulled me into the back seat and held me pinned with one arm. His strength was incredible.

He hadn't seemed vulnerable to me right after feeding. Apparently the Book of Protection had that part wrong. Except Marie had been able to chain Mya to the table. Did our blood affect vampires differently?

As we drove past Scott's body on the street, another explosion rocked the building where all the people I cared about were. I started to cry.

"Shut up," Mya hissed from the front seat. She looked like hell. Her face and neck were bleeding and her skin was a light green color. I watched the bones move in her face.

"I'm going to enjoy feasting on your cat while you watch. Then I'm going to feast on you," she hissed.

Isaac still held me effortlessly. His skin was flushed and my blood stained his lips. Energy rolled off him in waves. "This is what a Shadower's blood does, Kinsley. Think of how wonderful it would be if you could have power coursing through you all the time. The ability to be faster, stronger, more dangerous."

Great. I didn't really want to see Isaac stronger.

He used his other hand to caress my cheek and I recoiled. Grabbing my chin and yanking me within inches of his face, I smelled my blood on Isaac's breath and felt lightheaded. My wrist throbbed in time with the fast beating of my heart.

"I see you already appear to be healed from our run-in last night. Quite amazing. Maybe I'll have to break different bones in your body to see how quickly they heal. I wonder if you'll heal more slowly if I do it while I'm taking your blood." He grabbed my broken wrist and squeezed it again.

I whimpered. Isaac closed his eyes and breathed in. "I can almost taste the fear, Kinsley. You don't know what it does to me. Did you see Marie's scars? Did she show you what I can do?"

I closed my eyes and tried to ignore him. But I couldn't get the images out of my mind of Marie's scarred legs, Scott lying possibly dead in the street, Nate unconscious in the trunk, or the building blowing up. It was like the movie reel from hell.

"They're all dead, Kinsley. How does that make you feel?" Isaac said.

My eyes flew open as silent tears fell faster.

"They were all in that building when I had it blown up. Your doorman, Gerald. Your beloved cat, Raven. That dog, Ian. Your best friend, Rachel. And, of course, your precious Beckford. Burning to death right now."

As I sobbed and attempted to pull away from him, I focused on the fact he hadn't mentioned Marie being dead. Marie had to be alive somewhere if Isaac planned to make both of us blood slaves.

He threw me against the car door and laughed. I tried to open the door. It didn't budge. Isaac laughed harder, a loud and menacing sound in the small confines of the car.

I rammed my elbow into the glass over and over, but it wouldn't break. Finally my elbow started to bleed.

"Can't waste your blood," Mya said. She grabbed my arm and tried to lick my elbow. I hit her in the nose with the palm of my other hand as Isaac yanked me away from her.

Mya's nose bled and I smiled at her through my tears.

"You do not get the blood of the Shadower unless I offer it!" Isaac yelled at her.

Mya looked like she wanted to come over the seat and kill me. Mya was weak and I knew she'd be no match for me. If she got my blood that would be another story. How much stronger would she become?

"I'll share our lovely Kinsley after I've had my fill," Isaac said as he ran his fingers through my hair.

"I find your eyes amazing," Isaac whispered as he trailed a finger down the side of my face and gripped my chin in his cold, bony hand again. When I tried to close my eyes, he gripped my face harder. "There hasn't been a Silver Shadower in almost a millennium. I wonder what it would take to leach the silver completely from your eyes."

I had no idea what he was talking about. Silver Shadower? There hadn't been anything about that in the book. If I lived through this, I was going to find out what in the hell my destiny really was. The more I learned, the more confused I became.

Isaac lifted my pulsing wrist to his mouth and lightly pressed his teeth against the vein. The twin dots of blood looked almost black against my pale skin. Isaac gazed into my eyes while his tongue shot out and licked up the blood, instantly healing the tiny wound.

He did this three more times, licking up my forearm before I tried to pull away. That was when he bit me. My eyes closed in pain.

Punishment...I will have you...Silver Shadower is mine...

I tried to grasp his thoughts as they swirled through my mind like mist. Was I really reading his mind? What was happening to me?

Finally he stopped feeding, allowing me to slump in the seat as far from him as I could get.

We drove north, out of the city. I could barely keep my head up or my eyes open.

They were dead. They were all dead because of me.

Isaac sat next to me with his hand on my thigh. He mumbled to himself with his eyes closed. I knew he wasn't dreaming since he opened his eyes every time I tried to remove his hand.

I think over an hour passed before we pulled into a covered parking garage. I didn't even know which city we were in.

I heard Mya breathe a sigh of relief as the sun disappeared.

"Getting a little warm, Mya?" I asked. I had nothing to lose. "We could go for a walk in this beautiful sunshine."

She turned in the seat to slap me but Isaac stopped her.

"You keep baiting her and I may not be around to save you," he said to me.

"Maybe it's her who will need saving," I said as I glared into his black eyes. They had the blue-black flame look Beck's had held last night. "You've been communicating with the Sovereignty."

Isaac's eyes widened then narrowed. "You obviously know more than I gave you credit for, young Shadower." Then he turned to Mya and the driver of the car. "Let's get inside. I'll hold Kinsley while you open the trunk. Be careful, the cat might already be awake."

The locks clicked and everyone opened their doors. Isaac grabbed me around the neck, dragging me sideways out of the car. I tried to hold onto the door and realized my wrist was still hurt. I thought it would be healed by now. My internal injuries healed in less time than this.

Since I couldn't grip the door, Isaac had me out in no time. Mya popped the trunk and Nate lay naked in the back. He didn't move.

"Nate," I tried to say around the hand gripping my throat. "You better not have hurt him," I rasped.

"Or what?" Mya asked.

Nate leaped from the trunk, changing to a cougar in midair. He landed on Mya and snarled. His paws held her neck to the side as he snapped his jaws and went in for the kill.

"Kitty, kitty," Isaac said, "I wouldn't do that if I were you."

Nate looked over just as Isaac's fingernails grew to claws and swiped across my throat. He let my body drop to the ground and Nate ran to me. I couldn't breathe or talk. I put my hands to my throat and they came away covered in blood.

What was Isaac doing? If I died, he wouldn't be able to have any of my blood. Nate started licking the wound and healing me. Suddenly I could breathe, but it hurt like hell. I buried my head in Nate's fur. "Run," I whispered.

He shook his big head and nuzzled my neck.

"This is all very touching, but we have places to go." Isaac said. "Cat, you better not try anything or I'll slice Kinsley open again. You're the only one who can save her if I do that. My healing saliva can't handle such a large wound."

Isaac turned to me, "Kinsley, you better be a good little girl or I'll rip him open and you'll have to watch him die. You've never seen a shifter die and I don't think you'll like it."

Nate and I walked slowly behind the vamp who'd been driving the car while Isaac and Mya flanked us. I didn't know where we were going or what was going to happen next but I knew it wasn't going to be good.

We entered a small elevator and the silent vamp pulled out another syringe. Nate hissed and batted at his hand with a clawed paw. Isaac grabbed me and sank his teeth into my throat again.

I struggled, then heard him in my mind, "Sleep."

My neck was on fire and my knees buckled.

Chapter Thirty-Six

"KINSLEY! DAMN IT, KINSLEY, WAKE UP."

I could hear Nate's voice, but my body wouldn't cooperate. I couldn't open my eyes or figure out where I was or what was going on. I wondered if I was dreaming. Then the explosions and Isaac's attack rolled into my mind.

I forced my eyes open and saw Nate chained to a wall by his wrists. He was standing and no one had given him any clothes. I wasn't chained.

I sat up slowly and Nate let out a huge breath. "I didn't know if you were going to wake up. That bastard took a lot of blood from you. Do you feel lightheaded?"

"A little bit." My voice was gravelly and I wished for water.

I leaned my back against the cold brick wall and looked around. Nate and I were in a cell. Three brick walls and an iron barred door confined us. It was maybe ten by ten feet. I felt my neck gently and realized not only did my wrist still feel broken, I was bleeding slowly from the wounds on my throat.

"Why am I not healing?" I asked Nate. It hurt to talk.

"I don't know for sure. I think it's because Isaac keeps taking your blood. You've also been unconscious for over twenty-four hours. Can you move over here? I'll heal your neck. He leaves the puncture marks open on purpose." Nate didn't sound happy.

"Why?" I asked as I started to stand.

"For two reasons. One, you'll heal more slowly. Two, he knows I can smell you."

"What?" I looked at Nate. It had never occurred to me the shifters would be attracted to blood. It made sense. They were predators.

I looked at how Nate was chained to the wall. He was stretched out, his arms high above his head. And he was naked.

I went to him and pulled off my shirt. I wrapped it around his waist.

He smiled at my actions. "You're embarrassed by nudity? We're chained in a dungeon and you're concerned about my nakedness. That's funny."

"I'm glad you can find some humor." I leaned against his body and wrapped my arms around him. "Oh Nate. Isaac said they're dead, that he killed them all."

Nate rubbed his chin on the top of my head in a show of comfort. "They're fine. I promise."

"How can they be fine? Isaac said—"

"You're going to need to learn almost everything that comes out of that evil vamp's mouth is a lie. He's feeding off your emotions so he'll do and say just about anything to upset you.

"Beck and Marie sensed Isaac and Mya were coming. We hid Marie and Rachel in the basement with Ian and Gerald. Then Raven, Beck, and I waited for Isaac to attack. But he didn't."

"He called me on Rachel's phone. He told me he had her." Tears clogged my throat.

"I wondered why you and Scott showed up. I waited in the lobby while Beck and Raven went down to the basement to see if Marie or Rachel were able to get a hold of you. That's when the explosions started."

"Then you don't know if they're actually okay," I said. "They could all be dead, just like Isaac said."

"You have a connection with Beck. Close your eyes and concentrate on him. The sound of his voice, the smell of his skin. You'll feel he's still alive."

I tried what Nate said but didn't know what I was doing. I concentrated until I got light headed. Nothing happened.

Nate moved slightly then hissed in pain.

I looked at the chains. "Silver?"

"Yeah."

"I have an idea."

"I don't like the sound of that," he said.

"Hear me out before you say no. We don't have anything to lose. You know Isaac's going to eventually kill you," I said.

Nate nodded slowly.

"If my blood makes both the Monarchs and Sovereignty stronger, what would it do for a shifter?"

"No, absolutely not," Nate said. "I'm not taking your blood."

"Shut up and listen," I put my hand over his mouth. "How did it make you feel when you healed my neck earlier?" When he closed his eyes, I knew I was right. "I'm too weak. Think of how strong you'll be if my blood has the same effect on you as it does on vampires. I bet you can break the chains and get away."

He shook his head. I moved my hand from his mouth and rubbed my fingers on the open wound at my neck. I pushed my fingers next to his lips but he wouldn't open.

"Damn it, Nate! Quit being a hero and let's try this."

Finally he licked my fingers. He growled and closed his eyes again.

I watched his muscles flex and bunch. The sores on his

wrists started to heal. "I knew it!" I said. "With that tiny amount, think of what more could do."

"I felt different when I healed your neck earlier, but I thought it was just from adrenaline."

Before I could get him to take more, we heard someone coming toward the door of our cell. I turned so I was blocking his body from whoever showed up.

Mya and Isaac.

"So glad to see you're finally awake," Isaac said as he opened the lock.

They stepped inside, leaving the door open.

"Bite me," I said.

Nate's body tensed behind me.

"Such a tempting offer," Isaac said.

"Bite me and get out of here so you can save my ass!"

When Isaac realized I wasn't talking to him, his eyes widened.

Nate said, "I'm sorry." His fangs dug into the spot where my shoulder met my neck.

I cried out as Nate sucked and bit at me until I couldn't hold myself up any longer. I heard him roar and then the chains snapped as he changed into a cougar. He went for the door as Isaac yelled and Mya chased after him.

I slumped on the floor.

"That was stupid, little girl!" Isaac said. "You're not going to live if you keep letting blood be taken from you."

I could barely lift my head. "I've only let it be taken twice. Once by Beck and once by Nate. The rest has been taken against my will."

Isaac howled his displeasure and ripped me off the ground, slamming me against the wall that still held the jingling chains. "You let Beckford have your blood?"

"Are you upset you weren't the first?" I taunted.

"He didn't take it from your neck, I would have been able to tell."

"There are other places to get blood, Isaac. You know that." I let the innuendo hang in the air.

Isaac didn't need to know Beck had sucked a few drops from my finger. I'd let him think there was more going on between Beck and me than there actually was. I'd take whatever jabs I could get.

"You're going to pay for this!" Isaac shouted.

He dropped me and ran from the cell, shutting and locking the door behind him. I heard him yell for someone named Carl. Then I heard a woman crying and screaming.

The vamp who had driven the silver car came to my cell door with a naked blonde woman over his shoulder. My heart contracted in my chest because it was Rachel.

He dropped her to the ground and she screamed. It was someone much younger than Rachel, a teenager with dark makeup. The roots of her hair were black.

She saw me and started sobbing harder.

"Did you know," Isaac said from next to them, "the victims of the Seattle Ripper had burn marks on their bodies? At least that's what the police think they are." Isaac pulled out a knife and the blonde started screaming, kicking, and swinging her arms. "Carl, hold her down."

The other vampire put one arm across the girl's chest and one hand on her knees. His strength held her completely immobile. She screamed then whimpered. I closed my eyes as she screamed more.

"Kinsley, keep your eyes open and on her. She'll suffer less," Isaac commanded.

I kept my eyes closed as the girl screamed, over and over. I couldn't handle it anymore, so I opened my eyes. Her face, chest, arms, and stomach were covered in slices and puncture wounds. Isaac was getting ready to cut her again when he noticed my eyes were open.

"Good girl. I'll be gentler if you watch." Isaac began to lick the cuts on the girl's body. His saliva healed each one, leaving behind a welt-like mark.

The blonde whimpered but stopped screaming.

"You've been killing all those women?" I managed to say around the sick feeling in my stomach.

"Yes. It's been quite fun. No one believes in vampires. It's been wonderful to drain the blood of the humans and watch the police struggle to come up with a reasonable explanation." Isaac moved his head to the girl's neck and nipped at her skin.

She squealed. Isaac closed his eyes and drove his fangs into her throat. She screamed then went limp and quiet. After almost a full minute Isaac let go of her neck and looked at me with his glowing black eyes and blood covered fangs.

"You can have her now, Carl." Isaac moved to the cell door and opened it.

I crab-crawled backward until my shoulders hit the wall. My wrist collapsed in pain. There was no way it was broken if it had held my weight like that. Maybe I was finally healing.

Carl started taking off his clothes.

"No," I begged. "Let her go. You made your point."

"Not yet I haven't. Every time you do something I don't like, I'm going to bring a new girl down here and let you watch her die. Carl gets my leftovers, he likes it that way."

I covered my eyes when Carl dropped his pants. It took everything in me to bite back the sob building in my throat. I pressed the palms of my hands against my mouth. I'd always thought of myself as a strong person. I guess at some point we all learn what will break us. I was getting close.

Isaac sat down on the floor and dragged me into his lap so I looked at Carl and the blonde girl. Carl had his mouth on her breasts. Before I could turn my head or close my eyes again, Carl lifted his head and it was covered in blood.

I screamed and closed my eyes but Isaac forced my head up and placed his mouth at my neck. "You're going to watch, Kinsley. You're going to watch what you caused. If your cat hadn't run away, I wouldn't have done this." He bit into my neck and I screamed again.

"Yes you would have," I said through my tears. "That girl was here and you were going to do this anyway." I felt myself getting weaker and I welcomed the opportunity to pass out.

Isaac held my head and forced my eyes open with his fingers. Carl raped the blonde girl while eating from her neck. I started to gag, struggling against the roiling of my stomach. Isaac finally released me.

For once, he licked my wounds closed, but he left the tear from Nate's bite.

He tossed me to the side and laughed as he left. I kept my body turned as I heard Carl make noises I didn't want to identify. This time, I did throw up.

I heard some movement and then silence. After waiting a few more minutes, I looked through the bars of the cell door. There was blood on the floor but the two vampires and the poor girl were gone.

I swiped at the blood on my neck. I felt broken in spirit and body. My shirt was on the floor. It must have fallen off Nate. I crawled to the corner and tugged it over my head. Then I pulled my knees up to my chest, rested my head on them, and broke down.

I don't know how long I cried. I might have dozed off from exhaustion. I heard a key rattle and I lifted my head slowly. Carl held a tray with food. Like I was going to eat anything they gave me?

He set the tray inside the door then closed and locked it.

Carl stared at me through the bars with a sickening smile on his face. Finally, I looked away. His laugh as he walked down the hall made my skin crawl.

I stared at the food for endless minutes and tried to decide what to do. There was a bottle of water, a piece of bread, and a bowl of soup. If I starved myself, then Isaac couldn't have me. If I ate, I might get some strength back and be ready when someone came to save me.

Still undecided, I crawled to the tray and took a small sip of the water. I used it to rinse out my mouth. Then I poured some on my fingers and cleaned off my throat. I took one small swallow and used the rest to wash my vomit down a drain in the middle of the floor.

I picked the soup up and threw it at the bars. The bowl clanged and soup splattered on the floor to mix with the blood congealed there.

I crawled to my corner and rested my head back on my knees. I tried to find the connection Nate claimed I had with Beck.

All I felt was emptiness.

Chapter Thirty-Seven

TIME PASSED IN A BLUR. Minutes became hours, hours became days. I couldn't tell the difference between day and night. There was only a single light bulb outside my cell door.

I wanted to come up with something that would tell my muddled brain how many days it had been. I tried to use the delivery of meals, but I couldn't remember how many I'd had since it was the same thing each time.

Isaac would come in, wake me, drink my blood, and taunt me with my failure as a Shadower.

Why hadn't anyone come for me? Was Nate okay? What if he hadn't survived his escape? Maybe I should have had sex with Scott; at least I wouldn't die a virgin.

Carl appeared with another meal delivery. He leered at me and left the tray just inside the door like always. I didn't know what I would do if he ever stayed in my cell. I'd go down fighting, that was for sure.

Ever since Nate got away and that poor girl had been killed, I'd been throwing the soup out in front of the bars. No one had bothered to clean anything so it mixed with the blood and the smell was horrible.

I closed my eyes over another wave of nausea. I didn't have the energy to go to the tray right now.

"*Kinsley,*" a voice whispered through my mind and across my skin.

I had finally broken. Marie had made it twenty years and I hadn't even lasted a few days. Pathetic.

"*Kinsley.*"

"Leave me alone!" I screamed to the empty cell.

"*Kinsley, it's me.*" The achingly familiar voice made my heart clench.

"Beck? Where are you?"

"*I am trying to get to you.*"

I sobbed into my hands. "Is Nate okay?"

"*Yes. He was not happy when he got to me. He said you forced him to take your blood. That was very risky.*"

"You know, I thought I might be going crazy or maybe Isaac was messing with my mind. But only the real Beck would scold me when there are much more important things to worry about."

"*Are you speaking out loud?*" Beck asked.

"Yes." I closed my eyes and tried to picture Beck's beautiful face. "Talk to me some more," I whispered.

"*Because you are a Shadower and I am a Monarch we have the ability to communicate telepathically. Since you gave me blood of your own free will, it makes the connection stronger. However, you need to be able to speak to me with your mind and not out loud. Isaac cannot know we have connected.*"

I tried to speak in my head but nothing happened. "I can't do it. I don't know how."

"*Has Isaac been taking your blood?*"

"Yes," I said, stifling a sob.

"*Has he fed you at all?*"

"He's tried to, but I won't eat."

"*It has been four days. You need strength.*"

"Four days?" Time sure slips away from you when you're food for a sadistic vampire. "Why haven't you come for me?" My voice cracked again. I wanted to be in Beck's arms more than anything. Safe, protected.

Silence was my only answer. I counted my heartbeats thinking maybe I had made up Beck's voice to comfort me before I died.

"*I have been going mad knowing you are with him and I cannot protect you.*" I could feel Beck's distress through his thoughts. "*The first two days I did not know where you were. We searched all the places I knew Isaac had ever owned. Nathaniel arrived back to us at the end of the second day. He was badly injured from a fight with Mya. It took him hours to heal. After he healed, he told Masters and me where you were being held.*

"*It is an abandoned warehouse east of the city. I wanted to get you immediately, however Scott argued going in blind could get you killed. We have done reconnaissance of the area for the last day and a half.*" Beck paused. "*You haven't been moved, have you?*"

"No. I'm still in the cell Nate and I were in."

"*I cannot believe Isaac did not change your location when Nathaniel got away.*"

"Maybe he doesn't know Nate got away. You said that Mya injured him. Would she tell Isaac Nate was dead to save her own butt?"

"*Oh, yes, she definitely would.*"

I covered my face with my hands. "He told me you were dead, maybe he believes that. He wants Marie and me as his blood slaves. Isaac is the Seattle Ripper. I watched him kill a woman. You know Mya is here. And some vamp named Carl."

"*Have you seen anyone else?*" Beck asked.

"No."

"Isaac has humans guarding the building. It is a militia group known for 'blowing things up and asking questions later.' That is a quote from Masters."

"Are you and Scott speaking?" I asked.

"We are doing everything in our power to rescue you," he said. Not exactly an answer, but I wasn't going to be too picky in these circumstances.

I heard a noise. "I think someone's coming."

"I am going to stay right here with you. Try to get some food."

That was going to be easier said than done. I'd been throwing it out since I'd gotten here. At least I still had the latest delivery.

"Who are you talking to?" Carl demanded.

I leaned my head to the left and then to the right hoping I looked as crazy as I felt. "Myself," I answered quietly. "I got lonely." I laughed and clapped my hands as I channeled Marie.

"Very good." Beck's velvet voice whispered across my mind. I felt stronger knowing I wasn't alone.

"Isaac was worried about this. He said the other one went crazy after a few years in captivity but she ate and got to go for walks outside. You can't go outside because people are looking for you."

"Are they looking for me because Nate got away?"

"What are you doing? We don't want them to move you!" I could feel Beck's anger.

"Got away?" Carl laughed. "You think that dumb cat got away? Mya's better than you think she is. She killed your cat and skinned him. We're having him made into a rug to keep you company. I'll go see if it's ready yet."

I started screaming and crying as Carl left.

"Kinsley! Listen to me. Nathaniel is fine. Mya is conniving. It is exactly as you said. She knew Isaac would kill her if she let Nathaniel get away. She must have killed another shifter and told Isaac it was Nathaniel. That is why they have not moved you." His logic soothed my nerves.

"Beck, are you really here or am I going crazy?"

"I am really here, Kinsley, and I am coming to get you."

I still didn't know if he was real, but I took the small comfort I could get. "Okay. Hurry." But he was gone. I couldn't feel him in my mind anymore.

I crawled to the tray of food and lifted the soup bowl to my lips. The first few swallows made me gag since I hadn't eaten in days. I took a few sips of water and then some more soup. This time the soup went down easier. I dipped the bread in the broth that was left and ate everything slowly.

I heard footsteps coming down the stairs. I scooted away from the door with the bowl in one hand and the bottle of water in the other.

"I'm glad to see you've quit being so stubborn," Isaac said. "I can't have you die before I've completely enjoyed you. The next step was force feeding you."

Isaac looked over his shoulder. "How would you like a shower today?"

I knew there had to be a catch. "I'm fine," I said.

Isaac nodded to whoever was standing off to the side and I heard water splatter on the bricks. Oh shit.

Carl walked into view with a hose. He aimed it through the bars and drenched me before I could move. The water was ice cold and it soaked through my dirty clothes in seconds. I didn't have it in me to try and dodge the spray so I stood and turned my back.

I knew I'd taken all the fun out of what Carl had expected

to be water torture when he cursed and the water stopped hitting me. I looked over my shoulder and saw him wash the blood and soup down the floor drain.

Mya came to the door with a giant golden cougar pelt draped over her arm.

"No!" I screamed. I knew it wasn't Nate, but some cougar had been killed. I cried not only for that but also because Isaac needed to see my reaction.

They opened the door and tossed the pelt at my feet.

"Have fun with your kitty," Mya said. "I wanted to gut him in front of you but his little stunt upped my timetable."

I threw myself onto the pelt and sobbed.

They left me huddled in my soaking wet clothes.

I didn't want to give them the satisfaction of seeing me miserable so I peeled off my wet shirt and jeans. I wrung out my clothes the best I could. I put my wet shirt back on and left my jeans and tennis shoes to dry.

While sad that a cougar was dead, I was glad I had something besides wet bricks to sit on. I curled onto the pelt and fisted my hands in the soft fur.

I CAME AWAKE ABRUPTLY, pain in every part of my body, freezing cold. I shook out my jeans and yanked the gritty material up my legs. Shoes back on, I went to the cougar pelt and sat down.

I closed my eyes and cataloged the pain. My wrist didn't hurt anymore and the rip from Nate's bite was a square-lined scab on my shoulder. My neck ached where Isaac had been feeding from me, but it wasn't an open wound.

I thought about Beck like Nate had told me to. I pictured

his face and remembered the smell of his skin when we'd been dancing. I let the feeling of his lips on my neck take over my senses.

"*Beck,*" I whispered in my mind. "*Can you hear me?*"

"*You did it. Are you safe?*"

"*As safe as I can be,*" I answered.

"*What has happened?*"

"*Mya said she killed Nate and they gave me a cougar pelt. I also got a shower from a garden hose. That was fun,*" I said.

"*Your ability to keep your sense of humor is amazing.*"

"*It's part of going crazy; everything is funny.*"

"*You are not going crazy,*" Beck said.

"*Where are you?*"

"*Coming to you, like I promised.*"

I heard footsteps. "*Someone's coming,*" I said.

"*I know.*"

I opened my eyes. Beck stood at my cell door! I jumped up and ran to him.

"Are you really here?" I jammed my arms through the bars and pulled him to me. "How did you get in? Is Isaac dead?"

"Isaac is not dead." Beck's eyes held a hint of sadness.

"What's going on?" I asked.

"*Trust me, please,*" he whispered in my mind.

Isaac stepped next to Beck. "I can't just let her go, Beckford, you know that."

Beck turned to Isaac with rage in his eyes. "You said you would trade me for her."

"Technically, I said I would trade her for Marie. You offered yourself and I didn't refuse."

"No!" I yelled. "Leave, Beck, leave! Hurry!" I let go of Beck's arms and backed away from the cell door.

"Oh, Beckford. The world would be right again with you

dead and Marie back on my arm. Maybe I'll keep Kinsley around for a midnight snack."

Beck growled but didn't move.

Isaac laughed and lashed a clawed hand out. Beck's shirt shredded and five claw marks opened on his chest. Blood flowed freely as he fell to his knees.

"You seem to have forgotten I've been feeding from your Shadower for four days, Beckford. I'm stronger than you." Isaac kicked Beck in the head.

I screamed, "Stop it! Stop!" Beck lay there and let Isaac kick him.

Isaac stopped his assault and I heard another cell door jangle open. Mya and Carl came into view and dragged Beck's body out of sight. I heard him grunt in pain and then the cell door next to mine closed.

Isaac came into my cell and pulled me out. His arms held me immobile against his chest as he made me look into Beck's cell. Mya and Carl chained Beck up like Nate had been.

Beck's chest and face bled. His eyes were open and on mine.

I didn't utter a sound as Isaac forced his fangs into the side of my neck and began to feed. I was scared and I knew Isaac enjoyed it, but I tried to hide what I could. As he fed, my knees weakened.

Beck bellowed and pulled against the silver chains. Mya laughed and ran a finger down the side of his face. Beck snapped at her hand.

I was starting to get light headed when Isaac finally removed his mouth from my neck. "She told me she let you have her blood, Beckford, but I know you haven't had nearly as much as me." Isaac licked the puncture marks closed.

"I will kill you for this!" Beck pulled against the chains.

Isaac tossed me back in my cell and closed the door.

I thought I could hear Beck call my name but I couldn't tell if it was out loud or in my head. I was too weak to care.

My last thought before blackness took me was that rescues weren't supposed to happen like this.

Chapter Thirty-Eight

"KINSLEY!"

Beck's voice wasn't in my head this time. I opened one eye and realized I was sprawled on the concrete floor of my cell. The fact Beck was there came rushing back to me. I was relieved, angry, and sad all at the same time.

"What were you thinking?" I tried to yell, but it came out as a whisper.

"Kinsley, are you okay?"

"No, I'm not okay, you dumb ass. Now we're both trapped down here." My voice was louder this time.

"Listen to me for a moment."

"No, you listen to me!" I sat up, dizzy. I put my hand over my face and closed my eyes. "If we get out of here alive, I am so going to kick your ass," I said through my fingers.

He laughed! He actually had the guts to laugh. Finally he said, "I do not have a lot of time to explain, so you need to listen."

"What?" I snapped.

"I knew Isaac would not keep his word to trade me for you. I do have a plan."

"I'm listening," I said as I stood, leaning against the wall for support.

"I have been calling your name for at least an hour. Does Isaac always take that much?"

"No," I answered as I fought to stay conscious.

"You need some food."

"I need to get out of here," I said.

"Marie let me take her blood," Beck said.

"What?"

"She knew the only way I would be able to take on Isaac would be if I had the blood of a Shadower."

"How'd that work for you?" I asked. "Oh, wait. It didn't. You let him beat you up and chain you in a cell." Sarcasm was my new defense against death.

"I could not let him know I was stronger. I had to know you were okay."

I couldn't decide if Beck was telling me the truth or just trying to make me feel better.

"After they bring you your evening meal, I am going to snap the chains. I will need more blood to get us the rest of the way out and kill Isaac."

"Beck, he's been feeding on me for days. He's too strong. A little bit of my blood isn't going to give you enough strength to kill him." I dropped my chin to my chest.

"Kinsley," Beck said in a cautious tone.

"Fine," I snapped. "At least I can die knowing I did everything I could to get free. There's no point in waiting until my meal arrives, chicken broth isn't really a meal."

I heard Beck grunt, the sound of chains jingling, and metal on metal. "I do not know how much noise it is going to make when I rip open the cell doors. We may only have seconds."

"I'm ready," I said.

The sound of twisting metal and crumbling bricks filled the

hallway. Then my door was ripped out of the concrete. It sounded like a car smashing into a brick wall.

Beck pulled me into his body. Then he did something I didn't expect. Instead of driving his fangs into my throat, he kissed me. There was nothing soft or simple about it either.

His mouth landed on mine with a groan. I opened my lips and kissed him back. If I was going to die, I deserved a heart-stopping kiss, even if it was from a vampire. His hands cradled each side of my face as he tilted my head. His tongue swept across mine.

We heard shouts and Beck pulled back from my mouth. He kissed me quickly once more.

"I am so sorry," he whispered. Then he bit me.

It wasn't anything like Nate's rough invasion or Isaac's brutal attacks. I felt Beck's fangs slide into my skin like two tiny needles and then he was sucking on my neck. It was erotic instead of an unwanted assault of my body. Beck backed me up against the cold brick wall and continued to suck. Electricity coursed through my body in sensual ripples. I wanted him to keep drinking, keep giving me pleasure.

That's what scared me into action. "Stop," I whispered.

He kept feeding.

"Beck, stop." Finally my voice got through to him.

He pulled away and licked his lips. What had been revolting on Isaac was sexy from Beck. Maybe I had lost more blood than I thought.

"Lord, I am sorry." He closed his eyes and when he opened them they were glowing gold orbs. "Think of the most luscious tasting food or drink you have ever had; that is what your blood is to me. I should not have taken so much." He gently kissed my lips and the side of my neck before looking into my eyes again.

I watched his face sway in my vision and then split into

two. "There are two of you again and this time I don't have drugs to cause it."

"Damn it!" Beck said and picked me up in his arms. We made it through the door just before Mya came down the stairs.

She stared in shock for a moment and that was all Beck needed. While still holding me, he reached out and ripped a piece of the iron door off its frame. He held a nice metal stake in his left hand. Mya flew at us, feet not touching the ground.

Beck moved so fast I only saw that Mya stopped inches from us and then fell to the ground, the piece of iron rammed through her chest. She looked dead to me.

Beck broke off two more pieces of iron and handed them to me. My arms shook from holding such heavy stakes but I kept my grip because my life depended on it.

I buried my face in Beck's neck as he moved up the stairs so quickly it made my head spin even more.

Three vampires jumped in front of Beck just before he reached a large, wooden door. Would we run into the humans who were guarding the outside? I wasn't sure I'd feel bad about their deaths.

"I am going to set you down so I have both my hands," Beck said.

He made sure my feet were under me just as one of the vampires lunged at him. I was thrown to the side and landed hard on my hands and knees. One of the iron bars rolled out of my hand and clanged against the wall.

I looked up to see Beck grab the first vampire around his neck. In a move almost too fast for my eyes to track, Beck put one hand on the vamp's chin, one around his collar bone, and pulled.

The vampire's head landed next to me as the twitching body fell to the floor. I held back a scream. The next two vampires were no match for his speed and strength. Similar to the move with the first vampire, Beck snapped off both their heads in less than fifteen seconds.

I stood to move to him when I was kicked in the ribs and slid across the floor. Carl crouched five feet from me. I saw the other piece of iron out of the corner of my eye and reached for it as Carl lunged.

Beck yelled as I raised my hands in front of me. I had a piece of iron in each hand and Carl impaled himself on the spikes with the momentum of his body.

Shock crossed his face as the two pieces of iron drove into his chest. Blood ran from the wounds and covered my hands. Beck lifted Carl's lifeless body from mine.

"Are you okay? Did he hurt you?"

"No. Kill him like you did the others. I had to watch him rape a girl."

Beck turned and put his foot on Carl's chest between the spikes. He took his right hand and ripped Carl's head off.

I breathed a sigh of relief and tried to stand. I fell back to my knees. Beck wrapped his hands around my arms and lifted me to my feet.

I was worried we hadn't seen Isaac. As Beck lifted me into his arms once again, I looked around the huge brick and concrete room. No one else came from behind old machinery or dropped from the air to attack us.

Beck ran toward the large front doors and crashed through them with his shoulder. Splinters of wood rained down on us as we burst through. It was almost dawn, I could see the sun beginning to rise.

"How long can you be in the sunlight?" I asked.

"Between the blood I took from Marie and you, I could be out almost all day and not have any painful effects."

"Amazing," I said.

"You are amazing," Beck countered. "You would have killed that vampire with or without me."

"Yeah, but it was easier with." I closed my eyes. "I'm tired," I mumbled.

"I know. I will have you somewhere safe soon. Try to stay awake. You have lost too much blood."

I nodded and thought how nice it would be to just go to sleep. "How are we getting home? Is Nate waiting around the corner with a car?" Then I remembered I didn't have a home to go to. I opened my eyes and almost burst into tears.

"I did not know what kind of shape you would be in or how long it would take us to get out. Scott said he would set up surveillance and get to us when we escaped."

Beck looked back at the building we'd just exited then down at me. "We have to get out of here. I wanted to see if a car would show, but we must go before anyone else in that building notices we are gone."

He looked to the road then back down at me in his arms. "Some vampires are able to jump through time when they are at the height of their powers."

I pulled back as much as I could. "You mean like time travel?"

"No. Like teleport from one location to another. I have never done it, but I have never been this powerful. I think I could do it with both of us."

I didn't want to walk wherever we were going. Nor did I feel like waiting for a car in case Isaac or his human militia poured out of the woodwork. I was getting ready to tell him to try it when a black Hummer came squealing around the corner.

"Finally," Beck mumbled.

The Hummer slid to a stop with Oliver at the wheel. He saluted me with two fingers and smiled.

Scott jumped out of the passenger side and ran toward us.

Raven and Nate came boiling out of the back doors at the same time.

Beck wouldn't put me down as he walked toward the Hummer.

"How many of those do you have?" I asked Scott.

"You must be okay if you're picking on me," Scott said.

I'd never been so happy to see his smile.

"I've been better," I admitted.

"Let us continue this conversation on the way to Screamers," Beck said. He climbed in the back of the Hummer, keeping me in his arms.

Nate shut the door and ran around to the other side. Scott climbed in the middle and Nate sandwiched him in. That left Raven in front with Oliver.

"Blue Team, we're clear," Oliver said into a handheld radio as he drove. "Keep surveillance in place until you hear from Mr. Masters."

While Beck held me in his lap, Scott took one of my hands and pulled it up to his face. "I'm sorry I was such a bossy arrogant bastard. I had to tell you that. I thought I'd never see you again." He kissed my palm. "While Alexander and I don't agree about much, we agree you're incredibly special. Important. We're going to work together from now on so you'll always be safe. If we hadn't been split up, this never would have happened."

I looked to Beck for confirmation and he nodded. "Thank you," I said. Their fighting would be one less thing I'd have to worry about.

"I want Dr. Karlof to look you over. It feels as though you have lost over ten pounds in the days you were captive." Beck's arms tightened around me.

"Blood loss and lack of food will do that to you," I tried to joke.

"Then you're coming to my house until you're completely recovered," Scott added.

I expected an argument from Beck, but he locked his jaw and didn't say a word.

"Can I sleep now?" I asked.

"Yes," Scott said. "We'll be here when you wake up."

"You look like hell," Nate finally said. I craned my head so I could see him around Scott's body.

"You're not very good at following directions," I said.

"You don't have very good ideas," he shot back.

"It worked, didn't it?" I asked.

"Leave her alone, Nate," Raven said.

"Oh great, now she's calling me Nate." He pouted for a minute then looked at me. "I'm sorry I hurt you and I'm glad you're okay."

"I'm fine." And I was. I was with my guys and Raven.

Mya and Carl were dead. That would have to get me through until we could kill Isaac.

That was the only way Marie would ever be safe.

Chapter Thirty-Nine

I AWOKE in a soft bed with Beck's scent surrounding me. I rolled to my side and sighed contentedly, snuggling into the blankets and pillows. I wasn't quite ready to face reality. A masculine chuckle had me peeking from under the covers.

I was in Beck's office at Screamers and Scott sat in a chair beside the little bed. The single dimple in his cheek when he smiled made him look boyish, but I knew he was far from a boy.

"You probably shouldn't look at me like that, sweet thing," Scott said quietly. "I've decided to be altruistic and I can't do that if you're checking me out."

"You, altruistic? Do you even know what that means? I thought you were self*ish* not self*less*." I sat up and the blankets tumbled from my naked body.

Scott's eyes dropped down and stayed there. I pulled the sheet up and he laughed. "Raven and Rachel removed your dirty clothes and cleaned you up. Beck and I waited in the hallway."

"I'll take it as a good sign if you're calling him Beck."

"I told you, we'll get along for your sake." Scott wouldn't meet my eyes for a minute. "I want to apologize for my behavior on the day you were kidnapped," he finally said.

"No. I gave you the wrong idea. We slept together."

That's when Beck walked in, of course. He froze in the doorway with a tray of food and stared at me.

"It's not what you think," I said.

"You do not have to explain yourself to me, Kinsley. Nathaniel made you food. Eat as much as you can. Dr. Karlof gave you an IV of nutrients but you need solids."

I looked down my arms and, sure enough, there was a cotton ball taped to the top of my hand and remnants of medical tape. "How long have I been out?"

"Almost twenty-four hours," Scott said. "Karlof took good care of you. I didn't want to trust him, but Beck said he's good. Karlof wanted to take some of your blood."

"I told him he could ask when you were awake but that you were tired of sharing your blood with monsters," Beck said. He sat the tray of food on the corner of his desk and turned to leave.

"Beck, you're not a monster," I said. He stopped briefly, then walked out and closed the door behind him.

"You have to tell him nothing happened between us," I said to Scott.

Scott shrugged. "He's going to believe what he wants to believe. When you were missing, he told me your life would be better without any vampires in it."

"Well, we all know that isn't going to happen," I said.

Scott brought the tray of food to me. It was piled high with chunks of chicken, ham, and beef. There was a bowl of fettuccine with vegetables and a bottle of Gatorade.

I wolfed down the meat without using a fork. When that was gone, I drank half the Gatorade in four huge gulps. Then I started on the noodles. It took me about five minutes to empty the tray of food. I finished the last of the Gatorade and lay back on the bed with a sigh of contentment. I guessed a normal human would have been sick after not eating for so many days. But apparently not me and my rapid metabolism. I wanted more food but needed a shower.

"I'm going to take a shower. Will you go ask Nate to make me spaghetti and meatballs?"

Scott smiled. "That kid would fly to Italy and get you food if you asked him. I've never seen two more loyal friends in my life and they're not even human."

"Are you talking about Nate and Raven?" I asked.

When Scott nodded I glared at him. "Nate and Raven are human. All shifters are human. You need to get over your prejudice of paranormal creatures."

"I know," he said. "It's just that I've spent most of my life hunting and killing bad vampires and shifters. It's difficult for me to think of them as something other than the enemy." He stood with the tray and went to the door.

"Well, learn. These people are part of my life now. If you're going to be a part of it you have to accept them. All of them."

"I'll work on it for you. Go take a shower and I'll bring you more food. Anyone ever tell you you eat like a horse?" He laughed and left the room.

I waited until I was sure he wasn't by the door and slowly slid out of bed and to the small bathroom.

I took a long hot shower and washed my hair six times. I thought I could still smell blood and the dampness of the cell where I'd been. With my captivity and the day I'd slept, it had been a week since the Seattle Art Museum gala. A week ago I'd been in the most beautiful dress in the world, dancing with the most handsome men I'd ever known. It seemed like a lifetime ago.

My hand went to my throat as I realized the necklace with my parents' wedding rings was at the condo. I'd taken it off due to the halter top of the dress. The condo had to be leveled.

I'd watched explosions rip it to pieces. I had lost my parents' rings, my pictures, my dad's silver daggers, and everything else from my life before becoming a Shadower. Even my parents' ashes.

Tears threatened to overtake me. I should have just been happy I was alive. That the people I loved were alive. Material possessions shouldn't matter.

I twirled the ruby ring on my finger and took comfort in the fact I hadn't lost it. At least I had something of my mother left.

When I got out of the shower, there was a small bag by the bathroom door. Inside were some clothes and a toothbrush and toothpaste.

I put on a tank top and shorts then brushed my teeth. Twice.

Feeling under-dressed, I snagged a black terrycloth robe off the back of the door. The robe enveloped me in the scent of cedar and Beck's cologne. I pulled the collar up and inhaled the sharp smells. It comforted me like only Beck could.

When I came out of the bathroom, Marie, Rachel, and Raven were there. Marie, Rachel, and I screamed and ran to each other. We stood in a group hugging and crying. Raven watched from the edge of the office.

"Get over here and act like a girl with us," I said. She ran over and threw her arms around us.

We stood in our hugging, crying group until I couldn't breathe. "Okay, I need a tissue," I finally said.

Raven went into the bathroom and came out with a roll of toilet paper. We plopped ourselves on the floor, blowing our noses and wiping our eyes.

Finally Rachel pulled herself together enough to talk. "We were so worried about you. Marie was a wreck. More so than usual." She smiled and my eyes filled with tears again.

Marie crawled over to me and laid her head in my lap. "I

knew what you were going through. I hated you were at Isaac's mercy." I stroked Marie's head, looking down at her.

Her skin and hair shone in the dim lights of the office. I knew Isaac coveted more than Marie's blood. She was a beautiful trophy to him and I couldn't let him get his hands on her.

I wiped away some more tears. "Beck saved me. You all saved me. I wasn't there for very many days and only the thought of being with you all again kept me sane."

Marie kept her head in my lap as Raven took one of my hands. "I've never become so attached to a group of people, especially in such a short amount of time. Beck and Nate gave me a place to hide and come to terms with what I'd become. Now that you're all a part of my life, it's like I have a real family."

"See, Kinsley and I learned a long time ago family isn't just about the blood in your veins," Rachel said. "Family is the people you love and would do anything for. It's always been Kinsley and me. Well, and her parents. They're the ones who taught us you don't have to be blood to be family. We lost Tom and Claire, but we have Marie. Now some vampires, kitties, and wolves make more."

"Wolves?" I asked, temporarily distracted.

"Ian and Gerald," Rachel explained.

Raven let go of my hand and I went back to stroking Marie's hair.

"We almost translated the rest of the book while you were gone. It gave Marie and me something to do," Rachel said.

"The book? How could you have done that? I watched the condo blow up."

"Well," Rachel began, "Marie had a *bad feeling*. She grabbed some things before we were herded into that Fort Knox of a basement." Rachel nudged Marie with her toe and Marie sat up.

She put her hands behind her neck, fidgeting with something. When her hand stretched out, I saw light reflect off gold. A necklace. My necklace.

The rings were warm in my palm as she handed me the necklace.

"Oh, Marie! Thank you so much. I thought this was gone forever." I promised myself I'd never take the necklace off again.

Someone knocked at the door. Nate entered with a huge tray of food. I saw a pot of spaghetti and a loaf of garlic bread. I stood and went to Nate.

I waited for him to set the tray of food then I wrapped my arms around him and kissed his cheek. "Don't you ever risk your life for me again!"

He shook his head. "Not a promise I can make. I'll do everything in my power to protect you. That's what we do for our Shadower. I want you to know I'm never going to let you pull a stunt like that again. I'll never leave you alone with the bad guys."

I put my hand on the side of his face. "Sometimes we have to do things differently than we plan. No one could have saved us if you hadn't gotten away."

He covered my hand with his. "Yeah, well next time, we're going to figure out how to get you out."

"Next time?" I asked in horror as Nate laughed at me.

There were plates and forks on the tray with the spaghetti. Ian came through the door carrying a tray of drinks. When he set it down, I went to him.

He had on his dark sunglasses. I looked at him for a moment until he took them off.

His eyes seemed too big for his face, the corners turned down. Weepy brown eyes stared at me with such longing, I put my hand on his cheek. Ian nuzzled into my touch.

"Ian, I know we haven't gotten to spend much time together, but I've watched you be patient with Marie. You've put your life on the line to protect her and Rachel. Thank you."

Ian didn't speak. He nodded and stepped back out of my reach, moving to the corner where he liked to stand.

I turned back to the girls. "You're eating with me."

Nate started dishing out food and we all sat at the conference table and ate. I relaxed and enjoyed the comfort of being safe. I had trouble keeping my eyes open. My stomach was full and I almost felt normal.

Beck and Scott entered. Scott walked to me, Beck sat at his desk.

"I think Kinsley should sleep some more," Scott said.

I was equally sad and glad for the suggestion. I could have stayed for hours with my girls but I was exhausted. Scott helped me from my chair. I slid off the robe and climbed back in the soft bed.

Raven and Nate came over and each kissed me on the forehead then left. Ian nodded to me again and shuffled out behind them. Marie and Rachel gave me a hug and a kiss and then they were gone too.

Scott leaned over the bed and stroked my hair. "I'm glad you're back, sweet thing," he said. He kissed me gently on the lips. "I'm taking you back to my house when you wake up. Beck's got everything lined up to rebuild in a safe location, but that's going to take time. I'll rearrange things so you and Marie can each have your own room."

"Thank you, I'd like that," I said quietly.

Scott looked over his shoulder at Beck, gave me another quick kiss on the lips, and went out the door.

Beck and I were alone.

"I will do everything in my power to make sure you are never hurt again," Beck said from across the room.

"I believe you," I said. There were so many other things I wanted to say but I didn't know where to begin. It started something like 'Thanks for saving my life. Stay out of my head and don't ask to suck any more of my blood.' I just wasn't sure how it would end.

"I understand your need to be with other humans. I will not push you to come back to live near us. I will understand if you want to live with Scott."

"I'm assuming Rachel's staying with Nate, wherever that is?"

Beck nodded.

I took a deep breath and forged on. "I'd like to go over the plans for our new building with you. It would be a lot easier to have the entire top floor be one giant house, don't you think?"

"What are you saying?" Beck said.

"Scott and I both know vampires and shifters are more effective bodyguards. Rachel and Marie are safer around all of you, and I live where Rachel and Marie live."

"You are safer with us as well."

"I know that," I said. I pulled the covers around me like a shield. "Beck, we have to talk about what happened. This connection between us scares me a little."

"I know."

"I think we should stay out of each other's heads. And I don't want to give any more of my blood. To anyone. I don't want Karlof to study it right now. I don't want to be your open bar."

Beck smiled, which was what I hoped for.

"I understand," he said. "But when you are ready, please let Karlof examine your blood. Maybe he will be able to make a synthetic form. Then you would never have to share blood again."

Beck moved to the side of the bed. I thought he was going

to kiss me, but he only touched my lips with his fingertips. "You are safe now. Rest, relax, and heal. I will be here when you wake up. I will always be here." He turned out the lights and left the room.

"I know you will," I said to the darkness. "That's the one thing I can count on."

Chapter Forty

FOR THE NEXT TWO WEEKS, Marie and I lived with Scott. I felt fully recovered within two days but Scott and Beck demanded I wasn't quite 'perfect' yet.

Not only had Marie saved my necklace with the rings, she'd also lugged that fifty pound silver case to the basement with her; I had my dad's daggers. Rachel had grabbed a few pictures and the urn. I wondered how Marie knew things were going to go bad. There was no point in asking her, because I doubted she knew.

Rachel was completely recovered from the vamp attack. I didn't know if it was her past experiences or her ability to find the good in every situation, but she was mentally doing well. As usual, she impressed me with her ability to stay strong.

It helped she had Nate. They were living in an apartment above Screamers. She came to Scott's every day to workout with Raven and me. She had me updated on her love life in no time. She and Nate were serious about their relationship.

Today she hinted about the merits of sex with a shifter and Raven hooted her agreement. Something about stamina and size. I didn't really know what they were talking about and the conversation made me uncomfortable.

Of course I got even more uncomfortable as Rachel asked me questions about Scott and Beck. I ran on the treadmill, Rachel was on an elliptical, and Raven lifted weights. Oliver was nowhere to be seen, thank goodness.

"So, rumor has it you slept with Scott when you stayed the night at his house that first time." Rachel had never learned tact in delicate situations.

I almost fell off the treadmill. I lowered my speed and glared at her. "No, I did not. Where in the world did you hear that?"

"Nathaniel. He told me Beck was steaming mad but wouldn't give him any more details than you'd chosen Scott."

"I haven't chosen anyone. I don't want to choose anyone. Why are we even having this conversation?" I stopped the treadmill and moved to the free weights in the corner with Raven.

Rachel followed me. "Come on, tell me. You know all about my sex life."

"And why you think I want to know about it is beyond me. I didn't have sex with Scott. I haven't had sex with anybody!" I dodged her again and climbed on the elliptical she'd just abandoned.

"Kinsley, you need to learn to live a little. I know you want to save yourself for the *perfect guy*," Rachel made air quotes, "but the perfect guy doesn't exist. Just do it and then it won't be such a big deal."

Rachel and I had been having this discussion since we were fourteen, after she'd lost her virginity. I wasn't about to give in to her peer pressure. I had made it through my teen years. I wouldn't cave now that I was an adult. She must have seen the determination on my face because she gave up.

"Fine. Let's talk about dating, then. I know Scott and Beck

would both take you anywhere you wanted to go. Let's pick a location for your romantic rendezvous."

"With which one?" Raven asked.

"You stay out of this," I said to her. I was working so hard on the elliptical I could barely breathe and sweat ran in rivulets down my face, chest, and back. Maybe I would pass out, then I wouldn't have to listen to this conversation.

"Both of them, of course," Rachel said. "We're going to teach Kins to play the field, Raven. She needs to go out with men and experience life."

"Both of them? At the same time?" Raven asked.

"Ohh we need to share stories, girl," Rachel said with a touch of flirtation in her voice. "Kinsley wouldn't do that, though. I don't even think the boys would agree. They may have her best interests at heart when it comes to safety, but I don't think they'd share her body."

My cheeks heated and I slammed the machine to a halt. "Enough! We are not having this conversation ever again." I stepped off the elliptical and grabbed my towel and water bottle. "Stay in here for a while. I need a break from you." I walked out of Oliver's workout room and went to find him.

It was mid-September and summer was fading. Oliver shot his compound bow in the backyard. I know he heard me come outside but he didn't say a word.

"Ollie?" I asked.

He made his shot, lowered the bow, and turned to look at me.

"Scott says you're good with knives. Have you seen my daggers?"

He shook his head. "No, but I've heard about them."

"If I let you play with them, will you teach me to use them for killing vampires?"

Oliver looked at me closely then smiled. He went from

downright scary to handsome. What was it with these security experts? One minute they had the 'I'll rip your arms off your body and beat you with them' look. Yet a moment later they had a 'charm the panties right off you' glow.

"Play with them? You'd let me use Tom Preston's silver daggers?"

"Of course. But only if you teach me to use them."

"Deal," Oliver said.

"I also get to keep calling you Ollie."

He briefly glared at me but couldn't keep from smiling. "Get the daggers."

"Do I come back here, or will we do this in Scott's yard?"

Oliver pointed behind him. "Here. We'll use some of the bow targets for stabbing technique. I've got some rubber shooting mannequins we can use for slicing."

"You're a strange, strange man, Ollie," I said.

"I'm not sure you're one to talk, Kinsley," he countered.

I ran across the road and bounded up the stairs to my room. My entire wardrobe had been destroyed in the explosions and resulting fire. People had been picking up clothes here and there for all of us. Since I hadn't been allowed to leave the house, I was at the mercy of whatever happened to be hanging in the closet.

I changed into new, non-sweaty workout clothes, grabbed the case, and went back to Oliver's.

Ollie opened the case, running his hands over the daggers.

"You've got some drool," I said and reached my hand out pretending to wipe his chin.

He smiled, winked, then we got to work.

We talked about holding the daggers and testing balance. Ollie said the quickest way to end up dead was by having a knife that wasn't balanced. If they were too heavy or light at one end when throwing them, or even attacking in close combat, they could handle differently than you intended. Considering fights with vampires were going to be up close, I wanted all the precision I could get.

We worked for two hours. The first half hour was just talking about when to use the knives and key places to attack depending on if it was a vampire or shifter. While I had yet to meet any evil shifters, Ollie assured me there were many.

When it was time to practice using the knives, I got a little scared. Ollie took me to the kitchen and I sliced vegetables so I could see how sharp the knives were and feel them cutting things.

We washed the knives and then went back outside so I could practice stabbing into the archery target. We didn't get to throwing technique because Scott showed up saying it was time for lunch.

I thanked Oliver and went back to the house. Ian and Marie were in the living room reading books. Nate, Rachel, and Raven were nowhere to be seen.

"Who's making lunch?" I asked Scott. I mean, I could make my own lunch, but Nate's food was much better.

"No one, I'm taking you to Kirkland."

"Really?" I asked. Beck had been over almost every day. Yet whenever I asked anyone if I could leave they all told me no. Even Marie.

"Really. How long will it take you to get ready?"

I was racing up the stairs before he finished speaking. I took a shower, dressed in shorts and a sleeveless shirt with a pair of sandals. Thirty minutes later we were in his little black sports car on our way.

I looked at the trees as we came into town. Fall was coming early. Some of the leaves had started to change colors. Classes at UW started in a week and I hadn't registered. Regret sat like a rock in the pit of my stomach. My education had always been so important to me.

Scott didn't talk during the drive and we arrived at the restaurant after half an hour of comfortable silence. When we entered, there was a lunch crowd but we were immediately taken to a small table in the corner.

"Did you tell them I get cranky when I don't eat right away?" I asked.

"Yes. I also mentioned you were good with numerous weapons," Scott smiled and kissed my cheek as he held my chair out.

"So, why did you have to get me out of the house?"

"Figured that out, did you?" He winked as the waitress brought our water and menus.

When she left, I opened my menu and pretended to read the specials. "I've been under house arrest for two weeks and suddenly you let me come to Kirkland. Of course I figured it out. I suppose Beck is going to call or show up later and want to take me to dinner?" I knew I was right when Scott cursed under his breath and opened his own menu.

"What's going on?"

Scott shook his head. "Can we order and then have this discussion? You're easier to talk to when you're eating."

I was starving, so I agreed. Scott flagged the waitress over. He ordered a captain's plate with a variety of seafood.

"And for you, ma'am?" the petite teenage-looking waitress said. I was probably only a few years older than her, but I felt twenty years older.

"I'll have the Shrimp Louie salad," I paused to tell her the rest and she closed her order book and turned to leave.

Scott chuckled as I called, "Hey, I wasn't done."

The waitress was momentarily shocked then apologized.

"I'd like a pound of steamed clams, too."

She wrote it down and closed the book.

Now I was just playing with her. "I'd also like mozzarella sticks as an appetizer and why don't you whip up some spinach dip, too." I smiled as she scribbled everything down.

"Anything else?" she asked.

"Yeah, a bowl of clam chowder. And I want the Death By Chocolate cake for dessert. Thanks."

The poor girl stared at me. When she realized I wasn't kidding she scurried off to put in our order.

"Sometimes you're just mean," Scott said.

"The customer is always right," I said. "She didn't ask me if I wanted anything else, she just assumed I only wanted the salad." I took a drink of water. "Okay, what's going on?"

"Can't we wait until you at least have your soup or maybe your cheese sticks?"

"No. Spill it."

Scott put his palms on the table, moved them to rub his temples, and then moved his hands to his lap. "Alright. I know you haven't registered for classes yet and school starts in a week. Alexander is going to talk to you about a more rigorous work schedule for him so he can take your mind off the fact you're not taking classes. I didn't want you to be caught off guard and I figured we could brainstorm a good way for you to let him down easy."

"Let him down easy?" I asked. "What do you mean?"

"Well, you can't work for him. What if Isaac shows up while you're on campus? Oliver and I have other jobs to handle this fall."

I tried to keep from getting mad because we were in a public place. Maybe this was why he'd brought me to lunch.

"I'm going to keep working for Beck. I can't just sit at your house and twiddle my thumbs."

He ran a hand through his hair. "I thought you could find a hobby," he said. And he was serious.

I crossed my arms. "A hobby? Like what? Sharpening my daggers and writing manuals on how to kill vampires and shapeshifters? I have to have some normal stuff in my life or I'm going to go crazy."

I waved a hand in the air. "I've already given up the plan of becoming a teacher. I'll pick a different major and register for classes in the winter. I'm going back to live with my family when our new home is rebuilt. I intend to live as much of a normal life as I can."

The waitress came to our table with a basket of rolls and my soup. When she left I started talking again before Scott could.

"I'm not going to go out and look for vampires like you and my dad did. I'll live my life and if some bad creatures show up, I'll know how to take care of them."

His jaw was rock hard, but he nodded.

My new iPhone vibrated in my pocket. I pulled it out and saw it was Beck. I ignored the call and set my phone on the table. A few moments later, a text came through.

It was from Beck asking if he could take me to dinner.

I didn't respond. I finished my soup and the waitress brought the cheese sticks, spinach dip, and clams. Scott and I were eating those when another text came through. This one said he'd pick me up at eight.

Ugh! Men!

Chapter Forty-One

BECK TOOK me to Sky City, the restaurant at the top of the Space Needle. I'd never been there because it wasn't the kind of place poor college kids ate. I'd heard of it, but nothing prepared me for the view of the revolving restaurant. Every inch of Seattle during a September sunset cannot be described. Beautiful was all I could think of and that seemed inadequate.

The waiter arrived to take our drink order. Beck picked a bottle of champagne then waved the waiter away.

"I thought you might want to know a little about me," Beck said.

"Aren't we going to talk about work?"

Beck smiled. "I knew Masters would try to talk you out of working for me."

"I do what I want to," I said.

"You think I do not know that? It is one of the many reasons I am drawn to you. That, and the fact that you are not scared of me, or anything else for that matter."

I took a drink of water. "I'm scared of lots of things."

"That may be true, but you do not let your fear rule you," Beck said. "You try to make rational decisions based on what is the best course. Not what scares you."

"So we're not going to talk about work?"

"Not now, but we will," he said. "I know you have questions. What do you want to know?"

I leaned in and whispered, "How old are you?"

Beck laughed. "You went straight for the hard one."

"Why is it hard? Don't tell me you've forgotten what year you were born."

"Of course not. But when I was born, we did not keep track of dates the way we do now. I will say it was hundreds of years ago, in Europe, in the spring."

"How many hundreds? Five, seven?"

"A bit more," he said as the waiter returned.

Holy crap! Beck was more than seven hundred years old? He must have thought I was a total baby.

The waiter poured our champagne and set the bottle in a chiller between us. "Are you celebrating something special tonight?" he asked.

"I am always celebrating something special when I get to be alone with Kinsley," Beck said, looking at me. He lifted his champagne glass in a toast and our waiter left.

"You sweet talker, you," I said as our glasses clinked. "Speaking of which, I noticed your speech is a little different. You don't really use slang or contractions when you talk. You sound so educated. Is that a newly acquired education?"

"Are you asking if I come from a noble family?"

I averted my eyes. Hopefully he wasn't reading my thoughts again. I wasn't trying to romanticize him. Okay, maybe I was. It just seemed to me that for as old as Beck was, he must have come from a family with money to be so refined and educated. Of course he'd had many, many years to develop his suave ways.

"Do not think you have offended me. I did come from an

affluent family. They were not as important as they led themselves to believe, though."

"What happened to them? You told me your parents had also died in an accident." Would he share his family secrets with me?

"I think we will save that for a time when we are not having such a lovely dinner and there are not so many ears."

We both sipped. Another question came to mind. "The notes from the book say food has no taste to vampires, is that true?"

He nodded. "That is correct. Food and drink do not metabolize into our bloodstream and we do not have a regular digestive system." Before I could ask how he knew that, he said, "Karlof and I have dissected some of the vampires we killed to see if it could aid us with creating a blood supplement. In place of a stomach, we have an acid-like substance that deteriorates anything we eat or drink that is not blood."

"Some of this is grossly fascinating," I whispered. I looked around but everyone was immersed in their own conversations. "Why blood? And how?"

"Some of our kind believe we are cursed and damned. Created by the devil for punishment of a past life. I believe what the Book of Protection says: there are good and bad forces always at battle. Your religious humans would refer to God and Satan.

"As for the consumption of blood, our body does not produce its own. When we ingest blood, it goes directly into our veins, then our hearts pump it through our bodies. Our hearts pump at a fraction of the speed of a human's. The average is fifteen beats per minute. Blood goes into our tissues making us appear human. We must feed again when the tissues need more blood cells and oxygen."

I watched him with awe. Beck had taken the time, with

Karlof's help, to understand how a vampire body worked. Granted, it made him a more effective killer, but it also helped him survive.

"With the invention of modern technologies," Beck continued, "Karlof and I have made some amazing discoveries. Even fifty years ago, we did not know what we know now."

"Did you see where Rachel asked about animal blood? Could you drink that instead?" I leaned in closer, almost wishing we weren't at the restaurant so he couldn't dodge my questions.

His nose crinkled in revulsion. "It would be like bringing you two plates to choose from. One would contain a filet mignon and the other would have a pile of grasses sprinkled with dirt. For survival, you could eat the grass, but it is not appetizing."

He moved his chair closer to mine. "Vampires are designed to be the top of the food chain. We do not have to kill to feed, so we feed on what tastes best. Animal blood tastes like grass because that is what many of them eat. It does not have the same nutrients as human blood. There is also the added benefit of the thoughts, emotions, and feelings."

I shuddered as I remembered Isaac feeding off my fear. Beck's smile disappeared and his eyes softened as though he knew what I was thinking.

"What's it like? To feed off someone?" I whispered.

Beck's hand reached out and pulled mine until our palms pressed together. He interlocked our fingers and electricity danced across my skin. It traveled up my arm, across my breasts, and made a beeline down my body to more interesting places. I sucked in a breath.

Beck watched me closely. "It can be painful. Or it can be the most erotically satisfying, emotional experience of your life."

Muscles low in my belly clenched at his words. I remembered him kissing me and taking my blood. It had felt so good I hadn't wanted him to stop. What would happen if I let him feed from me when I wasn't weak and scared of dying?

"Some things are better left for non-dinner conversation, my dear," Beck said as he released my trembling hand.

Our waiter appeared, ready to take our order.

Beck ordered a steak, rare, and named some side dishes. Still in a daze, I chose the same. The waiter asked if we wanted more champagne. Beck declined, and once again we were alone.

I sipped from my glass, smoothed non-existent wrinkles in my lap, cleared my throat and took another sip without ever meeting Beck's eyes. I had to get myself under control and stop thinking about his hands on my body or his fangs in my neck.

Fangs. That did it. He had fangs and I couldn't let those anywhere near me.

"So what's it like to eat food with no flavor? I've noticed you only eat when you have to." I was impressed my voice sounded normal.

Beck looked out at the revolving skyline around us and then back to me. "It is just texture in my mouth. No flavor, good nor bad."

"What's the worst part about having lived for so long?" There, I could hold a normal conversation.

Beck looked surprised then he reached across the table to take my hand again. "No one has ever asked me that. The other vampires I associate with do not care to know. The shifters or humans who know my secret always ask what the best part is."

"Well, I'm going to ask that, too, I just thought I'd start with the bad." The electricity seemed to stay concentrated in our hands, which I was grateful for.

"No. Let us start with the good. Watching countries grow

and prosper. Seeing all the amazing inventions and technologies evolve has been amazing. I love to drive cars and watch movies in the theater. Help Karlof work in his lab and make new discoveries. Airplanes are impressive." He looked like a kid talking about Christmas or birthday presents. He stroked my hand and added one more item to his list. "I also love watching the human spirit. Individuals or groups fighting for what they believe in."

I squeezed his hand. "That's why you donate to charities, isn't it?"

"Yes. Nathaniel has quite the understanding of the workings of the stock market and a man can only spend so much money." Beck laughed.

"Okay, the not so good one. What's been the worst part of living so long?"

"The exact opposite of the good. Watching countries at war with themselves and others; watching people kill each other for foolish reasons like anger and greed. Life is short and precious. People should enjoy it for the gift it is, not waste it on hate and pain."

He was so eloquent it almost brought tears to my eyes. "Have you ever been in love?" I asked.

He let go of my hand.

"Beck? Have you ever—"

"Yes," he said. "Perhaps twice?"

"You don't know?" I said.

"Arranged marriages do not take love into account."

"Your marriage was arranged?"

"It was long ago. My bride and I only had a few years together before I was turned. I think I may have fallen in love with her."

I wanted to ask him how he'd become a vampire and when. I also wanted to know what happened to his wife. But

I didn't want to interrupt while he was being so open with me.

"I was in love with a human a few hundred years ago. She was killed by the Sovereignty."

"I'm so sorry," I whispered. I could see the pain in Beck's eyes. "Did she know your secret?" I asked.

"Yes. She wanted to become a vampire but I would not do it. Now I wish I had. She would still be with me."

I couldn't bring myself to ask anything else personal. I was on the verge of tears as it was. I could also tell that Beck wasn't used to sharing so many details about his life.

We sat in silence for a few moments. It was tense, unlike the comfortable silences I usually had with Scott.

Beck was getting ready to say something when the waiter arrived with our meals. He put our plates in front of us and asked if we needed anything else. When Beck shook his head, I think our waiter noticed the tension.

"Just wave me down if you need anything," he said as he retreated.

I had a few bites in silence. "I've never been in love," I volunteered. "Rachel's in and out of love every two minutes. I'm holding out for a love like my parents had. One that makes you weak in the knees and you know that you'd do anything for that person, even die."

Beck considered my words while he ate a small amount. "Let us talk about work."

"Okay." I sipped champagne and wished for the second time this month that alcohol had an effect on me.

"Will you stay as my assistant?"

Wow, a man who asked what I wanted to do instead of telling me. "Yes. I'd like that very much. I won't take classes this fall. I'll look at some new majors and maybe register for winter."

He nodded. "I can keep you busy. The fact you want to finish your degree is admirable. I also think you are courageous to give up your dream of teaching so you do not put any children at risk. The Sovereignty does not care how many innocents are hurt or killed in their quest to destroy the Shadowers and Monarchs."

I thought of the woman Beck had loved centuries before. I nodded, afraid I'd cry if I tried to speak. I was an emotional wreck tonight.

"When you are ready to look at some options, let me know so I may direct you to the heads of department on campus."

That made me pause. Dr. Gabriel Finch, a.k.a. Isaac, was head of the history department. I dropped my fork and leaned my head to Beck. "What's going to happen when Dr. Finch doesn't show for work?"

"That was something else I wanted to talk to you about. Apparently Dr. Finch's resignation arrived at the university yesterday. His letter described an ailing family member in England that he had to get to immediately. He recommended me as his replacement." Beck raised an eyebrow.

"Are you shitting me?" I was a little loud this time because a few people stopped talking and looked at us.

"He is up to something. I just do not know what," Beck said.

I whispered, "Isaac called me a *Silver Shadower*. What does that mean?"

"There is a prophecy among the Shadowers and Monarchs: *'The Silver Shadower shall emerge and call down Zeus. All who stand in his way will perish.'* There is no documentation in the Book of Protection to support it."

"Why would Isaac think I'm the Silver Shadower?"

"It must be your eyes." When Beck looked away from me, I could tell he was done talking about it.

"Okay, so more things to talk about in the comforts of our own home." Then I laughed without any humor. "Except we don't have a home."

"You do," Beck said, meeting my gaze once again. "You and Marie seem to be doing well at Scott's."

"I meant what I said before. I want to be back with you." I quickly made sure he knew what I meant. "Rachel and Marie are safe with you, Nate, and Raven. Plus, Scott can't cook," I tried to joke.

He placed his hands in his lap. "Are you sure that is what you want? Nothing would make me happier, but I want you to be sure."

"I'm sure. Now tell me about the building plans." As much as I wanted to learn more about the Silver Shadower prophecy, I had to let it go here. I was going to make a list of all the things he had avoided so I could make him tell me when we were alone.

A sparkle lit Beck's eyes. "Since I do not have a building to remodel like last time, we get to design it however we want. Luckily the underground section I had added was reinforced with concrete, rebar, and steel. The armory and shooting range are still intact and are being dug out to see what can be salvaged."

"Where are we going to build?" I said.

"I own property just outside the city for the shifters to hunt on. We will build there. Isaac does not know of this location."

I breathed a sigh of relief.

"For security purposes, I want a design similar to the condo. Except I thought we could have two levels this time, not counting the parking garage and basement."

"That would make jumping out the windows easier."

He smiled and continued. "The first floor will be a locked entryway opening to a foyer with elevators and doors. The elevator will go to the lobby and parking garage. If you have the codes, the elevator will go directly to our home on the second floor or to the basement and the armory."

"What about Gerald's room, the pool, and the workout room?" I was getting excited now.

"Gerald and Ian will have separate studio apartments on the first floor. There will also be the pool and hot tub in a glass enclosure, a separate workout room, and a separate sparring room.

"Nathaniel and I have designed the house to accommodate the two of us, Raven, and you three lovely ladies. Even though Nathaniel and Rachel seem to be doing so well, we will make sure everyone has separate bedrooms, bathrooms, and small sitting rooms for as much privacy as we can give. It will be similar to individual apartments within the home area."

"Don't forget the kitchen," I said.

Beck nodded. "Oh yes, that is Nathaniel's baby. He has total design freedom of the kitchen. We are going to have a large family room and then a separate living room for the television and gaming systems Marie has become addicted to."

"Oh, Beck, it sounds amazing."

"As an added security feature, all the closets are going to have removable panels allowing us into the other bedrooms in case of emergencies. The bedrooms will be a horseshoe around the perimeter of the building, with the bathroom and closets in between each one. UV filtering windows will also be installed so we can have the curtains open more often."

I couldn't wait. "How many years will it take?"

"You must remember I have a lot of money. We should move in by Thanksgiving."

I clapped. "You're kidding!"

"No. So how do you like the sound of our new home?"

"It's perfect." I slid out my chair and moved to Beck's side. I leaned down and gave him a kiss on the cheek, wrapping my arms around his shoulders.

I think he felt awkward because he stood. He pulled me back in for a hug.

"Thank you for helping take care of my family, Beck." I moved out of his arms and returned to my chair. After I sat, Beck sat.

Finally he said, "You are welcome. I would do anything you asked of me."

And that was the problem.

Because I was scared of what I might eventually ask for.

Chapter Forty-Two

WHEN BECK DROPPED me off at Scott's, no one met me at the door. Marie slept in her room and Scott's bedroom door was closed.

In my room, the Book of Protection was on my bed along with the notebook containing Rachel's notes.

Kinsley,

You're missing and Marie and I are going crazy. Since we don't have anything to do, we decided to translate the rest of the book until you get home. You will be coming home. Beck promised. (he's in a foul mood, by the way. so is Scott. it's like they're cavemen...I find that interesting)

As always, I'm overly optimistic in the outcome of good over evil. Whenever Marie starts talking about what happened when she was held captive by Isaac, I just give her more to read to me. (hopefully it's all going to make sense)

So, here's the last half of the Book of Protection translated, once again, by Rachel Fredericks and Marie DeVoe.

<u>More on shapeshifters</u>

- shapeshifters have healing saliva (as we know). For this reason, they are incredibly helpful to Shadowers. In the past, shifters built a bond with a Shadower family and protected them until death.

- With the loss of most of the Shadower families, many shifters separated and tried to live amongst society. Some bonded with vampires, either Monarch or Sovereignty. Some embraced their animal side and live in nature, rarely changing to human form.

- The larger shifters can kill a vampire because of their teeth and claws. Since vampires are faster this only happens if a shifter can somehow first immobilize the vampire.

- Shifters are created when a human is infected with a large amount of blood, or other bodily fluid, from a shifter.

The way Marie explained it made it sound like an STD. I asked Nathaniel so I'd know for sure. I mean, we're having sex and kissing....am I going to become a cougar? (He said no)

Nathaniel explained in the event of a shifter attacking a human (like what happened to Raven) the change is intentional. A wound is opened in a major artery, blood and saliva from the shifter is placed directly into the human's bloodstream, then the shifter heals the wound closed. They might bite other locations on the body so it looks like an animal attack.

Beck and the cougars have chosen to work together. Cougars are given sanctuary and protection while they are in his sector. (Nate told me that Beck's sector is all of Washington)

KINSLEY!! You're back and you're okay. Well, you look like death warmed over, but you're okay. I'm going to make you take notes on all your exploits; maybe we could write a book. We'd have to make it fiction because no one would believe any of this stuff is real! I love you and I'm glad you're safe!

<u>When a Vampire Feeds</u>

(Marie didn't explain the whole 'blood has flavor' thing very well before. Hopefully this is right...)

• Vampires have to have blood to survive, but they get an extra 'high' from the emotion the victim (food source? blood bank?) is feeling. It's been theorized the endorphins in the blood have taste which means emotions essentially have their own flavor.

- A vampire can render their victim unconscious when they first start feeding. If they take enough in the first swallow, the victim passes out from lack of blood to their brain, so the victim doesn't have a strong recollection of what happened.

- Since Sovereignty almost always kill their victims or turn them, they don't make the victim pass out because they want to feed on the fear or arousal.

Changing a Human

- The human is drained of almost all their blood. Just before their heart stops beating, they ingest a lot (Marie's scientific measurement) of vampire blood. The vampire blood infects the human's system, kind of like shifter blood. The human body either accepts and regenerates the vampire blood or rejects the blood and the human dies.

Nathaniel and Marie both said a vampire cannot be turned into a shifter and a shifter cannot be turned into a vampire. I asked if anyone had ever tried and they looked at me like I was crazy. I just wanted to know!

Vampire Powers and Myths

- Few vampire powers have been documented. Most don't want to give away their secrets and the Monarchs didn't think it would be smart to have it on paper.
- The Monarchs can move, or communicate, within each other's minds. If they band together, two or more can control the actions of another. (Nathaniel said you witnessed this when Beck attacked Scott and tried to attack you. I didn't know about this. Why didn't I know about this? You have to tell me EVERYTHING that happens to you when it involves Scott and Beck.)

Witnessed or experienced vampire powers:

- Flying
- Disappearing and reappearing
- The silent bubble thing Isaac can do
- Memory erasing
- Control of human actions
- Telekinesis
- Causing damage to someone without touching them (like Isaac choking Scott)

Other Stuff

- The older a vampire is, the stronger it is. (Beck said Isaac/Finch is older than him but Beck won't tell us how old he is). Beck also said there's a member of the Monarchs that is over 2,000 years old. He's the oldest known vampire.

- Vampires can have sex, but they can't get anyone pregnant or get pregnant (this was my personal question. I wanted you to know for future reference, you know, just in case)

- Myths - Vampires don't have to sleep in coffins or dirt. They can be awake any time during the day or night and only need a few hours of rest each day, sometimes going for days without sleep. As we know, they can tolerate small amounts of sunlight, but it could eventually kill them. Holy items don't have any effect. The thing about garlic being a deterrent is totally untrue. Vampires don't need permission to enter a dwelling.

(Well, everything we learned on 'Lost Boys' from the Frog Brothers is pointless...I'm very sad about this)

<u>Shadower Powers - not so much</u>

- Marie said something before about Shadowers having powers but she didn't explain it. That's because for the last three hundred years, no Shadowers have exhibited any powers beyond prolonged life, crazy strength, accelerated healing, and being able to sense supernatural beings. (Beck says the electricity thing you feel is your 'sense'.)

- Apparently the weakened bloodline caused

Shadower powers to become basically nonexistent. (bummer - I was hoping you really were going to be like a superhero...we could rob banks or some- thing! kidding, I promise!)

We finally made it to the end of the book, all 400 pages of it. Make sure you look at the pictures I told you about last time. Marie said she didn't translate it word for word, obviously, but now you have all the essential details. I think it was help- ful, but with the way Marie explains things, we might have been better off just getting information from our new family members.

P.S - you have to tell me how your dates went.

Rachel

I CLOSED the notebook and groaned. Rachel was not going to give up about the dates. Dates I hadn't even been on.

I'd never say it out loud, but Scott and Beck combined would be the perfect man. Beck was kind, caring, and sensitive. Scott was human. Both were to-die-for gorgeous.

Having to choose between the two of them seemed impossi- ble. I knew Scott was interested in me sexually. He'd come right out and said it. Beck seemed to be. He threw out little signals I'd take as being hit on if he were human.

I figured my best choice was to continue living vicariously through Rachel until I met a normal man and could start a rela- tionship. But then what if the 'normal man' learned what I was and didn't want me? Or what if Isaac showed up one day and killed whoever I had chosen for a boyfriend just because he was my boyfriend?

This was like the dilemma I had about being a teacher. Would I have to give up the chance at ever having a relationship too? Getting married and having kids?

I threw myself on my bed and closed my eyes. I was freaking out over nothing. I didn't need to have my whole life planned right now.

But what if I met the man of my dreams at a coffee shop tomorrow? I could fall madly in love after three dates and want to bring him home.

"Hi, I'm Kinsley. I live with a bodyguard and a crazy aunt. Want to come home with me?" That wasn't going to work. And I couldn't even imagine Scott's reaction if I showed up with a guy.

Or what if it was after Thanksgiving and I brought someone to our newly remodeled house? "I live with three other women and two men." I suppose that part wasn't really abnormal, we were roommates.

Of course when my date asked where the key coded elevator went I wouldn't be able to say, "Our shooting range and armory. We'll save that for date six."

I was freaking out again.

A shower. I could take a shower and relax. Then maybe I'd fall asleep. I gathered up my pajamas and tiptoed across the hall to the bathroom. Scott's light was off. Marie was talking in her sleep.

I showered, brushed my teeth, then decided I couldn't go to bed with wet hair. So I pulled out the hairdryer and started to dry my hair.

The bathroom door flew open and I was thankful I had put on my shorts and tank top before drying my hair instead of doing it naked like usual. Because all six feet and two hundred plus pounds of Scott Masters stood in the bathroom doorway.

He blinked rapidly at the bathroom lights and raised an arm to shield his eyes. "What in the hell are you doing?" he yelled. "It's after midnight and some of us have to work in the morning."

I stood there like a moron with the hair dryer still on, staring at his body. All he wore were a pair of bright red boxer briefs.

Scott ripped the hair dryer from my hands and shut it off. "Again, what in the hell are you doing?"

"Blow drying my hair," I said dumbly.

"I see that. The question is why you're doing it at almost one in the morning."

That's when my brain started to function. I noticed the scars on Scott's shoulder and side. Hadn't noticed those when I was in bed with him. Maybe because I'd been preoccupied?

"What happened?" I asked as I stepped closer.

"Vampires happened. Now go to bed."

I stared at him. "What flew up your ass?"

"You got home pretty late," Scott said.

We stood toe to toe in the bathroom and I wasn't ready to back down yet. "So?"

"So, I don't know. I hate it when I don't know where you are," he said. "I guess I should just be glad you came home."

I shoved past him and marched back to my room. "You two are starting to piss me off. I haven't slept with either one of you and I'm not going to!" I slammed the door and heard Scott curse down the hallway to his room, where he slammed the door too.

This was ridiculous. How would Scott behave when I was living with Beck again? And this time, I was actually going to live with him. In the same house. Yeah, there would be other people there, but I would be living with Beck.

What if I wanted to bring someone home? Oh, not this again! I climbed in bed and closed my eyes. All I could picture was some nice man standing at the door next to me. Then Beck, Scott, and Nate tearing him to shreds verbally and then literally.

Great. Just great.

Chapter Forty-Three

THE WEEK WENT by quicker than I expected. Probably because I avoided Scott and Beck, spending every spare moment working out or practicing with the knives and bows. Oliver would be tired of me soon.

The men were all worried Isaac would swoop out of the sky and kidnap me again. I was more worried about Beck and Marie. Isaac said he wanted Beck dead and Marie back. I was just an added snack. I also worried about Rachel's safety because Isaac knew he could hurt me by hurting her.

I insisted Nate always be with Rachel and Raven always be with Marie. In order to achieve that, I'd had to agree to always be with someone too. Mostly Oliver. But when I wasn't with him, Ian followed me around. He never really talked to me, but he was always in the background.

The morning classes started at UW, I sat on the steps of the history department building watching freshmen try to find their classes. Some walked with their parents, some were with friends, and some wandered alone, looking at their campus maps.

I hadn't seen Ian so I guessed Beck had him doing something more important than following me. Maybe the fact I could take care of myself was finally getting through Beck's thick head. I could dream.

For three hours I directed lost students to the correct buildings.

I was nearly done with lunch when I received a text from Beck asking me to meet with his secretary at the history department.

"Kinsley," Meredith beamed at me when I came through the door. "I set up a desk for you. This way you're within earshot of Dr. Alexander and myself." She was so happy to be the secretary to the new Head of the History Department she was glowing. "Everything you should need is on your desk. Holler if you need me."

"Thanks, Meredith." I looked at the stack of papers with student contact information on my new desk. I texted Beck and told him it would be easier for me to do everything at the office instead of trying to haul it back to Scott's.

I spent two hours checking class lists, drops and adds, making phone calls to wait-listed students, and organizing my little workspace. Meredith checked on me a few times to see if I needed anything.

I was getting ready to leave when my cell rang. It was Scott. I was surprised by his call after avoiding him all week.

"Alexander had me put a surveillance team on the building where Isaac kept you," he said.

"Okay."

"Sometime early this morning, it caught fire and burned to the ground. The police and fire department have been here since three this morning. It's being ruled an arson." He paused to speak to someone else. Then he asked me, "Has anything strange happened this morning? Any phone calls or weird feelings?"

"No. Why?"

"I don't know. I just have a bad feeling because this fire happened out of nowhere. Isaac's been hiding and now his torture castle is history. I don't think he ever left town. I think he's been here the whole time and now he's planning to leave. It's like he's cleaning up."

"He can leave. That would be fine," I said.

"I don't want him taking any guests with him. Like you."

"He doesn't want me. He wants Marie."

"That's your opinion," Scott said.

"I'll call everyone. Let them know to be cautious."

"You need to be cautious too. Where are you?"

"On campus. I'm completely safe."

"Where's Ian?"

"Around," I hedged. If I told Scott I hadn't seen Ian all morning, he'd probably show up guns blazing.

Scott snarled, "Damn it. Your safety is important. Is that little mutt with you or not?"

"Don't call Ian a mutt, you Neanderthal!" This is why I'd avoided him. Since the night I had dinner with Beck, we had argued about every little thing.

Scott mumbled something then spoke clearly, "Why do you have to make everything so damn difficult?"

"I'm not going to argue with you," I said. "Goodbye." I hung up.

Meredith looked at me. I smiled and she went back to working on her computer.

I thought about who to call first. I should call Ian and find out where he was. But I could do that after I checked on Rachel and Marie.

I called Rachel to meet me at the old condo site. I wanted to see how clean-up was going and I wasn't ready to go back to Scott's.

She didn't answer so I left a message.

As I walked to the car, I made sure to be aware of my surroundings. I got in the little Mercedes coupe Beck insisted I drive and went to the condo site. Ian's familiar bike never appeared in my rear view mirror.

The site was partially cleaned up. The basement had been dug out and a pile of debris sat next to a backhoe.

I parked carefully away from the mud puddles and large equipment. That's when I realized there wasn't another car. I went to call Rachel to see where she was when a movement from the construction site caught my eye. Ian stood where the front door would be.

I set my phone down and got out of the car to go to him. He looked strange. As I moved closer, I realized Ian's feet weren't touching the ground. His head hung low, his chin nearly touching his chest, and his sunglasses were missing.

The pieces of rebar formed a triangle poking out of his chest. He also had blood on his neck. I began to run toward him when a muffled scream stopped me.

Laughter made my skin tingle.

I turned. Mya stood on the roof of the building directly across the street. She held a tied and gagged Rachel next to her. I looked around wildly but didn't see anyone else.

"So glad you could make it. I wish you hadn't been so far away, though. My boys got bored and started playing with your dog." Mya laughed again.

"Let Rachel go. I'm here now."

"Oh, I don't think so. You see, I want to kill you. I want to kill you badly, but Isaac won't let me. So I get Rachel in place of you. I have some wonderful things planned. I think I might make her a vampire and then let her feed on you. Wouldn't that be ironic?"

Two men dressed in black appeared on the roof next to

Mya and Rachel. One stepped off the three-story building and half-floated, half-fell to the ground, landing in a crouch.

He showed me his fangs. "We were told not to kill you or drain too much blood. This should be fun." He sprang at me. All my training with Raven and Oliver took over.

The vampire went for me like he'd go for a regular human, head on. I planted my feet and drove my elbow into his stomach when he got close. Since I caught him off guard, he fell backward. I took advantage of his spread eagle state and kicked him as hard as I could in the groin.

Vampire or not, it's still the most sensitive location on a guy's body.

He howled in pain and jumped up to charge me. I leaned down and caught him with my shoulder, throwing him over my head and into the mud.

Since I didn't have a weapon, I slowly led him toward the work area. They'd killed Ian with rebar. I could use the same tool.

This vampire had to be young. He had the tattoos and clothes of a gang banger. He also didn't really understand his own speed and strength.

"Did anyone tell you I'm a Shadower?" I asked to taunt and distract him.

"Is shadow the new name for whore?" He laughed at his own joke.

Never putting my back to him, I maneuvered us toward a pile of lumber. "No, Shadower, you idiot. I'm faster and stronger than you."

"Look, bitch, did you see my fangs? I'm a fucking vampire. Ain't nobody faster or stronger than a fucking vampire." He lunged at me again and I swept his legs out from under him then dove for a two-by-four that had fallen off the pile.

I picked it up and swung it in front of me with more rage and strength than finesse. It had the intended effect.

I inched the vampire closer to a piece of protruding rebar. When he was about three feet away I swung my two-by-four with all my strength and hit him in the chest. The impact made him fly backward and the piece of rebar went through his throat. He was pinned to the concrete like an insect on a board.

I turned sideways and gripped the wood like a baseball bat. "Did you know I played softball in high school?" I swung for all I was worth and hit him in the ear. His head flew off and landed at Ian's feet.

Mya screamed her anger and the other vampire jumped from the top of the building. I didn't know what I was going to do this time since I was pretty sure there was no way this vamp was going to let me get him close to the rebar.

I needed to carry a knife on me at all times. A big one, one of dad's daggers. Maybe a gun. Even better? Both. I cursed myself for leaving my cell phone in the car. I couldn't even call anyone.

Call. I could call Beck with my mind.

Trying to concentrate while evading a vampire was much harder than I anticipated. I didn't run, because I knew he'd just jump on me. I kept my two-by-four up and stayed by the bodies of Ian and the dead vampire.

"*Beck.*" I tried to conjure his scent and the feel of his lips. "*Beck, damn it, I need you! Answer me!*"

"*Kinsley? What's wrong?*"

I was so relieved to hear his voice.

"*Call Scott, Oliver, Raven, Nate, and anyone else you can find. Hide Marie and come to the building site. Mya's alive and she has Rachel.*" I severed our mental connection because I couldn't concentrate on talking to Beck and watching the vampire at the same time.

This one had the same tattoos and demeanor as the first, but he took his time, stalking me. He'd been a vampire for longer than his buddy. The seconds ticked by and then he got antsy. He jumped at me and I swung my board before he landed. It connected with the side of his body and he fell back.

But he'd splintered my weapon and all I had left was about eighteen inches of jagged wood in my hand. It would make a great spike if I could get him to be still.

He moved more quickly from the ground than I expected, lashing out to grab my ankle. He couldn't throw me very far while on his back but it was far enough.

I landed in the mud and my head bounced off a rock. I shook my head to clear it and he was on me. He straddled my hips and showed his fangs. I rammed the flat of my hand into his nose and rolled away when he fell off me grunting in pain.

I heard a popping noise and electricity flowed down my arm and seemed to leak from my fingertips. Beck appeared next to me from out of nowhere.

He tried to grab me and I knew his intent.

"You are not taking me out of here without Rachel," I said. Then I screamed, "Look out!" because the vampire came at him from behind.

Beck turned and shot his arm out. He grabbed the puny little vamp by the throat and squeezed.

I turned my head and heard the sticky bursting sound of a beheaded vampire.

Mya screeched and jumped off the roof. In her haste, she left Rachel there. Mya didn't touch the ground as she flew at Beck.

I could hear them fight as I ran toward the building.

"Kinsley, behind you," Beck yelled just as Mya landed on my back.

I heard a vehicle and hoped to hell it was a black Hummer.

Mya wrenched my left arm behind me until my shoulder popped and I screamed in pain. She threw me to the ground, slamming her foot into the same arm, but down below my elbow. Beck pulled her away from me.

I didn't know if my arm was broken, if my shoulder was dislocated, or both. I just knew it hurt like hell.

Squealing tires were accented by gunshots. I looked up to see Scott hanging out the passenger side of the Hummer shooting at Beck and Mya. He was a good shot but even the best can miss when they're in a moving vehicle holding on with one hand.

I watched the back door open and Nate jumped out. In human form, he ran to the building, jumping and climbing the fire escape. I breathed a sigh of relief when he got to Rachel and pulled her back from the edge.

Oliver stopped the Hummer and now both men were shooting at Mya and Beck.

I watched a silver bullet rip through Mya's shoulder and embed itself in Beck's arm. She screamed and moved away from Beck, her skin smoking.

Beck dropped to his knees. "You damn humans and your guns!"

I ran to the lumber pile on my way to Beck and picked up another two-by-four. My left arm was completely useless and hung limply at my side.

Scott and Oliver continued to pepper Mya with silver bullets until I got closer.

The shooting stopped and I turned my head to see them running toward us. I swung the board and hit Mya in the head. Her limp body flopped to the ground. One-armed, I couldn't decapitate her like I had the other vampire.

As the board slipped from my fingers, I turned to Beck. "Are you okay?"

"I am now," Beck wrapped his right arm around me because his left was as useless as mine.

Thunder shook the sky and clouds rolled in like the night I'd met Beck. "Is it Isaac?"

Before Beck answered, Scott and Oliver were by us.

"Which one of you dumb shits shot me?" Beck said.

"I'm pretty sure it was me." Scott didn't sound the least bit sorry.

Mya moved on the ground.

"Kill her!" I yelled. "She's been nothing but trouble since I first laid eyes on her."

Oliver had pulled the nine inch sliver dagger from a sheath by his boot when the first bolt of lightning struck.

Isaac floated down and landed on the ground about fifty feet from us.

"Where's Marie?" I asked the men next to me.

"We left her with Raven," Scott whispered.

"Marie was never good at doing what she was told," Isaac said.

Chapter Forty-Four

"MARIE'S SAFE," Scott assured me.

I took the silver knife from Oliver's hand and used his and Scott's bodies as a shield. I slit open the wrist of my injured arm and offered it to Beck.

"What are you doing?" he demanded.

"Drink. I want you to kill that son of a bitch."

Beck took my wrist and pulled it to his mouth. Pain crashed through my entire left side but I ignored it.

I heard Isaac yell, "I can smell your blood, Shadower."

We didn't have much time until he figured out what I was doing. My wrist tingled from Beck's mouth.

Rain began to fall and another strike of lightning hit the ground. This one closer to Mya. Was Isaac trying to hit her with lightning?

Beck pulled his lips from my wrist and licked the wound closed. Then he launched himself into the air over both Oliver and Scott. Isaac jumped and they collided. Beck was stronger and they flew with his momentum until they slammed into the building Rachel and Nate had climbed down from.

I still held the silver dagger in my right hand and I went for Mya. Scott and Oliver were behind me as I ran for her. She crawled through the mud but managed to roll to her back, grabbing my injured arm as I swung the knife.

Because of the way she held me, I carved her shoulder instead of her neck. She screamed, her claws digging into my skin. Oliver grabbed me while Scott tackled Mya.

"No," I said, trying to get free. "She'll hurt you!"

Mya's arm hung from her body, almost completely severed at the shoulder. The wounds from the silver bullets weren't healing. She was bleeding and getting weaker by the moment, but she was still stronger than Scott.

Just when she would have tried to bite him, I wished more lightning would strike. It did. A bolt of lightning hit Mya. Scott flew backward and fell into Oliver and me.

Mya lay on the ground unmoving. Her arm now severed from her body.

"You did that, Kinsley," Beck said in my head.

"What?" I asked out loud.

"You are the Silver Shadower."

"But it's just a legend."

"What if it is not?"

"Marie!" Isaac yelled. "MARIE!"

"You'll never have her!" I screamed at him.

The lightning shot through the sky and this time hit Isaac. He flew thirty feet and landed on the ground by the Hummer.

"I loved you! You know I always loved you! I love you still!" He writhed on the ground holding his arm out toward the vehicle.

Did dying vampires ramble? Apparently.

There was movement from the bed of the Hummer. I looked to the building and saw Nate and Rachel hiding at the corner. What was moving at the Hummer? More vampires?

The world stood still as I watched Marie emerge from the back. "Nooo!" I screamed and ran for her.

Beck flew to me, lifting me off the ground. Scott and Oliver raced toward Marie. Oliver threw her over his shoulder and headed toward the building where Rachel and Nate were.

Isaac stood and flew to their running bodies. He plucked Marie from Oliver's arms and held her tightly in one arm then attacked Oliver. Isaac swung, hitting Oliver in the head. Oliver flew back at least fifteen feet and skidded through the mud and dirt. He didn't move.

"Let her go!" I screamed.

Marie looked kind of dazed but seemed unharmed as she stood in Isaac's arms. Scott moved toward them.

"I'm going to enjoy killing you," he said to Isaac.

"You can try." Isaac bit Marie's neck.

"Let go," I screamed at Beck. I twisted my body and clawed at his hands. As soon as his arms loosened, I pulled free and ran toward Marie.

Isaac lifted his arm in the air. I could almost see the invisible line that picked Scott's body five feet off the ground. I stopped, unsure of what to do.

Isaac lifted his mouth from Marie's neck and looked at me. "Which way do you want me to throw your human, Shadower? Toward the construction? Toward you? You won't be able to catch him with one of your arms not working."

Scott swayed above the ground and with a flick of Isaac's wrist, came hurtling at me. His body slammed into mine and we both tumbled to the ground. Beck tried to stop us but was only able to get an arm around me. Scott's body hit the ground and his leg snapped. His head bounced and he was knocked out.

A cougar with a green tuft of hair ran to Nate and Rachel.

I watched Nate jump and shift. Nate hit Isaac in the back with his paws but Isaac hardly moved. He swung his arm. Nate flew back and smashed into a dumpster.

"Enough!" Isaac yelled. "This isn't over." He flew into the air and disappeared with Marie.

"No, no, no, no!" I screamed as I hit Beck, trying to get him to put me down.

"She is gone. I am so sorry."

I screamed and cried as Beck carried me to the Hummer. How could this have happened? What was Marie doing here? She was supposed to be safe.

"Mya's gone!" Rachel yelled.

We looked behind us. All that remained of Mya was her severed arm.

Beck held me. Pain tore through my body, consuming my soul. Isaac and Mya had Marie.

I screamed, "What happened? Why was she here?"

"We will deal with that later. We need to take care of our wounded."

I struggled against Beck's hold. "No! We have to go. We have to find her. We have to do something!" I continued to pummel Beck's chest with my good arm.

"Kinsley, stop fighting me. We will get her back."

After one last scream at the empty sky I rested my head on Beck's shoulder and sobbed.

"You need to go to the doctor," he said into my hair.

I lifted my head and looked at our scattered people. "We all need to go to the doctor. Call Karlof."

"It will be faster if we put everyone in the Hummer and car then send a cleanup crew."

Rachel helped Nate up and they walked toward us.

"Is he okay?" Beck asked.

"Yes," Rachel said. "Just a little shaken up. I can't say the same about those two." Rachel walked to Oliver while Nate padded over to Scott.

"They're alive, right?" I asked.

"Oliver has a pulse but his head is bleeding badly," Rachel said.

"Scott—" I slid from Beck's arms.

Scott's leg was folded under him and I could see a gash above his right eye. As I got closer he started to stir.

"Don't move!" I yelled and ran to him, dropping to my knees. Nate moved away.

Scott's eyes were glassy. I cradled his face in my right hand. "I wish I could give you some of my healing powers," I whispered.

"Are you okay?" Again, the white knight, worried about me while he was laying broken on the ground.

A few tears slipped out. "Isaac took Marie."

"I'm sorry. I should have known she was back there." He winced when he tried to sit up.

I used my good arm to keep him down. "No one ever knows what Marie does or why she does it. I don't care how she got there, I care about how to get her back." I kissed Scott's forehead, next to the gash. "Does anything hurt besides your leg and head?"

"Everything in between," he closed his eyes.

"Beck," I yelled. "I don't want to move these two without doctors. Get Karlof up here!"

I sat with Scott and watched as three different cargo vans arrived. The first van drove toward the construction site. People got out and started getting bodies. Ian was separated from the vamps and wrapped reverently in a body bag. The vampires' headless bodies were tossed in the back of the van. Their heads were gathered into a big bag and that was also tossed in.

Beck directed the second van to Oliver and the third to where I was with Scott. When the back doors opened, I could see they were equipped like ambulances.

Someone tried to look at my arm but I told them Scott was first.

I went to Beck as the two different teams loaded up Scott and Oliver. "Thank you."

"I wish I could do more," he said.

We watched the organized chaos in silence. Nate went to the car, shifted back to human, and put on clothes from the trunk. Raven also had a change of clothes back there. I wondered how many shifters kept clothes in which of Beck's vehicles.

Raven slowly walked to me, head down, tears on her face. "I'm so sorry."

"Just tell me what happened," I said.

"Marie and I were at Scott's. When Beck called to say what was going on, Scott and Oliver jumped into action. The Hummer was in the driveway and they were loading it with gear. I was watching Marie." Raven wiped at her eyes. "She told me she had to go to the bathroom. I helped the guys finish loading the weapons and they tore out of the driveway. I went back in the house and waited a few minutes. When Marie didn't come back downstairs, I searched every room. She was gone." Raven closed her eyes.

If I was going to be mad at anyone, I had to be mad at Marie. She'd come here on purpose. Why? Did she think she'd be able to help?

I knew I had to stay strong or I wasn't going to be any help to Marie. I had to get my team up and moving so we could start looking for her.

"We will find her and get her back," Beck said.

"I know. I just can't stand the thought of her being with him for even a minute."

Raven looked at the vans, surveying the site. "I have to call Gerald and tell him Ian is dead."

"Were they close?" I asked.

She nodded. "They were brothers. Some of the last born wolves."

"Do you want to go to Screamers or the hospital facility?" Beck asked me as Raven walked away with her phone to her ear.

"Both," I said. "I need to know if Scott and Oliver are going to be okay. I want to devise a plan to save Marie."

"That is what I thought," Beck said. "First, you are going to be checked out to make sure everything is healing correctly."

"Then?"

"Then we try to figure out how to save your crazy aunt."

Chapter Forty-Five

AS BECK and I walked to the car, we both cradled our injured left arms. Mine moved in small increments but it throbbed. Beck stopped walking and hissed in pain.

"What's wrong?"

"I think your blood is healing me," he said.

I stood in front of him and watched as blood began to seep from the bullet wound in his shoulder. Muscles flexed as the silver bullet was pushed out of the hole and fell to the ground. The wound closed itself. The skin remained light pink in color, contrasting with the darkness of Beck's skin.

"My blood did that?" I reached up and gently ran my fingers over the now healed wound.

"This is what Shadowers do for their Monarchs. If I had taken more blood from you, it would have healed sooner. The more of your blood I have, the stronger I'll be."

"Beckford," Karlof's nasally voice said from behind us. I tensed, still uncomfortable around the old vampire.

"Yes, Karlof?"

"Nathaniel said you were shot. I need to look at your silver wound. If we don't get it removed, you could have severe damage..." Karlof trailed off as he looked at Beck's shoulder. "The blood of the Shadower?" he asked.

"She has a name, Karlof. Use it. And yes, Kinsley's blood did this."

The doctor turned his beady rat eyes on me. He eyed me like I was a piece of meat he was starving for. That was one reason I didn't like him. Karlof didn't think of me as a person. He considered me a magical blood source. Since the moment I'd met him, that's all he'd wanted from me.

Karlof turned back to Beck. "Think of all we could do, accomplish, if she would share her blood with us. We could take a few pints a day for consumption, storing up what we don't need, while I work on examining it, comparing it to human blood." At any moment, I expected him to rub his hands together like the evil villain from a movie. "I've never been able to study the blood of a Shadower with modern technology." I swear he licked his lips.

I stared at Dr. Frankenstein then looked at Beck. If he was even considering this ludicrous plan, I was going to shoot him with silver myself. Right after I severed Karlof's head.

Beck moved so close to Karlof there was hardly any space between them. Beck towered over the small man who now had the look of a deer in the headlights. "You will never suggest such a thing ever again. Do I make myself completely clear? Kinsley's blood is only to be given of her free will and never to be stored for consumption. Her blood will never be given to anyone other than a Monarch."

As Karlof trembled in front of Beck, I cleared my throat. "Actually, Beck, if I ever choose to share my blood again, you are the only vampire who will ever have it."

I said to Karlof, "You stay away from me." And walked to the car. I didn't know who was going to fix my shoulder at the hospital facility. I didn't care as long as it wasn't that creepy little vampire man.

Karlof slinked to the van in charge of the clean up as Beck got in the car with me.

He shut the door then gripped the steering wheel. "I am truly sorry about Karlof. He should have known better than to insinuate you were to be used like that."

The vans with Scott and Oliver pulled away. Nate followed them in the Hummer with Rachel and Raven.

"I don't want him anywhere near me. I mean it. Do you have another doctor who can look at my shoulder and arm when we get there?" I shivered.

"There are other doctors at the facility whom I trust. I will ensure you are taken care of," Beck said.

I wanted Karlof on his way back to England. But there were other things to worry about, as always.

Beck called Meredith as we pulled behind the other vehicles. I listened while he arranged to have a graduate student teach his classes. It was still only the first day of school. My life had been flipped upside down yet again.

As we drove, I tried to sort through my thoughts and keep calm. I wasn't doing a very good job.

The totally crappy thing about life is that it goes on. Whether you want it to or not, the world doesn't stop for your problems. Death, broken bones, the kidnapping of your aunt by evil vampires. The minutes still tick by and time still passes.

"You know I will do everything in my power to find Marie." Beck took one hand off the steering wheel to squeeze my leg. "Nathaniel and I have word out to our contacts that Gabriel Finch is not who he claimed to be and that he cannot be trusted."

I didn't say anything.

"He was a member of the Monarchs, or at least posing as a

Monarch. Now I am unsure who I can trust. Especially after they tried to control me to get your blood."

That night was not one I wanted to think about because it had made me question Beck's loyalty.

His hands clenched on the steering wheel. "Please, say something."

"We have to find Marie. That's all I care about."

We rode the rest of the way in silence.

Once at the hospital facility, Beck introduced me to a new vampire. Her name was Dr. Elizabeth Chavez. She was just a bit taller than me and had long dark hair and beautiful dark brown eyes.

"Miss Preston. I worked on you with Dr. Karlof the night of the SAM gala. I'm sure you don't remember me." She smiled, shaking my hand.

"Please call me Kinsley." I immediately liked her better than Karlof.

Beth, as she wouldn't let me call her Dr. Chavez, probed my forearm and shoulder. Quick x-rays showed my forearm had been snapped but was already healing. Miraculously, it was healing in place and wouldn't need to be re-broken.

My dislocated shoulder, however, was going to need to be put back.

"There's no point in giving you pain meds to do this. It will only take seconds to pop back in and you metabolize the drugs so quickly," Beth said.

I nodded and closed my eyes. I was tired of getting broken.

Beck braced my body from behind. Raven held my good hand while Nate and Rachel watched. I couldn't keep from screaming when Beth pushed on my shoulder with one hand and pulled my arm toward her with the other.

"Damn that hurt." I slumped my head on Raven's shoulder.

"You should ice that," Beth said with an apologetic smile.

"How are Scott and Oliver?" I asked.

"I've sedated Scott and his broken leg is being set. Oliver," she paused and looked over my shoulder at Beck.

"Oliver is not doing as well," Beck finished for her.

Beth smiled sadly. "We're going to get him hooked up to the monitors. First thing tomorrow we'll do some brain scans. My preliminary findings are that he has a concussion and possible swelling in his brain."

Karlof entered the room and narrowed his eyes at us.

"I'd like to go to Scott's room, please," I said to Beck. He had Nate and Rachel escort me.

Scott's leg was already in a cast and he slept peacefully. I stood by his bed and watched his chest rise and fall.

I don't know how long I stood there. Rachel was suddenly next to me and walked me backward to the other bed in the room. She pulled me down to sit beside her and she put her arms around me.

I cried.

I cried for Scott and Oliver. I cried for Marie. I cried for me. I cried until my throat hurt and my eyes were almost swollen shut.

I woke to the beeping of a heart monitor and the first rays of dawn peeking through the window shades. I was in Scott's hospital room sleeping on the other bed. Nate was asleep in the chair. Rachel was gone.

"Hey, sweet thing," Scott's voice was quiet.

Nate stirred.

I slid off the bed and went to Scott. "I'd ask how you're feeling but that seems like a really dumb question." I smiled and took his hand.

"Beth says I've got a couple cracked ribs to go with my broken leg. No deep breaths or laughing for me."

"Been there, done that. I don't envy you the long human healing process."

"I hate that you felt pain like this the night of that stupid party." He stroked his thumb over the top of my hand.

"I heal so fast that it's nothing compared to what you're going through."

"What's the word on Oliver?" Scott asked.

Beth poked her head in. "I can answer that." She smiled at Scott and checked all his vitals. Nate slipped out of the room, murmuring he'd be back to get me in a bit.

"Oliver has swelling of the brain. He is currently in a coma but I'm not too worried yet. The brain is amazing and this is its way of healing. However, the situation could quickly turn negative because the brain is so delicate. Oliver is getting the best care and we will do everything we can to pull him through. He also has a broken arm, which we've set." Beth turned to me. "Kinsley, how are you feeling?"

I rotated my shoulder. "Fine, actually."

"Mr. Masters, you should be able to go home tomorrow. You're in excellent physical shape and I know having to sit in this bed will drive you crazy."

"Wow, you just met him and you already know him so well," I said.

"Ha ha, ladies." Scott turned a hundred watt smile at the beautiful Dr. Chavez. "Beth, please call me Scott." Interesting. He knew she was a vampire, right?

"Do you want some books or magazines?" I asked.

"Yeah, just grab a couple books from my house."

"Okay, then. I'm going to make my rounds." Beth smiled at Scott. "Push your call button if you need anything." She nodded to me, touched Scott's good leg, and left.

Scott's eyes closed again and I snuck out of the room to find

Nate. I needed something to do. That, and I needed a shower and a change of clothes. Considering I didn't remember falling asleep in Scott's room last night, I had obviously been exhausted.

I wished for a moment I could fall back into a deep sleep and ignore what was happening in my life.

Chapter Forty-Six

WEDNESDAY. Another day since Marie had been taken. There'd been no sighting of the three of them. It was as though Isaac and Mya had dropped off the face of the earth with my aunt.

Honestly, I didn't really remember much of Tuesday. After we left the hospital, Nate took me to Scott's to get his books. Raven, Rachel, and I went grocery shopping for easy-to-make food. We cleaned Scott's house and rearranged a few things to make it easier for him to move around.

I was never alone because Raven, Nate, and Rachel wouldn't let me out of their sight. I suppose that was a good thing because I wanted to get in a car or on a plane and find Marie. The problem was I didn't know where to begin.

The next thing I knew, the sun had set and it was time to try and get some sleep, but I wouldn't be so lucky.

Every time I closed my eyes I saw the scars on Marie's legs or the blonde girl who had been raped and killed. The images kept running through my head.

Isaac had flown away with Marie. They had disappeared. Beck and Nate assured me they had people looking for them. Doing nothing made me feel useless.

Even though he hadn't done it, I felt like Beck had patted me on the head and told me not to worry. The big strong men would take care of everything. I was capable of finding Marie. I just needed a direction and a plan.

In the morning Raven took me to Screamers. We needed to go to the hospital to get Scott, but I wanted to check in with Beck first to see if he had any news.

When I walked in the office, Beck was hanging a world map on the wall. He started marking locations with a green pen and didn't bother with formalities. "These are all the places I know Isaac has lived or been."

I watched for ten minutes as Beck put X's on one hundred forty-two different cities spread out over fifteen countries.

Then he got a red pen and started circling some of the X's. "These are locations where I have people I trust. They are already on the lookout."

"Do they know what he looks like now?"

"I scanned and emailed his university photo and one of Marie's old photos."

"What did you vampires and shifters do before technology?" I asked.

"I do not remember," Beck said with a small smile.

"I'm taking Scott home today," I said.

He nodded. "You will want to stay with him."

"Yeah. Is that okay with you?" I said carefully.

"Anything you want is fine with me," Beck said. I think he meant it. Then he added, "I have hired four crews to work in ten hour shifts around the clock, seven days a week on our new home site. I tripled their regular wages and told them I would give them an extra bonus if they could get the building finished before October's end."

"Wow."

"I want us all home and in one place," Beck said.

"How's Gerald?"

"Upset over the loss of his brother. I gave him as much time as he needed to go be with his family. Wolves mourn differently than other shifters. He might not be back until Christmas."

We stared at each other for a moment.

"We need to develop battle plans when we work with humans," I said. "We should have put them somewhere safe with weapons while we were in the thick of things."

"I do not like you in the thick of things," Beck said.

"I know that, but let's look at the facts. Rachel could have been killed. Luckily she just had a few bruises. It's going to be weeks before Scott can even walk. Beth doesn't know when, or if, Oliver's going to wake up. You're healed, Nate and Raven are healed, I'm healed. Yeah it hurt at the time, but we're fine now."

"I understand your concern for the humans but they know what they are getting into."

"Are you trying to get Scott killed?" I asked.

"No, but it would make things easier. With you."

"What are you talking about?" I demanded.

Beck stalked toward me. I backed up until my butt hit the desk.

"Think of the satisfaction we could bring each other," he said. "We could live for hundreds of years going wherever you want. Think of the parts of the world I could show you." Beck pushed his body against mine and held my head in his hands. "Your blood is in my veins, heating me from the inside out, making me crave you like a drug. You are bonded to me and I want to have you. All of you." He brushed his lips over mine.

He was sin and pleasure all rolled into one and his timing sucked. I also really needed to know about this bonding thing yet wasn't sure this was the time. I assumed that was how we communicated in our heads. What else could there possibly be?

"We're not going to have this conversation," I said into his mouth, avoiding a full blown kiss.

"Do you want the human over me?" he demanded.

I shook my head. "Don't do this right now. Please."

He pulled me tighter against him and lightly kissed me again. Then he trailed his lips over my cheek and down the side of my neck. When his mouth latched onto the skin there, the electric feeling traveled from my throat down to my toes and back up again. It sent little vibrations of heat and pleasure to the core of my body. I moaned involuntarily.

"I can give you things the human cannot. I can make you feel things you have never felt before." He pushed his fangs against my throat but didn't break the skin.

That's what brought me crashing back to reality. I braced my arms between us.

"I don't want one of you over the other. I want Marie back. I want to live a normal life. We may have this conversation again after we find Marie." I pushed away from him and fled the room.

"This is not over, Kinsley!" Beck yelled at my retreating back.

When the office door closed behind me, I leaned against the wall and put my hand to my chest. My heartbeat so fast I felt light-headed. Damn man.

I closed my eyes and admitted to myself what I hadn't been willing to admit since I'd met Scott and Beck. I wanted both of them. That meant I couldn't have either.

"Raven," I yelled down the hall. "Let's go get Scott and take him home."

We used the Hummer so Scott could stretch his leg out over the entire back seat. The cast went to the middle of his thigh.

When we got to his house, Raven helped him out of the back. Scott stared for a minute at Oliver's house.

"He'll be okay," I said quietly.

"You don't know that," Scott responded as he pulled his crutches out of the back. He got himself to the front door, opened it, and stopped.

I waited while he took in what we'd done to his house so he wouldn't have to try and go upstairs.

He looked at us. "Who did this?"

Raven found her courage before I did. "It was Kinsley and Rachel's idea but Nate and I moved all the furniture."

Scott met my eyes. I walked to him and gently guided him into the house. "We moved your bed and dresser into the family room where there are fewer windows. Your TV, couch, and chair are all arranged in the living room. We moved your dining room table against the wall so you'll have more room to maneuver." I talked fast before he blew up.

"I wonder who you learned these strong-arm tactics from?" he asked with a smile.

"You're not mad?" I asked.

"This is what I'd do for you. You'd get mad at me because I wouldn't have asked your permission."

I glared at him because I knew he was right. "Fine, I get it," I conceded. "You do the things you do for me because you think they're helpful."

"No. I know they're helpful." He moved to the couch and lowered himself gently down. Then he flipped the lever and reclined the section he was sitting on. With his leg supported, he breathed a sigh of relief.

"Will you be here when I wake up, sweet thing?" Scott asked me with his eyes closed.

"I don't know," I said.

"I promise I won't try to get you into bed with me."

I glared at Raven when she laughed.

I brought Scott a glass of water and his pain pills. "Take two of these," I told him. "You're easier to deal with when you're drugged."

He smiled and took the pills.

I needed to go somewhere away from Beck and Scott so I could get my head on straight.

As Scott started to snore softly I turned to Raven. "Who's watching the house?"

She thought for a moment then said, "A bear from the north named Kevin. You haven't met him yet."

"Is Scott safe?"

"There's a bear watching his house. Of course he's safe."

"I need to get out of here for a while," I said. "What do you say you, me, and Rachel take a road trip out to the coast? We can talk about possible places to find Marie and how to get her back without the guys telling me no."

She was hesitant. "Beck'll have my hide if something happens to you."

"Nothing's going to happen to me. We're just going to plan. I can't think with all this testosterone flying around me. I know Beck is doing his best to find Isaac but I feel like I'm not doing enough to find Marie. I need some time alone to think."

"Okay," Raven finally agreed. "Let me pack our stuff."

While Raven went upstairs to pack I called Rachel and told her to throw some clothes in a bag and come get us. I told her not to tell Nate. She didn't ask where we were going.

I double checked that Scott could easily get to the food we bought. I wrote him a quick note stating I needed some time alone and that I'd be safe with Raven and Rachel. I underlined their names so he'd get the point that I wasn't going to be with Beck or him.

Rachel pulled up out front in the four door Mercedes.

Raven carried two duffel bags down the stairs and went out the door.

I stood over Scott and ran my fingers through his short hair. He didn't move. I kissed his forehead and left.

Raven took the wheel, I called shotgun, and Rachel climbed in back. We drove west toward the ocean. Raven turned on the stereo. Raven and Rachel were silent, respecting my need for privacy.

I stared out the window and tried to solve the problems of the world as I watched traffic. Then I gave up. I needed to relax, get my mind back in the game, and find Marie. Everything else was going to unfold according to fate.

My mom believed in fate, chance, and destiny. I twirled the ruby ring on my finger and then gripped the rings hanging on the chain around my neck. Maybe it was time for me to let the world do what it wanted to do. It's not like I'd been able to change anything so far.

"Okay guys. I don't even know where to start looking. Ideas?" I asked.

"Raven, shut off the stereo. Kins, I have an idea. But you're probably going to think I'm crazy," Rachel said.

Raven turned off the music and looked at Rachel curiously in the rear view mirror.

"Right now, crazy is better than nothing," I said, turning sideways.

"I brought the Book of Protection and Marie's photo album with all the letters and old pictures. So I've been hauling this thing around for how many days now? This morning, I moved them off my bed and I accidentally dropped the photo album," she said. "But it was good because look what happened!"

Rachel showed me the back of the old leather album. There was a tear by the seam at the binding. "It ripped," I said. Was she happy because the one-hundred-plus year old album had ripped?

"It's not a rip. Look closer."

I pulled the book to the front seat and looked. It was a slit that had been sewn over with a hidden flap. I stuck my finger inside. Only wide enough for maybe two fingers and it was still tight. "There's nothing in it," I said. "So what's the big deal?"

Rachel smiled her mischievous smile that had been getting us in trouble since we were five. "This was in it!" She held out an old rusty key.

"What does it go to?" I asked.

"I don't know, but I think I have an idea. I spent a lot of time with Marie while she rambled about these books. She really was in love with Isaac before she found out he was evil. He bought her a house while he had her in captivity."

Now Rachel had my attention. "He bought her a house? Where?"

"On the Oregon coast."

"Do you know where?"

Rachel smiled again. "Why do you think I didn't ask where we were going on this road trip? I already had a destination in mind."

"Beck, Scott, and Nate are never going to agree to this," I told her.

She looked right and left. "I don't see them. Do you?"

Raven laughed. "This is crazy. Are you proposing we go try to find Marie? Alone?"

"Why not?" Rachel asked.

"Raven just told you. It's crazy," I said. But part of me wanted to do it.

Rachel waved her hand at us. "You know what's happening to her every hour of every day. We can't do *nothing*."

I looked at Rachel and decided I wasn't good at letting fate take the wheel. I'm not quite human and it was time to embrace that part of me.

"We can do this," I said.

"Are you trying to convince me or you?" Raven asked, barely taking her eyes off the road.

"We can do this. Rachel knows where we're going. You and I can kick Isaac's ass. Then we're going to kill him," I told Raven.

Raven shook her head. "We should have Beck with us. And Nate. Isaac is very powerful. We can't just *kick his ass.*"

"Beck and Nate aren't going to let us go charging into a potentially dangerous situation. When we get back with her, we'll have proved we can do things on our own."

"You mean you'll have proved you can do things on your own."

Sometimes Raven was too damn intuitive.

"Besides, she might not even be there. In which case we can tell the guys we have a lead." I smiled.

"No," Raven said. "I will not put you and Rachel in danger."

"Ecstasy," Rachel said.

"What?" Raven asked.

"Ecstasy, Oregon. Seems fitting, don't you think? Compromise: Let's just go. We'll make a plan on the way. If we need the boys, we'll call them."

Rachel knew how to convince me to do just about anything.

"I guess we're going to Ecstasy," I said.

"This is a bad idea," Raven said. "And who names a town Ecstasy?"

"You're talking to girls who grew up in Paradise," Rachel told her.

"I can't sit around and do nothing," I said.

"If we go," Raven said, "there will be no confronting Isaac if he's there. We will see what the situation is and then call Beck. He can come with the others."

I nodded. We'd see once we got there. If Isaac and Marie were there, I was going to kill Isaac. I didn't need Beck.

"Don't think, just drive," Rachel said. "Everything will be fine. You'll see."

"Famous last words," Raven said. But twenty minutes later she took I-5 South instead of North.

We were going to Ecstasy, Oregon.

Epilogue

HAVE you ever stared death in the face? Has He looked at you with His dark, hooded eyes and made your blood pump faster, your stomach free fall, your heart spasm? I have. And I lived to tell about it. Barely. It changed me forever.

Marie is missing, Ian is dead, Oliver is in the hospital unresponsive, and it will be weeks before Scott can walk on his own. I hate being reminded how fragile life is. There's nothing I can do for Ian, Oliver, or Scott right now.

But I can help Marie.

Beck says it's not over. I know he's right.

It won't be over until I have Marie back and Isaac is dead. I know Beck meant more than that, but all I care about right now is finding Marie.

And I *will* find her.

A Note From The Author

Thank you so much for picking up your copy of *First Death*. I want you to know that without you, this adventure would not exist and I appreciate you more than I can say. You matter to me as a reader! As an independent author, your reviews of my stories matter too. I depend on the honest reviews readers like you leave on Amazon (just scan the QR code below) and Goodreads. Other readers use your insights when choosing what to read and will appreciate hearing your opinions of my book. I, of course, would love to hear from you as well. Please leave a review to let me know what you think.

Wishing you all the best,
Kyona

Acknowledgments 2012

For my personal editors: Jo Jiles, Kara Gross, Kim Freel, and Charity Becker. Your hours of devotion helped make this story amazing and my writing stronger. Any mistakes are my own.

Thank you to the Kalispell Crew who were with me when *First Death* began. To Beth, Karly, and Sharon for our lunch talks and all your encouragement. To Beth and Sarah for reading my manuscript, offering suggestions, and feeding my ego (like my ego needs feeding). I miss you all!

Charity: Thank you for your support, guidance, editing, and amazing art.

Hayden Family: There are no words to explain what the unconditional love you share means to me. Years of friendship and family are forever. Special thanks to my bestie and muse, Erin. Carla, you've always had my back. I love you guys!

Jake: Thanks for everything! (you know what I mean)
   Mom: I love you and like you!

About the Author

As a teacher, Kyona is always writing stories and reading books for work and fun. Reading gives people an opportunity to relax and escape the pressures of everyday life. She lives in Eastern Washington with her loving husband and crazy dogs.

Life is short; enjoy it any way you can.

Also by Kyona Jiles

Running Series

Outrunning The Hunter

Running Out of Time

Vampire Shadower Series

First Death

Second Chance

www.ingramcontent.com/pod-product-compliance
Lightning Source LLC
Chambersburg PA
CBHW022005310726
48972CB00006B/1532